P9-BXV-860

THE MASTERPIECE

Also by Fiona Davis

The Dollhouse

The Address

THE
MASTERPIECE

A Novel

FIONA DAVIS

DUTTON

DUTTON

An imprint of Penguin Random House LLC
375 Hudson Street
New York, New York 10014

Copyright © 2018 by Fiona Davis

Penguin supports copyright. Copyright fuels creativity, encourages diverse voices, promotes free speech, and creates a vibrant culture. Thank you for buying an authorized edition of this book and for complying with copyright laws by not reproducing, scanning, or distributing any part of it in any form without permission. You are supporting writers and allowing Penguin to continue to publish books for every reader.

DUTTON and the D colophon are registered trademarks of Penguin Random House LLC.

LIBRARY OF CONGRESS CATALOGING-IN-PUBLICATION DATA
Names: Davis, Fiona, 1966– author.
Title: The masterpiece : a novel / Fiona Davis.
Description: First edition. | New York, New York : Dutton, 2018. |
Identifiers: LCCN 2017060556 (print) | LCCN 2018000513 (ebook) |
ISBN 9781524742966 (ebook) | ISBN 9781524742959 (hc)
Subjects: | BISAC: FICTION / Historical. | FICTION / Mystery & Detective /
General. | FICTION / Literary.
Classification: LCC PS3604.A95695 (ebook) | LCC PS3604.A95695 M38 2018
(print) | DDC 813/.6—dc23
LC record available at https://lccn.loc.gov/2017060556

Printed in the United States of America
1   3   5   7   9   10   8   6   4   2

Set in Bell MT Std
Designed by Cassandra Garruzzo

This book is a work of fiction. Names, characters, places, and incidents either are the product of the author's imagination or are used fictitiously, and any resemblance to actual persons, living or dead, business establishments, events, or locales is entirely coincidental.

R0452818699

For Tom

THE MASTERPIECE

CHAPTER ONE

New York City, April 1928

C lara Darden's illustration class at the Grand Central School of Art, tucked under the copper eaves of the terminal, was unaffected by the trains that rumbled through ancient layers of Manhattan schist hundreds of feet below. But somehow, a surprise visit from Mr. Lorette, the school's director, had the disruptive power of a locomotive weighing in at thousands of tons.

Even before Mr. Lorette was a factor, Clara had been anxious about the annual faculty exhibition set to open at six o'clock that evening. Her first show in New York City, and everyone important in the art and editorial worlds would be there. She'd been working on her illustrations for months now, knowing this might be her only chance.

She asked her class to begin work on an alternate cover design for Virginia Woolf's latest book, and the four ladies dove in eagerly, while Wilbur, the only male and something of a rake to boot, sighed loudly and rolled his eyes. Gertrude, the most studious of the five members, was so offended by Wilbur's lack of respect that she threatened to toss a jar of turpentine at him. They were still arguing vociferously when Mr. Lorette waltzed in.

Never mind that these were all adults, not children. Whenever Wilbur made a ruckus, it had the unfortunate effect of lowering the entire class's maturity level by a decade. More often than not, Clara was strong enough to restore order before things went too far. But Mr. Lorette seemed possessed of a miraculous talent for sensing the rare occasions during which Clara lost control of the room, and he could usually be counted upon to choose such times to wander by and assess her skills as an educator.

"Miss Darden, do you need additional supervision again?" Mr. Lorette's bald pate shone as if it had been buffed by one of the shoeshine boys in the terminal's main concourse. The corners of his mouth curled down, even when he was pleased, while his eyebrows moved independently of each other, like two furry caterpillars trying to scurry away. Even though he was only in his early thirties, he exuded the snippety nature of a judgmental great-aunt.

He'd been appointed director three years earlier, after one of the school's illustrious founders, John Singer Sargent, passed away. The school had increased in reputation and enrollment with each new term, and Mr. Lorette had given himself full credit for its smashing success when he'd interviewed Clara. She'd been promoted from student monitor to interim teacher after Mr. Lorette's chosen instructor dropped out at the last minute, putting her on uneven footing from the beginning. It hadn't helped that the class had shriveled to five from an initial January enrollment of fifteen. Ten of those early enrollees had walked out on the first day, miffed at having a woman in charge.

Mr. Lorette's dissatisfaction, and the likelihood that she'd not be asked back next term, mounted each week, which meant tonight's faculty show would probably be her last opportunity to get her illustrations in front of the city's top magazine editors.

Since coming to New York the year before, Clara had dutifully dropped off samples of her work at the offices of *Vogue* and *McCall's* every few months, to no avail. The responses ranged from the soul-crushing—"Unoriginal/No"—to the encouraging—"Try again later." All that would change, tonight. She hoped. By seeing her work in the hallowed setting of the Grand Central Art Galleries, alongside the well-known names of other faculty members, the editors would finally appreciate what she had to offer. Even better, as the only illustrator on the faculty, she was sure to stand out.

Mr. Lorette cleared his throat.

"No, sir. We don't need any assistance. Thank you for checking in." She maneuvered around to the front of the table where she'd been working, in an attempt to block his view of her own sketches.

No luck. He circled around and stood behind it, his nose twitching. "What is this?"

"Some figures I was working on, to demonstrate the use of compass points to achieve the correct proportions."

"I thought you'd covered that already."

"You can never go back to the basics enough."

He offered a suspicious nod before winding his way through the tables, his eyes darting from drawing board to drawing board. Her students stood back, hoping for a kind word.

"Why is it each student seems to be drawing something completely different from the others?"

She nodded at the novel she'd left out on the still-life table. "The assignment was to create a cover for a book. I encouraged them to use their imaginations."

"Their examples of lighthouses and beaches are apropos. Yet you are drawing undergarments?"

Even if he had been a more sympathetic man, there was no way to explain how the hours stretched painfully long with her having so few students. How the skylights diffused the light in a way that made each day, whether sunny or overcast, feel exactly like every other. She routinely made the rounds, suggesting that a drybrush would work best to create texture or offering encouragement when Gertrude became frustrated, but at some point, the students had to be left alone to get to their work. Which was why today she'd pulled a chair up to a drawing table and sketched out the figures for her latest commission from Wanamaker Department Store: three pages of chemises for the summer catalog. The work paid a pittance, but at least it was something.

"This is for tomorrow's class," she lied. "As we do not have a live model to work from, I was planning on using a work of my own to guide them."

As she hoped, the mention of her standing request for a model redirected his attention.

His voice rose in pitch to that of a schoolgirl. "The students are free to take a life class at any time. This is an illustration class, and right now our models are reserved for the fine arts classes. As you said, they can use their imaginations, no?"

"But it is not ideal. If we can have a model to understand the anatomy underneath the fashions, to have the model begin nude and then add layers of clothing, we could build upon what we've learned already."

She never meant to be ornery, but somehow Mr. Lorette brought out a stubbornness in her every time.

"As yours is a class of mixed genders, taught by a woman, having a nude model would be most inappropriate. I'm sorry you find our school so deficient, Miss Darden." He clucked his tongue, which made her want to reach into his mouth and pull it out. "The other instructors, who have vastly more experience than you do, seem to manage just fine."

The other instructors—all men—had their every whim met by Mr. Lorette. She'd seen it in action, the director encouraging them to stop by his office for a smoke, the group laughing at some private joke, the director's feet propped up on his desk in an attempt to convey casual masculinity. Clara didn't fit the mold, which made her vulnerable.

"I'm sure we can manage, sir."

He shuffled off, closing the door behind him.

She directed the class to continue. Gertrude's work had only three rips from her overuse of the razor for corrections, a record low for her.

"Your stormy clouds are exquisite, but where would the lettering of the title and author go?" Clara asked.

Gertrude rubbed her nose with her wrist, leaving a gray streak at the tip. "Right. I got so caught up, I forgot."

Clara pointed to the top edge. "Try a damp sponge on the wet areas to lift out some color."

The girl was always eager, even if her strong hand was better suited to clay or oils than to the careful placement of watercolor, where mistakes were difficult to correct. Use too much water, and a brilliant cauliflower pattern would bloom where a smooth line ought to have been. Too dry, and the saturated color would stick to the page, resisting softening. But Clara loved watercolor in spite of, or perhaps because of, its difficult temperament. The way the paper shone after a wash of cool orange to convey a sunset, how the colors blended together in the tray to form new ones that probably didn't even have a name.

Finally, five o'clock came around. The students stored their art-work in the wooden racks, and once the room was empty, Clara hid her own sketches up on the very top of the storage cabinet, away from Mr. Lorette's prying eyes.

Starving, she headed downstairs to the main concourse, where cocoa-pink walls trimmed in Botticino marble soared into the air. Electrically lit stars and painted constellations twinkled along the turquoise vaulted ceiling, although the poor artist had inadvertently painted the sky backward, a mistake the art students loved to re-mark upon.

The first time she'd entered the hallowed space, stepping off the train from Arizona last September, she'd stopped and stared, her mouth open, until a man brushed past her, swearing under his breath at her inertia. The vastness of the main concourse, where sunshine beamed through the giant windows and bronze chandeliers glowed, left her gobsmacked. With its exhilarating mix of light, air, and move-ment, the terminal was the perfect location for a school of art.

Since then, she'd been sure to glance up quickly before joining in what seemed like an elaborate square dance of men and maids, of red-capped porters and well-dressed society ladies, all gliding by one another at various angles, yet never colliding. She liked best to lean over the banister on the West Balcony and watch the patterns of people flowing around the circular information booth, which sat in the middle of the floor, its four-faced clock tipped with a gleam-ing gold acorn.

Her stomach growled. She followed a group of smartly dressed men down the ramp to the suburban concourse and into the Grand Central Terminal Restaurant, where she secured a seat at the counter.

"Miss Darden?"

A young woman wearing a black velvet coat trimmed with fur

hovered behind Clara, offering an inquisitive smile. "Yes, I thought that might be you. I'm Nadine Stevenson. I take painting classes at the school. You're having a bite before the show?"

"I am, Miss Stevenson."

"Oh now, call me Nadine."

Nadine's nose was large, her eyes close together and deep-set. Her right eye was slightly larger than the left, and the asymmetry was unsettling but powerful. Clara couldn't help but imagine how Picasso might approach her, all mismatched cubes and colors. Next to her stood an Adonis of a man whose symmetrical beauty offered a fascinating counterpoint. Shining blue-gray eyes under arched brows, hair the color of wheat.

"And this is Mr. Oliver Smith, a friend and poet."

Even though Clara had hoped to eat dinner in peace, she didn't have much of a choice. "Lovely to meet you both; please join me."

They took the stools next to her as the waiter stopped in front of them, pen in hand. Clara ordered the oyster stew, as did Oliver. Nadine requested peeled Muscat grapes, followed by a lobster cocktail.

Many of the young girls at the Grand Central School of Art had enrolled only so they could list it in their wedding announcements someday—a creative outlet that wouldn't threaten future in-laws. Nadine seemed to fall into that category, with her airs and pearls.

"Miss Darden is the only lady teacher at the Grand Central School of Art," said Nadine to Oliver. "She teaches illustration." She turned to Clara with a bright smile. "Now tell us about what you'll be showing tonight."

"Four illustrations that depict four seasons of high fashion." Clara couldn't help but elaborate. She'd put so much thought into the drawings. "For example, the one for winter depicts three women draped in fur coats, walking poodles sporting matching pelts."

"Well, that sounds pleasant."

Was Nadine making fun of her? Clara couldn't tell. She'd hardly had time to socialize, other than occasionally trading a few words with some of the other women artists who lived in her Greenwich Village apartment house. She'd been far too busy trying to make a living.

Nadine placed one hand on the counter and leaned in closely. The citrus scent of Emeraude perfume drifted Clara's way. "Did you know that Georgia O'Keeffe—she does those astonishing flowers—was a commercial artist at first? There's no need to be ashamed of it, not at all. Illustration is a common stepping-stone into the true arts."

"I'm not ashamed in the least." The audacity. Clara didn't enjoy being talked down to by a student. "I don't intend to do the 'true arts,' Nadine, as you put it. I enjoy illustration; it's what I do best."

"Well, I adore my life drawing and painting class. I'm learning so much from my instructor, Mr. Zakarian. He made me class monitor, and he's magnificent."

Jealousy pinged. None of Clara's students would describe her in such superlative terms, of that she was quite certain. "Class monitor, that's quite an honor. Do you plan on becoming an artist, then?"

Nadine gave out a squeak of a laugh. "Oh dear, no. I'm only taking classes for personal enrichment."

The waiter dropped off their bowls, and for a moment nothing was said. If Clara had been alone, she would have surreptitiously folded a dozen or so oyster crackers into her handkerchief, to have something to snack on before bed.

The poet, who'd been silent the entire time, finally spoke. "My mother was an artist, although my father insisted she give it up after they married. She's been sick lately, but she very much misses going to museums and exhibits."

"I'm sorry to hear that," offered Clara. "Nadine mentioned that you're a poet?"

"Nadine is too kind in her description of me. Struggling poet, you might say. I suppose I take after my mother in that regard, having an innate love of the arts. My father is hoping I'll give it up eventually and go into banking."

Nadine placed a protective hand on his arm. "Oliver was accepted to Harvard and refused to go. Can you imagine? Instead, he's slumming it with us bohemians."

By all accounts, Nadine was hardly slumming it. But Clara understood firsthand what it was like to disappoint your family. "When I told my father I was moving to New York, he told me to not bother coming back. It's not an easy decision, but I'm glad I made it."

Oliver's blue eyes danced. "So there's hope for us miscreants?"

"Never."

They shared a look, a quick, knowing smile, that sent Clara's pulse racing.

Usually, men didn't give her a second glance. Her father generously described her as "ethereal" for her blond hair, pale skin, and towering, skinny figure. Her mother said she looked washed-out and encouraged her to wear clothes that added color to her complexion, but Clara preferred blacks and grays. Her ghostly pallor and height had always been sore points, embarrassing, and she preferred to avoid drawing attention to herself.

Oliver tucked into his stew. She did the same, embarrassed. She must have imagined the exchange.

Nadine took over the reins of the conversation. "Now, where are you from, Miss Darden?"

"Arizona." She waited for the inevitable intake of breath. The

American West might as well have been Australia, for how shocked most East Coast natives were at her having come all this way.

"You've come all this way! Gosh. What does your father do? Is he a cowboy?"

"He sells metals."

Clara deliberately used the present tense instead of the past when speaking of her family's fortunes—now their misfortunes. Her father's fraudulent scheming was no longer any of Clara's concern, nor of anyone else's. Luckily, Nadine went on and on about her own father's real estate business, more for Oliver's benefit than Clara's, as Clara quickly finished her meal.

She looked up at the clock. "I must go; the doors will be opening soon."

But there was no slipping away. Nadine locked arms with Clara as they walked out of the restaurant, as if they'd been friends for years. To the left and right, ramps sloped back up to the concourse, framed by glorious marble arches, and a vaulted ceiling rose above their heads in a herringbone pattern. Clara had tried to duplicate the earth-and-sable tones of the tiles in one of her illustrations to be shown tonight.

"Wait, before we go, stand over there." Oliver pointed to a spot where two of the arches met. "Face right into the corner and listen carefully."

Clara had no time for games but watched as Nadine did as she was told. Oliver took up a spot at the opposite corner and mouthed something Clara couldn't hear. Nadine giggled.

"What's so funny?" Clara asked.

"You've got to try it. We're in the Whispering Gallery."

Begrudgingly, Clara took up Nadine's position.

"Clara, Clara."

The words drifted over her like a ghost. Oliver might as well have been standing close by, speaking right into her ear. She looked up, trying to figure out how the shape of the ceiling transmitted sound waves so effortlessly. She faced the corner again. "Recite a poem to me."

For a moment, she wasn't sure if he would. Then the disembodied voice returned.

> *That whisper takes the voice*
> *Of a Spirit, speaking to me,*
> *Close, but invisible,*
> *And throws me under a spell.*

She swore she could feel the heat of Oliver's breath. They locked eyes as they met once again in the center of the space.

"Thomas Hardy. The poem's called 'In a Whispering Gallery,'" Oliver volunteered.

Nadine crossed her arms, indignant. "You didn't recite verse to me."

"I'll regale you next time, I promise. For now, I must head to a poetry reading downtown and amass further inspiration."

Clara shook hands and they took their leave, the poem still echoing in her head.

—⚭—

The mob of nattily dressed art lovers trying to squeeze their way through the gallery's doorway had already backed up to the elevator by the time Clara and Nadine arrived. They toddled through, taking small steps so as not to get their toes crushed, until they were safely inside.

The Grand Central Art Galleries predated the school by two years, when a businessman turned artist named Walter Clark had enlisted the help of John Singer Sargent to convert part of the sixth floor into a massive exhibition space, a kind of artists' cooperative where commissions were kept to a minimum. Clara stopped by at least once a week to see the latest works, and she encouraged her students to do the same. The rooms were rarely empty, as visitors to New York and everyday commuters continually drifted through.

Tonight, the room buzzed with energy. The faculty's work would stay up for a week, before being replaced with the students' work, a celebration of the school's spring term and its growing prestige. Clara's illustrations would be on the same walls that once displayed Sargent's portraits. The thought made her giddy.

Located on the south side of the terminal, the Grand Central Art Galleries were four times as long as they were wide, a warren of rooms and hallways, twenty in all, that encouraged visitors to circulate in a counterclockwise manner without ever having to double back. Clara scanned the walls of the first gallery for her work, with no luck. In the middle of the space, the sculpture teacher stood beside a table featuring two nymphs, both nude, one standing on a turtle.

"Now, that's unremarkable," said Nadine.

Clara agreed but kept her mouth shut. They continued on, to where a group of students surveyed an oil of an ungainly horse. Towering above them all was the artist, an instructor for the life drawing and painting class.

Clara had seen him a few times before. A foreigner, he was known to sing loudly during his classes and even dance about at times. This evening, he stood to the side, listening with intensity as his acolytes buttered him up, every so often tossing his head in a futile effort to flick a thatch of hair out of his eyes. Indeed, he was more horselike than the horse in his painting.

"That's my teacher. Mr. Zakarian." Nadine sidled up next to him. Clara had seen women like her before, flinging themselves into the orbits of handsome or powerful men to fend off their own insecurities. Clara had no time for such nonsense.

Back to the task at hand. The air had become stifling as more people crammed in. She ventured into room after room before circling back, and still she didn't see her illustrations.

A flash of panic seized her. Her job with Wanamaker was ending soon. They'd recently announced that they'd be using only in-house artists going forward. Her salary of seventy-five dollars a month from teaching covered her expenses, but not much more. And she could not count on the next term.

She wormed her way back one more time through the mazelike space. Nothing. Down one hallway, off to the right, was a door marked SALES OFFICE. She'd passed by it in her first go-round, assuming it to be a place for clerks to write up invoices. The door stood halfway open, the lights on. She peered inside.

It was more a closet than a room, with a scratched-up desk against one wall and a wooden file cabinet wedged into a corner.

There, above the desk, equally spaced apart and centered on the wall with great care, were her illustrations.

By the time she found Mr. Lorette, Clara's limbs shook with rage. He was in an animated conversation with Mr. Zakarian while Mrs. Lorette looked on. Clara had met her in passing at one of the faculty get-togethers, awed by the puffy, out-of-date pompadour that perched on the woman's head like a long-haired cat.

She inserted herself into the group. "Mr. Lorette, my illustrations have been hung in a back office. A back office!"

While Mr. Lorette sputtered at her rudeness, she continued on. "I am a faculty member of the School of Art, and yet my work has been placed in a cave where no one would think to go."

"I am sorry, Miss Darden. We were in a tight spot, you see." He paused. "Quite literally."

As Mr. Lorette laughed at his own joke, Clara noticed the editor of *Vogue* headed for the exit. For certain, he'd never even seen her work.

Mr. Zakarian spoke up. "Where was her art hung?"

"Just off a main gallery," said Mr. Lorette. "They are illustrations. We concluded they were more suited to an intimate environment."

"Perhaps you could guarantee her a spot here in the first room next year, to make it up to her?" Mr. Zakarian held out his hand to Clara. "I don't think we've met. I'm Mr. Levon Zakarian, one of your fellow teachers."

She shook it without looking at him, her glare fixed on Mr. Lorette. "Next year it'll be too late. It's already too late."

Unlike students such as Nadine, for whom the Grand Central School of Art was just a pit stop on the way to marital bliss, Clara had sunk every ounce of energy into her career as an artist. Against her parents' wishes, she'd arrived in New York, knowing no one, and done everything she could to make it as an illustrator. What made it worse was knowing she'd been given a shot that other artists would have been envious of—to teach at the Grand Central School of Art, to show her work at the galleries—only to see it vaporize.

Mr. Lorette shrugged. "I can't seem to please anyone tonight. We will make it up to you; my deepest apologies, Miss Darden." He turned to Mr. Zakarian. "Have you seen Edmund's latest work? Come with me. I assure you it'll give you something to think about."

"I believe Miss Darden may give you something to think about, if you try to shake her off." Mr. Zakarian wore a crooked smile. "I have an idea. Let's take down one of mine, and we'll replace it with her work. Get it right out there in the center."

She didn't need one of the faculty stars to swoop down and protect her. The very thought made her sick with embarrassment.

Unwilling to give Mr. Lorette any further satisfaction at her distress, Clara stormed out without uttering a reply.

CHAPTER TWO

New York City, November 1974

When Virginia signed with the Trimble Temp Agency, desperate to fill her empty days as well as her dwindling bank account, she'd expected to be sent to one of the fancy skyscrapers where lawyers conferred in hushed tones with their elegant, efficient secretaries. Not the dumpy train station that squatted like a toad beneath the New York skyline.

But she'd shown up at Grand Central at 9:20 the following morning and, as directed by the agency, taken the elevator near track 23 up to the seventh floor. A wooden door marked PENN CENTRAL IN-HOUSE LEGAL DEPT opened to a reception area where a pretty blonde with Joni Mitchell hair sat.

"I'm here from the Trimble Temp Agency."

The receptionist motioned to the chairs along one wall. "Please take a seat. You can hang your coat in the closet."

Not very fancy, this law office, with its oatmeal-colored carpeting and matching walls. But still as good a place as any to start a career. She liked to think she was changing with the times. The 1950s, when she got married and had her daughter, Ruby, were all about family. But the seventies, as Ruby liked to inform her, were about finding yourself. Of course, Ruby was more than busy finding *her-self* these days, having withdrawn from Sarah Lawrence less than a month into her freshman year, telling Virginia she needed a breather. For now, Virginia had to admit she liked having her back in their apartment. Someone to take care of again. Fuss over.

She'd do the same with her new lawyer boss. Over time, she'd joke with his wife that they knew him better than he did himself, share a chuckle over the phone about how he'd forget his daughter's birthday if they weren't there to remind him. Just as she'd done with Chester's legal secretary once upon a time. The tables had turned: She was now the secretary, no longer the wife, but what was life without a little shake-up? She sat up straighter and tried to believe it.

A woman around her own age, with tight curls and a rough voice, walked into the foyer. "Ms. Clay?"

"Yes." She hated her married name but couldn't imagine changing it back. After all, it'd been her identity for almost two decades. Still. Virginia Clay. Sounded like something you dug up in a quarry.

"Right. Follow me."

The woman explained she was the head of human resources at Penn Central, the company that owned Grand Central Terminal, and that Virginia would be working for one of the lawyers whose secretary had left to have a baby. If all went well, Virginia had a chance of being hired full-time, once her contract with the temp agency was up.

"Have you worked for attorneys before?" asked the woman.

Virginia had already forgotten the woman's name. She really needed to pay more attention, now that she was a part of the business world. "Yes, for a firm in Midtown."

She'd said the same lie to the man who ran the temp agency, but she figured being married to a corporate lawyer for the past nineteen years was pretty much the same thing. He'd spent most weekends and evenings on the phone with clients and associates, and some of what she'd overheard must have seeped into her brain.

The woman led her to a desk with a typewriter and a fancy phone, with one of the plastic buttons lit up in red. "Mr. Huckle's on the phone, so I won't interrupt him to introduce you. He'll be out when he needs something."

Virginia tucked her purse into one of the lower drawers and explored the others, which contained pencils, pens, Wite-Out, and carbon paper, all the usual accoutrements of the modern secretary. Behind her was a big metal filing cabinet. As she rose to see what was inside, a man barreled out of one of the offices. He had movie-star eyes, a brilliant blue, and a thick head of hair. Not what she'd expected, and she tried not to gawk.

"You the new girl?" He eyed her, from her scuffed gray pumps to the top of her head. She tried not to squirm under his gaze. Earlier this year, she'd had her brown hair cut in what she hoped was a trendy shag, but without regular trims, it had curled into a bird's nest.

Mr. Huckle's gaze traveled back to her midsection and lingered there. Even if her nose was slightly too wide and her eyes deep-set, she'd always had a remarkable figure. Her waist stayed thin even after having Ruby, her chest double D's. Single D, now, she'd remarked to Chester after the operation. He hadn't laughed.

"How old are you?"

The question was unexpected. "I'm thirty-five." Shaving off five years didn't seem too egregious.

"Fine." He took one last survey of her hips and motioned for her to follow him. "Come into my office. Bring your steno pad."

The nameplate on the office door read DENNIS HUCKLE. She grabbed the steno pad from her desk and followed him in, her stomach queasy. Mr. Huckle began rattling off dictation, but she had to stop him almost immediately.

"In Ray?"

He looked at her as if she were mad. "What? Yes."

"Is there a last name?"

He didn't dress like the other attorneys she'd met before, at business dinners and off-site conferences. The top button of his shirt was undone, his striped tie loosened, exposing the strong tendons of his neck. But in-house lawyers probably didn't need to impress the same way ones at white-shoe firms did. The client was already guaranteed. "This is a memo to files. There's no last name."

"Then who's Ray?"

He leaned back, breathing like a dragon about to roar. "*In re.*" He spelled out the words. "It's part of the subject line of a legal memorandum."

"Right, sorry, I misheard. Never mind. Carry on."

Back at her desk, she put a piece of clean white paper in the typewriter and looked down at her notepad. She'd tried her very best to keep up, but the squiggles meant nothing to her. Steno wasn't something she'd ever learned, so she'd simply written the important words as quickly as possible and skipped the unimportant ones.

An hour later, Mr. Huckle came out of his office. "Where's that memo?"

She yanked it out of the typewriter carriage and held it out to him, then sank back into her chair once his door was closed. She waited.

Thirty seconds later, she heard him screaming on the phone to someone. Kathleen. That was the human resources person's name. At least now she knew. The woman tore down the hall and asked Virginia to follow her back to her office.

Virginia was already making excuses to tell the temp agency. The man was unreasonable, it wasn't a good fit, personality-wise. She'd do better next time.

Kathleen sat behind her desk and folded her hands in front of her. "Mr. Huckle said you have no idea what you're doing."

Virginia shook her head. "I'm still catching up on my stenography, you see. Maybe if he spoke a little slower I could do it. I'm happy to try again."

"You're wasting everyone's time." She looked Virginia straight on, but not with anger.

With pity.

Somehow, in her head, Virginia had imagined herself as one of those fancy secretaries in the temp agency ad, sporting a lithe figure and knowing smile that emanated capability and discretion. When in fact she was a middle-aged frump in a pilled sweater set, a laughingstock. Ever since the divorce was finalized a year earlier, she'd tried so hard to maintain control. To prove to Ruby that they'd be just fine, you wait and see. When in fact their world had been shattered by Chester's desertion.

She didn't want to think about that, but the images came flooding to mind anyway. Ruby popping out of her room, singing some bittersweet Donny Osmond song, while she and Chester stood at the kitchen counter like frozen statues, knowing they were about to rip her world to shreds. Ruby had instantly sensed something was wrong. "Did I do something?" she'd asked.

Then, as Chester explained the situation, that they were getting divorced, Virginia had watched her crumple. That was the right word, the only word. *Crumple.* Bit by bit, muscle by muscle, a puzzled agony had worked its way down her darling daughter's face: Her forehead crinkled, her nose went red, her chin wobbled. The worst was trying to keep her own expression calm and capable, to show that this was just another day, nothing was wrong, we'd all be fine. Ruby's eyes went pink and wet, and she ran out of the room, slamming her bedroom door shut.

They'd done that to her. Chester had done that to her. Virginia would never stop trying to fix it for Ruby. To make up for the devastation they'd wrought.

Now, Virginia tried to keep her own face from crumpling, but the effort only made it worse, and finally she let out a strangled, choking sound. "I'm sorry. I don't know what I was thinking. My husband is a lawyer. My ex-husband, I mean. I thought I could handle it."

Kathleen looked up. "You're divorced?"

"Yes."

A hushed moment passed, like in church right before the choir begins to sing. "Me, too."

The woman looked down at some papers on her desk. "There's another position available, one that doesn't require typing or steno. Would you be interested?"

Even if she were locked in a windowless room to file papers eight hours a day, she'd take it. Something to do each day, a place to report to. A reason to wake up in the morning. "Of course. Thank you." Kathleen's sympathy only made her want to weep more. "Do you mind if I freshen up first?"

"Ask Annie out front for a key to the bathroom. Take your time."

The receptionist yanked open a drawer full of keys and handed one to Virginia. Outside in the hallway, Virginia turned left and then right, trying to remember the woman's mumbled directions. Around the corner, then third door on the left. Or was it the fourth?

She tried the third door with no luck. On the fourth, her key slid in the lock.

She stepped inside and fumbled for the light switch, expecting to see a row of porcelain sinks and grungy tile walls. Instead, she stood in a small foyer, where a painted sign along one wall read THE GRAND CENTRAL SCHOOL OF ART in gold letters. Handsome art deco ceiling pendants threw a warm light down a long hallway off to her left. She ventured farther inside, curious, her despair momentarily forgotten.

At the first doorway, it was as if the art school were still open, a dozen easels at the ready for the next day's class, paintings and drawings hung on one wall, a ceramic vase on a table in the center of the room. The only sign of abandonment was the coating of dust on everything, the vase an ashy green. A faint scent of chemicals made her sneeze, or maybe that was the dust. A large storage cabinet for artwork lined one wall, a mix of slots for framed canvases at the bottom and shelving above.

She checked each room, counting five studios in total, amazed at her find: a mummified art school at the top of Grand Central. The last room was some kind of storage area, filled with wooden crates stacked haphazardly on top of one another. The crate closest to her had been opened; a crowbar lay on the floor nearby. Inside, Virginia discovered course catalogs, accounting ledgers, and notebooks filled with names of students and tuition figures. A winter catalog from 1928 offered a snapshot of life right before the Depression, when a portrait painting class cost fourteen dollars a month.

She shouldn't linger; Kathleen was waiting for her and she had yet to find the bathroom. But as she turned to go, an entire wall filled with artwork stopped her in her tracks. Still lifes, portraits, landscapes, some on yellowed canvas and others on brittle, tea-colored paper. Her eye was drawn to a familiar tableau that Virginia recognized as a Renoir, the festive one of the boating party, but in this version a figure clutched a bottle of Coke, of all things.

Surrounded by such ruined beauty, the faded artifacts of students who had once worked diligently and were now God knew where, Virginia burst into tears. At her recent failures, at the way her world was no longer within her control.

She grabbed a tissue from her purse. As she wiped under her eyes, she caught sight of a sketch of women wearing vintage tailored suits, like something from an old newspaper ad. *For the Well-Dressed Secretary* was written at the very top. While most of the models looked off to the side, the one in the center stared straight out. Her posture—shoulders flung back, chin raised—spoke of strength and character. On the bottom right-hand corner the name Clara Darden was scrawled.

Virginia struck the same pose, laughing at herself, but doing so gave her a burst of energy and confidence. Whatever Kathleen had in store, she could dig down and find the courage to face it. Today's wasn't the first humiliation she'd faced since her divorce, and it probably wouldn't be her last. But at least she was putting herself out there in the world.

When Virginia returned, to her surprise, Kathleen led her out of the offices, back down the elevator, to the concourse level. She pointed over the crowds. "We need some help in the information booth."

"The information booth? Right in the middle of the station?"

"Yes. It would be from nine to five, a trainee position. There's a night shift as well, but I don't recommend that for a woman. You don't want to be hanging around here too late."

Virginia didn't want to be hanging around there at all. The

circular booth stood smack in the middle of the main concourse like a little spaceship, the bottom half the same grungy-looking marble as the floor, the top covered in dull glass. She'd be totally exposed if she went in there. People would be able to see her. People who were headed off to their houses in Connecticut or taking the train to Boston. People she knew.

"There's nothing else, nothing in the office? I thought I was hired by Penn Central."

"Penn Central owns Grand Central Terminal and runs the railroad, so you would be working for us. The only opening right now that doesn't require experience is as a trainee clerk for the railroad."

"I don't know anything about the trains or the station."

"You won't deal directly with the public, not yet. Just do what the head clerk tells you, answer the phone when the corporate office calls down, and restock the schedules. It's not a fancy job, but it pays one hundred and eighty dollars a week. To the agency, of course. I don't know what you'll get from that."

Around $120, Virginia figured. As a legal secretary, she had been promised $200.

As they neared the booth, Virginia kept her head down, hoping no one she knew was nearby. Kathleen waved to one of the people inside, who opened a small door and ushered them in.

Two of the clerks sitting closest to the door stared at her before turning back to the mob of people that encircled the booth. The interior was cramped, with hardly enough room to maneuver between the high stools where the clerks perched. A large metal cylinder rose up in the middle of the booth, taking up even more room. Decades of shuffling feet had worn the floor around the tube into a circular groove, while the marble counters inside the perimeter were scratched and sticky-looking.

Under the countertop, brown paper lunch bags sat next to dirty rags and newspapers in open compartments, like the storage cubbies in Ruby's old kindergarten. Kathleen and Virginia stood near the door, practically touching, as there was nowhere else to go.

Kathleen pointed to a dapper older man sitting two windows away. "That's Terrence. He's the head clerk. He'll tell you what to do and can sign your time sheet on Fridays." Kathleen gave her a sympathetic pat on the arm and was gone, swept away in the swarm of commuters outside the information booth.

Virginia sidled over to Terrence. He held out a hand to stop her from speaking while he explained to a woman the best way to get to St. Patrick's Cathedral.

He turned a WINDOW CLOSED placard to face out and swiveled around, using the countertop as leverage. "Who are you?"

She held out her hand. "Virginia Clay. I'm the new trainee."

The clerk sitting on the other side of Terrence glanced over at her. The two looked like brothers, both stick-thin, close in age, each sporting a shock of gray hair. Both wore the same dark blazer, white shirt, and tie.

The brother sniffed the air. "This one uses perfume. I think I may be sick."

"Enough, Totto." Terrence cocked his head. "No more perfume, okay? He's very sensitive."

She'd sprayed a little Charlie Eau de Toilette that morning, hoping to suggest an air of mystique and class. What a mistake. Claustrophobia washed over her. She feared she could not spend another minute in this place without screaming.

"You okay?" Terrence asked, not unkindly.

She nodded, unable to speak.

Terrence gestured to Totto. "Ignore him; he's always looking for trouble. You can put your purse there." He pointed to one of the cub-bies. "Right above, on the counter, is the Information Clerk Hand-book. Take that and memorize everything in it. If you pass the test after a year, you get a promotion. For now, you can sort all the time-tables by the door. The night crew knocked over a box of them and didn't do anything about it. When you're done, go outside and refill any of the stacks that need it. Can you handle that?"

The sorting helped calm her down, her focus drawn to the differ-ent colors and letters. All those *H*'s, the Hudson, Harlem, and New Haven Lines, the pastoral names of towns she'd never been to, Val-halla, Cos Cob, Beacon Falls, and her favorite, Green's Farms. She could sell her apartment and buy a place there, where life was easier and simpler. Though Ruby would never agree—her daughter was a city girl, all the way.

Virginia stepped outside the booth with her cardboard box of sorted timetables. Metal holders lined the counters. She circled the booth slowly, the box digging into her hip, as she matched up the piles in her box with the ones already set out, eavesdropping on everyone who came up to ask a question.

The inquiries she overheard were, for the most part, dull. Direc-tions, train schedules, where to get a taxi. One couple wearing matching Hawaiian shirts asked about tickets for the next train to the Statue of Liberty. The clerk behind the window—a tetchy, sal-low woman in her late sixties, sporting an ill-fitting black wig—laughed in their faces before sticking out her tongue at Virginia for staring. Not much in the way of customer service, this crew.

But she reconsidered after watching the one with the name tag WINSTON, who had a southern accent that rumbled easily through the glass barrier. He seemed to know the answer to any question without having to check the timetable book first, and he gave Virginia a wink as she circled by.

She committed the four clerks' names to memory: Terrence and Totto, the fearless leader of the crew and his snarky brother. Winston, the sweet black gentleman from the South. Doris, with the fake hair and nasty laugh. All four seemed like they'd been working in the booth for as long as the station had been standing.

Back inside, Virginia took an empty stool and leafed through the handbook while she waited for another assignment. She studied the map of the layout, figuring she should know her way around. The gates for the trains were arrayed on the north side of two large concourses, the one she was on and the one directly below it. The ticket windows ran along the south side of the main concourse, below an electronic board displaying departures and arrivals. A cavernous waiting room, filled with street people and addicts, loomed on the far side of the ticket windows, the shrieks and screams within cutting through the din of commuters at least once an hour. She'd be sure not to venture that way.

To the west, a once-grand stairway led up to Vanderbilt Avenue, which she knew from experience was its own kind of hell, with drug dealers pushing their wares right outside the doors and along the narrow street. The Oyster Bar, which years ago was her parents' favorite restaurant, sat directly under the waiting room, off the lower concourse. She overheard Winston advise a traveler looking for lunch to take the ramp to get there and bypass the lower concourse entirely, so as to avoid getting mugged.

According to her map, the train operations offices were all located on the upper office floors, which ran in a rectangle around the main concourse. That art school was up high in the east wing, labeled on the map as STORAGE. Other than the law offices for Penn Central, most of that floor appeared to be uninhabited.

The main concourse reminded her of Times Square at night, the billboards and brightly lit ads for *Newsweek* and Kodak a flamboyant contrast to the tarnished walls and blackened ceiling. The immensity of the space was broken up by a Chase Manhattan bank booth a few hundred feet away, next to a freestanding display for Merrill Lynch.

She had feared feeling like she was in a fishbowl, exposed on all sides, but in fact the information booth acted as a kind of bubble of invisibility. No one looked her way, not a soul. She stared at all the faces, not recognizing anyone, and in no fear of being recognized herself. By eleven thirty, the crowd had thinned considerably. Terrence closed up his window and slid off his stool. "You did all the timetables?"

She nodded. "Do you mind if I ask how long you've worked at Grand Central Station?"

"Terminal."

"What's the difference?"

From behind him, Doris snickered. "Rookie question."

"The difference is that a station is a place where a train passes through, on the way to somewhere else. A terminal, as the name suggests, is the end of the line."

"I see. Grand Central Terminal. Got it. How long have you worked here?"

"Since 1942. Why don't you do a coffee run? It's in the Station Master's Office, under the stairs that way." He pointed west. "That's also where you should use the restroom if you have to. Whatever you do, don't use the public bathrooms; it's too dangerous."

The tube in the center of the booth began to vibrate. Virginia gasped and almost fell off her stool when a wiry man with thick black hair emerged and stood not two feet away from her, as if he'd appeared out of thin air.

Terrence handed him some papers, and then he disappeared back inside. "That's Ernesto."

"But where did he come from?"

Doris mocked in her high-pitched squeal, "But where did he come from?"

"Enough, Doris. There's a set of spiral stairs that connect us to the information booth on the lower level."

"How many people work down there?" She glanced at Doris to see if she'd do another echo, but a traveler had stepped up to her window and she was otherwise engaged.

"Just the one. He's only part-time, though. Back in the day, we had fourteen clerks up here, two below. Not a lot of elbow room."

Indeed, if each window had a clerk sitting behind it, the booth would have been impossibly crowded. Until now, she hadn't noticed how many spots were empty.

Winston spoke up. "The average clerk answers 167,440 questions a year."

"Wow." Virginia tried to look suitably impressed.

"We don't get nearly that many now, though." Terrence's voice had a hint of nostalgia. "That was back when trains, not planes, were the way to get around the country."

"You must know everything about this building."

"Probably do."

"I heard there used to be an art school in Grand Central." Better not to mention that she'd been inside; she didn't want to get in trouble on her first day.

He nodded. "The Grand Central School of Art, it was called.

Every September and January we'd get students asking how to get to it. East wing, top floor."

"You have a good memory."

"That's why they pay me the big bucks."

"Why did it close?"

"World War II, probably. No one had time for frivolous vocations during the war. There were Nazis right in the terminal, trying to sabotage the trains by dumping sand on the power converters. Luckily, we caught them just in time."

Doris cocked her head. "'We'? Did you personally make the arrest?"

"Well, the police did. But you bet I would have caught them, had they asked a question."

"Like '*Vo ist de* power converter?'" Doris broke out in a full-throated laugh.

Terrence smiled. "Exactly." He had a dreamy, faraway look in his eyes. "Back in the day, Grand Central was the beating heart of New York City. Soldiers, artists, businessmen, all dashing to get where they needed to go."

Winston piped up. "Did you ever see Jackson Pollock?"

"Afraid not."

"Winston, do you know a lot about art?" asked Virginia.

"I like the ones who splash all the paint about."

"Right." The jump from Nazis to abstract art made her head spin. Of course, it probably should come as no surprise that the info booth clerks were chock-full of facts, many of which had nothing to do with trains. Nature of the job.

"The art school, though. They say it's haunted." Totto's eyes were narrow slits. "An art teacher was killed in a train crash and all the art-work was destroyed. They say the ghost of the artist haunts the place, and no matter how hard Penn Central tries, no one will rent it."

Doris tossed an empty paper cup into the garbage. "No one will rent it because this place is a dump, and who wants to have offices in a dump? Hey, trainee, I need more coffee."

Virginia took the coffee order, writing it down on the back of one of the train schedules, and walked to the Station Master's Office. The inside of the terminal was dark, even at midday, the ceiling stained by decades of cigarette and cigar smoke and the bare-bulb chandeliers encrusted in soot. The whole place felt noxious.

Even so, hints of its former grandeur existed. A railing dripped with delicate brass filigree, topped by a scratched oak handrail. Even flaking paint couldn't obscure the ornamental detail of the metalwork. Virginia found the coffee machine in the Station Master's Office and trundled back out, balancing five paper cups on a plastic tray. Once back in the booth, she bolted the door behind her and handed out the coffees. Totto even said thank you.

The rest of her day went by fairly quickly. She tidied the area around her, grabbed a hot dog outdoors for lunch in order to get out of the gloom, refilled the schedules again, and answered the phone, which was usually for Terrence.

A few minutes before five, Terrence told her to head home. Not until she was outside the booth did she realize she didn't have her coat. She'd left it in the closet at the Penn Central legal offices.

Spun around by the crush of commuters, Virginia decided to take the elevator on the far side of the station rather than fight her way across the concourse. She got off on the seventh floor and stepped into a long hallway with trash piled up high against the walls and a general air of disuse. She headed right, figuring she'd end up at the offices soon enough, but only found more of the same. Had she gotten off on the wrong floor?

She turned another corner and froze. Three men sat in an alcove, sharing a joint that turned the air acrid and sweet. They wore jeans and leather jackets. Virginia's mother had always warned her to check the footwear of men who lurked about. "If they're in sneakers, it means they're planning to rob you and make a fast getaway."

Typical of her mother to make such a sweeping generalization. But all three wore sneakers. Her mother's words seemed to ring true as Virginia stared at their jagged faces.

"Whatcha doing here, lady?" The tallest one spoke up, pointing his finger at her like it was a gun.

They rose, slowly, the way cats move when they don't want to startle their prey.

She turned around and ran.

CHAPTER THREE

April 1928

Clara stood on the corner of Forty-Second Street and Vanderbilt Avenue, enraged. The sight of her illustrations, which she'd taken months to plan, design, and execute, hanging on the wall of the gallery's sales office like some cheap prints, ran through her head like a newsreel, followed by Mr. Lorette's sniveling face and that teacher's feeble attempt to mollify her.

"Wait!"

Levon Zakarian emerged from the terminal, wearing a long dark coat that flared behind him like an eagle's tail. Five of his students, including Nadine, trotted to keep up with their hero. "Where are you off to? I feel awful about what happened up there." He gestured with his thumb to the roof of the building.

"You didn't have anything to do with it."

She hadn't noticed how tall he was. He had about four inches on her, she guessed. At six feet tall, Clara wasn't used to having to look up to anyone. Her mother would have called him a swarthy man and not intended it kindly. But his pointed chin and nose created an elegant profile that counteracted the very bulk of him.

She'd never seen eyes so black, like ink, that it was hard to distinguish his pupil from his iris. His heavy eyelids lent him an air of recalcitrance or amusement, she wasn't sure which.

He smoothed his mustache, as thick and dark as the hair on his head, and regarded her. "As a fellow teacher, I feel the need to come to your aid." She couldn't place his accent, eastern European, perhaps.

"I don't need your aid. I needed the editor of *Vogue* to see my illustrations and offer me a contract, which did not happen because Mr. Lorette buried my work."

"You're so confident that this editor would have hired you on the spot after seeing your work?"

"I am."

"Very well, then, you belong with me. Come downtown with us. We're going to Richard's, which is full of people who hold similarly high opinions of their own work. You'll fit right in."

A few moments ago, all she wanted was to go back to her studio on East Tenth Street, rip up all her sketches, shove over her drawing table with its paints, trays, and rags, and watch the rubbish clatter to the floor.

It would probably be better for her art supplies if she avoided going home until her rage subsided, and part of her wanted to pick a fight with this man, who seemed sure of himself and his place in the world.

She squeezed into a taxi full of jabbering students, Nadine perched up front next to Mr. Zakarian, and stared out the window until it pulled up to a basement restaurant off West Fourth Street. The place was full, but the owner ushered them to a room at the back, where Mr. Zakarian took a seat at the head of a long table while the rest pulled up chairs around him, shouting out orders to the waitress.

Clara hung back and watched Mr. Zakarian's disciples jockey for the seats nearest him. The only other teacher present she recognized was Sebastian Standish, who had achieved a modicum of fame with his flattering portraits of newly wealthy businessmen and their families. He led the antique drawing class, where beginner students were taught to draw from cast models of Greek and Roman sculptures.

"It's old news," Mr. Zakarian announced, in response to a question Clara hadn't heard. "The Armory Show was the death knell to representational art. Anyone who doesn't think Picasso is a genius will be left behind, sketching and resketching four-hundred-year-old nudes until their pencils wear down to a nub as the rest of us move on to cubism, modernism."

The Armory Show. Where the work of avant-garde artists like Duchamp, Matisse, and Picasso had graced America's shores for the first time. Among a certain faction of the art world, the exhibit had caused a seismic shift in theories and approaches.

Mr. Standish bristled. He had at least twenty years on Mr. Zakarian, and his Newport plaid suit stood in marked contrast to the other teacher's shabby lumberjack shirt. "The Armory Show was fifteen years ago, Levon. If the curators intended to shock those of us who believe that a realistic drawing of peasants working in a field is a truer work of art as compared to a mishmash of shapes and colors signifying nothing, they have failed. I'm in no fear of being left behind."

"If a student has talent, they need inspiration, not rigid rules: 'Draw the finger like this and the torso like this.'" Mr. Zakarian's mimicry drew laughter.

"You must admit that classical techniques ought to be mastered first. Can you at least admit that?"

Mr. Zakarian relented. "We agree on that point. But if my student wants to draw a fish on the head of his figure, why shouldn't he?"

As they railed back and forth, the students breaking out into smaller arguments among themselves, Clara leaned against the wall. She had nothing to add. The hierarchy in the art world had been established hundreds of years ago: Oil painting trumped watercolors, portraits trumped landscapes. And all of that, summed up as "fine" art, trumped commercial art. Illustrators lay at the very bottom of the totem pole.

Mr. Zakarian had probably invited her along to show her how little her tantrum mattered in the rarefied world of high art.

"You must declare your affiliation and stand by it," said Mr. Standish. "Academic art has been around for far longer than your cubist goulash. In a hundred years, it will still be the standard-bearer for great art."

One of Mr. Zakarian's students chimed in. "You don't understand how fast the world is changing. Pretty pictures are no longer of interest, except to stodgy collectors."

Back in Arizona, taking classes at her provincial art school, Clara dreamed of meeting other artists. No one in her family understood her passion for drawing. How sometimes at night she'd lie awake, thinking about the line of a cheekbone on a portrait she'd been struggling with, imagining the exact brushstroke she'd use the next day.

But this discussion, if you could call it that, was far beyond anything she'd been taught. She didn't have the vocabulary to join in, even if she wanted to. A part of her knew this was why she'd kept to herself this past year. Everyone else in New York was so polished.

She was not, her family hailing from hardscrabble stock who endured the blistering heat of desert summers.

But even if she didn't speak like they did, her confidence and passion in her own work were unwavering. When she drew or painted, it was as if an unseen hand guided her own. She'd never been able to explain that to anyone. To her, painting was an internal expression, not a political or social one. She didn't have a manifesto or an affiliation, other than to please herself doing what she loved to do and make money doing it. The first part was easy—the second, more elusive.

"Picabia is no better than an illustrator." The speaker was Nadine. Her friendly smile from earlier that evening had disappeared.

Mr. Zakarian's gaze swung Clara's way like a lighthouse beacon. "An interesting supposition, Nadine. Luckily, we have a distinguished illustrator here. Perhaps Miss Darden has something to say in her own defense?"

Clara was only vaguely familiar with Picabia's early drawings of machines, which resembled instruction manuals and were of no interest to her. But that wasn't the point here, and Levon knew it. He was challenging her to prove herself.

Her heart pounding at the attention, she went on the attack. "I assume you rarely have illustrators join in your cozy after-hours gatherings, but my guess is that's because illustration requires both talent and discipline. Which in turn requires honing your craft instead of staying up all night talking about it."

Mr. Zakarian grinned; her audacity seemed to please him. "You can only work so many hours in a day. If you don't know *why* you're working, what's the point?"

"I know exactly why I'm working. To please the client. Illustrators have to be malleable experts at all styles and subjects." The silence that followed only fed her disdain. She wouldn't be working at the school much longer, anyway, so what did it matter? "I'd like to see you get a commission, figure out the approach and execution, then do it all over again the next day, with a different client with a different set of expectations. You wouldn't last a week."

"Fine, it's a tough field," said the student sitting to Mr. Zakarian's right. "But you can't call it art. It's a magazine cover or an ad, and then it's trash."

She stood firm. "One day, illustrations will be as venerated as the works of Matisse."

Mr. Zakarian laughed. "So you're saying that one day, an ad for pea soup will be framed and hanging on the wall of a museum?"

"Maybe. What I'm saying is that many illustrators are more proficient, more skilled, than fine artists."

"Let's prove it. I dare you to come to my life drawing and painting class. Tomorrow." Mr. Zakarian's words had an edge that belied the smile on his face.

Mr. Zakarian had no idea whom he was dealing with. Clara had been born into a family of great wealth and indulgence in Phoenix, and she vividly remembered screaming as a child of three when her mother refused her a sweet. Her father had adored her ferocity, encouraged it. When his embezzlement scheme—selling shares in a copper mine that never existed—finally unraveled, it had only made Clara more demanding. For fifteen years, the world had revolved around her, and then suddenly she was an afterthought, her tyrannical ways no longer effective at getting attention or a pleasing response. But she could summon up the familiar fury at a moment's notice, if necessary. "I'd be delighted."

The students cheered. Or, more accurately, jeered.

She'd show them. "In return, you can come to my class and spend a day as an illustrator."

Mr. Zakarian rubbed his mustache with his hand in what she suspected was an effort to hide his amused surprise. "Very well. We'll see who is the better artist then."

"We certainly will."

"What will be the wager?"

The answer came to her in a flash: a way to make up for the dismal evening, even if it meant laying bare her vulnerability before everyone. "If I win, you must speak with Mr. Lorette and convince him to keep me on next term."

"Do you think I have that kind of pull?"

"I do."

"Very well, then." He paused. "And if I win, I get the opportunity to paint you."

Someone let out a low whistle. She ignored it, as well as the insinuation of his wanting her to be his model. Everyone knew what he meant, and she noticed the muscles in Nadine's neck twitch.

She nodded. "Very well."

Out on the sidewalk, Clara took a moment to get her bearings. Even this late at night, the narrow Greenwich Village street was punctuated with people who seemed to be in no rush to get home. A couple linked at the arms brushed by her as if she wasn't even there, the woman laughing loudly at something the man said. She watched them walk away, their movements slightly off, as if they were walking on a ship's deck, a sure sign that they'd visited one of the many speakeasies tucked under stoops and in back courtyards.

The door to the restaurant opened, and Mr. Zakarian flew out, followed closely by Nadine.

"You're leaving?" Nadine's voice was short and sharp, a recrimination.

Mr. Zakarian threw Clara an apologetic look and held up one finger before turning back to the girl.

If God created a woman who was the exact opposite of Clara, Nadine would be the result. Short, with a stocky build, full bosom, and thick black hair, she was of the ground, of the earth, in spite of her fashionable clothes and well-bred airs.

Nadine put her hands on her hips and glowered up at Mr. Zakarian. "You're going with her?"

"I'm planning on discussing the school with another faculty member. You don't need to be jealous."

Clara had no desire to get involved in the drama of a lecherous teacher and his needy student. "I don't need an escort home, thank you very much."

She headed east at a good clip.

Only ten seconds passed before she heard Mr. Zakarian's footsteps. He pulled up beside her as she reached the next intersection. "Sorry about that. But I did want to speak with you further. First, I want to apologize for putting you on the spot like that."

"I rather enjoy watching spoiled young artists declare their manifestos. If only we could all meet again in three years when they realize what a pointless enterprise it was and that the time would have been better spent in the studio, Mr. Zakarian."

"Please, call me Levon." His dark eyes sparkled in the lamplight. "I agree. Although I admit that I do my share of declaring. Isn't it a good idea to have a sense of what you want to accomplish?"

She stopped walking. "I have had a very long day, and the last thing I wish to do is continue on with that ridiculous conversation. We have drawn our lines in the sand, and I look forward to taking your class. But for now, I must get home and finish up my commissions so that I can afford to buy more paint."

He joined her again, loping along like a Saint Bernard. "Just take it from the teachers' supply closet. They'll never know. I do it all the time."

She could only imagine the glee in Mr. Lorette's eyes, catching her with a satchel full of purloined paints. "Mr. Lorette may give you that liberty, but he wouldn't do the same for me. You really ought to go back to your audience."

"Nah, they're probably still torturing Sebastian." They fell into step together. Like her, he took long strides. "I have students who love me and those who hate me, but the past few years teaching, I've earned my audience. I suspect you'll have your own group of fawning students before the semester is out. Part of the job."

"Speaking of fawns, how old is Nadine?"

He had the decency to look abashed. "Just turned nineteen."

"And how old are you?"

"Twenty-five."

She'd figured he was over thirty. "Oh. So am I." Her assessment of his talents reordered themselves. At twenty-five, he was still new on the scene. The show earlier this evening was probably as important to him as it was to her. "Did you get any interest tonight?"

"Who knows? Who cares?" His voice rose, the questions quivering in the cold night air. He did care.

She refused to soften. "What are your ambitions, then, if you don't care?"

"To change the way people look at the world."

She tried not to laugh, but he caught her smirking.

"Don't make fun of me. I bet you feel the same way." He carried on. "But your idea of changing the world is to have someone buy a product. A dress or a hat or a can of soup, no?"

His naivety rankled her. "You'd like them to buy your painting. Is that any different?"

"Of course it is. Because they will buy their soup and take it home and eat it, while my work will hang on their walls and give them joy for years."

"Or no one will buy it, and it'll languish in your studio. Because there are a hundred other artists who are trying to do what you do."

He stopped walking. "What is it that I do?"

"Draw like Picasso." She couldn't help herself. The works she'd seen on the walls of the Grand Central Art Galleries signed by Levon Zakarian were far too similar to those of the Spanish genius.

"Why not? He's the greatest painter of our time. What is wrong with paying homage to him?"

"Nothing at all. But if someone wants a Picasso, they can buy one." She waited for a retort, but none came.

"I want to show you something."

"Now?"

"Yes. My studio isn't far from here. Right off Union Square. Will you come with me?"

She studied him. Levon was almost giddy, like a child on Christmas Eve, but he wasn't attracted to her; she was sure of that. Aside from her brief frisson with Oliver earlier that evening, most men weren't, and it didn't bother her much now that she was away from her mother's heaving sighs of disappointment. In this case, it was a relief, as she was curious to see his studio, and the wager to paint her, while bold, was probably the best he could come up with under the circumstances.

Levon led her into a building on the north side of Sixteenth Street. They trudged up several sets of stairs and down a long, dark hallway to the door at the very end. Levon's studio, to her shock, was as clean as a hospital. The parquet floor had been newly scrubbed. Two massive easels stood in the middle of the floor, the center of attention, while jars of brushes and paint cans lined a windowsill like a row of inert spectators. A bank of leaded windows slanted down on the north side, where a daybed and a large dining room table had been shoved aside, the furniture merely an afterthought.

Clara shrugged off her coat and wandered over to a bookshelf near the fireplace, trying not to appear too impressed. Levon had obviously done well to be able to afford such a massive studio. He was probably subsidizing his salary from the art school with private lessons. How easy it was for him, to have come to New York and found respect, a steady income, and an enormous place to work.

Levon lit the burner under a kettle on the small kitchen stove. "Would you like some tea?"

"No, thank you." She paged through a volume on Matisse before placing it back on a different shelf. Levon opened his mouth to say something but busied himself with his tea preparations instead. He was so easily provoked, for a moment she regretted teasing him. Any artist who so tightly controlled his studio—the alphabetized books, carefully spaced jars, and scrubbed floors—was trying to keep something else in check, and she wondered what it could be.

Eventually, he approached one of the easels and gently lifted the dustcloth from it. "I'd like you to see this, Miss Darden."

She waved one hand at him. "Please, call me Clara."

He gave her a solemn nod and stepped back, offering her the prime spot in front of it.

She'd expected another wild, Picasso-like flight of fancy, not a portrait. Two figures looked out from the canvas, a boy holding something in one hand, standing beside a seated woman whose gaze was as dark as death. A boy and his mother. The boy had a dark mess of hair and the same pointed widow's peak as Levon's. He wore a yellow overcoat and a funny set of slipper-like shoes, his feet turned slightly away, as if he hoped to escape as soon as possible.

The woman, though, was solid, unmoving, going nowhere. Her hands rested on her knees but appeared unfinished, as if she were wearing mittens. The lack of detail existed only from the neck down, however, as her face had been drawn in with an elegant line from eyebrow to nose, heavily lidded eyes, encircled by an ocean-blue headscarf.

The boy, unsure and self-conscious, was turned in on himself, while the woman's energy was directed outward at the viewer: accusatory yet hopeful.

"This is you and your mother?"

He nodded.

"It's beautiful, heartbreaking, Levon. Why didn't you show this tonight?"

He pulled the cloth back over it. "It's not finished."

On a table nearby, she spotted a photograph. "Is that what you're working from?"

He snatched it up and stared hard at it for a couple of seconds before reluctantly passing it over. Clara held it carefully at the very edges. The same figures, but filled with details. The woman's hands had thick, working-class fingers. The boy held a small bouquet of flowers. The boy looked more certain and the woman less so. "Tell me the story behind this."

Levon prowled away from her, then back. "My father was a

cobbler; he came to the United States from the shores of Lake Van, in Turkish Armenia. He was going to send for my mother, sister, and me once he was settled. While we waited, my mother had this photo taken in the hopes that he wouldn't forget us."

"Why wasn't your sister in the photograph?"

"Girls were not as important. I was the boy, his son. My mother hoped it would remind him of his duties."

"I see."

"But before we could send it to him, we were forced out by the threat of a civil war, and headed east. My sister wore boy's clothes, for safety's sake, and together we made it to a city called Yerevan, where we lived in an abandoned building. If it rained we got wet, and we tried to make do, but it was very difficult to find food." As he spoke, he circled the entire room several times. Clara stayed still as he grew more and more agitated.

"My mother became ill, and one day she died. She'd given all her food to us, and we'd eaten it. Taken her life. We were selfish."

The day's complaints and petty jealousies fell away. "She would have wanted to feed you first. Any mother would have. When did you come to the States?"

"Soon after. As orphans, we were bumped up to the top of the list. We lived with relatives in Providence, and I never did find my father. Never cared to. Our relatives said he'd taken up with another woman and moved away. I drew, went to art school there, and then came here. I studied at the Grand Central School of Art and became a teacher within months."

The return of his bravado cheered Clara. "Of course you did. This painting is remarkable. You must continue."

"You must as well."

"How can you say that, when you've never even seen my work?"

"I can see in you that you are like me. Strong. I must give you my advice, though."

"Okay."

"Get out more. Don't sit in your studio all day; it's not good for the soul. Also, don't let your students come first. Your work comes first, always."

"I'll do my best."

"And when you come to my class, don't worry if you don't do very well. These students, my students, are trained by the very best. Me."

And the pomposity was back with a vengeance. "I'll see you tomorrow at ten."

As she left, she saw him reach for the mop leaning against the wall. His voice, singing some kind of folk song in a foreign tongue, rang down the stairwell. She imagined him mopping away their footprints, scrubbing away his sad tale, well into the night.

CHAPTER FOUR

April 1928

Clara walked into Levon's studio at the Grand Central School of Art ten minutes early. She'd woken with a burst of nervous energy and wanted to get this ridiculous bet over with. If she was going to make a fool of herself in a roomful of his students, so be it. She'd torture him in her own class. Although, looking around the studio, she saw that her humiliation would take place in front of four times as many onlookers.

Levon's class was held in one of the biggest studios in the school, a testament to his popularity. A couple of dozen easels encircled the model's platform in the middle of the room. Nadine, as class monitor, directed Clara to an easel in the front row, with a scowl.

"Levon wants you here."

Clara shrugged off the girl's rudeness and busied herself with organizing her brushes and paint. She'd loved everything about being in a studio ever since she'd attended her first art class several years earlier. The sharp tang of turpentine, the oily residue of paint on a palette, and even the scuffed-up floors awed her. You never knew what might come to pass after four hours of diligent concentration: a work of art, or a canvas to be scraped and reused for next time?

Soon after her family had fled to Tucson, she read about a new art school in the newspaper. Located in an abandoned factory just outside of town, where every summer, monsoon rains pounded the shellacked earth, the school attracted a fair bit of notice and Clara begged her father for permission to go. She'd filled notebooks with silly doodlings as a young girl, and later, when the family's fortunes fell, the act of drawing had become an escape of sorts. Her father allowed her to go to one class—that was all they could afford—but the director, Miss Alice, recognized her talent and allowed her to come back whenever she liked. Miss Alice taught her to be quiet for a moment before putting brush or pencil to paper, to wait and listen to the voice in her head before beginning. Once Clara discovered her passion for art, there was no going back. She was determined to make it her career, her life.

Levon entered in a rush, shouting out for Nadine. She leaped forward and took his coat, hanging it on the rack near the door. Levon looked about. "Where's our model? Not here yet? Well, let's not fret about that."

Levon stopped in front of Clara, blinked a couple of times, and moved on. She was relieved he didn't call attention to her. Being parked in the front of the room was bad enough.

For five minutes, Levon spoke in a torrent of ideas, touching upon the best works to view in the Met and Gallatin's Gallery of Living Art, of Cézanne, Picasso, and Braque. He called on students to offer their opinions before shredding them to pieces. What had she been thinking? This was no painting class; it was a cult.

The students appeared to enjoy the show. Several tried to offer counterpoints, and Levon prodded them into expanding on their ideas before shooting them down, always with a smile on his face.

The door opened, and the robed model walked in.

Usually, the men and women who got paid to pose were on the far side of desperate. Washed-up dancers or actors, with folds of flesh that spoke of indulgence or limbs bony with age. Last year, as a student at the school, Clara had quickly gotten over the shock of a nude man or woman posing for class. The challenge of capturing a sagging breast or rounded buttock on paper or canvas quickly overtook the embarrassment of gawking at a naked human being.

But this wasn't a down-on-his-luck stranger. It was Oliver, the poet from the restaurant.

As Oliver's robe fell to the floor and he stepped onto the platform, a collective hush fell around the room. Every line of his body, the one that ran above his hip, the one that differentiated the long muscles of his thigh, resembled those of the antique casts that stared down at them from the studio's shelves.

She caught Levon watching her and looked at her canvas, unsure of where to begin, overwhelmed.

She wasn't the only one. A couple of the women gaped openly, which made her smile. Back to the work at hand. She had a bet to win, and she wasn't about to let a swell-looking fellow throw her off-balance.

"Don't be bound by what you see," said Levon. He came to a stop beside Oliver, who stood with his arms crossed, as if waiting for a bus. Levon whispered something, and he struck a pose, shifting his weight on the left leg, a hand on his hip, his eyes looking up and out.

Levon nodded and addressed the class. "I want you to sketch what you feel."

Clara had to bite her cheek to keep from smiling at the vagueness of his words, so typical of pompous art teachers. Imagine if she said such a thing to her illustration class? They'd have looked at her as if she had two heads. All around her, the students dove in, knowing that time was limited and eager to please their master. As they worked, Levon drifted from easel to easel. He stared for a long time at the canvas of a young woman at the end of Clara's row. "You're trying to be clever again, and I don't want that. I must break you of that habit. For the next class, when we turn to oils, I want you to use a large brush for the details and the small brush for the fill."

He moved down another easel, to a young man whose hand was wildly moving about the paper. Levon took the pencil from him. "Permit me."

Clara stifled a gasp as he drew over the student's work. His arrogance astounded her.

She sharpened her pencil, the sound like a low rumble in the quiet room, and immediately regretted calling attention to herself. Levon was getting closer. He looked over and flashed a big smile her way, stuck his thumb up in the air like a clown. She should never have agreed to this—she'd placed herself at a disadvantage, and by failing here, she'd further erode what was left of her standing in the school.

Clara looked at her own blank canvas, then back up at the model, only to discover he was looking right at her. She was the only one not doing anything, frozen in place. He winked at her, and, reflexively, she smiled back.

Levon shouted at a skinny boy to her right. "No, no! You have to consider the negative space. Stupid, stupid." He was closing in.

One thing was certain: If he dared to draw on her canvas, she'd pick it up and smash it over his head.

Clara remembered her father, who'd taken to belittling Clara and her mother once his fortunes fell, as if their reduced circumstances were their fault. He went out very little, other than to his menial job at a hospital, while Clara's mother took over all the tasks the servants had done in Phoenix, cooking and cleaning and polishing his shoes. Clara watched with horror and revulsion as her mother kowtowed to his every need, doing whatever it took to defuse his foul moods, often making them worse in the process.

Levon was similar in temperament: his impetuousness, the cavalier disregard for everyone around him, his certainty in his own talents. She had to put him straight, let him know that she was not to be bullied. No doubt, if she didn't do well under this ridiculous test, he'd lose interest in her. For some strange reason, the thought annoyed her even more.

She took a deep breath, reminding herself that she was a teacher, not a frightened pupil. When one of her own students seemed stuck, she'd tell them to stop believing that everything they did was precious. If you want to make a living at it, she'd say, you must sit at the drawing board, brush in hand, and simply do it.

She put the pencil to the paper and began sketching out the proportions, the same as she would approach a Wanamaker drawing. The boy was so angelic, the line of his limbs so much the ideal, that before she knew it, the figure on the canvas was almost completed. What a relief not to worry about the correct drape of a coat, or the texture of a pair of pants. This was simply skin, bones, and musculature.

Once she was satisfied with the outline, she picked up the palette and began experimenting with the oils. While watercolors were her favorite medium, oils came in a close second. She'd stepped in as a teacher for Miss Alice every so often after a couple of years of study, and she relished the challenge, switching from oils to watercolors to etching. She gave all her earnings to her father, which only seemed to make matters worse, adding to his humiliation.

When she showed up at art class with a bruised wrist after one of their arguments, Miss Alice insisted she apply for a scholarship at the Grand Central School of Art in New York City. Together, they selected her best work and sent it off in the post. The letter of acceptance arrived a month later. It was for only one term—after that, she'd be on her own—but Clara jumped at the chance. Her father had railed at her for trying to sneak away, but she was certain he was secretly pleased to get rid of her. Her mother was openly relieved, as it meant one less person to provoke him.

"You'll never make it there," he said over her last dinner at home, a measly meal of stringy, overcooked chicken and some kind of mashed vegetables. Her mother knew she couldn't compete with the lavish dinners of their former cook, and she didn't bother to try.

"Why shouldn't I?"

"Because you're a girl and you're a dilettante. That city will devour you."

She'd arrived in New York on a bright September day, still reeling from the train trip, where she'd learned to carry a book whenever she got up from her seat, the better to fend off the advances of male passengers who took advantage of any sudden lurch for a quick grope. A hard bonk ensured they behaved better the next time they passed each other in the aisle. Grateful to finally be discharged from the claustrophobic train cars, she'd found her way to the door of a small apartment building on East Tenth Street that leased rooms only to women. The landlord had shown her to the top floor, her very own studio, and Clara almost danced with joy. She began her illustration class the next day with Mr. Wendle, who was kind but bland. She learned later he was ill, which explained his hacking cough and lack of enthusiasm: For the first three weeks, he insisted the entire class draw shoes. Over and over. Mary Janes, oxfords, satin slippers, and mules, followed by men's leather dress shoes. At night Clara dreamed of soles and laces. She did as she was told and was made monitor of the class, which made the other students jealous, but she didn't care.

Armed with her drawings and desperate for rent money, Clara made the rounds of the magazines and big department stores, and Wanamaker had immediately assigned her to do an advertisement for children's shoes. Unlike the other, less ambitious students, the ones who were unsure of their work and required Mr. Wendle's constant hand-holding, Clara had one goal: to make money off her art and prove her father wrong.

As the fall wore on, New York grew colder and wetter. The tree outside her apartment scraped its stripped branches against the dull stone walls. Christmas Day she spent alone in her studio drawing gloves, a step up from footwear, or so the advertising executive told her, and made just enough to pay for the next semester's classes. In January, when Mr. Wendle didn't show up to class, she offered to fill in, citing her experience in Arizona and her commissions from Wanamaker. Mr. Lorette had hesitated before agreeing that, for now, she might serve as a substitute. No doubt her lower salary had also factored into his decision.

It had all seemed so easy at the time. But her hope had faded fast. She'd plateaued early and hadn't been able to move up since. No increase in commissions, possibly no class to teach next term, and no fashion magazine cover.

A shuffling sound brought Clara back to earth, back to where she stood in front of an easel at the Grand Central School of Art, her painting finished. She turned around to see the entire class clustered behind her, Levon at the fore, his arms crossed. She had no idea how long they'd all been standing there.

But she knew from the way his eyes traveled over her painting, from the right shoulder to the detail of the left foot and back up, that she'd more than held her own.

⁓⦿⦿

The assignment in Levon's class freed Clara from her recent gloom. She couldn't explain it, other than she'd regained a touch of confidence that her time in New York had steadily eroded. Her brashness had gotten her through doors, but beneath it all had been a desperation to succeed at all costs, and pushing that hard had caused her to stall, just like her father's decrepit Model T used to do. He'd kick the tires and curse while she waited inside, cocooned in the tufted leather seat.

Levon's assignment had forced her to dig deep back into her creative well and do something unusual: Draw for the sake of beauty. It wasn't about accurately capturing the curve of a leather T-strap but the curve from waist to hip, the simple beauty of the human form. In any event, the few hours in Levon's class had offered her a reprieve from her impending financial doom.

In front of his students, Levon had pointed out how she'd captured the model's character, not just his construction. "Do you see the romance, the spirit, the fine truth?" They'd all nodded, as Clara stood by, squashing any outward sign of satisfaction. At the end of class, she'd hovered, hoping to thank Levon for his graciousness, but he'd been corralled by a student in the far corner, and she'd left without a word. Oliver had dashed the moment the students had been told to put down their brushes. Thank God, for she didn't think she'd be able to look him in the eyes without blushing.

Over the weekend, the news of the bet had spread throughout the school, and she'd arrived at her illustration class heady with expectation. Yet Levon lumbered in late, shaking the hands of the students he knew, like a polished politician. She watched with irritation as her tiny class fell under his spell.

Levon seemed to think that he could charm his way to a win. "I'm sorry to be late; my apologies to our venerated professor."

Gertrude giggled.

"You may take any drawing table you like," offered Clara.

"So many to choose from."

He wandered about, taking his time, as if selecting the best seat in a restaurant. The man took up too much room. Not because of his height or build but because he simply demanded more attention than anyone else, which was saying a lot in a school for artists. Clara ignored his overacting and continued describing the day's assignment.

"I'd like you to take a close look at Renoir's *Luncheon of the Boating Party.*" She placed a print of it on an easel and slid it forward. The work was one of her favorites, the way Renoir had captured the flirtation of youth, hands almost touching, languorous looks, a man with bare arms straddling a chair. The heat of a summer's day seemed to rise from the painting's surface. "You're to rework this to the modern day and place a bottle of Coca-Cola in one of the sub-ject's hands."

A murmur went around the room. Gertrude spoke up. "Do we have to re-create the entire composition?"

"No, you can narrow down your focus to whichever character or group appeals most to you."

Levon stood. "You cannot be serious."

"I am serious. If you want to focus on only one character, I understand."

He gasped a couple of times, like a fish on a hook. If he had gills, they'd be fanning themselves madly. This was far easier than she imagined.

"This is blasphemy. You're defiling a master. You can't ask your students to do this; it's not dignified."

"It sells soda."

"No, it doesn't. This is a class, not the real world."

"For illustrators, there is no delineation. They may be asked to do something like this, so they might as well get used to it." She paused. "You're lucky I didn't choose *Les Demoiselles d'Avignon*."

At the mention of his beloved Picasso, Levon almost levitated off the floor.

"If you'd chosen that, I would have walked right out that door."

"And you would have lost the bet. Now, class, please get to work."

For some time, there was no sound other than pencils scribbling away, followed by the soft whoosh of brush on paper. Wilbur, true to form, grumbled every so often, but the girls stayed focused on the task at hand.

"Watercolor is like a performance," she said, speaking to no one in particular. "The wash is constantly changing, drying with every passing minute, and you must be able to move quickly, make a large field fast if you want the color to be consistent. The preparation—the right brush, the right amount of wash, the correct mix of colors—is key, but you must work with speed and confidence."

Levon lit a cigarette and sat back in his chair, gazing up at the ceiling. She ignored him and watched over Gertrude's shoulder as she painted the orange flower on the woman's hat. "Flowers are certainly your forte, Gertrude."

The girl smiled. "They're my favorite."

Levon stubbed out his cigarette and leaned over the drawing board, pencil in hand.

He drew a few quick strokes before leaping up and leaving the room.

Was he throwing the bet? She sidled over and looked at his paper, where he'd deftly captured the figure of the man straddling the chair. But he hadn't opened up one jar of paint yet.

She checked her watch. He had plenty of time.

What if he regretted the wager, of using her as his model? It had certainly been an impulsive declaration. What if, upon further thought, he'd come to the conclusion it would be a waste of time? Clara wasn't a typical model. "A pair of large feet and hands attached to a string bean," her mother used to say.

Levon returned ten minutes later, took his seat, and picked up a brush.

What did it matter what his motives were? She hardly knew him at all, and this bet was a means to an end.

Much of Clara's time was spent with Wilbur, helping him attain the flesh-colored tone of the faces. Finally, the bell sounded for the end of class.

Levon squirmed in his chair, stood, and put on his coat. Clara walked over to his table, standing as tall as she possibly could, her spine long and stiff, and looked down at the paper. The other students, curious, gathered around her.

He'd made so many mistakes she didn't know where to begin. His impatience with the amount of time it took for one color to dry before working on the adjacent hue meant that they'd bled into one another, forming what seemed to be a hazy sunset, not a human being. The bottle of Coca-Cola looked like a bouquet of roses that had wilted in the heat. No advertiser would accept this. Her own students had done much better jobs.

And he hadn't thrown the bet. He was red-faced, fuming, and silent.

"Interesting." She couldn't help herself. "An unusual approach."

He twirled about, grabbing the paper and ripping it in half. "Watercolor is a child's medium."

She tried, and failed, to keep a satisfied smile from spreading across her face. "So you'll speak with Mr. Lorette in the morning?"

He took a deep breath and gave her the slightest nod before storming off.

She'd won.

CHAPTER FIVE

November 1974

Virginia ran as fast as her high heels could take her, away from the three men huddled together in the seventh-floor hallway of Grand Central. They yelled after her, calling her terrible names. She took the corner fast, slamming her knee into the opposite wall. A door a few yards away opened slowly, and she slid to a stop. One of them must have taken a shortcut, knowing she'd never make it to the elevator in time. It was over.

But instead of a thug, the lawyer from this morning emerged. Mr. Huckle. He was wiping down his hands with a paper towel, on his way out of the men's room. He looked as shocked to see her as she did him.

He looked past her to her pursuers, and in a split second, his entire visage changed. He stood up, tall. Huge, in fact. She hadn't noticed how enormous he was back in his office, surrounded by all the papers and books. He filled the narrow hallway like a boulder in a crevice.

"What the hell do you think you're doing?" he bellowed. Virginia ducked behind him, not sure if she should stay put or make a run for the elevator.

"We're cool, man. Just trying to help out a lost lady." The three men began backing up almost immediately. Now that she had a chance to study them, she could see they were teenagers with acne over pallid skin, raging with testosterone-fueled bluster. She imagined Mr. Huckle barreling toward them, a bowling ball aimed at three skinny pins.

"They were going to attack me," whispered Virginia.

Mr. Huckle glanced around at her. "Stay put. Don't move."

One of the men swore. "We're going, we're going. Don't get all bent outta shape."

"You're going to be bent out of shape by the time I'm done with you. Get the hell out of here before I call the cops."

After they'd turned the corner, out of view, Mr. Huckle put a protective arm around Virginia. It felt heavy but good. "Are you all right? Did they hurt you?"

She shook her head. "You appeared just in time."

"We better get out of here. Follow me." He led her down the hall, around another corner—by now she was completely turned around—until they reached the door to the legal department. "What are you doing wandering around up here? Everything's empty, closed up in this section."

"I took the wrong elevator trying to get back to my coat. I left it in the closet."

The shock of what she'd just been through hit home now that she was in the fluorescent lights of the offices, somewhere safe. Her mind replayed the scene in her head, the dank smell of the hallway, the shininess of their black leather jackets.

Her head felt foggy. What was she supposed to do now? Get out of here. Virginia slid her coat off the hanger.

"What were you doing here all day?" asked Mr. Huckle. "I didn't see you."

"Kathleen sent me down to the information booth."

"Did she?" He frowned.

"Yes. Since we didn't work out. I'm sorry about that, by the way, Mr. Huckle." She turned to leave.

"Call me Dennis. You shouldn't go out there alone. In fact, we should go to the police and report these guys. I don't like the idea of them wandering around up here with the other office workers. Let's go down and we'll make a report, see if we can actually get them to do their jobs in this hellhole."

She looked at her watch. She was supposed to meet her friend Betsy in an hour. But if she didn't do anything, her would-be attackers might waltz past the information booth one day and spot her. She was safe with Dennis. Nothing was going to happen to her as long as he was nearby, so she might as well keep him nearby for as long as possible.

They took the elevator down to the mezzanine level and walked through a set of doors with the words TO VANDERBILT AVENUE / THE CAMPBELL APARTMENT etched in the marble above them. He cut a sharp left, and she followed him up a narrow set of stairs. The placard on the door read METRO-NORTH POLICE.

Dennis greeted a man in a blue uniform who sat beneath a row of television monitors showing grainy black-and-white footage of train platforms. Cheap wood paneling divided the entryway from another, larger area behind him. In the smaller space, uneven shelves held files and binders, messier than in the information booth. Virginia stifled an impulse to straighten them out, clean up the messy piles. She hated to see disarray, which was why she avoided going into her daughter's bedroom as much as possible, where bell-bottoms and peasant tops were strewn about like the cast of *Hair* had just cavorted by.

A sliding window looked out into a holding pen. Inside, a couple of bums had arranged metal folding chairs as beds and were asleep or, more likely, passed out. One man groaned, and the police officer slammed the window shut.

"Dennis, what's going on?" asked the cop.

"We had a problem up on seven. Couple of thugs tried to attack one of our employees." He motioned to Virginia.

The officer barely reacted. Just another day in the city. "Sorry to hear it. Let me call the sergeant, see if we can't have some guys go up and do a sweep. Hold on a sec." He picked up the phone, spoke in a thick Brooklyn accent to someone on the receiving end. "They're on it. In the meantime, let me get you some paperwork to fill out; we'll see if we can catch these guys." He looked around and swore. "Be right back."

When they were alone, Dennis looked down at her, a reassuring smile on his face.

She pretended her neck itched, covering her right breast with her arm. Her reflexive, protective gesture. Chester had hated when she did that. He'd tell her to sit up straight, stop worrying so much, that she looked fine.

They'd lived what she thought was a wonderful life together until he went to a party in the Village one Friday night on a whim, dragged downtown by two winsome girls from the secretarial pool in his office. What he saw there, he said, opened his eyes to his own true nature. He didn't want to be pinned down anymore; he wanted his freedom instead. The timing of his ridiculous announcement, just a few years after her recovery, had left Virginia dizzy and breathless. He'd insisted it had nothing to do with her disfigurement, but she'd known better. He'd taken her to the Oyster Bar for dinner one night—probably on his way to some key party up in Connecticut—and told her it was over. She'd shielded herself with her arm, sat back in her chair and looked up at the vaulted ceiling, wondering if it would amplify her screams. But she hadn't screamed. Just looked at him, agreed, insisted that they tell Ruby together.

Chester hadn't settled down with one woman, and for that she'd been grateful. She hadn't been replaced by a younger, prettier version. She'd heard through the grapevine that he'd cycled through dozens of girls and was living the high life.

"Have some water." Dennis reached over to the water cooler propped up in the corner, filled a paper cone, and handed it to her. "You okay?"

"I think I'm a little freaked-out, to be honest." She took a sip, stifling a giggle. "My daughter always tells me I have the wrong reaction to things. Like laughing at a funeral, crying at a funny movie. My ex-husband would tell me that I tend to babble on when I'm nervous. Talk, talk, talk. And sometimes hum. Boy, that drove him crazy. Because I can't keep a tune. Or is it hold a tune?"

She was making a fool of herself.

"Try me. Hum something, and let's see if I can recognize it."

Lips pursed, she launched into the chorus of "Seasons in the Sun," which had been circling around her brain ever since it came out.

Dennis listened, blinking with concentration. "'Time in a Bottle'?"

She shook her head. "No! Oh dear. It's that one about—" She stopped herself mid-sentence. "I'm sorry I'm taking up so much of your time; you must want to get home to your family."

"Don't worry about it. I'm divorced, so there's no rush to get back to my place in Yonkers."

"Yonkers?" She'd imagined him, like all the lawyers she knew, living on the Upper East Side or off in the distant suburbs.

"Where my family's from originally. I live near my ma, take care of her. Probably why I'm getting divorced, if you want to know the truth."

As he spoke, he rolled up his shirtsleeves, exposing thick forearms. She'd always been a sucker for a rolled-up sleeve on a man. Something about the thatch of short hairs against a crisp white shirt made her knees wobble. "How did you become a lawyer?"

"Studied, got into City College and then Fordham Law."

"My ex-husband is a lawyer. Columbia." Even though they'd been divorced for a year, she still sometimes dropped that into conversation, out of habit. As if they were still a unit and his accomplishments were synonymous with her own. Dennis didn't seem all that impressed, which made her like him more. "How long have you been working for Penn Central?"

"Since I got out of law school. Started as an associate. With this lawsuit still pending against the Landmarks Commission, it's been crazy, but there's a light at the end of the tunnel."

"Why's there a lawsuit?"

"The Landmarks Commission says that Penn Central has to keep the terminal exactly like it is. Which is absurd. The place is a money pit. If all goes according to plan and we win this case, I'm going to be promoted to head of the department."

One of the guys in the holding cell began to moan. She wondered if the cop was ever going to come back, but in a way, she didn't mind. "What's the big plan?"

"Once we shoot down the notion that the terminal is protected by landmark status, we're going to put up a new skyscraper on this very spot. Fifty-five stories. It's going to be massive. The city will give us a huge tax write-off for improving the district, and we'll be making serious money from the rent. Much better than this old mausoleum." He gestured around him.

"They'd tear it down, like Penn Station?" A little less than ten years ago, she'd been as surprised as many others in the city to find that Penn Station, a glass jewel of a train hub, was to be demolished. The few voices raised in protest had made no difference.

"The new building will rip through part of it, the side facing Forty-Second Street, and rest on top, like a hen sitting on its eggs." To demonstrate, Dennis held out one hand in a fist and settled the other lightly on top of it. His fingernails were trimmed and clean.

She studied the odd shape formed by Dennis's hands, unable to picture what he described. A couple of years ago, Betsy had insisted Virginia join her in signing up for the ladies' committee to Preserve Old New York, or PONY, as it was known. They met in a member's overdecorated living room once a month and listened to a guest speaker, nodding with concern while getting buzzed on generous pours of rosé. The day of the Grand Central lecture, the historian described how Cornelius Vanderbilt constructed the original station, called Grand Central Depot, in 1871, and that the one that stood today was completed in 1913. He showed them photos of the pristine waiting room right after it was built and the Whispering Gallery, where the unique design of the vaulted ceiling carried even the smallest sound to the opposite corner. The historian, surveying the room of tipsy wives, had proclaimed that women, in particular, should recall that whispers carry and can have tremendous power, even if their voices were weaker than a man's. Virginia wasn't sure if he was being encouraging or chauvinistic.

Still, Grand Central had such a rich history. "You're putting a modernist skyscraper on top of a beaux arts building. Won't that look strange?"

"It's the future. The city's got to move forward. At the moment, there's a ton of empty space in here that's completely unusable. That's lost revenue for Penn Central."

Like the art school.

She thought of Terrence and his clerks. "What about the employees who work for the railroad?"

"Anything to do with the trains gets buried underground. The terminal goes down ten stories, so there's a lot of room to play with. Next time you come up to my office, I'll show you a model of the new building. Incredible. Hey, if you play your cards right, I'll get you a cushy job."

"As long as I don't have to do stenography."

He laughed. "I'm sorry I was hard on you this morning."

"Don't be sorry. I had no idea what I was doing. But I like this idea of a cushy job. I could answer phones, say. I'd be a great receptionist." She pretended to pick up a phone. "Mr. Huckle's office, how may I help you?"

"I like that." He stared at her a moment too long.

He was flirting with her. The realization came with a rush of confusion. She hadn't flirted since 1953.

How different he seemed now than when they'd first met, seven hours ago. But how could she ever consider being with another man? How would she talk about it? *I had an operation. What you see is not what you get.* He'd laugh, thinking she was joking, and then he'd try to look concerned. All while trying to conceal his horror.

The cop came back, and they filled out the paperwork, describing the incident and the men they'd encountered. As she repeated the details, it became less a frightening experience and more a story, something that had happened and was over. She could handle almost being mugged; it had happened to almost everyone she knew at one time or another. It was amazing she'd avoided it for so long, being a lifelong New Yorker.

Handling Dennis's flirtation, though, was truly scary. They signed the documents, and the cop said he'd make sure his guys patrolled the hallways regularly from now on.

Dennis walked her to the taxi stand on Vanderbilt Avenue. She couldn't afford a cab, but she was running late to meet Betsy and today of all days she deserved a little treat, a comfort that she took for granted all those years she was married.

He opened the car door for her. "Thank you, Dennis." She avoided his eyes, tucked herself into the back seat.

As the door shut, he called out, "Hey, maybe I'll stop by and see you in the information booth tomorrow."

The cab pulled away before she could answer.

✦

When Betsy ordered the third round of martinis, Virginia knew it tripled her own odds of revealing the truth about her day, but she hadn't eaten since the street vendor's hot dog that afternoon and the thought of three more olives in her belly was incentive enough.

"Oh my God, Vee, I've been blathering on." Betsy jangled the wooden beads that hung around her neck. "Tell me what you've been up to." She had that strained look on her face that meant she was trying to focus even though she was already buzzing from the gin. A few drops sloshed onto the already sticky bar as she brought the glass to her lips.

They'd met years ago when their husbands worked at the same firm. Both lived on the Upper East Side and had run into each other at corporate and school events over the past two decades. What they had in common was also what kept them from truly being friends: humble beginnings. Virginia's home was a Hell's Kitchen tenement that she'd shared with her parents and younger brother, Betsy's a two-bedroom in Stuyvesant Town. They'd discussed it once and never again, a shameful secret. Betsy knew the drill as well as Virginia did. You kept certain things quiet, for appearance's sake. Instead, they had attended barbecues in Greenwich and private dinners in four-star restaurants, and Betsy even began talking like the other ladies, as if her jaw had been wired shut. Virginia's own accent had been tempered as an underclassman at Barnard College. After meeting Chester at a Columbia mixer, she'd toned it down even further.

As the fog from her post-divorce haze had cleared, she'd understood that what Betsy really wanted was the dirt: a detailed list of what had happened to send Virginia's life careening downward, in order to avoid the same fate. When Betsy called last week to arrange a girls' night out, Virginia had eagerly agreed, knowing she'd be coming straight off her first day on the job. She'd imagined their meeting as the exclamation point on her new life as a successful workingwoman.

Sticking with the script, she pasted a bright smile on her face. "It's been a whirlwind. I started working at Penn Central this week, right in Grand Central Terminal. Can you imagine?"

Betsy frowned as she dabbed at the bar with a cocktail napkin. "You're working now?" Her lipstick matched her ruffled top, the color of orange sherbet, which she'd pulled down to expose her shoulders even though it was November.

"Ruby's quite independent, and I enjoy having a sense of purpose in life."

"I haven't been to Grand Central in ages, because we take the car up to North Salem on weekends, but I hear it's ghastly these days."

"The building's seen better days, but the office is quite grand. You take an elevator right up, so you don't see any of the street people. Perfectly safe."

So far, so good. Especially learning that Betsy and Cliff rarely used the train. Less chance of being discovered.

"Cliff's seriously considering that we move out of the city. I don't blame him." Betsy rummaged through her bag, placing her wallet, a tube of lipstick, and a small book on the bar before locating her compact. "The other day, I noticed graffiti on 820 Fifth Avenue. That grand building, marred by spray paint! Horrible people running around." She checked her appearance, clicked the compact shut, and swept everything but the book back into her purse.

The bar had filled up since they'd arrived. Single men with exposed chest hair chatting up women with exposed cleavage. The room teetered a little, and Virginia placed both hands on the bar to steady herself. She glanced down quickly at her own chest, to make sure that her bra hadn't slid up again. With only one breast, there was nothing to hold the other side in place. The woman at the specialty shop who'd sold her the bra had promised it would look completely natural, but Virginia wasn't so sure.

Betsy stared with concern. The only friend Virginia had told about her operation was Samantha. If Samantha were here, Virginia would have a different story to tell. But Sam had moved to California just as Virginia's life was imploding. Sure, they tried to speak on the phone once a week, but long-distance phone calls were expensive. Their letters had trailed off, which was to be expected, really. A holiday card at Christmas was probably the best Virginia could hope for, at this point.

Virginia picked up the book Betsy had left on the bar, diverting her attention. "What's this?"

"It's the spring auction catalog for Sotheby Parke Bernet. Take a look; there's a ton of great art in there."

Virginia leafed through, pretending to consider the possibilities. "Really great." She handed it back to her. "Are you going anywhere for the holidays?" Always a safe question.

Betsy made a face. "I'd rather go to Europe, but Cliff is insisting we go somewhere warm for Christmas. He just got us a suite at the Habitation Leclerc, in Haiti." Betsy's voice rose in both volume and pitch, either to make herself heard above the crowd or to impress those seated nearby. "It's where Bianca Jagger goes, apparently. And you? I hope you get some time off."

"Ruby and I were just talking about hitting the slopes. Maybe Tahoe this year." As if they could afford the airfare, never mind the cost of a hotel. What a joke.

"Oh dear." Betsy put a hand up to her lips. "I think we may have taken your skis. How awful. I can give them back if you need them."

"What?" For a moment, Virginia thought she'd misheard. The ski equipment was stored up in their country house, in northern Westchester. Officially Chester's country house, these days. Back when Ruby was young, they'd go up every weekend to let her explore the garden, take family hikes in the woods out back. She fondly remembered sitting under the porch, holding Ruby in her lap, and listening to the raindrops tap on the leaves.

Betsy leaned in. "Chester had a big estate sale a couple of months ago. Didn't he tell you he's selling the house?"

"Oh right, I forgot." Virginia steeled herself. He hadn't told her. Not that he was required to, anymore.

"Everything was laid out in the driveway. Pretty much everybody from the street stopped by; it almost became a kind of party."

Virginia stiffened at the thought of the detritus of their marriage strewn across the driveway for the neighbors to pick through. The skis, the water guns, the Slip 'N Slide that Ruby had played with summer after summer. The basketball, which she'd dribbled a few times and then ignored. Their bikes, the three of them riding along, waving at neighbors like the happy family they were supposed to be, Ruby's with metallic purple tassels streaming from the handles.

Betsy laid a hand on Virginia's leg. "We snatched up Ruby's skis for Libby. I probably should have asked you first."

Strangers had come in and fingered through their stuff, offered cash. Loaded it up in their station wagons and driven off.

A familiar wave of shame and loss rippled through Virginia. Her made-up story, about how great her job was, how happy she was, was a farce. She could no longer tidy everything up, put on a brave face. If she didn't leave now, she'd expose the truth. That, in fact, she was a failed temp, relegated to the most basic job in a grungy, dangerous place. A failing mother, struggling to make ends meet. A failed wife, a failed woman.

Right now, all she wanted was to take a long shower and wash the grime of Grand Central out of her pores. God knew what lurked in that information booth, the clerks all breathing the same stale air, customers marking up the counters and glass with their dirty fingers.

At one point that day, around noon, a single shaft of sunlight had seeped in from one of the high, half-moon windows, the only one that hadn't been painted over, streaming in like a beam from heaven. Virginia had stared at it, transfixed, until she realized that she was really looking at all the cigarette smoke and dust particles that hovered in the air: a sparkling ray of filth, an illuminated pollution.

CHAPTER SIX

November 1974

"But if I don't have a darkroom, I can't print my photos."
Ruby threw herself facedown on Virginia's bed.

Virginia watched her daughter through the mirror of her vanity while trying to clip a rhinestone onto one earlobe. Ruby had figured out early on that the best time to ask for something was when Virginia was most vulnerable. When she was rushed, like now. Or stressed, like now.

Back when Ruby was a little girl, she'd lie on the bed and watch Virginia get ready for a night out on the town, laughing with glee when Virginia touched a dot of perfume on the inside of her daughter's pale, delicate wrist. Since then, Virginia's daughter had lengthened and filled out into a creature she sometimes wasn't sure she recognized. A beautiful, changeable creature with caramel-brown hair down to her waist and big hazel eyes. Not to mention the stubbornness of a bull.

Virginia's first date since the divorce was in forty-five minutes. When Dennis had stopped by the information booth that morning—

only her second day on the job—and asked her out, she'd been both embarrassed and pleased. He'd rapped hard on the glass to get her attention. Terrence and Totto had exchanged looks, and she'd quietly stepped out to chat with him, elated to be pursued by such a dashing man. When Doris inquired about him, she'd simply said, "He's with Penn Central; we used to work together." They had, for about ten minutes, so it wasn't a lie.

Virginia knew needling her daughter wasn't the best tactic, but she couldn't help herself. "If you hadn't dropped out of school this semester, you'd have a darkroom. At Sarah Lawrence."

Ruby turned her head to the side. "Yes, Mom. I remember where I went to school."

"Well, it'll still be there if you decide to go back in January, so you'll just have to hold out until then."

When she'd picked Ruby up at school only a few weeks into the semester, she expected to bring her home for a long weekend at most, to make her favorite meals and offer some maternal advice before sending her right back. But Ruby had steadfastly refused to return to school, saying she was only going to fail if she did, so what was the point? In the end, Ruby's tearstained face and abject misery had warranted a stronger plan of action, one that Chester loudly objected to: Withdraw for the semester and look for a less rigorous program. Virginia still held a small sliver of hope that Ruby would decide to give Sarah Lawrence another try in the spring. She'd given up so easily, so early. The official school withdrawal slip still sat on Virginia's desk, unsent.

Yet the girl had always struggled in school, socially and academically, and Virginia was fairly certain the only reason she got into Sarah Lawrence in the first place was that Chester's mother had pulled some strings. Virginia often fretted that her own worries about fitting in had rubbed off on her daughter. Throughout high school, Ruby had maneuvered through the world behind the safety of a camera lens. The yearbook was full of her photos of her classmates—the debate team, the theater club—but none of Ruby. Other than the official school photo, which for some reason broke Virginia's heart: her daughter's angelic face raised at a slight angle, as if in disbelief that someone's attention was on her, her eyes bright with excitement. When Virginia asked Ruby what she'd been thinking of, Ruby had said she'd been chatting with the professional photographer about f-stops and apertures.

They'd grown even closer after Chester left, but now their relationship was fraying. Ruby had become irritable and secretive, disappearing for hours at a time. She fumed and stormed off whenever Virginia asked about going back to Sarah Lawrence or transferring into a new school. And now this.

"I need money to help pay for the darkroom. We're going to set it up ourselves."

"Who is this 'we' you refer to?" Virginia wiped off the lipstick she'd just applied. Too pink. Best to stick to her everyday rose.

"It's a group downtown. Like an art collective."

Smart girl, that Ruby, to bring up the artistic angle in her argument. Virginia's first love was art history, which she'd studied at Barnard, specializing in medieval art. But she wouldn't be swayed so easily. "I would have to meet these people first. I'm sure you understand my concerns."

Ruby scowled. "They're not like that. They'll laugh at me and kick me out if I say that they have to come uptown and meet my mom." Her eyes narrowed. "You've been on my case for not doing anything these past two months. Now I'm working with my hands, making something real, and you don't like that either."

She had a point. She was nineteen, after all. It was nice to see her striking out on her own, following an artistic passion. Virginia hated to shoot her down. "How much?"

"A hundred dollars."

Virginia turned to face her, her mouth open. "You're kidding, right? What on earth do you need a hundred dollars for?"

"I told you, to set up a professional darkroom. We're all chipping in."

"You're being swindled. No. Even if I had the money, I wouldn't give it to you. Where is this art collective you go to?"

"The East Village. East Sixth Street."

Had she lost her mind? Virginia pictured a group of heroin addicts shooting up in an abandoned building, eyeing Ruby and her camera as easy prey. "It's dangerous down there. I don't like the idea of you wandering around that neighborhood."

"God, I'm not a child anymore. Forget it, then." Ruby bounded off the bed and out of the room, her exit punctuated by the slamming of her bedroom door.

Her daughter was lost, searching for some meaning in her life, and Virginia knew what that was like. She shouldn't have overreacted. Ruby didn't know how much they were struggling financially. Virginia had shielded her from the truth as much as possible, calling her job hunt a "fun lark." She dreaded introducing the additional stress into her daughter's life.

But for now, she was late for her date.

The restaurant Dennis had chosen was located close to Grand Central, which made sense since he lived on the Hudson Line. Virginia knew it took around thirty minutes to get to the Yonkers stop, depending on whether you were traveling at peak hours. Not a bad commute.

He was already inside, near the back, at a booth. He stood and kissed her on the cheek, a mix of soap and aftershave she'd always found appealing. The scent brought back memories of hot summer nights up on the roof of her parents' apartment building, necking with her high school crush.

Dennis ordered a wine for her and a beer for him. "You been staying out of trouble, little missy?" he asked.

"Luckily, yes."

"I bought you a present."

Her heart thumped as he reached into his coat pocket. She hadn't received a gift from a man in ages. Whenever it had been her birthday, she'd gone out and bought herself whatever she wanted and told Chester what he'd gotten her, so as not to be disappointed by his forgetting the day entirely.

Dennis placed a can of something on the table. "Mace. For your protection."

Not what she'd expected. Still. "How thoughtful. And practical."

"How's the job going so far?" He passed a menu to her.

She searched for something interesting to say that might impress him. "I've been reading through the handbook for info booth clerks. Did you know that there's a newsreel theater opposite track 17, and that until the 1960s, CBS had a television studio in Grand Central?"

"Sure did. You can't surprise me with anything about that place. I know it all. But why are you learning about stuff from the 1960s? It's not like a passenger is going to come up and ask that."

"Oh, we get all kinds of strange questions. You'd be surprised. But the handbook is ancient, probably from the 1950s. Whenever it needs updating, Terrence just adds in more pages at the front. I like the older stuff, to be honest, finding out what it was like way back when. There's even a photo of the information booth back before the terminal opened to the public. Turns out the metal frame on top is supposed to be shiny brass, not black."

In fact, after studying the photo, she'd picked up some brass cleaner during her break and spent the afternoon wiping down the exterior detailing until it reflected her face back to her. Totto and Doris, the most caustic of the booth's employees, had snickered at her while she worked, but she didn't care. Terrence had given her a thumbs-up from behind the window.

She shrugged. "Anyway, it's a job. I'm not sure I'm much help."

They both ordered the shepherd's pie, then clinked glasses.

"How do you like working for Penn Central?" she asked.

"It's interesting enough. My grandfather was a conductor, so we have a family legacy in the railroad, you could say. But that was back when train travel was something special. Did you know that they used to roll out a red carpet for passengers on the Twentieth Century Limited, which ran between Chicago and New York? That's where the phrase 'roll out the red carpet' comes from."

Virginia smiled at his boyish excitement. "You're a real train buff, then?"

"Even had an electric train set as a kid. I loved that thing." He took another swig of beer. "Ironic that I'm the one ripping the place apart."

She thought of her ladies' committee, how the historian had spoken with such reverence about the architecture. "Do you have to rip it apart?"

"Time marches on. There's no money to fix it up, so the alternative is to let it collapse in a heap."

"I guess we don't want that. How soon do you think they'll start building the skyscraper?"

"Whenever the court case wraps up. Hopefully, next year."

"Terrific. I'll make sure my steno is up to snuff by then."

A cloud of confusion crossed his face.

"For my new job, remember?"

He laughed, and she breathed a sigh of relief. "Of course. We can't have you stuck in that information booth forever. You can count on me to get this building up and running. It's in the bag."

"How's that?"

"I'm working with the numbers guy, and it's all about the numbers." He leaned in, as if the waiter was in danger of eavesdropping. "We've put together the financials to show the terminal's upkeep is a huge burden on Penn Central, one that's draining all our resources. These liberals say it should be a landmark, but it's not like we get any economic benefits from the landmark designation. It's killing us. Once we win, we'll use the building as a base for something better. Just like the Romans used to layer villages one right on top of another."

The reference to ancient Rome made her less worried about the idea of the terminal being totally subsumed. "Progress, then?"

"Progress. Just goes to show that you can be a corporate stiff and be creative at the same time."

"What do you mean?"

"Let's just say we've had to massage the numbers some, to increase the likelihood the court decides in our favor."

"Is that legal?"

He laughed. "We're lawyers; of course it's legal."

She poured a good helping of ketchup on the edge of her shepherd's pie as Dennis changed the subject to his favorite television shows. They both liked *M*A*S*H*, and she made him laugh with her impression of the uptight nurse Margaret Houlihan. She told him he reminded her of Trapper John.

"You're easy to talk to." He took the bill from the waiter and reached for his wallet. "Even if you can't surprise me with anything when it comes to Grand Central. You're talking to the expert, here."

She racked her brain for something he might not know. "Did you know about the ghost?"

"What ghost?"

"There's a ghost that haunts the old art school, up in the east wing of the seventh floor."

"What art school? That's all storage space."

She'd got him. "The map of the terminal calls it a storage space, but in fact, it's a school of art, frozen in time. I was in there yesterday—I took a wrong turn on the way to the bathroom—and it's amazing inside. Later, the guys in the info booth told me that it's haunted."

"Is that so?"

She couldn't hide her delight at his surprise. "So there. I've topped you. I know something you don't."

"You could be fooling me." He reached across the table and took her hand, rubbing his thumb so lightly over her skin she shivered. "Prove it."

"You want me to show it to you? It means returning to the scene of the crime."

"You up for that? I'll take care of you. I promise." Was that a double meaning behind his words? "Come on. Now you've got me intrigued. Let's go explore."

—◈—

Virginia had second thoughts as Dennis led her across the concourse. He squeezed her hand and pulled her slightly closer to him, as if he sensed her reluctance. Anyone in their right mind would be reluctant, entering Grand Central after hours like this, when the mob of commuters had thinned out. The waiting room, never safe on a good day, was filled with homeless people lying on benches, some even stretched out on the sticky floors. A fight broke out between two of them, something about stolen shoes, and she was glad when they made it safely into the alcove of elevator banks. Dennis pressed the button to the seventh floor before pulling her close and landing a soft kiss on her lips.

She'd been unprepared and couldn't relax enough to enjoy it. When the elevator doors opened, she pulled back with a giggle of relief.

They walked down the hallway, made a right, and she counted to the fourth door before fishing in her pocketbook for the bathroom key, which she'd never returned.

Inside, she clicked on the hallway light switch and watched him explore. In the darkened studios, the light from the skyscrapers surrounding the terminal poured in through a line of skylights, giving off an eerie glow.

"Did you see a ghost when you were here?" Dennis asked.

"No. But it's easy to imagine a ghost of an artist wandering through, right?"

"Wearing a beret and a smock, no doubt."

"I think it's wonderful, that it's unchanged." There was something romantic about this place, forgotten yet preserved, that pleased her. She touched a set of brushes on a workbench. "It seems so odd that people would come up here, in a train station, to paint."

"You know anything about art?"

"I was an art history major in college. But my focus was on art from the Middle Ages. Frescoes and mosaics and that sort of thing."

"I knew you were a smart one." Dennis had shifted so he was standing behind her, his hands on her waist. She leaned back slightly and pressed her back into him, and he responded by wrapping his arms about her stomach. She hadn't experienced a man's touch for so long, and she'd missed it. They stood together for a while, his chin resting on her head, and as long as she could cover his arms with her own, keep them from sliding up, she was fine. But the thought of him trying to touch her chest made her want to run screaming out of the room.

She couldn't reveal the scar to him. It was too long a story to tell. The concerned way her doctor looked at her as he prodded her breast. The visit to the oncologist, to the surgeon. Trying to remember what they were saying and then putting a positive spin on it over dinner with Chester and Ruby. The lovely sensation of going under on the operating table, like she'd just drunk seven martinis, followed by the pain and confusion of waking up.

The recovery, putting on a brave face with Ruby when she came home from school that first week at home, pretending that she wasn't in terrible pain, and refusing to take the pills the doctor had prescribed because she didn't want to lose control.

For once, here in this strange room with practically a stranger, she wanted to lose control. Everyone else did these days. Why couldn't she indulge like most of America was doing, from the suburban key parties to the sex clubs downtown?

Because she was deformed. No one would want to touch her.

"You're beautiful," he murmured as he slid his hands upward.

If she had to distract him with another body part, so be it. Virginia leaned down and pulled up her skirt, turning her head to look at him with what she hoped was an enticing smile.

Dennis stepped back, caught off guard. Her actions made her look like a brazen hussy, as her mother would've said, but at least they kept his hands off her chest. A hunger in his eyes soon replaced his surprise, and he ran his hands along her bare thighs, slowly.

Now, this wasn't so bad, after all. She'd forgotten the kind of electricity that passed between two people when they were on the precipice of something new.

Just to her right stood a large storage cabinet. She slid sideways and hinged slightly at the waist, placing her hands on the shelf in front of her. While Dennis fumbled behind her, she caught sight of a tattered copy of Virginia Woolf's *To the Lighthouse* on the shelf at eye level. Virginia had read it in college, and for the first time all semester raised her hand during class. She couldn't remember what she'd said, but low snickers had traveled around the room when she mispronounced the *ch* in *nonchalance* as a hard *k* sound. She'd never heard the word spoken out loud, only read it in books. The embarrassment had derailed her confidence the rest of the year, until she'd met Chester.

From the sounds Dennis made, he seemed to be enjoying himself immensely, and that made her happy, even if she didn't feel the same heat. Not yet, anyway. Maybe next time she'd be less nervous and lose herself the way he was now.

Good thing they were isolated back here, as his groans were of a decibel level and pitch that rivaled the folk singers Ruby liked to listen to in her room, her record player's volume turned all the way up. When he finished, he turned her around and held her close. "Amazing."

She pulled down her skirt. "It was."

He cocked his head toward a lumpy-looking chaise lounge pushed against one wall. "Come lie down with me for a moment; I want to cuddle."

A man who liked to cuddle. How could she say no? They settled in, both lying on their sides. Virginia perched on the very edge, trying not to sneeze. Dennis wrapped his hand around her and fell promptly asleep.

Not what she'd expected when she'd gotten ready that evening. She'd imagined them at a candlelit dinner, him giving her a chaste but yearning kiss and putting her in a cab afterward. The hint of something more on both their lips. Yet there she was, huddled on an old couch in a forgotten, ghostly art school.

What the hell; she was proud of herself. This is what life was like as a divorcée in the seventies. It's what all the books and movies talked about. Quickie sex with someone you just met. Already, she was rewriting the scene in her head for the next time she saw Betsy. A gal-on-the-town having a passionate tryst with a stunner of a guy.

A shock of color sticking out from the side of the storage cabinet caught her eye. Cobalt blue, on what looked like a corner of drawing paper that was wedged between the back of the cabinet and the wall, at knee level. Quietly, carefully, she disentangled herself from Dennis's arms and extricated the paper from behind the cabinet. On one side was a pencil drawing of a glamorous woman that looked like it was from the 1920s or thirties. The woman lay on the same chaise lounge Dennis was currently stretched out on, her limbs long and languorous.

At the very bottom was a signature. *Clara Darden*. The artist who'd sketched the secretary advertisement from the other room.

The paper was stiffer than the others, and when Virginia turned it over, she saw the reason. The other side was covered in paint, the blue that she'd spied from the sofa. Watercolors, she guessed. The figure vaguely resembled the well-dressed woman on the other side, but with more movement and color; it both horrified her and drew her in. Something terrible, violent was going on, but the shapes weren't clear.

She tiptoed into the storage room and found the drawing of the secretaries that had caught her eye the day before. Both shared the same signature. *Clara Darden.* But something was off. It took her a minute to realize that the wall of art had changed. A few of the paintings she'd seen yesterday were missing, replaced by others. Including the Renoir reproduction with the soda bottle. She looked around for it. Nothing was on the floor; it hadn't fallen off. Someone had rearranged things.

The ghost?

She told herself not to be silly. *Probably the cleaning crew messing around.*

No. The place was covered in dust. No cleaning crew had been inside the school in decades.

She studied the painting in her hand. She'd seen it before, but where? The audaciousness, and the blue colors, pleased her. The woman figure was bold, just as Virginia had been lately. Taking risks, a shape-shifter. If she took it, would anyone care or notice? Probably not. The painting had been stuck behind a cabinet for this long and would have eventually disintegrated if she hadn't spotted it. Instead, she could save it, preserve it.

Framed, the painting would fill a blank space in her living room, one that had bothered Virginia ever since she'd moved in. It would serve as a reminder to stay strong and welcome change into her life. Virginia rolled it up and carefully tucked it inside her sisal handbag before waking her sleeping giant with a kiss.

CHAPTER SEVEN

May 1928

Clara had seen Levon only twice since he'd taken her class five days earlier: once in a crowded hallway, where he'd given her a salute as he brushed by, and another time on the concourse of the terminal, where she was certain he'd spotted her but pretended not to.

His puerile behavior annoyed her. She had no way of knowing if he'd upheld his end of the bet and insisted that Mr. Lorette keep her on.

But the signs were promising. Mr. Lorette had pulled her aside as she was leaving yesterday and told her that he'd arranged a live model for her illustration class the next day. She jumped at the opportunity and altered her lesson plans accordingly.

As she entered the school the next morning, Oliver was sitting in one of the chairs outside Mr. Lorette's office. She'd secretly hoped he would be her model, while also fearing it. She'd intended to start with the model in the nude, but there was no possible way Gertrude and the others would be able to focus if this man disrobed.

She wouldn't be able to, either. It was one thing to be a student, tucked behind an easel, but another entirely to be the instructor, out in front discussing grids and proportions. And what proportions. Absolutely not.

"Oliver. Lovely to see you." She swallowed. "Again."

"Miss Darden. I hope you weren't too put off by my modeling here. Nadine had suggested it; she said it would be a good way to meet artists, break into the bohemian crowd, if you will."

"No doubt she did."

"Anyway. Would you like me to change into a robe?"

He wore a polished wool flannel suit in dark brown, his slim figure perfect for the fashionably wide Oxford trousers. "No. We'll draw what you have on. See you inside."

She spent the first fifteen minutes pointing out the details she expected the class to capture in their drawings, tugging on the jacket's lapel as she explained the best approach. "You'll want to do the suit in an opaque wash and the hat and face with a transparent one."

She adjusted his tie and stepped back. "Would you mind putting one hand in a pocket?"

He did so, his eyes shining as if posing were a delight, not a physical ordeal. Standing still wasn't easy, and she appreciated his enthusiasm.

"Whatever you need, Miss Darden." He winked at her, and the class giggled.

She would not be made fun of. Why should she get flustered and feel strange when the male teachers never did? If a female model flirted with Levon, he probably flirted right back.

She reached up and touched his face, adjusted his hat. This was power. To be the one in control. She liked it and didn't care if her students noticed. Let them talk.

"I suggest you use a Gillott 170 pen point for the figure and add the black with a No. 8 brush." She scanned his body one last time and then began making the rounds.

The rest of the class went smoothly, and the students turned in some of their best work yet. Finally, their drawings showed more than two dimensions. After dismissal, she stopped by Mr. Lorette's office, but before she could express her gratitude, he asked her to step inside and close the door.

She spoke first. "I'd like to thank you for allowing a live model in our class. The work was terrific. I hope you'll stop by and see."

"Right. Good to hear. I want to let you know that we'd like you to carry on in the fall with the illustration class. There will be two sessions, one on Tuesday and Thursday mornings and another in the afternoons. You can have both."

He threw out the words as if they were part of a script. Not heart-felt. But Levon had made good on his bet. Even if Mr. Lorette was keeping her on against his better judgment, it was no matter. She'd have money to buy more time in New York City.

As long as she made it through the summer.

"Thank you, that's wonderful news. Are there any summer classes available?" She knew she was pushing it, but better to ask than not.

"We bring a small number of students and teachers to Maine in the summer. So, no."

Fine. She'd manage.

"Also, you'll be giving out the illustration award tomorrow night at the May Ball, correct?" The ball, held in the art galleries, was an annual event for students and faculty. Student work was displayed, and awards were announced. Clara had been dreading going, but now, with the news she'd be staying on at the school, she didn't mind.

"Yes. Looking forward to it."

A student barged in, complaining to Mr. Lorette about a missing artwork. "I spent five weeks on it and it was finally finished, drying overnight, and now it's gone."

"Now then, Cyril, I'm sure we'll track it down."

"Same thing happened to Graham Hanover earlier in the term, Mr. Lorette. It's an epidemic."

"Let's not be too dramatic, now. Come inside, tell me what's going on." Mr. Lorette waved Clara off. She thanked him once more before heading out.

Outside the office, Oliver stood speaking with three of her students, all of whom looked as if they wanted to devour him whole.

She heard Oliver laugh and say good-bye to his fan club. He caught up with her in front of the elevator. "Where are you off to?"

The arrow above the elevator door hit 5. She was heading home. Of course. As she always did, day after day. "Why do you ask?"

"I'd like to take you somewhere surprising."

"I'm sure Gertrude or one of the others would be pleased to accompany you."

He laughed. "Not them. You."

She wanted to get back to her studio and work. But his excitement intrigued her, and she was flattered by his interest.

"You don't have to leave Grand Central, Miss Darden. Even better, the crowd is an illustrator's dream. Will you come?"

An illustrator's dream.

She nodded and let him take her elbow as the elevator doors opened.

They crossed the concourse and went up the stairs of the West Balcony. "I thought you said we didn't have to leave Grand Central," said Clara as he ushered her out the doors that led to Vanderbilt Avenue.

"Not exactly." He made a sharp left up a narrow staircase to a set of wrought iron doors.

"What is this place?"

"You'll see."

Inside the doorway stood a man holding a tray of glasses filled with bubbles.

It couldn't be. "Champagne?"

Oliver put a finger to his lips. "Not at all. Prohibition, re-member?"

"Right."

She took the glass he offered her and let him lead her through a small anteroom, where she stopped cold.

She was no longer in the heart of New York City but in a thirteenth-century Florentine palazzo, the floor covered by a massive Persian rug. The painted wood ceiling soared a good twenty feet above her head, and everywhere were strange treasures: six-foot-tall vases, bronze sculptures, petrified tree trunks, and, up in a balcony, what appeared to be a pipe organ.

"What on earth is this?"

"It's called the Campbell Apartment, but it's an office."

"For someone who works for the railroad?" She imagined a Van-derbilt installed here, running the trains from this magnificent headquarters.

"Not really. A financier who's on the board of New York Central. He likes to throw parties every so often. I thought you'd get a kick out it."

"More than a kick. This place is breathtaking." She took a sip from the glass. The real thing. "How did you get in here?"

"I know someone who knows someone."

A woman in a peach-colored chiffon gown spotted Oliver, and

Clara watched as she drank him in, her fat-cat husband oblivious to his wife's greedy leering.

New York City was full of people like Oliver: beautiful men and women used to being stared at, who politely looked away so you could drink in your fill of exquisite cheekbones or blue eyes. In Oliver's case, both features.

When the woman's eyes shifted to Clara, they registered something else entirely. Disdain. As someone who was used to being gawked at, for her height and her awkwardness, Clara knew the other side of the coin. Her defense was to stare back, widen her eyes, run her hands through her hair so it stuck up more than usual.

She did so, hard, until the woman turned away. When Clara turned back to Oliver, she caught her reflection in a smoky mirror on the wall. No wonder she drew stares. Her serviceable broadcloth frock had a rip in the elbow and the hem was coming loose. She'd meant to fix it but had never gotten around to it. She looked like a waif from the streets.

Before they'd moved to Tucson, when times were flush, Clara had watched her mother dress for balls and dinner parties. Truth be told, it would have been easier if she didn't know how badly she stood out, if she were naive when it came to fashion and class. She'd enjoy herself, ignorant and blissful, pleased to have gained entry to high society instead of wishing she could crawl underneath the massive antique desk and hide.

She turned back to Oliver, wanting to focus on anything else but herself. "Tell me about your family. They don't appreciate having a poet for a son?"

"I'm afraid not. I could tell, when we first met, that you understood what that feels like. Trying to please for so many years and then, ultimately, disappointing."

She certainly did. "But your mother, she must be happy at your chosen path."

"Quietly, she might be. But she married into wealth and subverted all her creativity. She'd adore you, though. You're her dream. A woman artist out in the world. Not easy, I presume."

"You presume correctly." If he only knew. The champagne was making her tipsy, as though she could float away. Another woman looked her up and down, dismissively. Boy, was Oliver lucky. Money and looks, quite a combo. Even if he didn't appreciate it now. "Could you give me an example of your work?"

"Now?"

"Why not?"

He paused, then spoke in a clear, soft voice.

Thin fingered twigs clutch darkly at nothing.
Crackling skeletons shine.
Along the smutted horizon of Fifth Avenue
The hooded houses watch heavily
With oily gold eyes.

There was more to this sweet pea than she expected. She swallowed, trying to hide her shock. "What's a smutted horizon?"

He threw back his head and laughed. "I'm not sure. I have to confess, those aren't my words. It's a poem called 'Autumn Dusk in Central Park' by Evelyn Scott."

She tried to take this turn in stride. "It's remarkable."

"I don't have any of mine memorized. They're more of a work in progress. You put me on the spot and I was desperate to show off."

"Why would you be wanting to impress me?" What a coy thing to say. Tingled by champagne, she was coming off as silly as Gertrude or Nadine. She continued before he replied. "You've been blessed with wealth and education, so I'm not sure what the problem is. Write your poems and get on with it already."

He grinned. "You've summed it up perfectly. Yet I'm dismissed by the artistic set for my wealth and by the wealthy set for my artistic aspirations." The words came out as a statement, not a complaint. But underneath lay a whiff of misery. The same she would have felt if she'd remained in Arizona, her creativity squelched.

The droning of the organ stopped, and a man with a tall forehead and hooded eyes leaned one hand against the imposing stone fireplace and asked for everyone's attention. Apparently, this was the famous Mr. Campbell, who had an office that he called an apartment in the middle of Grand Central. He thanked everyone for stopping by, and when he finished, the crowd clapped with gusto—the alcohol certainly helped in this regard.

Clara looked to the exit, hoping they could sidle their way out.

"My dear Oliver!"

A skinny older woman snapped her head in between them, blinking hard at Oliver. Her dusky fur, which hung loosely over her shoulders, was the same color as her hair, and the overall effect was that of a posh ferret.

Oliver opened his mouth to reply, but the woman spoke first. "Mr. Campbell and I were wondering if you were going to appear. Where have you been gadding about these days, and with whom?" She peered at Clara. "I get my answer right off. You are an artist, I'm guessing."

"How did you know?" asked Clara.

"The smudge of something on your cheek and on your hands. We've been worried about our Oliver, slumming in the Village." She chuckled. "Oh, ignore me, I'm being a silly goose."

Clara swiped at her cheek and glared at Oliver.

"Now, Oliver, my dear nephew, we must see you more often up in Rye." She droned on about an upcoming race at the yacht club while Clara fumed. Finally, the woman sauntered off.

"Why didn't you tell me I had paint on my face?" Clara growled. "Bad enough I'm not dressed correctly."

She turned to go, but he took her hand and pulled her up a small staircase to where the organ sat. The organist was packing up his music and barely regarded them before slipping away.

She stomped away from Oliver, staring down over the balcony.

He cleared his throat. "I'm sorry for making you feel awkward. That wasn't my intention at all. I just wanted you to see this place. To share it with you. I wanted to impress you with the room. Not the people."

"Oh, please. You're one of them. Why bother pretending to be a poor poet?"

"I'm not pretending anything. I don't want to be known for this." He gestured out over the crowd. "I want my work to stand on its own."

"Why poetry?"

"Why art?"

She thought about it for a moment. "Because I have a passion for it and I can make money doing it. Or so I thought."

"What's got you stuck?"

"I don't have connections. I can't seem to break in."

"And I can't break out." He looked dejected, beat. "I'd rather be like Walt Whitman, a workingman, than an overeducated twit who loves verse."

She couldn't help but laugh. "Your idea of being a workingman is taking off your clothes in front of a bunch of artists."

"If that means I can meet people like Levon Zakarian and Sebastian Standish, then yes. Unfortunately, that crowd doesn't let in outsiders easily. Especially not guys like me."

He had a point. They were a caustic, judgmental bunch. Herself included.

Oliver touched her hand. "I loved watching you teach. I never know what you'll say or do next. You're brimming with confidence, and that's not something you see every day in a gal. Do you happen to be in the market for a muse?"

She tried not to smile. "They tend not to come to very good ends, you know. Artists are a fickle lot."

"I can hold my own."

"Can you?"

He leaned in and kissed her. Having never been kissed before, she was eager to see what the fuss was all about.

They were about the same height, and at first it felt strange, like kissing a mirror image, but he pulled her to him and explored her mouth with his tongue. It was glorious, the sensations and the wetness of their mouths, the quiet moans. The warmth of his touch was all too accessible through the thin fabric of her dress.

But her mother's admonition to be careful, spoken in a hushed voice up in Clara's bedroom the evening before her trip east, stuck in her head. She pulled away, laughing.

He looked hurt.

"I'm not laughing at you; that was marvelous," she said.

"Then why laugh?"

"Because I've never met anyone like you before. You are so beautiful."

His mouth turned down. "You keep saying that."

"It's the truth. You belong with some pretty little child, one of my witless students, perhaps. Not with me."

"Why don't you see us together? I can help you."

She regarded him. "What do you want from me in return?"

"Nothing. Nothing at all." He kissed her again, pulling away just as the heat began to build. "Say, there is one thing."

"I knew it."

"Will you go to the May Ball with me tomorrow night?"

Clara imagined showing up on Oliver's arm, returning to the scene of last week's humiliation with her head held high.

And said yes.

CHAPTER EIGHT

May 1928

Clara had planned on wearing her nicest frock to the May Ball, a sensible two-piece crepe de Chine, the same one she'd worn to the exhibit a little over a week ago. But that morning, Oliver rang her apartment and offered to buy her something special. "My first role as muse," he'd said with a laugh. She considered his offer. The tepid reception at the Campbell Apartment still rankled Clara, and tonight she wanted to shine, to show Mr. Lorette and Levon and the rest of them that she was someone to be taken seriously.

A new dress would help.

She'd expected a trip to Wanamaker or Lord & Taylor, but Oliver brought her to a small shop on Fifth Avenue with the name PEGGY HOYT on the window.

Clara steeled herself before entering. Peggy Hoyt was a marvel at gown design, far beyond the reach of any starving artist. Peggy Hoyt gowns got mentioned in the social columns of the newspapers with regularity. The women who wore them were all dolled up in diamonds and smug smiles, knowing they counted in the world.

To her surprise, there were no dresses in sight. It was as if they'd stepped inside someone's dark, quiet living room, with thick silk curtains and a rose-covered chaise angled toward a marble fireplace.

A middle-aged woman wearing a simple black suit appeared from a back room. She greeted Oliver warmly and offered a kind smile to Clara. "Miss Hoyt sent her apologies, but she's in Paris this week. I told her I'd take good care of you, though."

"You're too kind, Mrs. Fletcher, and Clara and I appreciate your accommodating us on such short notice." Oliver was quite the man-about-town, comfortable in his own skin and as elegant as Mr. Campbell. No wonder he'd been rejected by the hard-nosed poets of Greenwich Village as a dandy. A dire mismatch of personality and profession.

Mrs. Fletcher guided Clara to the back of the shop.

"You have the perfect figure for a Peggy Hoyt dress, I have to say." She began pulling gowns from a rack. "Long and lean."

Clara shook her head. "I'm far too tall. I doubt any of them will fit me." When she was sixteen and still squeezing into too-small clothes, as there was no money to replace them, she'd stolen a pair of stable hand's overalls to work in the vegetable garden. The freedom of movement exhilarated her, as did the fact that she could finally take a deep breath without feeling pinched in the waist. Until her mother had caught sight of her and howled like a coyote and Clara retreated inside to change.

Mrs. Fletcher responded with a reassuring smile. "We'll find the right thing, don't you worry. In fact, there's one gown in particular that I think will look smashing on you. Here it is."

She held up an aquamarine silk with a chiffon overlay embroidered with copper-colored thread. The threading extended in a peacock feather design from just below the waist to the hem of the dress, where gold and silver beading formed the eyes of each feather. A similar beading adorned the neckline, rendering a necklace superfluous.

Clara prayed for it to fit. It did, the inner lining slipping over her hips with ease, the hem brushing just below her knees.

"It's perfect." She'd been holding her breath since spying it in Mrs. Fletcher's arms, and her voice came out in an unladylike exhale.

Mrs. Fletcher laughed. "Most women would be overpowered by the peacock design, but you have the height and authority to carry it off."

She walked into the other room, where Oliver sat reading the newspaper as if they were an old married couple who did this kind of thing every other week.

He jumped out of the chair like a jack-in-the-box, the paper fluttering to the floor. "You look astonishing."

"Doesn't she?" asked Mrs. Fletcher. "We have shoes and an evening bag as well."

"We'll take it all. Put it on my family's account, please."

After slipping out of the dress and handing it over to Mrs. Fletcher to wrap, Clara re-joined Oliver. For all she knew, Clara was one of a line of creative women whom Oliver took under his wing, bought trinkets and gowns for, and then dropped when his artistic ambitions didn't come to fruition.

Clara's mother would be horrified at the thought of her daughter being dressed and kissed by a man, even a wealthy man, when any intentions were strictly nonmarital. But the world had changed. Free love wasn't necessarily as outrageous, at least among the bohemians, as it might have been ten years ago. Just as waistlines had disappeared from fashion, the restrictions of courting had loosened considerably.

At least in New York.

And among the more scandalous set.

Oliver broke into her thoughts. "I know this seems crazy, but I'd like you to meet my mother."

"Your mother?"

"Yes. I'm expected for tea at my parents' in a half hour. I know you'll hit it off, and it would help. You're a real working artist, and it would give her a lift that she sorely needs."

"That seems rather fast." All thoughts of having Oliver take her to his apartment and make love to her dissipated. With disappointment, she had to admit. In the end, she relented, after he described the fresh scones to be served. Her diet the past many months had been one of baked beans and cold meats. High tea at Oliver's parents', no matter how it went or why he was so insistent she go, would be an extra meal she didn't have to pay for.

His motives for the visit worried her, though, as he ushered her inside the elevator of a handsome limestone apartment building. What if he was doing this to shock his parents—show them what a bad boy he was, hobnobbing with the arty set? Better to be aware of his immaturity sooner rather than later, she supposed. If so, she'd at least gotten a swanky dress out of the deal.

The operator pulled the lever to bring them up to the tenth floor and shared an easy repartee with Oliver, ribbing him about his muddy shoes and how much dirt he was tracking inside. Oliver didn't take offense, joking back that he'd return with a broom and clean it right up, like he used to do as a little boy.

"I wanted to work as a doorman since I was about three, I'd say," he told Clara, turning to the operator for confirmation. "I'd dress in my fanciest suit and join them in the lobby, holding the door open and greeting the residents."

The very idea made her smile. They stepped off into a wide hallway with a marble floor, the door slamming hard behind them. "I'm surprised your parents allowed it."

"My father didn't know; he was off working. My mother, well, you'll see."

The minute Clara entered the apartment, a more feminine, older version of Oliver greeted them. "Oliver?" She looked over at Clara, confused.

"Mother, I'd like to introduce you to a friend of mine, Miss Clara Darden, who's on the faculty of the Grand Central School of Art. Miss Darden is an esteemed illustrator."

"An artist. Aren't we lucky?" She was a ghost of a woman, thin and pale, a suggestion of sadness in her mouth and eyes, which were the same blue as her son's. Her hand in Clara's was cool, her fingers fragile and light.

Oliver placed a protective hand on his mother's shoulder. "I told her you also paint."

She shook her head. "Used to paint. In my youth. Not anymore. But my goodness, you teach art. Are there many women teachers?"

"Just me."

A much older man with a rheumatic cough and milky eyes emerged from a doorway without bothering to acknowledge the stranger in the room. "Come, I'd like to drink my tea before the sun sets." His voice rumbled like the subway. Underneath the pillowy folds of his face and neck, Clara recognized the slice of Oliver's cheekbones. If there were two more mismatched spouses in the city, Clara would be surprised.

After introductions, the four settled at a dining room table with a sweeping view of Central Park. It was all Clara could do to keep her gaze on the table's occupants and not get distracted by the lush carpet of new green leaves outside the window. April had been a dull, rainy month, and she hadn't ventured uptown in a while. The bright pink shock of cherry blooms excited her. She wished she could just stand at the window and drink in the colors of spring.

Mrs. Smith beamed as a maid passed around the plate of warm scones. "How long have you been teaching at Grand Central?"

"Since January. I started as a student last fall."

"A quick promotion."

"I suppose." The tinkling of silverware on china and the way the scone melted in her mouth brought memories rushing back. After all, she'd been raised in luxury and in many ways felt at home here more than in her stark artist's garret. While the ostentatiousness of the Campbell Apartment had thrown her off-balance, the Smiths' refinement closely mirrored her mother's.

"I did love painting." Mrs. Smith dabbed at a crumb that had fallen onto the tablecloth. "I never could get people right, faces seemed to elude me, but I loved painting landscapes. Turner's my favorite, the way he paints the sea and the sky, simply breathtaking."

"*Cologne from the River*," suggested Clara.

Both women sighed at the same time, then laughed.

"Never mind that." Mr. Smith's gruff voice practically rattled the Tuscan china. "Where do you come from? Where's your family?"

Oliver threw her an apologetic look. "Father, you don't know anyone in common, so don't start fishing to see if she's a debutante."

Clara wasn't about to let Oliver speak for her. "My family is in copper; we've invested in several mines out west, including a lucrative arrangement with the Brawleys of Phoenix. Perhaps you're acquainted with them?"

Mr. Smith sat back, suspicious. "I don't know them personally, but of course I've heard of them." He looked over at his wife. "Own the biggest mines in the country."

Clara launched into a protracted explanation of the speculative copper industry out west and her father's partnership with the Brawleys, watching with satisfaction as the man's eyes widened with surprise. Her father had taught her well. Of course, she skipped the part about his attempt to swindle the Brawleys out of thousands of dollars. Hopefully, enough time had passed that the fraud was no longer remembered outside of Maricopa County.

Oliver, laughing, finally cut her off. "Enough about metals. Father seems to have met his match." He turned to his parents. "Miss Darden and I have a ball to attend, and I was hoping she could get dressed here."

"No, I couldn't intrude."

"Please, we insist." Mrs. Smith practically levitated from the table with excitement. "My Rose can set hair like no one else in this town, and you can borrow whatever you need, lipstick, rouge. I have it all."

"That would be lovely."

By the time the maid was finished with her, Clara could hardly contain her surprise. She thanked the woman profusely and entered the parlor where Oliver waited.

"You look exquisite." Oliver stuttered over the last word.

Her hair, set in regular waves along her skull instead of flying about, was like a sleek helmet. The beads of the dress gave it a weight that offset the silky lightness of the fabric, and she'd borrowed a pair of pearl-colored gloves to go with her shoes. For once, her height worked in her favor, just as Mrs. Fletcher in the shop had predicted. She was a smooth, aquamarine column of elegance.

Mr. Smith took her hands in both of his to say good-bye and urged her to return at any time.

In the taxi, Oliver kissed her lightly on the cheek. "You were wonderful."

"You thought you were bringing a silly artist to tea in an attempt to shock your parents. Shame on you." She was only half joking.

He pursed his lips. "I will admit, part of my intention was to expose them to a different side of New York. I'm trying to get them used to the idea that I won't be a banker. But you seem to be able to switch back and forth between worlds with ease."

"I wouldn't go that far. I didn't mention this to your parents, but my father lost his fortune ten years ago, so I understand both sides. Great wealth—although I was just a girl at the zenith—and great poverty. If anything, though, it makes me useless in either world. I'm certainly no socialite. This is the fanciest thing I've worn since I was a little girl." She plucked at the fabric of her gown. "And I'm far from being a successful artist."

"Let's see what we can do about that. As your muse, I'm at your service. You made my mother very happy today."

Just outside the Grand Central Art Galleries, Gertrude stood sentry with a clipboard in hand. As they approached, her jaw dropped, and she stared, first at Oliver, who wore a handsome double-breasted wool suit, and then back at Clara.

"Welcome to the May Ball," the girl finally said. "You can go right on in. My goodness, Miss Darden, you look ritzy. That dress is the bee's knees."

Inside, the faculty art had been taken down and replaced with student work, and Clara was thrilled to see some of her class's illustrations on the far wall of the first gallery, a place of honor. Wilbur, ever her troublemaking student, sauntered over and slipped Oliver a silver flask. "Ollie, a little hooch for you?"

Oliver took a sip and handed it to Clara. She looked about. Mr. and Mrs. Lorette stood off to one side, speaking with Edmund Greacen, one of the school's founders.

Clara took a discreet sip from the flask and tried not to cough as the liquor burned her throat.

"You look sensational," said Wilbur. "The belle of the ball."

Oliver pulled her close and murmured in her ear, "I'm going to have to model for you every class, just to keep these dogs in check."

She swatted him away. Inside one of the middle galleries, iron chairs and tables were scattered about to replicate a Parisian boulevard café. A band played in the corner, and couples tripped about the room in time with the crooner singing "My Blue Heaven" in a warbled tenor.

Oliver asked her to dance, and together they trotted about the floor, which was becoming more and more crowded. A dark shadow appeared at the edge of the room. Levon.

She tried to avoid his gaze, annoyed at his churlishness the past few days. But he was staring at her, oblivious to dear Nadine, who was on her tiptoes, trying to chatter into his left ear.

He lifted his chin, and Clara offered a swift smile in return. Bad idea. He was upon them a moment later, the unsteadiness of his balance evidence that he'd had his fair share of someone's flask.

"May I have this dance?" He did a little jig, and she couldn't help but laugh.

"You may. Oliver, do you mind?"

If he did, Oliver gave no indication, smiling broadly and stepping to the side.

Dancing with Oliver, Clara had formed an equal part of a pair, the two of them moving in perfect synchronization, the steps even and steady. In Levon's arms, she was swallowed up, consumed. He wore a thick black sweater that only made him feel more hulking, yet underneath it, she could feel his body twitching, twisting. He danced with the same gusto with which he painted, the thick brushstrokes replaced with stomping feet.

"Are you doing some kind of Armenian folk dance?"

He blushed. She hadn't meant to be mean. Somehow everything came out wrong with Levon.

She continued, not letting him respond to her remark. "I hear you dance in class sometimes. I'm sorry you weren't doing so when I attended."

"I'm sorry I was such a bad loser. You did an excellent job. I failed miserably."

"You spoke with Mr. Lorette, and I haven't had a chance to thank you. He's offered me a position for the fall, and I know you were behind that. I can't tell you what a relief it is."

"I have honor, if nothing else."

"You do."

"You should be on the cover of a magazine, in that dress."

"Thank you. A friend bought it for me."

"A good friend. I would have bought you one myself if I could. I would paint you in it as well."

"In watercolor or oil?" She couldn't help teasing.

"In verdigris, like the ancients did. Reclining on a bed, the dress pooled around you, like a tropical puddle."

His overfamiliarity was tempered by the serious look on his face, an expression she recognized. He wasn't studying her as a woman but as a subject for a painting. She'd done the same when Oliver posed for her class.

Oliver and Nadine sat at one of the tables, chatting and eyeing the dance floor. Clara tried to lighten the mood. "How would you paint the room, maestro?"

He scoffed. "Not possible. All these silly characters. A waste of good paint."

She imagined trying to capture the scene swirling around her, the way Renoir had done with his boating party. The room made her head swim: the sparkling jewelry, the garish smiles, and the flash of bare arms and necks.

Levon was right. It was too much. She closed her eyes, reveling in the symphony of sensations, the sounds of music and laughter, her dress swinging with each step.

Instantly, she knew what she had to do to make her magazine covers stand out.

Up until now, she had included too much, so the viewer never knew where to look, what was important. Instead, she would focus on one figure, and with minimal detail. Pare it down. Cut out everything extraneous.

One woman in an aquamarine dress. She'd capture, on paper, not only what the dress looked like but also what it felt like on. Thighs lightly brushed by silk, beading like Braille under a fingertip.

Simple lines, a simple focus. Thanks to Oliver's buying spree and Levon's brilliance, she'd figured out a fresh approach.

She couldn't wait to get started.

⁓⚬

Clara arrived at her appointment with ten minutes to spare. She took a breath, checked her hair in the reflection of a bookseller's shop, and spun through the revolving door of 420 Lexington Avenue.

The Graybar Building, home to *Vogue* magazine.

In the taxi with Oliver on the way home from the ball, Clara had explained in between luxurious kisses that she'd had a breakthrough and that if she didn't get the image inside her head down onto paper, she was certain she'd lose it. She'd jokingly promised him more if she got an appointment at *Vogue*, and he'd used his contacts to get her in the door five days later. Which meant for five days straight, she'd spent every free moment at her drawing table.

She told Oliver that as a muse, he was more than remarkable. She didn't mention that she'd had her revelation while in Levon's arms.

She tucked her portfolio against her chest and waited to be called in to the fashion editor's office. This time, she wasn't just dropping off the illustrations to a secretary. She had a face-to-face appointment with a Mr. Charles Whittlesley, and Oliver had even offered to accompany her. She'd turned him down. Her work would stand on its own this time; she was sure of it.

She'd dressed for the occasion, getting her hair done, putting on some bright lipstick, and filling in her brows with the pencil that Mrs. Smith had given her. Four o'clock on the dot, Mr. Whittlesley called her into his office.

"Miss Darden." He gestured for her to take a seat. She lay her portfolio on his desk and held her breath.

He didn't open it right away. "I understand you're a family friend of the Smiths?"

"I am. Oliver Smith and I became acquainted at the Grand Central School of Art, where I teach illustration." She'd dropped the mention of the school right away on purpose. Mr. Whittlesley was doing the Smiths a favor by agreeing to see her and was probably expecting some breathless, inexperienced girl.

He harrumphed.

"How many women illustrators do you use?" she asked.

He shook his head and untied the ribbons of her portfolio. "Not many."

"Right. Georges Lepape, Charles Martin, Paul Iribe." The names flew off her tongue; she'd practiced this speech in front of her mirror this morning. "How many of them have worn a Chanel gown?"

He laughed and looked up. "I hope none of them."

"That's where I can help you sell magazines. I want to invite women inside the world of fashion, not just aspire to it. They should look at your cover and understand what it feels like to wear a fox fur stole. The softness on the back of the neck, the luxuriousness."

He opened the portfolio to her mock cover of the blue dress. A lithe woman with a secret smile on her face stood in front of a Parisian café. The background was faint, the emphasis on the lone figure. With her cocked hip and caved shoulders, she resembled a treble clef, all curves and movement.

"A Peggy Hoyt."

"Yes."

His eyes traveled from the woman's face to her hands, along the vertical feathers in the dress and back to her face.

He carefully moved it to the side. The illustration beneath showed a woman in an enormous fur coat and matching cloche, wearing mustard-colored long gloves. The lining of the coat, which peeked through the draped sleeves and the kicked-up hem, was a shocking scarlet that matched the woman's lipstick and ruddy cheeks. The overall effect was of the woman being quite happily devoured by the coat.

Mr. Whittlesley stared hard at both, going back from one to the other. Winter and summer. Summer and winter.

Clara didn't move, didn't breathe.

He picked up his phone and barked into it. Within ten seconds, another man walked in. The introductions were so fast, she didn't catch his name, but he leaned over Mr. Whittlesley's shoulder and whistled.

"Can we bump July?" asked Mr. Whittlesley.

"We could. We should."

Mr. Whittlesley looked up at Clara. "We'll take them both."

Clara sold both on the spot and promised to come back in two days to sign a contract for more.

As she approached her building, she spotted Oliver waiting outside, smoking a cigarette and pacing like an expectant father. A surge of joy spread through her, for having found him. They spoke the same language, of parental disappointment and artistic ambition. His support, right when she needed it most, had changed everything. She walked up to him and kissed him on the mouth, not caring that her landlady was staring out of her first-floor window.

"We did it."

"You did it," he answered.

They went upstairs, giggling like children, and she slid off her dress, remembering the image Levon had described as they danced, of a dress pooling on the floor. She pushed the thought of Levon aside.

Oliver sat on the bed, watching greedily. At first, his caresses were careful, too careful for her reckless mood, but with her encouragement, he grew bold until she matched him, touch by touch, wave by wave.

CHAPTER NINE

November 1974

The next day at work, Terrence presented Virginia with her very own clerk's blazer. She stuttered out a thank-you but inside reeled with shame. If any of her old acquaintances saw her, she'd be the laughingstock of the Upper East Side.

Her urge to clean, though, overrode her humiliation. Now that the brass trim that circled the booth had been buffed to a shine, the marble underneath looked dingier than ever. She'd brought in the marble cleaner she'd used (or, more specifically, her cleaning lady had used) in her old Park Avenue apartment and did a quick patch test. With a little elbow grease, a creamy pink hue, like a baby's bottom, emerged from the brown grit. The situation was too tempting to pass up, so she spent the morning half-bent over, spraying and rubbing until her back ached, hoping that Dennis wouldn't stop by and catch her scrubbing away like a charwoman. She occasionally popped up to scan the crowds, adjust her shift dress, and try to appear nonchalant. God, she hated that word.

She straightened up, needing a break. Totto gave a high-pitched yelp and almost fell off his chair from fright, while Terrence just laughed.

Totto fixed her with a stare. "What the hell are you doing out there, crawling around the floor?"

She held up the spray can and rag. "Cleaning."

He shook his head. "There are people who do that already. Jesus."

Doris made a face. "That rag is disgusting."

"I know, right? And I'm only halfway done."

"Why you want to touch anything out there is beyond me," said Doris. "You'll catch some kind of bug."

"The plague, probably," added Totto. "Why are you cleaning the booth? The better it looks, the more people will show up, asking questions, which means more work for us."

Terrence shushed him. "Maybe by then, you'll have learned the answers to some of the questions, instead of passing the buck to me all the time." A weary look crossed his face. "Uh-oh. Here she comes."

Virginia watched as a woman dressed in a black-and-white Chanel suit clicked over to Terrence's window. She looked like any other Upper East Side matron, except for the fact that an enormous parrot perched on her right shoulder, while another, slightly smaller one, balanced on the top of her pillbox hat.

"Do you know anything about birds?" the woman asked Terrence with a clipped English accent. The larger bird stretched out one wing, and Virginia marveled at the gradation in color of the feathers, which started out teal near the chest and progressed to a deep sapphire blue at the tip.

He nodded. "There are approximately 372 different species of parrot."

"Thank you." She turned and walked away, the shoulder with the parrot slightly lower than the other.

Virginia stared in amazement. "Who was that?"

"The Bird Lady," answered Terrence. "Stops by once a week, I toss out some random fact, and off she goes."

"Who is she? Why does she do that?"

"Makes her happy, I guess. Trust me, she's on the low end of weird characters we encounter."

"Wow. You must see a lot." Virginia let herself back into the booth and put the cleaning supplies away. "Between all of you, you could write a book about this place. Terrence has been here since the forties, right? How long for the rest of you?"

Winston whistled. "I'm next, here for twenty years. Then Doris, how long have you been here, you lovely woman, you?"

Doris's caustic side disappeared; she even batted her eyelashes at Winston. "Seventeen, you old flirt, you." She dropped the charm and pointed at Totto. "He's the newbie."

"No. She's the newbie." Totto pointed at Virginia.

As Doris and Totto launched into the inevitable bickering, Virginia pulled out her handbook but couldn't concentrate. After all her worrying, Dennis hadn't shown up at all. Maybe he'd had a tough day at work, fighting to build his new skyscraper, or maybe he'd had to go down to court. A pucker of disappointment rose in her.

The Bird Lady had stationed herself at the top of the West Balcony. Other than from a few small children who stopped and stared, she garnered hardly any notice. The birds' feathers were a jolt of color against the faded afternoon light and reminded Virginia of the painting she'd found at the art school. When she'd gotten home last night, she'd tucked the painting inside an old art portfolio of Ruby's to keep it safe. This weekend, she'd take it to a frame shop.

Those blues. The painting. With a rush, she remembered where she'd seen it before.

The auction catalog. The Sotheby Parke Bernet auction catalog Betsy had had with her when they'd met for drinks. She was certain of it.

Before heading home, Virginia stopped off at the auction house. The girl behind the counter didn't look up until Virginia cleared her throat. Ever since her marriage had fallen apart, Virginia had felt invisible. As if without the magic ring on her left hand, she was no longer worthy of attention. Ridiculous, she knew.

"I was hoping I could get a copy of your most recent auction catalog, please."

The girl handed one over.

"Thank you so much. Have a great day." *Try killing them with kindness.* The girl remained mute and unseeing. Like a robot. Virginia was tempted to reach her hand over and slap the girl upside the head. All that rancor between Doris and Totto had gotten to her.

Back at the apartment, she went into her bedroom and compared the photo of the painting in the catalog with the one she'd found in the old art school. The similarity was uncanny. Yet hers was made using watercolors, while the one in the catalog was an oil painting.

A thumping noise from down the hallway broke her concentration.

"Ruby?"

Another thump, more metallic this time, and then the sound of a door slamming.

She sighed. A good mother would go and see what was going on, check in. At dinner, she vowed to have a serious talk with the girl. For now, she needed some quiet time alone. She was bone-tired from working an eight-hour day in that tiny booth. Shoving people together like that wasn't healthy, which was probably why there was so much squabbling.

She turned back to the catalog. The painting was attributed to Levon Zakarian, an Armenian immigrant who'd taught at the Grand Central School of Art. He'd had some early fame as a pioneer of abstract expressionism before dying young, on April 11, 1931, when he was just twenty-eight years old. The untitled work for auction had been only recently discovered and was estimated to sell for $300,000 to $350,000.

She'd hoped to see Clara Darden's name in the catalog, since that was the signature on the drawing on the back of the painting. Still, excitement sizzled through her. The Grand Central School of Art reference directly linked Zakarian, a faculty member there, to the watercolor. Maybe he'd been working on it while teaching, using a piece of scrap paper that Clara Darden had tossed out.

She checked her watch. The library was open for another half hour, and Virginia didn't want to wait until tomorrow. Unfortunately, the art section didn't yield much more on Zakarian, maybe because he'd died young. Nothing on Clara Darden, either.

The library lights blinked twice: closing time. She'd fix something nice for Ruby, maybe pineapple chicken, and encourage her to sit and chat over dinner. She'd ask her lots of questions about this art collective, really try to engage with her daughter. This little side trip into the world of art history had given Virginia an unexpected burst of energy and deepened her understanding of Ruby's passion for a darkroom. Maybe this would bring them closer together.

Virginia didn't smell the smoke until she turned the key in the lock. Something was burning. Maybe Ruby had started dinner, but that would be a first. No. Something was terribly wrong.

She shoved the door open. A thick gray fog coiled toward her, like an apparition. Virginia screamed into the apartment, and then there was Ruby, running toward her, covering her mouth with her arm, coughing.

Virginia pulled Ruby out into the hallway, slamming the door shut.

"Are you all right?"

Ruby coughed hard, unable to answer. At least she was standing and breathing. Virginia pulled her down the hallway, pausing in front of the fire alarm to pull the lever. As the neighbors poured out of their doors, Virginia led the charge down the stairs, all ten flights, until they were in the lobby. Firemen burst in, ordering them outside.

Huddled with the other tenants on the opposite sidewalk, Virginia put her arms around her daughter, partly to keep her warm but also to keep her as close to her as possible.

"What happened?" Virginia tucked a lock of Ruby's hair behind her ear, just like she used to do when she was a little girl.

Ruby could barely get the words out. "I was trying to turn my bathroom into a darkroom."

"What?"

"Dad gave me ten bucks, and I bought the chemicals and a light and some red gel to put over it. I figured I'd make my own safelight. But I must've bought the wrong kind of lamp, because the gel caught fire, and before I realized it, the shower curtain next to it was burning." Ruby began to cry. "I'm sorry. I tried to put it out, but it was smoky and I couldn't breathe."

Virginia reeled. Ruby could have burned down the entire complex. She wanted to shake her. What the hell had she been thinking? But she was too relieved that she'd arrived home in time. "It'll be fine. The firemen are here now."

After they were given the okay to reenter, the firemen told Virginia to check in with her insurance company. The damage was mostly from smoke—nothing structural had been jeopardized—but for now the apartment was uninhabitable.

Together, they went back upstairs and wandered through the apartment, which smelled like the inside of an ashtray. Ruby's room was gray with soot, but they tossed some clothes into a garbage bag to take with them. Virginia stuffed what she could into a Samsonite suitcase. Right before shutting it tight, she placed the portfolio with the sketch inside on top of her clothes.

She fought back tears, not wanting to make Ruby feel worse. This apartment in the East Sixties had been her one extravagance after the divorce. The cost was a little out of her budget, but it had light, big windows, and floors the color of a sandy beach, the complete opposite of their old apartment, with its dark moldings and maze of rooms. Every time she walked through the door, even after a long, miserable day in the information booth, her heart gave a little jump. This was her own place. To begin anew.

She tried Betsy, who lived a few blocks north, but the phone just rang and rang. To be honest, she really didn't want to deal with Betsy right now, have her see what a mess her life really was. But a hotel was too expensive. She didn't have that much cash to spare.

"We'll have to show up on Betsy's doorstep and wait for her to get back," she said out loud, finally.

Ruby yanked the garbage bag up and over her shoulder. "We have another option."

Virginia sighed. "No. We can't go to your dad's."

"I know that. That's not what I meant. Trust me, I have a solution, which is only fair, as I'm the one who caused the problem."

"Where do we go?"

"Follow me."

~&~

The taxi pulled up outside the Carlyle Hotel, on Madison and Seventy-Sixth. As the driver hauled their garbage bag and suitcase out of the trunk, Virginia stared up at the handsome terra-cotta tower. "We can't afford this."

"We're not paying."

Ruby grabbed her bag, and Virginia followed her through the revolving doors, unsure whether to be appalled or impressed by her daughter's confidence. Terrible thoughts popped into her head: Her daughter was a high-priced call girl and this was where she worked. Why else would her daughter be so familiar with a hotel that was way out of their price range?

Ruby spoke briefly with the bellboy. "Give him your suitcase; they'll hold our stuff for now."

She did as she was told, partly from shock.

"Let's stop in at the bar."

The sound of the piano drifted out as they approached. Then a voice. A voice Virginia knew too well.

"Is that your uncle Finn?" She stopped short.

"Yes. That's the surprise. He's in town, and I bet we can stay with him."

Virginia racked her brain to figure out how long it had been since she'd seen her baby brother. Since before her diagnosis, so at least five years, although he always called on Christmas from whatever European city he was living in at the time.

"How long has he been back in the city?"

"Not long. He called the apartment to say hello, and I swung by here last week."

Finn had come to town and met up with her daughter, and no one had bothered to mention it to Virginia. "When were either of you planning to tell me?"

The music stopped, replaced by applause. "Come on, he's great. You'll love this."

Virginia had never been inside Bemelmans Bar, although she'd read about the murals painted by the eponymous author and illustrator back in the 1940s, in return for lodging. *Whimsical* was the word that came to mind: Central Park scenes where elephants ice-skated and giraffes lifted their hats in greeting. The gold-leaf ceiling reflected the glow of the lamps perched on each cocktail table.

Finn began playing again, a Cole Porter tune that was perfect for his warm tenor. In the dark, Virginia and Ruby slid into two seats at the black granite bar. Finn's hands tripped along the keys of the Steinway, the long fingers as familiar to Virginia as her own.

The last time she'd heard him play was on the sturdy, well-worn upright in their parents' apartment. After years of studying classical piano—Finn had been a quiet, good boy who practiced for three hours a day, like clockwork—he'd transformed at seventeen, wearing white leather pants, staying out until all hours, and driving their parents batty in the process. Virginia had been a sophomore in college at the time, clueless to the chaos. She'd come home one weekend to find her mother and Finn at each other's throats, him refusing to accept his scholarship to Juilliard, wanting to be a Broadway actor instead, and her mother threatening to throw him out on the streets if he did.

He'd left, cutting off all contact with their parents. Virginia tried to stay in touch, but he traveled around so much, it was hard to know where to send the letters. He didn't come back for the funerals, when their parents died within months of each other. A gig in Madrid kept him away, apparently. After Ruby was born, he made more of an effort, and they'd met up for lunch whenever he came into town, but Chester's sullen disapproval of his lifestyle—by then, Finn was openly gay—left the few family reunions fraught with tension.

She missed him and should have made more of an effort. But Finn had pulled back as well, never responding to the letter she wrote telling him about her cancer. No doubt it'd been lost in the transatlantic mail—it wouldn't be the first time—and by the time their annual Christmas call came around, she was up and about, healthy, and ready to move forward. Her "affliction," as Chester called her bout with cancer, was over and no longer needed to be brought up.

After ending with a flourish, Finn stood and made his way through the crowd, shaking hands and flashing a white smile. Like Virginia, he hadn't thickened with age. Instead, his slim shoulders and hips remained lithe, further emphasized by the elegant line of his tuxedo. He belonged in a black-and-white movie, dancing across a ballroom with some starlet. When he spotted Ruby, he grinned from ear to ear and gave a wave.

"Surprise!" Ruby gave him a big hug. "Look who's here."

"You. And your mom!" Finn and Virginia embraced. He smelled of cologne and cigarette smoke, and she breathed him in.

"I didn't know you were in town until about two minutes ago," Virginia said.

Ruby cut in. "Listen, I did something terrible. I almost burned down our apartment building."

Finn's eyes widened in alarm. "You did not!"

"I did. So now we have to stay with you and Xavier, just for a while, until they clean it up." Ruby turned to her mother. "Xavier's his boyfriend. He's incredible; you'll love him. Just wait until you see their place."

Virginia put a hand on her daughter's arm. "I'm sorry, Finn. I didn't know about this and wasn't sure where to turn, and then Ruby insisted we come here but wouldn't tell me why—"

"Stop. Don't say another word. You're safe with me, ladies."

He chatted briefly with the maître d' and motioned for them to follow him. A bellboy filed in behind them, bearing Ruby's garbage bag as if it contained gold coins, and they headed up in an elevator to the top floor. "We're staying in a friend's place here. The joys of home combined with the perks of a hotel." He opened the door.

Virginia didn't know where to look. A tiger-skin rug spread-eagled across the living room floor. Bright red walls reflected glints from the oversize chandelier that rose above a snow-white velvet sofa. It was all too much, from the lacquered chinoiserie to the disco music blaring on the stereo.

"Xavier!" yelled Finn. He turned down the volume as a bell-shaped man wearing a hotel robe appeared. Virginia guessed he was about a decade older than Finn and had about thirty pounds on him as well, sporting a head of hair so black it must be dyed and a matching mustache. Virginia blinked a couple of times, adjusting to the idea that this was her brother's boyfriend.

"Are we having a party?" Xavier pulled Ruby to him, planting a kiss on her forehead. "Ruby, how lovely to see you again."

"Xavier, this is my sister, Virginia."

"Oh no!" Xavier covered his mouth with both hands.

Virginia startled. "'Oh no' what?"

"Your hair!"

Virginia patted her head. "What about it?"

"Ignore him, he's being dramatic." Finn clinked some ice into a glass at the bar cart. "Tom Collins, anyone?"

They arranged themselves in the living room, as Ruby recounted the story of the fire to Finn and Xavier.

"Of course, you must stay here, but only if I can cut your mother's hair," announced Xavier.

Finn nodded. "He advises salons all over the world, but originally he was a hairdresser. You'll love what he does."

"Yes, sure." Anything to stop them from staring at her. "Tell me how you two met."

Finn took Xavier's hand. "In Monaco. He was consulting for a grand opening of the Hotel Metropole's hair salon; I was playing at the bar. True love. When I got the gig at Bemelmans, I was excited that the three of you would finally get to meet."

"You lead quite the peripatetic life, then."

"We do. When I get a gig, we go there; if he gets put in charge of opening a new salon, we go there. From Amsterdam to, well, Xanadu! Now, how long do you need to stay? We're here for four months, until March."

"We'll definitely be out of your hair by then." This weekend, Virginia would have time to figure out the insurance for the apartment, arrange for cleaners. The co-op board might write her a warning or something—she wasn't sure how all that worked—but soon enough it'd all be back to normal.

"I want to be *in* your hair, darling." Xavier scooted over and ran his fingers through her unruly mane. "What were you trying to do, here?"

"It's a shag."

"It's a shag rug. Let me play, won't you?" He returned with a towel, scissors, and a chair, which he placed in the middle of the rug. "Sit."

"I don't need a haircut at the moment."

"Go on, Mom." Ruby wouldn't relent, so Virginia, again, did what her daughter told her to do.

"How are you guys doing these days?" asked Finn as Xavier snipped away.

Ruby snuggled in next to her uncle. While Virginia was happy that her daughter and brother had established a close connection, she couldn't help but feel she'd been kept out of some private club.

"We're okay. And Mom's totally fine now. Right, Mom?"

"What does she mean?" Finn swiveled around to face Virginia.

From the concerned look on Finn's face, Virginia could tell he didn't know about the cancer. Her letter must have gotten lost. But now was not the time. Virginia answered, keeping her head as still as possible. "I'm enjoying the single life. I have a job, working for Penn Central, which runs Grand Central Terminal. In the information department."

"That's great, Vee."

Thankfully, Ruby stepped in, asking Finn about Europe, and he regaled her with stories about careening through Naples on a Vespa and dining on octopus in Portugal. What a shame their parents weren't alive to see what a success he'd made of himself: a worldly, charismatic musician who made money playing the very songs they had loved.

Finn interrupted himself mid-story and pointed to Virginia. "You look way better than you did before."

Xavier stepped back. "My work here is done."

Virginia went over to a gilded mirror in the front hallway. He'd cut it short, in a boyish pixie. The lack of hair around her neck highlighted her chin and jawline. "I like it. Thank you."

"Like it? You look fabulous." Xavier gave her a hug.

Finn showed them to the guest room, where a daisy-print coverlet clashed with the foil-patterned wallpaper.

Ruby changed into a pair of pajamas and snuggled under the covers while Virginia unpacked. "You're not mad at me, are you, for bringing you here?"

It was way better than the alternatives. "Of course not. This was a good idea. I'm glad you and your uncle are close. You did well."

Ruby turned over and curled into a ball, whispering, "I love you."

"Love you, too."

Virginia wandered back out into the dark apartment, not ready to sleep. She quietly made some tea and sat at the lemon-yellow Formica table, reading through the insurance company binder she'd brought from the apartment, trying to make sense of the legalese.

Damn.

The deductible for the apartment policy was huge. She'd been trying to cut costs in order to afford her dream apartment. Which was now ruined. She'd be able to pay it off, but just barely. And not right away.

Her neck itched from the haircut, and the overwrought decor made her jumpy. There was no way she could sleep. She let herself out and took the elevator down to the first floor. The bar was still hopping, but she found a single seat.

A man with a thick head of white hair tended the bar. A silver fox. That's how Betsy would describe him. One of the lucky ones who wasn't losing more hair with every passing decade.

"What would you like?" He spoke with an Irish lilt that reminded Virginia of her grandparents.

"I'll have a Jameson. Where are you from?"

"Dublin. Came over a few years ago." He held out his hand. "Name's Ryan."

Virginia introduced herself. "My parents were Irish. Lived in Hell's Kitchen, and my dad owned a pub there."

"That so? I'm impressed."

"Don't be. It was a dive." Her father had owned the bar on the ground floor of their building his entire life, showing up every day in black pants, a white shirt, and a tie, as if he were an accountant. His sad, hound-dog eyes—which Finn had inherited—and quiet demeanor seemed completely wrong for the owner of a West Side Irish bar, but they worked in his favor. His regulars knew they were the focus, that they'd be listened to and sided with as they ranted about their jobs or their wives, that he'd laugh at their jokes. Seeing Finn again made Virginia ache for her father. She shook it off. "This place, though, is fabulous. The murals are the perfect touch, low-key but lovely."

"Done by a man named Ludwig Bemelmans."

"Hence the name of the bar."

"Hence." Ryan's skin was smooth, unlined. Must be from all that Irish fog. Put him on a trawler in a fisherman's sweater and he'd make a great ad for frozen fish sticks.

She rambled on, driven by edgy exhaustion. "I came in with my daughter earlier; we met up with my brother, who plays here. I haven't seen him in ages."

"That's right, I saw you before with Finn. You're his sister?"

She nodded. "We're going to be staying with him for a little while. Him and Xavier."

"That's great; maybe we'll see more of you, then. Great haircut, by the way. Suits you."

She touched a tendril near her ears. "Thanks."

A new group of customers burst through the doors, tourists carrying shopping bags, cameras slung around their necks. Virginia took another few sips of her drink before waving good-bye to Ryan and retreating to her brother's lair.

CHAPTER TEN

November 1974

Virginia filtered through the lunch-hour crowds outside Grand Central. Thanksgiving was in two days, and the pedestrians bustled about with pre-holiday zeal. Yesterday, in between stacking brochures, she'd snuck in a whispered call to the Art Students League, one of the top art schools in Manhattan, and to her surprise, she had gotten a meeting with a curator there. She figured if the watercolor was worthless, the curator would tell her without making her feel like an idiot, as opposed to presenting herself as a laughingstock to the people at Sotheby Parke Bernet. If so, that would be fine. She'd frame it and enjoy looking at it just as much as if it were worth a thousand dollars. And if it happened to be worth something, as much as she'd hate to part with it, perhaps she'd have enough to pay off the deductible on the insurance. In any case, she wanted to know more about Clara Darden and Levon Zakarian and how the canvas might have ended up stuck behind a cabinet at the Grand Central School of Art.

She'd been inside the Art Students League many years ago,

during a field trip for an undergraduate seminar, but she had never really studied the grandeur of the exterior. The embellished five-story building looked like it belonged on a Paris boulevard, not on Fifty-Seventh Street, but the ornate detailing did seem fitting for an art school. Inside, she encountered a hive of activity, with students of all ages, from eighteen to eighty, passing along the hallways, calling out to one another.

Virginia waited in a second-floor gallery where students' work was on display, as well as a small pamphlet on the history of the school. It had been founded in 1875, and artists like Pollock, O'Keeffe, and Norman Rockwell had studied there.

A young woman with long black braids approached. "Ms. Clay?"

"Yes."

"I'm Janice Russo."

"You're the curator I'm supposed to meet with?" Not what she expected. The girl was young and so pretty.

Janice clearly heard her surprised tone. "That's right. I have a PhD in art history, and I'm the curator for the school."

"How fantastic. Good for you."

"Thanks."

Virginia kicked herself for assuming it would be a crusty old man, for falling into the trap of assuming such a thing. It made her feel older than ever.

"They said you had something to show me?" Janice led her into a small office off the gallery, where a desk took up most of the space. One wall was devoted to bookshelves, with oversize art books taking up the bottom row, and the thin spines of auction catalogs lined up in date order along the top. "Have a seat."

Virginia pulled the portfolio out of her bag. "I found this artwork the other day and was curious about it. I noticed it looks a lot like a painting by Levon Zakarian that's up for auction." She took out the auction catalog and opened it to the earmarked page. "I was hoping you'd take a look and tell me what you think."

The curator opened the portfolio and let out a sharp breath. She pulled the painting close and examined it carefully, not touching anything but the very edges, looking back and forth from the catalog to the paper. "What strikes me is that the brushstrokes are quite similar. Like it's a trial run for the real thing. It's watercolor, though, not oil. To my knowledge, Zakarian only worked in oil, using the impasto method. He was known to have detested watercolor, for some reason."

"What's impasto? Sounds like a noodle dish."

Janice laughed. "No, it's a technique where the paint is laid down very thickly, so that the work has a lot of texture. Like Van Gogh's *Starry Night*. Basically, it's the opposite of watercolor."

"Huh. I was wondering if maybe this is a real Levon Zakarian, what with the auction coming up." She added, quietly, "That maybe it might be worth something."

Janice reached into her desk drawer and took out a magnifying glass. She peered through it, paying special attention to the bottom right corner. "Unfortunately, there's no signature, neither Clyde nor Levon Zakarian."

"Who's Clyde?" asked Virginia. "I thought the artist was Levon Zakarian."

Janice turned and scanned the bookshelf, pulling out a thin catalog. "This exhibition catalog is one of the few remaining records of the Clyde paintings that were shown in New York in the early 1930s, although at the time, no one knew who the real artist was. He preferred to remain anonymous. The paintings were a huge hit, heralded as one of the first direct links between the School of

Paris—cubism, for example, or fauvism—and the New York School, where abstract expressionism got its start."

Virginia's head spun. If only she'd studied modern art instead of medieval, this might make sense. "Cubism is Picasso, right, and fauvism is Matisse?"

"Exactly. Cubism was an early-twentieth-century movement, where the artists portrayed an image from many different angles, broken up into cubes." She pulled out a book on Picasso and pointed to the cover. "*Girl with a Mandolin* is the name of this one."

"It's jarring."

"Sure is. That's the School of Paris, an umbrella term for all the remarkable artists who lived and worked there at the beginning of the twentieth century. The New York School, which includes abstract expressionism, came later, after World War II, with men like Pollock and de Kooning, who turned away from using a figure entirely. Pollock's drip paintings, for example."

"You're saying that this Clyde artist was a bridge between the two?"

"Yes." She pointed to the watercolor. "Look at the way the figure is barely suggested. Even less so than the Picasso painting. It might not be a figure at all."

"How are Clyde and Levon Zakarian related to each other?"

"As I mentioned, at the exhibit in New York in 1931, the artist behind the Clyde paintings insisted on remaining unknown. Not until a second exhibit in Chicago was he supposed to step forward. Of course, there was great speculation, as the paintings had made an enormous impact with art critics."

"What happened?"

"The train carrying the works from New York to Chicago crashed, ended up in a river. A horrible accident. All the paintings were destroyed, and the art dealer who represented the artist died on the train, along with Levon Zakarian. It was easy enough to put two and two together. Ever since, Clyde's work has been attributed to Zakarian."

Levon Zakarian must be the ghostly presence that Totto had mentioned her first day on the job.

"How terrible." She thought for a moment. "You said all the paintings were destroyed. But what about the one that's for auction?"

"That surfaced recently. Happens every so often; something comes to light that's been stored in an attic for decades. Usually, the owner's family never realized it was valuable. Even though the one that's for auction wasn't listed in the original exhibition catalog, the experts examined it and agreed it's a Zakarian Clyde painting."

"What are the chances mine is also a Zakarian Clyde? A study for the oil painting?"

"Hard to say. As I mentioned, he didn't like watercolors. It could be a really good reproduction."

Virginia turned over the watercolor. "What about this drawing on the other side?"

"How strange. Clara Darden, of all people." Janice's brow furrowed. "Darden was an illustrator who did magazine covers and that kind of thing. During her day, she was considered a huge commercial success." She picked up a history of illustration from her bookshelf, turned to the section on Clara Darden, and handed it to Virginia.

In the black-and-white image, Clara Darden was wraithlike, her pale eyes, hair, and eyelashes hardly distinguishable from the gray background. The defiant look on her face, though, was familiar. Virginia recognized it from the illustration of the secretaries she'd seen on the wall of the art school her first day. The model in the center of the drawing had been a self-portrait, she was certain.

Janice continued. "Both Zakarian and Darden were on the faculty of the Grand Central School of Art, but Darden wasn't in the same league as Zakarian, artistically." She examined the signature at the bottom right-hand corner of the drawing, then did the same for the image in the auction catalog. "This is odd, though." She picked up the magnifying glass again.

"What's that?"

"The letter *C* in the signature lines. Take a look."

Virginia examined both signatures, *Clara Darden* on the sketch and *Clyde* in the auction catalog. Both *C*'s had an extra swirl at the top. "They both curl around, more like a swirl than a letter *C*."

"Yes." Janice looked up and blinked a couple of times. "That's unexpected. Astonishing, really." She turned the page in the illustration book. "Here's one of Darden's illustrations for *Vogue*."

Virginia's eyes went right to the signature. "A curly *C*."

"A curly *C*." Janice pointed to the watercolor. "Your drawing is dated as well, 1929."

"But the exhibit wasn't until 1931."

"Right."

Virginia couldn't contain herself. "So it probably wasn't a reproduction. What if Clara Darden was Clyde?"

Janice raised her eyebrows. "The similarity in the name is interesting. However, it could be that Clara Darden did the sketch, and then Levon Zakarian took the paper and made this as a kind of study, in watercolor, for the final work. Artists often reused supplies and canvases in order to save money. The whole thing is quite odd."

"But you said yourself he didn't like watercolor. And why would they both use a curly *C*?"

"The curly *C* points to both works being by the same person, that's true. I have to admit I'm stunned by the close correlation between the drawing and the watercolor."

The way Janice drank in the painting, practically devouring it with her eyes, gave Virginia a surge of excitement. She really should be getting back to work, but this was worth being late. She might be in possession of a valuable work of art. To hell with Terrence's scolding. "In that case, Clara Darden might be the original painter, not Levon Zakarian. After all, the train crashed before the artist was officially revealed, right?" Virginia's thoughts rushed over one another. "Why would Levon Zakarian want to stay anonymous in the first place?"

"Good question. Maybe because it was so unlike his earlier work, for shock value. Bear in mind this was during the Depression, when no one was buying art. At the time, a lot of folks wrote it off as a publicity stunt to boost sales."

Virginia shifted to the edge of her seat. "Is Clara Darden still around?"

"I'm afraid not. Nothing was heard from her after 1931."

"The same year of the train crash. Maybe she was on the train."

"You would think it would've made the newspapers. After all, she was one of the most successful female illustrators of that era. What's really strange is that we know what happened to all the other illustrators in this book, but for her, there's nothing. Like she just disappeared." Janice touched the painting, gently, as if it were a relic. "You've discovered something important, I think."

"Is it valuable?" Excitement rose in Virginia's belly, like the quickening she'd felt while pregnant with Ruby.

"If it's a Zakarian, a study like this could fetch more than a hundred and fifty thousand dollars."

"Wow." The number floored Virginia. It was more than she could have imagined. She took a moment to gather herself. "What if it's a Darden?"

Janice sat back in her chair and blew out a breath. "Then all bets are off. It means that a little-known female artist had an instrumental influence on the progression of art in the twentieth century. A revelation like that could be incredibly valuable."

To prove that a woman had been the driving force between two art movements was exciting, and not only because then the watercolor would be worth even more. Virginia had followed with great interest the news coverage of the women's movement, how the Equal Rights Amendment was certain to be ratified. When Chester made stupid jokes about women marching in the streets, she and Ruby had scolded him into submission.

For more than forty years, Clara Darden had been shoved to the sidelines, overshadowed by a man. Just as Virginia had felt overshadowed by Chester during their marriage. Perhaps this was Virginia's chance to make something of herself in the wake of Chester's desertion, and bring Clara out into the light.

"There is someone who could help you figure this out, who knew them both," said Janice.

"Who's that?"

"Irving Lorette. He used to run the Grand Central School of Art. I saw him recently at an opening. He and his wife live downtown and are still active in the art world. You could start there, to get a sense of whether Darden and Zakarian knew each other well, get some backstory. They'd be able to point you in the right direction."

"I'll do that."

"Use my name when you do. I have to admit, this is exciting, what you found." She paused. "Where did you get it again?"

Virginia's mind went blank. What should she say? That she'd accidentally trespassed into the Grand Central School of Art? The truth was complicated. "Um, an aunt of mine had it for years. We just discovered it after she passed away."

"Good for her for saving it. When you think of the remarkable works that have been lost to the garbage heap."

"So true." In fact, if Virginia hadn't found the watercolor, it would have eventually been destroyed by a demolition crew. The thought alleviated her guilt a smidgen. Virginia tucked the portfolio under her arm and left, promising to keep Janice in the loop.

—◦◦◦—

"I'm calling for Dennis Huckle, please. It's Virginia Clay."

Virginia covered the mouthpiece with her hand as she waited to be connected. Privacy was not an option in the information booth, and she certainly wasn't supposed to use the phone for personal calls. But she'd been sweet-talking Terrence since she arrived that morning and had delivered the ten-thirty coffees to the staff at ten fifteen, even stealing a couple of sad-looking donuts from the employee kitchen at the back of the Station Master's Office.

She'd already called the Lorette residence and briefly explained the situation to Mrs. Lorette, who seemed quite kind and set up an appointment for Virginia to stop by on Friday. But that was two days away, and in the meantime she'd decided to reach out to Dennis, stop waiting around for him to call her. After all, she was a modern woman.

This morning at breakfast, her brother and Xavier had cracked each other up, laughing at some story in the paper, and their silly joy had made her miss having a partner. She wouldn't mind trying another round of sex as well. The first one had stirred up something in her that she hadn't felt in years. On top of all that, she was dying to show off her new haircut. The crew in the booth had given it two thumbs up. Well, all except Doris, who told her she looked like a boy.

Long lines starfished around the information booth. Thanksgiving was the next day, the concourse brimmed with passengers, and Doris had even put down her nail file in order to keep up with the constant inquiries. These weren't the regular commuters, who knew where they were headed and wouldn't be caught dead asking a question. Instead, the terminal teemed with train travel neophytes who showed up at the information booth helpless and harried, unsure of where to buy a ticket or how to get to the correct platform. But the swarm kept Terrence off Virginia's back for being on the phone twice in one morning.

"Virginia!" Dennis sounded pleased to hear from her, and she breathed a sigh of relief. Terrence glanced over at her, and she held up one finger and mouthed, *I'll be quick.* A man in line at Terrence's window rapped on the glass to get his attention, complaining he'd been pickpocketed.

"Hi, Dennis. I hope I didn't catch you at a bad time."

"It's a madhouse up here."

"Down here as well. Everyone's heading out of town at once."

"We're preparing to file a brief with the court next week, so I'll be lucky if I get any turkey at all."

She heard the sound of shuffling papers through the phone. "What are you filing?"

"We're asking the judge to declare the landmark designation unconstitutional."

"If you have time for a quick break, I was hoping I might pop up and take a look at the model of the new building, like you'd promised." She hoped she didn't sound too needy.

The pickpocket victim spotted a policeman and barreled over to complain to him instead. Terrence peered over at Virginia.

Dennis took a beat. "Sounds great. It'd be nice to see you."

She hung up the phone, unable to hide the huge smile on her face.

"One of your paramours?" asked Terrence. Totto's ears perked up, and Winston shifted around so he could keep one eye on his line and the other on what was going on inside the booth.

"No. That was just a friend." She offered him the last donut, but he shook his head.

"How's the studying going?" Terrence pointed to the binder.

"Fine." While she loved the historical summary, the dry facts bored her. "How long did it take you to learn all this?"

"About a week."

"You're kidding, right?"

"Terrence has a photographic memory," offered Totto. "Sees something once and never forgets it."

"Do you as well?" asked Virginia.

"Me?" Totto looked confused. "No. Why would I?"

"I thought you were brothers."

Totto laughed. "You kidding? I'm way better-looking."

"He is," added Terrence. "I'll give him that."

By now, Virginia knew what to expect from her coworkers: Doris bemoaning her sciatica and the sister-in-law who lived with her and her husband in Queens; Totto's constant cursing how the city had changed and how rude New Yorkers were these days; Winston missing the warmth of Savannah; and Terrence keeping them all in line. Once she'd gotten over her initial claustrophobia, she'd found it was nice to be with people during the day, even if the job was a bore. Back when her days were wide-open, she'd filled them with nonsense, like committees that accomplished nothing.

She opened the binder but wasn't in the mood to study. "Terrence, have you heard about this plan to demolish part of Grand Central and put up a skyscraper on top of it?"

Terrence propped up the WINDOW CLOSED sign and directed the next customer over to Totto. "Never gonna happen."

"What do you mean?"

"This place has a legacy; it's an important part of New York City's history."

"I happen to know one of the lawyers involved in the court case, and he says it's a shoo-in." She didn't mean to sound like such a know-it-all. "I mean, the place isn't exactly a shining example of New York City anymore. Everyone tries to avoid it if they can."

She thought Terrence would get mad, as he seemed to take any affront to the terminal personally. But instead, he lowered his voice. "You don't see it the way I do. You know how when you've known someone a long time, you still see them as youthful?"

She knew exactly what he was talking about. To her, Ruby was frozen in time, the happy girl with grand plans and knobby knees, even when she knew Ruby was a grown woman. "I get what you mean."

"I still see this place as it was in the forties." Terrence looked about, and she did as well, trying to picture what he described. "Gleaming and beautiful. A masterpiece. The red carpet rolled out for the Twentieth Century Limited to Chicago right there on track 34."

She smiled as if she hadn't heard the same thing a week earlier from Dennis. Boys and their trains.

"You see up there?" He pointed to the blackened ceiling. "That used to be a vivid turquoise color."

Virginia laughed. He was teasing her. "No way. I don't believe that one bit." But he didn't crack a smile. "In any event, it's like a cave now, dark and scary. I don't think many other people see it the way you do."

"I suppose so." His face took on a sad cast.

An irate man in a black top hat banged on the window. Terrence sighed, removed the WINDOW CLOSED placard, and patiently explained that the man's mastiff would not be allowed on the train to Greenwich, under any circumstances.

After work, as Virginia waited for the elevator to the Penn Central offices, the metal grillwork above the doors caught her eyes. Like the filigree, the design was complicated and showy. A slew of wrought iron vines twisted around the floor indicator, and recessed in the marble trim immediately above was a leaf-and-acorn wreath in bronze. The terminal was like a giant gallery of hidden art; you just had to know where to look. What was that expression from her art major days? Memento mori, where an object in the artwork served as a warning of death. Usually, it was a skull or an hourglass, a bowl of rotting fruit. Grand Central, in its decaying splendor, was the embodiment of a memento mori work of art. If it came down, Terrence's heart would be broken.

Virginia put on fresh lipstick as the car rose. She asked the receptionist to announce her to Dennis and planted herself in the same chair she'd waited in a week ago.

Dennis shambled out, looking tired, but when he saw her, he put his hands on his hips and laughed. "Look at that haircut. I love it. Very French."

"Thanks."

"Come right this way. I don't have much time, but I think you'll be impressed." He put his hand on the small of her back to guide her, leaving it there a little longer than necessary, and she felt a zing of desire.

On a table inside his office, a large white model rose up three feet. Dennis's description of the proposed skyscraper was apt. The building literally sat on top of the front half of the station, with long supports like spider legs jutting out onto the transverse. It was rectangular, windowed, and boring.

"What do you think?" Dennis asked.

She thought for a moment. "It's very modern."

"You bet. Think of all the rent money that will pour in, as well as the taxes for the city. It's good for everyone."

"Where will your office be?" she teased.

"Right there." Dennis pointed to the top floor.

He leaned in and gave her a quick kiss before his phone rang. "Give me a sec."

While he spoke, she studied the model further. Grand Central would become even darker, with the new building blocking most of the windows. Terrence and Winston and the others would be stuck belowground, like mole people.

Dennis hung up the phone. "I'm sorry, I have a meeting I have to get to."

"Of course."

She wanted to ask more questions about the new building, find out how exactly it would affect the railroad terminal, but before she could speak, Dennis kissed her, long and slow. When they drew apart, she was glad for his arms around her, or she might have wobbled to the floor.

She really shouldn't have waited as long as she did to get out in the world after her divorce. With men like Dennis around, smart and just the right amount of burly, a woman could get everything that she didn't get in a marriage: compliments, sex, and downtime when she could just be herself. Of course, he still didn't know her secret. But for the first time, she could imagine telling him about the cancer. About her missing piece. As she walked down the hall, knowing he was watching her, she added a little kick to her step, a sway to her hips. It was nice being wanted.

Instead of going back down by elevator, Virginia headed to the art school, clutching the can of mace Dennis had given her last week, just in case any hoodlums might be lurking about. She tucked it back inside her purse as she wandered through the rooms, keeping an eye out for anything that might help identify the artist behind the watercolor. The lockers contained ancient paints, brushes with hardened bristles, and other detritus of no value. The narrow wooden slots for storing large canvases were mostly empty, and the few artworks that remained had faded, paint chips forming a mosaic beneath them. How sad for this place to be lost to time, with no one left to mourn it. The same could be said for the entire terminal, if Dennis got his way.

She combed through the desks in the small offices but discovered nothing other than a fountain pen, a jar of dried black ink, and a couple of pencils. She wasn't sure what she was looking for, but in any case, nothing jumped out as important.

At the entrance to the storage room, though, she froze. Two new crates had been opened and pulled into the center of the room. The wall of artwork had changed again. Two bright monochromes in orange, which definitely hadn't been there before, were tacked up in the very center. Someone had been in here, digging through the crates, putting paintings up and taking them down. Looking for something.

This was no ghost.

A muffled moan sounded from another room. She froze, hoping to hear Dennis's baritone calling out her name. Had she locked the door behind her? She couldn't remember.

Those thugs, the ones she'd encountered last week, might be back. If she screamed, who would hear her? No one.

She was trapped. She unzipped her purse to retrieve the can of mace, the sound louder than expected, and heard footsteps in response. A shuffling, followed by a loud bang.

Now there was no doubt in her mind.

Someone else was inside the school.

Virginia ran through her options. Whoever else was inside was somewhere between her and the front door. She looked about for a place to hide, a closet or under a desk. But the thought of staying put terrified her.

Running as if she was on fire, Virginia made it to the exit without looking right or left, staring straight ahead at her goal, sure that at any moment an arm would reach out and grab her hair, her clothes, and yank her backward.

She fumbled with the doorknob, breathing heavily, her hands shaking, and finally turned it. Bursting into the hallway, she headed right, to safety.

A man in a suit stood in front of the elevator. Thank God. Not Dennis, but not a thug. She looked behind her for the first time since her sprint. No one was there; no one was coming.

"Are you all right?" The man's eyes showed a wary concern. She could only imagine what she looked like, rumpled, her face red, eyes wide.

"I'm fine, thank you." The elevator opened.

"After you."

She rushed inside, breathing hard, relief setting in only after the doors had closed.

CHAPTER ELEVEN

May 1929

T hey'll be here any moment, Clara. Do hurry."

Clara nodded at Oliver through the reflection of her vanity mirror. He looked as handsome as ever in a natty yellow bow tie and two-toned oxfords, his face flushed with excitement at the arrival of their dinner party guests and from the martini he'd drunk while dressing.

He drew close and kissed her on the top of her head. "Sorry. I know you must be tired. You've been working all day, and now I'm forcing you to hobnob with strangers. You aren't mad, are you?"

"Of course not, my love. I know how you enjoy your salons." She tilted her face up, and he kissed her properly, slowly, until she was dizzy and breathless. It still amazed her that this beautiful boy was all hers.

So much had happened since she'd signed the contract with *Vogue* last year. At times, Clara's new apartment at 25 Fifth Avenue was unrecognizable, the squeaky cot from her Tenth Street studio replaced with a macassar bed fit for a queen, with an inlaid parchment headboard. Oliver had laid eyes on it in some uptown furniture store and insisted she take it. They weren't exactly living together—he still had his bachelor pad in the Village—but he spent most of the day and many of the evenings here, answering her correspondence, arranging social events like tonight's dinner, and generally making her life run as smoothly as possible.

"What were you working on today?" He sat at the edge of the bed and adjusted a cuff link.

"They want a dozen new illustrations for a piece on the 'Well-Dressed Secretary.' And of course, the September cover."

All day she'd been working on the cover, a woman at the wheel of an automobile facing out, the door open, one hand casually resting on the steering wheel and the other on the back of the seat. The figure had come easy enough, but she'd been struggling over the details of the car when Oliver had told her it was time to wash up and dress. Like an obedient child, she'd cleaned off her brushes and palette and closed the door of her studio behind her.

She'd never have attained the success she had without him. Between the commissions and teaching, she was even able to sock money away. The school term would end in a few weeks, and she was thrilled to have had a class of thirty this term, with no dropouts at all.

She slid a pair of crystal combs into her unruly mane. "I forgot to mention, Mr. Lorette at the art school said my class would be moved to a bigger studio in the fall. To fit the additional students."

"Isn't that tiring, though? Why teach when you don't have to?" The smile on his face belied his concern, she knew. Lately, he'd complained they didn't spend enough time together, suggesting a long weekend at Compo Beach or a jaunt to Europe. But now that she finally had the work she had craved for so long, she couldn't bear to walk away.

She also had a terrible fear that it was all going to be taken away at any moment. That was what had happened to her father, after all. One day they were eating steaks and caramel custard, the next she was scrounging in a vegetable garden for potatoes to make soup. She understood that, rationally, it was her father's own fault. But that sense of fragility, of everything all coming crashing down, stayed with her always. She was like one of those squirrels in Washington Square Park, tucking nuts in their cheeks and burying the rest of the bounty. The taste of success had only increased her urge to accumulate more. More work, more money.

And it had all come so quickly. The months flew by in a blur. Yet every morning when she rose, she peered out her bedroom window, the rectangular buildings and conical water towers sharp against a blue sky, and gave a moment of thanks for Oliver, for her work, and for this lovely city.

She didn't mention the other reason she enjoyed going to the School of Art twice a week. Sometimes after class, she and Levon would meet for a coffee in the Grand Central Terminal Restaurant. Or they'd sneak off for a quick smoke away from the students, in her favorite place in the building: a secret room behind the huge Tiffany clock that overlooked Forty-Second Street. While there was no reason to keep this from Oliver—after all, she had friendships with many male artists these days—Oliver and Levon never seemed to get on. They'd run into each other at a couple of faculty dinners at the Lorettes' brownstone in the Village, where Levon had drunk too much and carried on about the superiority of Armenian poets over American ones. Clara didn't blame Oliver, really. While she admired the depth of Levon's knowledge and his natural exuberance, he could become a tedious conversationalist when his authority was questioned. Clara often teased him that he'd win even more admirers than he had already amassed if he could only pretend, on occasion, that he thought slightly less of himself.

But Levon was even more defensive and self-aggrandizing now than he had been when they first met. He'd been stuck in an artistic rut for some time, painting the mother and child over and over, unable to move forward. Clara's good fortune made her want to assist in some way. She'd insisted he be invited to that night's dinner party, even though the thought made her nervous. The guest list was eclectic, a mix of poets and singers as well as a couple of moneyed husbands and lovers. If Levon was in a charming mood, he might be able to entice a potential buyer to a studio visit.

She patted some rouge on her cheeks and smiled. Oliver enjoyed pulling together people from different walks of life; he was a natural as a host, even though sometimes she wondered if his energies might be better put into his poetry. "I do appreciate you bringing the mountain to Mohammed. To have a dinner party in my own home without having to lift a finger? You've been a dream. Who are we expecting tonight?"

The doorbell rang, and Oliver leaped to his feet. "A banker and his ode-writing poet mistress, an automobile executive and his opera-singing wife. A fellow alum from Andover and, of course, Levon." The last name hung in the air. "I'll make the introductions. You won't have to worry about a thing."

He disappeared, off to help her maid greet the guests.

They were eight around the dining room table, a shiny walnut number with a matching sidebar, where a silver-plated cocktail set and tray sparkled in the candlelight. Another of Oliver's finds. Levon strode in late, catching Oliver up in an awkward hug and kissing Clara's hand before diving into a conversation about European politics with the Andover classmate.

Seated to Clara's left was Mr. Cavanaugh, the banker, a man with a penchant for expensive clothes and inexpensive dentistry, judging from his yellowed teeth. He gushed over Clara, remarked on her latest cover, asked her about the Paris fashions. "My wife goes over every season, you know. She adores your work, has even had several framed for our house in Glen Cove."

She smiled and answered his rapid-fire questions with as much grace as she could muster. After all, how lovely it was to be sought after, instead of desperately seeking.

"Framed? I'm touched. How kind of her."

"Yes. Like they're real art."

Real art. As if her imagination, technique, and execution were false.

"What are you working on now, Miss Darden?" The banker's mistress, a slight, redheaded woman named Sally, chirped from the other end of the table.

"Another cover. And another one after that." Each had to be better than the last, more whimsical. Illustrators were glorified factory workers, she'd complained to Levon just that week. There was always someone new coming up the ranks, offering a unique angle. Just as she had.

Oliver piped up. "Clara's contracted through the end of this year with *Vogue*, and I have no doubt they'll renew for another year."

The banker's mistress took several puffs from her cigarette holder, her eyes glittering. "I loved the latest issue. The cover was gorgeous, of course, but there were also so many delightful photographs. One layout, do you call it a layout?"—she didn't wait for Clara's response—"showed the most divine tweed suits. I swear I could see every thread."

Mr. Cavanaugh held up his wineglass for the maid to refill. "Do you think eventually magazines will be all photographs? What would all the illustrators do then?"

"It'll never happen." Oliver looked over at Clara, silently apologizing for the turn in the conversation. "Photography is far too expensive and not nearly as expressive."

Mr. Cavanaugh slapped the table. "Good to hear. Speaking of expression, how is your poetry going, Mr. Smith? You and Sally are in that literary group together, aren't you?"

Oliver hadn't written anything new in months. Clara had told him he didn't have to do so much for her, that he ought to take time out for himself, but he'd brushed her off.

"Perhaps after dinner you both could read some of your work," she suggested. One of the other guests was going to sing; the Andover alum had brought a guitar. If she could persuade Oliver to share his work, get some approbation, he might be newly inspired.

Sally squealed with delight, but Oliver shot Clara a worried look. "I'm still in the early stages, I'm afraid. I've been so busy lately."

She tried again. "Maybe one of your earlier poems?" She looked out over the table. "He's an extraordinary talent."

"Don't, Clara."

The other conversations at the table, including Levon's, quieted down as the tension rose.

She hadn't meant to put him on the spot. Clara turned to the guest to her right, a gentleman who manufactured and sold Studebaker automobiles, to take the attention off Oliver. Mr. Bianchi was his name, and his wife was the singer in the group. "Tell me, Mr. Bianchi, what's your favorite poem?"

The man chuckled and wiped his mouth with his napkin. He wore round spectacles that echoed his bulbous nose. "I do love the Italian Decadents, D'Annunzio and the like." Mr. Bianchi winked at her.

Levon's fork clattered to the table. "The fascist?"

"Sometimes you have to ignore the politics and focus on the poetry."

"Is it possible to ignore politics?"

"I'm sorry, I've upset you." Mr. Bianchi shrugged. "What can I say? I like beautiful things. Beautiful poetry, beautiful art, beautiful cars."

The maid began serving dessert, an upside-down cake, as Clara grappled to gain control of the conversation. "What's your latest automobile model?"

"Ah, that's quite exciting. It's a lower-priced one called the Dictator."

Dear God.

Levon spoke with his mouth full of cake. "Really? You can't be serious."

Clara noticed Oliver wince at his bad manners. She should have never invited him.

Levon finally swallowed. "You want to speak of dictators? In the last decade of the last century, Sultan Abdul Hamid II of the Ottoman Empire concentrated power into his own hands and ordered the massacre of the Armenian people."

A startled Mr. Bianchi turned red. "We don't mean that kind of dictator. We're imagining someone like Mussolini, a man of strength, of power. Our lines include the Commander, the President, and now the Dictator. It 'Dictates the Standard.'"

Oliver stepped in. "Of course, that makes perfect sense."

"It's an uphill battle." Mr. Bianchi shook his head. "The market is saturated. Everyone owns a car these days. Our hope is that a cheaper model will encourage families to buy two." He waved a chubby hand at Clara. "In fact, next week we're bringing in a consulting group of lady decorators to help us figure out the best way to appeal to the wives. You should come on board; we could use an artist in the group."

Clara thought of her current cover. A close-up look at the latest car model might inspire her. Also, as much as she didn't want to admit it, the banker's mistress had a point about the threat of photography. Clara could envision a time in the future when magazine illustrators were reduced to scrambling for crumbs. Branching out into consulting work was a wise idea. But she didn't want to be lumped in with a group of "lady decorators." She had more to offer Mr. Bianchi than that. "I'd be happy to get involved. In fact, I bet I can solve your problem."

"How so?"

"It's all in the ad campaign. I bet I can create one that will make your Dictator the bestselling car of the year." As she spoke, her excitement grew.

Mr. Bianchi sat back and studied her. "You could, could you?"

"Of course she could. You're talking to Clara Darden, one of the finest instructors at the Grand Central School of Art!" Levon raised his glass to her, and Clara bowed her head slightly in response, hoping to temper his enthusiasm.

"Do you really have time to do car advertisements?" Oliver again. "Your schedule is quite booked already." He was trying to save her, thinking she was being bulldozed. But he was wrong. She wanted this. Something new, something that would provide some contrast to her magazine covers.

"Plenty of other illustrators do designs for more than fashion magazines. I don't see why I can't as well."

Sally giggled. "But automobiles? It's not very feminine work."

Clara sat back, crossed her arms, and shot Sally a look that made her choke on her laughter. "Maybe it should be."

A week after the dinner party, Clara was picked up by a gleaming Studebaker, sent by Mr. Bianchi, and driven to the factory where the cars were made, a massive, drab cement structure about an hour away from the city. Mr. Bianchi's well-appointed office, however, was a pleasant surprise, replete with geometric paneling and Ruhlmann chairs. Finely detailed toy cars dotted the bookshelves.

Four other women, two of whom were renowned designers, sat in chairs in a semicircle around Mr. Bianchi's desk. Clara made her way to the empty seat as introductions were made.

"I'm so pleased you could join me today. Would anyone like a drink?" Mr. Bianchi's nose twitched.

All the women, save Clara, declined the offer.

He poured a couple of Scotches from a bar concealed behind one of the panels, then handed a glass to Clara. She drank a sip, careful to not let him see how it burned her throat.

"On my desk you'll see the latest design for the Dictator. Take a look and let me know your thoughts. We want to know what's the best way to market it so women will encourage their husbands to snap one up, over all our competitors."

The ladies huddled around the desk as Mr. Bianchi made his way to the back of the room. Better to study their figures, Clara surmised. This was all a sham so he could announce to the world that he'd designed a car using the input of women. He really didn't want to hear what they said.

The drink made her bolder than she might have been otherwise, more easily outraged, but she patiently waited her turn to study the drawings. Each page offered a different view: the exterior, the interior dash, details of the hardware. "Who is your ideal buyer for this car?" asked one of the other consultants.

"A family that requires a second so the wife can toodle around town while the husband's at work. Or a family that's just starting out, that can't afford our more expensive lines."

Clara spoke up. "What's the price point?"

"I see you've studied the terminology. Well done. Around twelve hundred dollars."

The ladies spoke over one another in an effort to impress. "You must have an advertisement of a man opening the door for the lady, and maybe she's dressed like Cinderella going to a ball."

"How about a woman behind the wheel with a little boy on her lap, pretending to drive? That'll warm the hearts of the mothers."

While they brainstormed, Clara wandered over to an observation window to the right of the desk, which looked down at the factory floor. Below, hundreds of men attended to the assembly lines, lifting parts from trolleys and affixing them to metal chassis, an intimate dance of muscles and machinery. She touched her fingertips to the glass. "I'd like to go down on the floor."

Mr. Bianchi blanched. "You don't want to go down there. You'll get grubby. I'd hate to see you spoil your lovely dress."

She insisted, and he called in a foreman, who handed her a smock as they headed down several flights of stairs to the floor, where the noise level almost burst her eardrums and the smell of grease and sweat threatened to overwhelm her. Instead of covering her nose, she inhaled deeply. This is what car-making was all about. They were machines, and the design was secondary to the utility.

But that didn't mean the design was superfluous. The foreman, unlike Mr. Bianchi, didn't rush her. She got down on her hands and knees and peered under a finished car, curious what she would find. Another worker pointed out the various locks and hinges of the hefty doors, and she ran her fingers over the cold metal. As a fashion illustrator, she had learned to pay attention to material, color, line, and anatomy. An automobile, which was almost like a coat of armor, was no different from a coat of fur. Protection against the world.

Back in Mr. Bianchi's office, the other ladies were long gone. He looked up in surprise. "Miss Darden? I'd forgotten about you entirely. What on earth have you been doing?"

Clara pulled off the smock and pointed at the drawing. "Not even the cleverest advertisement will work if the interior of the car isn't functional for women. Right now it's not. There are too many knobs that stick out, gears that get in the way. It's too easy for her to catch a sleeve on a gear shift or a glove on an instrument gauge."

He regarded her warily. "We thought women might like all the styling. The rosettes, for instance, on the robe rail. Don't you think they're pretty?"

"There's too much frippery entirely. Women don't want to be riding in a stagecoach from the Georgian age. This is a new, American mode of transport and ought to reflect that. Look at our clothing. No more bustles and corsets." Mr. Bianchi blushed, but she kept on, picking up a fountain pen and drawing right on the plans. "You want only clean lines inside the vehicle, an art deco approach. Get rid of the boxiness of the dash and curve the edges. Everywhere." Her pen raced across the paper, her hand sure and even. "The door handles could look like this. Tuck the ashtray away, here."

He studied them for a long moment, his brow furrowed. "Do you really think this will sell?"

"Let me go back to my studio and come up with some proper sketches for you. Let's make the 1930 Studebaker something that everyone will talk about."

"I'm not sure; this is rather overwhelming."

If she were a man, no doubt he'd give her opinion more consideration. She stopped drawing and gestured for him to sit. He did so, blinking with uncertainty.

"You can use me to sell it."

"Use you?"

"All this past year, I've been telling women what looks good, what's a quality product, and why they should buy it, through my illustrations. I can do the same for you. Hire me for the interior design of the Dictator, as well as the advertisement campaign. In the ads, we'll use my name. 'Styled by Clara Darden.' They'll trust my taste and insist their husbands buy your car."

He looked at the plans, avoiding her stare. He was balking. "Well, I'll have to see."

As a girl, she'd listened while her father bamboozled potential clients and had picked up some of his techniques. Time to close the deal. "Here's what you do. Go home and ask your wife. Tell her about our conversation. Then call me tomorrow and we'll talk numbers."

A strong handshake, and she was out the door.

That evening, Clara shared the day's events with Oliver as they lay in bed.

His face stayed still, inscrutable. "Is this why you came to New York City, to design car door handles?"

"It's not just the handle. It's the entire interior, possibly the exterior as well. I'm shaping the car, you see. Like a sculpture."

"If you want to do sculpture, then do that. Don't pretend that prettying up an automobile is art, though."

His words hurt. But he didn't understand. She tried again. "I'm not 'prettying it up.' Machines can be beautiful. Just like furniture, which can be pleasing to the eye and functional at the same time. A Marianne Brandt teapot is gorgeous, right? And useful. It's called industrial design, and you oughtn't pooh-pooh it. What I'd be doing is hard work, but my guess is that it'll pay off grandly. With a company, with a product, I have an infinite number of possibilities. They change car designs every year. Which means a new opportunity to make my mark."

"And another reason to avoid spending time together."

"Don't be silly. We're together right now."

"You're working all the time, either in class or in your studio. Now this car project."

"You could work as well, on your poetry."

She expected him to rage out of the room, but instead, he sighed. "I'm sorry. You're absolutely right. I have no right to stop you from exploring whatever you want. I'm taking out my own writer's block on you. It's just that you're so prolific. Whatever you do turns to gold. As for me, I'm a champion at dinner parties. No different from my father."

She'd never admit it out loud, but his words contained a kernel of truth. Clara wasn't a struggling teacher anymore, was finally making her own way, but every so often, she got the impression that Oliver didn't approve of her independence. His happiness at her early successes had soured with the more recent ones. He'd seen his mother's independence stifled by his father, and sometimes Clara worried he was falling into a familiar pattern. If only his work would sell. "How about you try a different form? A short story, perhaps?"

"Don't you worry about me. I've got all kinds of things up my sleeve. We'll hear good news soon; I'm sure of it."

She certainly hoped so.

They kissed, and she wrapped herself tightly around Oliver, her head on his shoulder, before falling fast asleep.

Clara could hardly wait to get home after her illustration class the next day, to see if Mr. Bianchi had left a message for her. If he accepted her offer, she'd get paid not only for the advertisements but also for the interior design of the car. She'd be able to add "industrial designer" to her title, charge a princely sum. Maybe even convince Mr. Lorette to let her teach the subject. Her head swam with the possibilities.

As she burst through the doors of Grand Central onto Forty-Second Street, she spied a familiar figure leaning against one of the lampposts, inhaling a cigarette.

She marched over. "How's Grand Central's most famous Armenian painter doing these days?"

He lifted her off the ground in an enormous hug. "My dear Clara, there you are!"

He set her down on the pavement with a thud, and she stumbled briefly before finding her footing. "Enough, Levon. Shake hands like a normal person, will you?"

"You're a vision. We must walk together."

She'd planned on taking a taxi, one of the perks of having a constant stream of income. Last year, she would have taken the subway to spare the expense, but now it was no longer a second thought. She considered asking Levon to join her in the cab, but it was a brilliant May day. A walk would do her good, and whatever Mr. Bianchi had to say could wait. Better to make him wait, probably. They turned onto Fifth Avenue.

Usually, maneuvering along Fifth Avenue this time of day was a matter of dodging tourists and pedestrians coming the other way, not to mention human cannonballs careening out of doorways with no regard for the regular flow of foot traffic. But walking with Levon was much like being one of Moses's followers, she suspected. His mass, his posture, caused the river of humanity to flow around him. He moved in a straight line, which meant she did as well.

"How is your illustration class going this term?" he asked.

"Some are brilliant, others less so. But I had a very productive meeting with the head of Studebaker cars yesterday."

She recapped the meeting, keeping her excitement in check, in case Mr. Bianchi didn't follow through.

He grinned down at her. "Fantastic, my girl. I hope you don't forget me when you're the toast of the town."

But something in him was off. Levon's strides were hurried, as if he wanted to get away from her. She regretted reveling in her enthusiasm, her success. A year ago, he'd been the hero of the school and had used his influence to help her. She shouldn't crow. "Tell me, what are you working on these days?"

"I'm a whirling dervish in the studio. No one can stop me." The usual bravado came out forced.

"I don't believe you."

He made an exasperated sound, like a horse fluttering its lips. When he spoke, the words were so soft she had to strain to hear them over the din of the streets. "That photograph, the one of my mother and me. I can't seem to get the painting of it right. I finish one and then immediately start on another."

"Can I come see?"

His face darkened. "No. I don't let anyone come to my studio anymore. I'm not ready."

She remembered how she'd been stymied until Oliver had lent a hand. "You're stuck. Maybe I can help."

"You'll have me put a bottle of soda in my mother's hand, is that your answer?"

"Don't be petty. You're a great artist. Are you sleeping?" The dark circles under his eyes told her what she knew already.

"Not really. I can't finish it; it will never be right, and I'll keep going on and on and I'll never be able to afford bread and tea again."

They were both propelled by childhood memories of hardship, Levon's far more ghastly than her own. Which was probably why she had been able to overcome the fear of failure, while Levon was succumbing to it. "There's plenty of work out there; times are good. Don't do this to yourself. Is Nadine a help?"

"She went off and got engaged to a stockbroker. I don't blame her. How's your lapdog?"

For a second, she was unsure what he was talking about. "Stop. That's not kind. Oliver is a sweetheart." They passed a bench, set back from the street in a shady spot. "Do you mind if we sit for a moment?"

He sank onto the wooden bench like a puppet released from its strings.

She angled toward him, one arm draped over the back of the bench. "Your work is strong, Levon. Why not let others see it? What if they think it's wonderful?"

"What if they don't?"

"It's worth the risk, trust me."

"You wouldn't know."

She did her best to maintain an even tone. "What do you mean by that?"

"What I do, I do from my heart. What you do, well . . . it's business."

She remembered their debate that night in the Village, in front of the students. There was no reason for him to have changed his mind. Not Levon. "Oh, for God's sake. I won't apologize for my success. I won't apologize for my ambition. Why fight me on this?"

He tensed with a catlike ferocity. For a moment, she thought he was going to leap into the middle of the street, end it all under the wheels of a passing car.

Instead, his head dropped onto her shoulder. "I'm done for, Clara."

She bent her arm around him, averting her eyes from curious stares of passersby. What a sight they must make, a pietà of giants, all long limbs and wide shoulders, the man silently weeping.

CHAPTER TWELVE

June 1929

As she'd hoped, Mr. Bianchi offered Clara the chance to reinterpret the interior of the Dictator, as well as take the lead on the advertising campaign. She immersed herself in the job, stopping by the factory twice more, staying up all night sketching out dashboard designs and advertisement ideas. Even though her schedule was packed, Clara made a point of stopping by Levon's studio every few days, dropping off some bread and cheese or soup, waiting until he'd eaten it all before heading back out. From what she could tell, he still hadn't made much progress on the paintings, but she made a point of not speaking about art, either his or her own.

Today she'd brought an apple and some cold chicken drumsticks, wrapped in brown paper. A lazy heat had settled over the city in the past couple of days, and she didn't want to have to turn on Levon's stove. Striped awnings kept her own apartment cool, but she knew his top-floor studio would be sweltering.

She knocked twice before letting herself in with the spare key, which she'd pilfered after he'd refused to answer the door one day.

She'd had to pound away until he finally let her in, looking morose and surly. This week had shown signs of improvement: He'd had other visitors one day, and on the others, she'd found him reading a book or newspaper instead of indulging in his melancholy.

"Here. Eat this before it spoils." She laid the bag on the table as she unpinned her hat.

Levon wore a white undershirt and blue serge trousers. He reached for his shirt, which lay over a chair, sweeping it about him like a cape and tucking one arm through.

"You don't have to do that for me. It's too hot for long sleeves."

"I'd never be so gauche as to eat in front of a lady with my arms bare. I may have been raised in a dirt hut, but even peasants have standards."

She laughed. "You're about as far from a peasant as any man I know. You're a secret member of the aristocracy, no? Russian, perhaps? I've always suspected that accent wasn't quite right."

"If only. My father was a cobbler, not a duke." He sighed, hiding a smile.

"What was he like?" She'd found that getting him to reminisce often lightened his mood. Which was especially odd, as most of his memories were sad, bordering on grim.

"Simple, but strict. He fled before the worst of the persecution began. I remember once, a few months after my father was gone, a Turk tried to steal from one of my neighbor's homes. In the darkness, he hit his eye on a nail, blinding himself, and was caught. The Turk went to court and insisted that my neighbor was responsible for his accident, and the judge agreed. They pinned him down and gouged out his eye as well."

When he ranted like this, it was best to stay neutral. "How biblical."

Levon burst into peals of laughter. "That is why I adore you, my Clara. You are not afraid of anything. You don't cower like the rest of them."

"What happened to your father? Did you ever find out?"

"He started a new family in the States. When my sister and I finally came here, she wanted to try to find him. But what was the point? He had left us behind in that morass. I wanted nothing to do with him."

"How did you manage, when you first got here?" If she could remind him of his resiliency, maybe he would break free from these doldrums, return to the passionate man she'd first met.

"I found work in an art store. I've always drawn, even when I was young. I made paints from whatever I could find, pear juice and peels, from egg yolks. You're the same way, no?"

"I suppose."

He lurched over to the painting of his mother. "What if I can never finish it?"

She stood behind him. Sections of the canvas shone like porcelain, from the application of multiple coats of paint, followed by scraping and sanding until only a reflective layer remained. While arduous, the technique worked—the finish showed depth that she'd seen before only in the work of Vermeer.

"Who says you have to finish it, anyway? Why not keep on painting for as long as you like?"

"You're saying that so that I do the opposite, right? That I fight back and say that I must finish it."

He was impossible. "Do whatever you must, Levon. It's too hot to argue with you today. Let's go out."

"Where?"

She opened her leather satchel and pulled out a sheaf of papers.

"The Heckscher Building. Three society ladies are creating a museum of modern art there later this year, and I was asked to stop by and give my opinion on some works they're considering."

"Which artists?"

"Cézanne, Gauguin, Seurat, and Van Gogh." She handed over the list.

He scanned it voraciously. "So many."

"They're aiming for a hundred artworks. Can you imagine? We can see them firsthand, right here in New York, and they already have a dozen at the gallery. It's an exciting prospect. You should come."

"What exactly are you doing for them?"

"Mr. Lorette told them I'd take a look at the space, offer my thoughts on the light. That sort of thing."

"Why didn't he ask me?"

Good. The old, competitive Levon was seeping through. She tried not to smile. "Because you've been a miserable wretch the past month and he was probably afraid to approach you. Like almost everyone else at the school."

"But not you."

"No. Not me."

In the gallery space, a woman in her sixties, with a frizz of caramel-colored hair poking out from under a hat, greeted Clara and Levon as they entered.

"I'm Miss Lillie Bliss; you must be Miss Darden. I do love your covers. Such an air of whimsy to them."

"Thank you. May I introduce you to Mr. Zakarian, also of the Grand Central School of Art, and a painter?"

"Pleasure."

Miss Bliss turned back to Clara and began rattling on about

frames, shipping fees, and storage. Clara already regretted bringing Levon, who sulked quietly behind her like a fretful bear. She wished Miss Bliss had at least recognized his name.

A slight man with crooked teeth and a high forehead approached.

"Ah, Felix. You've arrived." Miss Bliss greeted him warmly.

"I certainly have and am eager to offer my strong opinions and have you shoot them down." The words came out in staccato stabs.

"Miss Darden, Mr. Zakarian. You must know Felix Hornsby."

Of course. Oliver had pointed him out to Clara during a cocktail party as one of the city's most distinguished, and successful, art dealers. His unremarkable presence, more like that of a plumber who'd come to fix the sink, caught her off guard at this second sighting.

Clara held out her hand. "Mr. Hornsby. We have a mutual acquaintance, Mrs. Alston Smith." Oliver's mother had recently purchased several Steichen photographs from Mr. Hornsby for the Newport house.

As expected, the man regarded her with a great deal more interest now. Connections, always connections.

Miss Bliss waved her gloved hand. "Such a small world, we art lovers. Everyone, please follow me. I just received a special piece from France, and you'll be the first to see it."

In the next room, two assistants lifted a frame out of a wooden crate with care. They all leaned over to examine it.

A Van Gogh.

"This is *Madame Ginoux*," said Miss Bliss. "What do you think?"

In the painting, an older woman in white, wearing a mint-green scarf and matching cuffs, rested one elbow on a table. Her craggy closed fist supported her cheek, and she seemed both amused and sad. The strong eyebrows and coal-black eyes reminded Clara of

Levon's mother's portrait. But this woman had not been abandoned. Her face showed resilience and a fading beauty. It was not a plea for rescue.

Clara took in the clarity of the painting like a drunk to whiskey. This is the woman she wanted to be in forty years. She wasn't a beauty, or at least hadn't been spruced up to be prettier than she was, the way the famous portraitists of the time tended to do. She was hardy, wary, and tender.

"If you like this, you really should visit Levon's studio." Clara addressed Mr. Hornsby directly, avoiding Levon's openmouthed stare. Daring him to defy her boldness. "His work is exquisite."

Mr. Hornsby nodded. "I've heard many good things about you, Mr. Zakarian. I remember your work in the Grand Central Art Galleries last year." He slapped Levon on the back.

Levon didn't bellow or storm out as she feared he might. Instead, he remained strangely mute as they wandered through the rooms, while the rest advised Miss Bliss on lighting and paint color.

After the tour, Levon made his excuses and left without waiting for her.

Here she was, giving him the opportunity of a lifetime, and he'd blown it. What bothered her most was that his work was terrific— she hadn't embellished her admiration.

"Mr. Hornsby, I'd like to invite you to see Mr. Zakarian's studio."

Mr. Hornsby looked confused. "Wouldn't he normally invite me himself?"

"He would, but he was in a rush to get back and paint. Why don't we meet there tomorrow at one?"

She'd drag Levon with her into the blinding glare of success, in spite of his moods and lack of any social niceties. Just as Levon had unknowingly inspired her at the May Ball, she would prop up Levon for as long as she could stand him, offer him access to her contacts and her sway. His works deserved to be seen and sold, she was sure of that, and perhaps one sale, or even an encouraging word from someone like Felix Hornsby, would lift him out of the darkness that pulled him back to the pain of his past.

He'd be furious. But she didn't care.

Clara let herself in with the key to Levon's studio and looked about. The weather hadn't cooperated one bit. Dark storm clouds brewed beyond the slanted windows, rendering the place more like a vault than an airy artist's loft. But she'd have to make do. Mr. Hornsby would be there any moment, and she wanted him out by the time Levon returned from teaching his class at two.

A lightning bolt cracked like a warning as she arranged the easels in a U-shape before turning to the dozens of paintings leaning against the walls. She examined each canvas carefully before deciding either to place it on an easel or prop it on top of any empty shelf or mantel, as close to eye level as possible. Levon's breadth of talent astounded her. So many different ideas, wrangled and rewrangled, resulted in a powerful array of images. Except his imitation Picassos, which she tucked out of view in the small bedroom.

Clara stepped back and surveyed her efforts. Not bad at all. But where was Mr. Hornsby?

She waited, hopeful at first, but after forty-five minutes, she began to panic. Her plan was to amaze him with the artwork, get him to agree to represent Levon, and then show him the door so she had time to right the room. She'd tell Levon the good news when he returned from teaching.

But time was getting tight.

A fierce bang on the studio door brought her to her feet. She sprang for the latch. Mr. Hornsby stood on the other side, rain dripping off his hat and down his shoulders.

"I couldn't get in. I've been waiting downstairs for five minutes. I was about to leave when someone came down and let me in."

"I'm sorry." She must not have heard the buzzer over the chain saw of rain slamming on the roof. "Please, I'll get you a towel."

She ran to fetch one from Levon's tiny bathroom, where a delicate child's brush balanced on the edge of a pedestal sink, strands of black hair entwined in the bristles. The unexpected intimacy brought tears to her eyes. For all she knew, he'd brought it with him from his homeland, carried it all that way. The image of a young Levon running it through his thick mane in an effort to appear presentable, in the midst of so much turmoil, pained her. The fact that Levon, as a grown man, used it still was unbearably sad.

She pushed it from her mind and went back out, offering tea and cookies, anything to swing Mr. Hornsby's foul mood.

"No. I don't have much time. Where's the artist?"

"Levon is running late. But why don't we start here, with the still lifes?"

Mr. Hornsby surveyed them, various arrangements of pears and figs in bold, almost garish, hues. They moved on to the drawings, including one of a woman in bed, the covers pulled up to her chin. Then landscapes, a couple of self-portraits. He didn't speak, didn't nod, offered no sign of his reaction whatsoever. Finally, they reached the painting of mother and child.

"That one's of his mother when—"

Mr. Hornsby cut her off. "Don't tell me anything about it."

He moved closer, then back. She stayed quiet. Mr. Hornsby was right; there was no need for words. She could tell the figures on the canvas haunted him, just as they had her.

The rain ended, and a powerful silence descended over the studio, broken by a faint scratching sound.

For a second, she thought maybe a mouse had skittered across the floor. But no. It was Levon's key in the lock.

He entered with his back to them, closing a large umbrella and giving it a final shake in the hallway.

He turned around, staring at Clara, then Mr. Hornsby, and back again at Clara. She wished she could fall into a hole, disappear.

Mr. Hornsby held out his hand, practically skipping across the room. "Mr. Zakarian. What a pleasure." Levon didn't respond. Mr. Hornsby looked over at Clara. "Is something wrong?"

She implored Levon with her eyes, keeping her voice measured, pleasant. "Mr. Hornsby is here to see your work. I arranged for him to come by."

Mr. Hornsby's expression turned from confusion to suspicion. "Mr. Zakarian didn't know I'd be coming, did he?"

She shrugged, waiting them both out. It was too late now. Let the games begin. Levon barged across the room, and to Mr. Hornsby's credit, he ignored him. The man clearly had experience with temperamental artists.

"How did you achieve the luminescence in the background of this one?" Mr. Hornsby pointed to a still life.

Levon stopped in his tracks. She recognized the desperate look in his eyes. Wanting acclaim. Wanting success. If Mr. Hornsby played him carefully, this just might work.

They began discussing viscosity and tints. Levon's words began measured, precise, but soon they tumbled out, just like in his paint-ing classes. The two men shared the same vocabulary, which helped break down Levon's defenses.

The still lifes vibrated with energy, the self-portraits murmured with pain and loss. She finally understood why Levon was reluctant to put his work up for inspection. His art was a direct reflection of his very being, which meant an analysis by someone like Mr. Hornsby was in fact an examination of Levon's soul. Clara's illustra-tions were a completely different animal, outside of herself, a sepa-rate product. A business, as Levon had put it.

They approached the mother-and-son portrait. "It's not finished." Levon's words grew clipped again, all goodwill fading away.

Mr. Hornsby ran his index finger over his bottom lip, staring hard. "No. To finish it would destroy it. It's the rawness, the empty spaces, that make us grieve for this woman and this boy. It should never be completed."

That pinprick of approval, of understanding, shredded Levon's carefully constructed facade. He stormed away, grabbing a pitcher from the table and hurling it across the room. "I'm done with this. Get out. I didn't invite you here, and you should never have come."

"Levon, he understands. Let him stay. Don't do this." Clara shook with disappointment and fury.

"Out. Now."

She grabbed her bag and hat and retreated, Mr. Hornsby skitter-ing behind her.

To her surprise, Mr. Hornsby accepted her apologies out on the street, patting her hand. "Don't fret, Miss Darden. I've been kicked out of many an artist's studio in my time. At least I didn't get hit by a palette covered in wet paint."

But she couldn't let it go. Clara stewed during her illustration class the next day, angry at the unwarranted drama of it all. She'd done Levon a favor, even if he didn't recognize it.

She clapped her hands together. "All right, class. The break is over; please take your places."

Thanks to a favor from a *Vogue* editor, the students had been treated to a true fashion model today, a sylphlike girl who'd appeared in the pages of the magazine in the latest editorial layout. The model puffed on her cigarette holder before resuming her position on a green chaise lounge that the students had dragged to the front of the room.

Two more hours of class. Knowing she'd go mad if she didn't do something with the extra energy coursing through her body, Clara sat down at a drawing table near the back of the room, where she could survey her students' efforts while keeping her own work private.

The model wore a cerulean blue Georgette crepe dress with a dropped waist and neckline, wide sleeves, and a matching ring of rosettes that encased her hips. A turban covered most of her black hair. Her features were tiny and pointed, allowing the clothes to take center stage. Clara took up a pencil and sketched an outline, filling in details, taking her typical approach: elongating the neck, sloping the shoulders, and deemphasizing the head. The final rendering was all curves and froth. Out of habit, she signed her name on the bottom right corner, along with the year.

She stepped back and tried to view it as if it were one of her students' efforts. Pedestrian. Rote. An object to be looked at once in a magazine and then tossed in the trash. A calling card for a business proposition.

Turning over the paper, she tried again, this time from a purely artistic standpoint. How would Levon see it? Instead of sketching with fluttering, light lines, she pushed down hard, not caring if it didn't align with the editorial perspective. The model became an afterthought the longer she concentrated, her focus staying on the paper and the drawing. She wanted to paint like Levon, from the inside. The model was exquisite, which only made Clara's irritation grow. Why did she have to be pretty? What did it mean, that this woman was considered a beauty?

The woman in the Van Gogh painting wasn't pretty, and that was why the artist chose her. Because she had lived a life and it showed on her face, in her posture. A smooth face was a bore. Drawing a set of perfectly bowed lips was fun the first time, but what if this time she made the mouth garishly wide? What then? And what if the fingers were thick stubs instead of long tapers?

The drawing was a mess, but a good one. She unscrewed some paint jars, chose a flat brush, and swept a light water wash across the background. No. The water diluted the brushstrokes. Working dry, she mixed the blue for the dress and laid it down fast, knowing it was a race against time before it set. The deadline worked in her favor, preventing her from second-guessing her decisions.

So this is what Levon felt as he worked. Once she banished the running commentary of an editor's critique from her mind—"The model needs to be thinner," "Enlarge the masthead"—her imagination was free to play. She took what she saw in front of her and attacked the paper with little forethought. The rush stayed with her until class came to a close. She thanked the model, checked in with her students, and made sure the room was cleaned up before tucking the painting on top of the storage cabinet.

Oliver was waiting for her by the clock on the concourse floor. They were due to catch the train to Newport, to spend a weekend at his parents' country house.

"Oliver, I've had the strangest experience."

Her words came out in a tumble, how she'd approached the painting in a new way, a more instinctive one. "It was almost mystical, the sense that this creation was erupting from inside me. Not outside. Does that make any sense?"

He laughed. "Good for you, I guess."

"What do you mean?"

He counted on his fingers. "The magazine work, your teaching, the Studebaker job. Are you about to shoot off in another direction? Maybe you'd rather stay in the city and skip our Newport trip? Again?"

She did. But she'd never admit it.

"You're diluting your energies, Clara. Be careful."

He had a point. A physical and mental heaviness weighed on her after those two hours of concentration, unlike anything she'd experienced before.

As she gave him a reassuring smile, Levon came into view.

She braced herself for another round of derision. Or maybe he'd just ignore her and walk right by them.

Instead, he took Oliver's hand and shook it heartily. "How are you? And Miss Darden?"

"We're both well. Off to Newport. And you?"

"Meeting with my dealer in the restaurant."

Clara threw Levon a look. His dealer? What was he talking about?

Levon stuck his hands in his pockets. "I'm working with Felix Hornsby after all. Two landscapes to start. We'll see where it goes from there."

"When did all this happen?" she asked.

"I went to his office, after you left. Told him I wanted to work with him. He made a couple of calls and, like that"—he snapped his fingers—"I was flush."

"What changed your mind?"

"I needed to eat."

That would do it. She was glad he came to his senses. "And?"

"And I guess I should thank you for making the introduction." He bowed in her direction. "And for breaking into my studio and showing my work without my consent. At the time, I was worried I'd allowed goats on my roof."

"Goats on your roof?" She had no idea what he was talking about.

He gave them both a hug, smiling broadly, before striding away. The old Levon was back.

"Strange man." Oliver shook his head as Levon disappeared into the crowd. "Let's just hope his English skills improve soon."

CHAPTER THIRTEEN

November 1974

O vernight, the scare Virginia had at the defunct school of art faded slightly. The sound was probably rats scurrying around. Not a person. As a matter of fact, she'd seen several large rats scrounging for food around the terminal's garbage cans. In her head, she replayed the scene. Had those been footsteps? No, just scurrying. What about the bang on the door? Just an old paint can that had gotten knocked over by a rodent.

Virginia stumbled out of bed and into Finn's brightly lit kitchen, where Ruby sat eating a bowl of cornflakes. Finn poured her coffee without saying a word, knowing that it took her ten minutes before she was fully cognizant. Xavier tossed the newspaper on the table, and they each took a section. "Are we ready for Turkey Day?"

That's right. It was Thanksgiving. When Finn had suggested last weekend that they all go to a restaurant for Thanksgiving dinner, Virginia insisted on cooking instead. She wanted to give Ruby a traditional holiday, as a way to prove that they were still a family, even if they were missing her father. At the same time, drumming up a feast was a perfect way to thank Finn and Xavier for letting them crash at the Carlyle.

Xavier continued. "I bought everything we need, but I'm not lifting a finger to cook. You do not want me in the kitchen."

"True." Finn patted him on the arm. "Last time he tried to cook a steak, it ended up so raw I swear it moved."

"That's truly disgusting." Ruby turned to Virginia. "I want marshmallows on the sweet potatoes."

"That is the plan." Virginia almost chastised her for not saying "please" but held her tongue, not wanting to embarrass her.

"Is there anything we can do to help?" asked Finn.

"Not a thing. I've got this."

After showering and fluffing her hair per Xavier's detailed instructions, Virginia threw on an apron and got down to work: prepping the turkey and getting it in the oven, figuring out where the pots and pans were, and deciding which serving dishes were most festive. She could hear Finn, Xavier, and Ruby in the living room watching the Thanksgiving Day parade on the television, cheering when their favorite balloons drifted by.

After Xavier announced the Bloody Marys were ready, she joined them in the living room, setting a tray with some Ritz crackers and cheddar cheese on the coffee table.

Finn patted the cushion beside him. "Sit, Vee, and tell us about your new job."

She tucked her bare feet underneath her and sipped the Bloody Mary. Strong but good. "It's interesting, more so than I expected. But it's pretty straightforward. I help out, make sure the supplies are filled, get coffee."

"Where do you work in Grand Central?"

"I'm in the information booth."

Xavier leaned forward. "The one with the clock on top of it? Right in the middle of that big space?"

"The concourse. Well, yes."

"How on earth did you end up in there?" asked Finn.

She stifled the familiar drumbeat of defensiveness. "Long story. The people who work there are a quirky bunch, to say the least, but I don't mind it. The building has so much history behind it, I like being part of it."

Ruby wiped some crumbs off her skirt, not looking her mother's way. "That time I took the train back from Sarah Lawrence, I was so scared. The place is creepy."

"It's not creepy once you get used to it. Although I am careful. In any case, it's a paycheck." She shrugged. "Who knows how long I'll be there."

"Why the uncertainty?" Xavier asked.

"The building might lose its landmark status, in which case the owner wants to put up a skyscraper. They'd move the train station down belowground and build up above it."

"They shouldn't tear Grand Central down," said Finn. "They'll just regret it, like with Penn Station."

"But why keep something that's old and crummy?" asked Ruby. She'd been edgy since waking, flinging her clothes around their shared room because she couldn't find the right outfit. She was probably missing her father for the holiday, Virginia realized with a rush of guilt.

"It's not all old and crummy." Virginia couldn't help but spring to the building's defense as if it were an aging, disagreeable dowager, one who deserved a grudging respect. "Parts of it are gorgeous. If they tear it down, it would be like taking down the history of New York with it."

"What if they said that back in the eighteen hundreds?" countered Ruby. "New York would still have cobblestone streets, farms, and tenement buildings. It's called progress."

"Your daughter has a good point," said Finn.

"I guess so. Maybe we can find some kind of happy medium." She thought of Dennis's model, with the skyscraper perching on top of the terminal. Would that qualify as a happy medium?

No. The more she considered it, the more she wanted the terminal to stay as it was. Not only for Terrence, Totto, Winston, and Doris. But so that in fifty years, the city's residents could appreciate the grandeur of the olden days the same way she did now.

Finn laughed. "Remember when Mom and Dad took us to the Oyster Bar?"

The memory flooded back. "But then wouldn't let us order oysters, because the month didn't contain an *r*? We had minestrone soup instead."

Finn turned to Xavier. "She was certain that if an oyster passed our lips in July, we would fall deathly ill. Never mind all the advances in refrigeration. Our mother was always one for a potential crisis. Whether it was that our dad might be robbed at gunpoint, or the city was about to fall into the sea, she was always thinking three steps ahead. She didn't see the glass half-empty; she saw it as laced with angel dust, which she'd heard on the news made you want to jump off buildings."

Virginia waggled a finger at him. "There wasn't angel dust back then. Now you're being ridiculous."

Finn shrugged. "You know what I mean. To give her a little credit, it really didn't bother her much when I came out. She took that in stride. Blowing off Juilliard, however, that caused an earthquake."

The earthquake had occurred on a sweltering Indian summer of a day, when Finn was seventeen. He'd been banging away on the upright piano all afternoon, struggling through a Bach piece, slamming his hands down hard on the keyboard when he made a mistake, the neighbors below pounding on the ceiling with a broom handle. Everyone's nerves were frayed. When their mother told Finn to get his act together and stop behaving like a child, he'd erupted, telling her that he wanted to go into theater, not to Juilliard. Their parents had cut him off right there and then, and he'd run away, heading to Europe with only a backpack.

"Here's to Meryl O'Connor, flawed as she was." Virginia raised her glass in a toast.

"Here's to Meryl." Finn echoed her, and the others joined in.

"Her funeral was nice. So was Dad's. All the neighbors came, at least the gang that was still living from the pub days."

A shadow crossed Finn's face. They were moving into dangerous territory, but Virginia couldn't help herself. She was two-thirds of the way through the Bloody Mary, and the vodka made her brave.

"Right," he said. "I just couldn't swing it."

"We missed you."

As children, they'd played together constantly, either with Finn's tin soldiers in the middle of the living room or lounging out on the fire escape in the heat of summer while Virginia read out loud from her Nancy Drew books. But once his musical talent was discovered, she'd lost him to the piano and the daily practice that ate up all his free time. She'd hoped, after their parents' deaths, that she and her brother would become closer, but that hadn't happened. No doubt Chester's conservative outlook hadn't helped matters; the man was far from welcoming. In any event, they had spun in completely different orbits until now.

She checked her watch. Time to get back in the kitchen. She

ruffled her brother's hair on her way out, a gesture of love and for-
giveness. He took her hand and held it a moment, and they smiled at
each other.

At dinner, the conversation flowed from politics to music to Finn's
success as an entertainer. Xavier held court, raving about the inter-
national audiences and the steady gigs, Finn regaling them with
impersonations of drunken patrons who insisted on singing along.

The dinner was going as well as Virginia could have hoped. Until
Finn asked Ruby when she got into photography.

Ruby crinkled her nose. "Right when I started high school, Dad
bought me a camera. At the time, Mom was going through chemo
and one of my first photos was of her wearing a crazy scarf to cover
her bald head. I probably still have it."

At first Finn didn't react. He chewed and swallowed, blinking
fiercely, before turning to look at Virginia. "You had chemotherapy?"

A shiver of guilt passed through her. This was not how she
wanted to break the news to him. To be honest, she'd never wanted
to break the news to him. It meant dredging up all those old fears.

The shock of waking up after surgery still haunted her. She'd
known, going in, that if they found cancer during the biopsy, they'd
perform a radical mastectomy. "Perform a radical mastectomy." The
surgeon's words at first had sounded like it was some kind of symphony. Something involving lots of timpani. She'd woken up in a
postsurgical haze to see Chester hovering over her. Her right side
felt as though a cement truck had parked there. They'd taken not
only the breast but a portion of the chest wall muscle. She'd been
carved out and had felt lopsided ever since, physically and emotion-
ally, lurching through the world unbalanced.

Still, life had moved forward. "I had cancer. Breast cancer. But it
was five years ago; it's over and done with."

"Why didn't you tell me?" asked Finn, his eyes wide.

"I tried. I sent you a letter. When I didn't hear back, I figured I'd just drop it. There was nothing you could have done."

"I never got the letter." He laid down his fork and knife on the plate. "I can't believe you wouldn't tell me."

Ruby piped up. "I just assumed you knew, Finn. Mom, why didn't you tell your own brother?"

The accusatory tone in Ruby's voice was unwarranted. Virginia was the one who'd had cancer, yet she was the one being brow-beaten? "Because he was never around. What could he have done? Nothing." She immediately regretted her harshness. Once Virginia was home from the hospital, stiff and sore, unable to raise her arm or lift anything, Ruby helped bolster her spirits. She'd read from fashion magazines and fussed over the bed linens. Chester was there, too, of course, but as her recovery failed to meet his expectations, he stayed out at business dinners more and more, a pattern that be-came ingrained even after she was fully healed. "You were a big help, Ruby, and I thank you for that. Now I'm fine. Period."

The doorbell sounded, like an angry cicada. Virginia leaped up and opened the front door, thankful for the interruption.

Ryan, the bartender from downstairs, stood in the hallway.

"Come on in, take a seat." Finn waved him in and pointed to an empty chair. "We told Ryan to stop by on his break."

Virginia shot her brother a look. It would have been nice if he'd told her.

Ryan ducked his head, hands together, like a supplicant. "I hope you don't mind. I can't stay long, but I couldn't pass up your invita-tion."

"Stay as long as you like." Virginia took her seat. "We're not go-ing anywhere." She passed him the bowl of string beans.

"How's the family reunion going?" he asked.

"Woo-hoo." Xavier waved one hand weakly in the air. "Great."

"Finn, do you regret not going to Juilliard?" Ruby poured herself some wine.

Her second glass, Virginia noted. At least the cancer talk was over, for the time being.

Finn held out his glass for a refill as well. "No. It would've stifled me. My life's not easy, and sometimes I'm scrambling, but I do love it."

"Scrambling?" Virginia motioned around the room.

Finn laughed. "Don't let the trappings fool you. We're staying in the fabulous apartment of a friend because the timing worked out. That's sheer luck. Xavier's business is struggling, as is everything these days. Thank God my tips are in cash."

Virginia had assumed they were flush, living large and traveling the world. If they were struggling, they didn't let it get them down. An admirable trait, one she could use more of.

Ruby placed her hands in her lap. "I have an announcement. I hope you'll understand, but you probably won't."

Dear God. What now?

"I'm not going back to college."

"To Sarah Lawrence?"

"No. To any college."

So that was why Ruby had been truculent all day. She was waiting until they were all around the dinner table to bring up what should have been discussed in private. Hoping to find safety in numbers.

Virginia refused to be manipulated. If Ruby wanted to have this conversation now, so be it. "You didn't even give college a try. How can you drop out when you were only there for a few weeks? When we agreed to you taking the semester off, it was on the condition you either found another school or went back to Sarah Lawrence in January."

"Finn didn't even put in a day at Juilliard. He knew it wasn't for him, just like I do."

Finn opened his mouth but didn't say anything. Ryan looked like he wanted to crawl under the table.

"Ruby, you've been doing absolutely nothing these past two months. What exactly would you replace college with?"

"I want to be a photographer."

"If you really wanted that, you would be out taking photos."

"I can't develop them, remember?"

"Then enroll in some class that offers access to a darkroom. I think you're using this to avoid whatever difficulties you faced at Sarah Lawrence."

"I'm not. And I can't afford to take a class."

Her list of excuses was endless. "Then you could have gotten a job to be able to pay for a class."

"You're missing the point."

"I don't think so. You want to drop out?" Virginia had had it. She was tired of tiptoeing around the family's long list of conversational minefields. She'd watched Finn walk out of her life, and now her daughter was using him as her role model. The thought made her sick with panic. "Fine. You can drop out. Go right ahead. Run off to Europe, like Finn. You can team up and travel the world, take photos of him playing the piano in Monaco and Madrid. Leave me to sweep up the mess."

Finn held out both hands. "Hold on a second. One thing at a time." He turned to Virginia. "I'm sorry if I did that, but I had to get away. I really don't think Ruby's planning on running away from you."

She took a swig of wine. "I assume you two have teamed up to figure out the best way to maneuver around me on this."

"No, Mom." Ruby sat straight in her chair. "I haven't talked to Finn about this at all. I want to be a photographer. I don't want to go to college."

Before the fire, before the new job, Virginia might have excused Ruby's outburst—smoothed things over and made peace—to save face in front of a stranger, to prevent her daughter from pulling away. But Ruby's lack of direction infuriated her, even more so now that Virginia was scrambling to get by, including taking a job as a trainee, for God's sake. "So you'll just camp out at home until someone magically calls to offer you a job as a professional photographer? You're a grown woman now; you can't be wasting your time." She paused. "Get a job or enroll in college. You have until January."

"I swear I'll try." Ruby's voice was a squeak. "But there aren't many jobs out there."

Everyone was staring at Virginia as if she was crazy. Maybe she was. But she didn't care. Saying her mind, drawing a line in the sand, gave her a head rush, like when she'd acted so brazenly with Dennis. "Hey, I found a job. I show up every day and put in my hours. You're a smart girl; you'll figure it out." She stood. "Ryan and Xavier, sorry you had to be part of the family drama. Happy Thanksgiving to all."

She walked to her room and sat on the bed. Virginia often had a delayed reaction to any outburst, her own or someone else's, similar to when you made a transatlantic call and had to wait for the other person's voice to kick in. Like realizing she was burning with fury the day after Chester came home from a business dinner smelling of perfume.

This time, though, there was nothing but relief. Virginia had acted in the moment, an unusual occurrence. She'd said her piece and was done with it. Ruby was probably angry, her brother upset. Ryan must think she was the worst mother in Manhattan. But who cared anymore? Let the family fall apart. She'd spent too much energy pretending to hold it all together, to be civil with Chester in front of Ruby when she wanted to rip out his tongue, to be peppy and cheerful with her daughter when she wanted to cry.

Eager to do something with her hands, she began tearing through the pile of mail she'd collected from their apartment yesterday and left on her nightstand. On the very bottom was a white envelope, no return address. She opened it and unfolded a plain piece of paper. No date, no address, no signature. The words were scrawled along the diagonal.

> Hand the painting over to the Lost and Found in Grand
> Central by noon on Friday, 11/29. If you don't, you'll be sorry.

~◈◎

Virginia stood next to a phone booth on Lexington Avenue, staring at the peeling paint of a tenement building and considering her next move. A dry wind had swept the sidewalks clear of pedestrians like an unseen broom, and most everyone was inside watching football or gorging on pumpkin pie. Ruby had left to see her dad, having previously arranged to split the holiday between their two households. As Xavier and Finn cleaned up in the kitchen, Virginia had collected herself, slung on her rain jacket, and headed out into the night.

She stepped into the phone booth and slid the door shut, blinking in the harsh fluorescent light.

Someone wanted her painting. Whoever sent the note knew she'd been in the school, knew she'd taken the painting, and knew where she lived. Those weren't rats she'd heard; another person had been in the art school with her.

Whoever it was had thought ahead, as the Lost and Found of Grand Central was the perfect place to pick up an item while remaining undetected. Located at the foot of the Vanderbilt ramp, the place was legendary for its efficiency and vast stores of umbrellas, suitcases, and various other detritus. If she turned it in, the painting would be carefully cataloged and safely stored away until whenever the letter writer chose to claim it. Just the other day, Terrence had regaled the information booth clerks with a gruesome story of a surgeon who'd accidentally left a body part on a train, in a container with dry ice, and gotten it back a few hours later.

Virginia checked the postmark on the envelope: It'd been sent earlier this week. The deadline was the same time tomorrow as her appointment with the Lorettes.

The painting had to be valuable. Somebody wanted it badly enough to send her a threatening note. She needed to talk to someone, get a second opinion.

Virginia heaved open the phone book and looked up her own name. There were three Virginia Clays, one in Manhattan and two in Staten Island. Which made it easy enough for whoever sent the letter to figure out her address.

She turned to the *H*'s. Dennis Huckle. Yonkers. Her need to confess to someone overrode her shyness in calling him. He was a lawyer, he worked for Penn Central, and maybe it was time for her to come clean and let someone else take over, let them figure out the provenance and worth of the watercolor. In any event, he would have some solid advice.

The phone rang twice before a woman's voice answered, throwing Virginia at first. But he'd talked about taking care of his mother; she must be over for Thanksgiving dinner.

"Is this Mrs. Huckle?"

"Yes, it is. Who's this?" The words didn't crackle with age.

"I'm sorry. Is this Dennis's mother?"

"His mother? No. This is his wife. Who is this?"

His wife. He wasn't divorced. He'd lied.

Virginia couldn't think of what to say next.

"Jesus Christ. Not again. Dennis!"

The phone went dead.

Stunned, Virginia hung up the phone and rubbed her hand on her jacket, as if the sordid exchange could be wiped off. She pulled the folding door open, not without a struggle, and squeezed out.

Where now? She wandered back to the hotel, unwilling to go up just yet. A stiff drink might help.

Inside Bemelmans Bar, Ryan nodded. "What can I get you?"

"How about a Jameson?"

He grinned. "Sure."

"Sorry you had to witness the O'Connor family meltdown."

"Seen plenty of my own." He set a glass on the bar and reached for the bottle. "Sunday dinners back in Ireland were a full-out war."

"Right."

Dennis was a liar. He'd deliberately misled her, knowing full well that she was fresh from a divorce. Virginia missed the strict rules of the old days, when you got married and that was that. But even before Chester had left, their marriage had been fraying at the edges.

The confusion of the modern-day world was too much. Everyone did whatever they wanted. In spite of who got hurt.

And somehow, Virginia was always the one who got hurt.

"You okay?" Ryan placed the drink in front of her.

"Not really." She didn't want to go into it. He probably got a version of the same sob story every day. "Why did you come to New York?"

"Opportunity."

She laughed in his face. Couldn't help it. "There's no opportunity here. We're hitting rock-bottom."

He seemed unfazed. "Maybe for now. But it won't always be like this. In ten years, who knows what'll be going on? It's not like Dublin, which has been around since the age of the Druids."

"At least there you have tradition."

"A tradition that makes people want to kill each other. If that's tradition, I want no part of it."

"The Troubles."

"Right."

"Strange how unimpactful your name for the conflict is. 'The Troubles.' Like heartburn or something."

"Unlike you Yanks, who prefer to scream to the mountaintop."

"Not a lot of good either method does."

"True."

They fell into a comfortable silence. The sting of the whiskey soothed her.

"I'm sorry about the argument with my daughter. She used to be levelheaded, before the divorce. Sometimes now I don't recognize her."

"Happens to everyone at some point."

She eyed him. "Do you have children?"

"None."

"Wife?"

"Ex-wife."

Sure. She'd heard that before.

He winced. "What's that look for, then?"

"Sorry. Nothing. Troubles of my own."

"Sorry to hear that."

"I wish Ruby could settle down, find a practical way to pursue what she enjoys doing." She sighed. "I shouldn't have given her a deadline."

"Your logic made perfect sense to me. If it helps, she's already found a job."

"Where?"

"Here. We got to talking, and I told her that the manager was looking for an extra barmaid."

"Here?" She tried to imagine Ruby toiling behind a bar, just like her grandfather. None of her classmates would be caught dead doing something so working-class.

"Don't worry. I'll keep an eye out for her."

"Thanks for doing that. She's not an easy girl these days."

"That's all right. The tougher the better."

Virginia finished up the last drop of whiskey. Her daughter had a job. Virginia had laid down the law, and the world hadn't fallen apart. Sure, she still had her trials ahead of her, including a wretched love life, a mysterious stalker, and the looming decision of whether to turn in the painting, but, for the moment, everything seemed a little less painful.

CHAPTER FOURTEEN

November 1974

Virginia woke up the next day with one purpose in mind: Get her family life in order.

Over breakfast, she apologized to Finn for not telling him about the cancer and promised to keep him in the loop going forward. He'd choked up and told her that he'd always be there for her.

"I love you, Vee."

They'd never, ever exchanged those words before. The O'Connor family was one of "Sleep wells" and "Very good, thens." She silently thanked Xavier for having made her brother feel safe and brave enough to say it first.

"I love you, too."

When Ruby arrived back from her dad's, Virginia suggested a walk in the park. Warily, her daughter agreed.

They circled around the pond where, in the warmer months, model sailboats zigzagged across the shallow waters. The morning was brisk; frost grayed the tips of the grass.

"I hear you've got yourself a job already."

Ruby dug her hands into her pockets. "Yup."

Virginia had a hard time imagining her shy daughter working in a bustling bar. She hoped it would be a good fit. The very fact that Ruby had accepted Ryan's offer was a good sign, though. "That's great."

"Once I start getting paychecks, I'm going to take a class at the New York Institute of Photography."

"You seem determined."

Ruby nodded, staring out across the water. "I want to prove to you and Dad that this is the right path for me."

"Did you mention it to your dad last night?"

Ruby made a noise like fireworks, her hands splayed out.

"I take it the idea went over well."

A reluctant grin spread over Ruby's face; then she laughed. "He lost it. I almost came back home to you."

Virginia spoke quickly, grateful for the opening. "You can always come home to me. I won't lose it. I have to admit I'm impressed. It's not even been twenty-four hours and you have a plan." She paused. "Can I ask what happened at Sarah Lawrence? I know you were upset about academics, but was it something else?"

For a moment, it looked like Ruby was about to turn sullen, close back down. Virginia waited, hoping the storm would pass quickly. Eventually, her daughter let out a quiet, resigned sigh, one that made her seem more like an ancient woman than a coltish girl. "I felt like I was falling behind from the very first day of classes. That I'd never catch up. Late one night, I was sitting out in the hall outside my dorm room, trying to study, and I heard my suite mates talking about me inside. I thought we were all friends, but they were saying that they couldn't wait until next year so they could replace me with someone else. That I was a drag, a dimwit."

"I'm so sorry." Virginia put an arm around her. "They obviously didn't get to know you."

"I only got accepted there because Grandma pulled strings. I don't belong. It's like Finn at Juilliard—he knew it wouldn't be a good fit."

"I understand."

"Do you, really?" Her chin jutted out, a challenge.

"You felt like you were in over your head. I was the same after the divorce."

"You were? How?"

"I bought an apartment that was over my budget, as a way of trying to prove that I was something that I'm not. To prove to you that our lifestyle wouldn't change. Well, it has. And no matter how much I pretended otherwise, I'm the daughter of an Irish bar owner, not some fancy East Side lady who lunches."

"Don't be embarrassed by that. I'm proud of you."

Her words brought tears to Virginia's eyes. She hugged her. "I'm proud of you, too. So much so, I want to offer you your first professional photography job. Although I can't pay you much."

"What are you talking about?"

"I want to go to Grand Central together one weekend and have you take some photos of the place before it loses its landmark status and gets destroyed. Will you do that for me?"

The idea had come to Virginia last night, in a furious flash. Even if the building came down, she'd have a visual testament to its beauty. It was a way to preserve the memory of the terminal as well as show Ruby that she supported her photography with more than hollow words.

"You really have a thing for that building, don't you?"

Virginia smiled. "I do."

"Well, then, I'm in."

An hour later, Virginia waited in line at the Lost and Found in Grand Central, clutching the art portfolio with the watercolor inside, unsure. When the man behind the counter offered to be of service, she stammered out an apology and turned away.

The decision not to answer the letter writer's threat, and instead keep her appointment with the Lorettes, wasn't an easy one, but Virginia didn't feel unsafe. The fire, in a strange way, was a blessing, because whoever was threatening her didn't know that she'd relocated to the Carlyle, which meant they didn't know how to find her outside of work.

Her curiosity kept her moving forward. She wanted to learn more about Clara Darden and Levon Zakarian and how the artwork came to be. If the Lorettes dismissed it as unimportant, then she'd turn it in and be done with it, just to get the ghost of Grand Central off her tail. If they didn't, she'd have another risky decision to make.

For now, it was time to hightail it downtown.

❦

A cold rain began to fall as Virginia made her way to the East Village address Mrs. Lorette had given her, the very same neighborhood that Virginia had warned Ruby about. She tucked the portfolio under one arm while struggling to open her umbrella.

"Give me that."

She looked up, surprised to see a gaunt man standing in front of her. Did he want the umbrella? She was about to ask when she caught sight of the knife in his hand. Her first thought was exasperation, not fear. Really? She was getting mugged twice in two weeks?

"Hand it over!"

Right. She needed to think clearly, not do anything stupid. The street was empty of other pedestrians. The knife shook in the man's hand, his nails dirty, his clothes ragged. She avoided his eyes, trying to convey that she was not a threat. "Okay, okay. You can have it. Take it, I won't bother you."

She lifted the strap from her purse off her shoulder.

"No. The other thing."

She let it drop back down to her shoulder. "You want my umbrella?"

"Fuck, lady, no. The other thing."

"The portfolio?"

He nodded.

"But I have money." She unzipped her purse, reached inside.

"I don't want money. Give me that other thing."

The watercolor. He wanted the watercolor.

"Did you send me that letter?"

He blinked several times, confused. "I don't know what you're talking about, bitch. Just hand it over."

He reached for the portfolio at the same time she yanked the can of mace out of her purse and squeezed the trigger, hoping she had it pointed the right way.

She did. Her assailant screamed and covered his eyes, falling to his knees. Virginia ran as fast as she could. The steps up to the front door of the Lorettes' brownstone were cracked and chipped at the edges. She took them two at a time and hit the buzzer hard.

An older man with a mahogany cane answered the door.

"You must be Virginia Clay," he said.

"Someone just tried to mug me; let me inside, please." She looked to her left. Her assailant was staggering in the opposite direction, his hands clutching his face.

Mr. Lorette peered out, resting a protective hand on Virginia's arm. "My God, please, come in."

He led her into a parlor. "Shall we call the police? Are you hurt?"

Virginia shook her head. "I'm fine. Just shaken up."

The mugger had wanted the painting. Not her purse. She took a seat near the fireplace, hugging the portfolio to her, trying to make sense of what had just occurred. Had the letter writer sent someone after her when she didn't return it to the Lost and Found by the deadline? Was she being followed?

She shivered and studied the room while Mr. Lorette called for his wife. The simplicity of the furnishings stood in contrast to the remarkable paintings, drawings, and sketches that covered the walls. Some seemed familiar, but she didn't dare ask in case she made a silly error and came off like a dolt. Most of the titles and painters she'd crammed into her head as an art major had dribbled away over the past twenty years. Funny how art acted as a separation between those who deemed themselves cultured and those who did not. Virginia at the very least knew to keep her mouth shut and not give away her ignorance.

Her thoughts were racing from shock. She took a deep breath to calm herself.

An elegant older woman, her thick hair piled on top of her head like an Edwardian maiden, entered carrying a tea tray. Mr. Lorette introduced her as his wife, and she offered Virginia a plate of jam cookies. "I'm sorry to hear you were accosted outside. The neighborhood has changed over the years—I don't think I can remember when it's been so dangerous. You are sure you're all right?"

Virginia nodded. "I'm fine." She thanked them again for seeing her.

"Our pleasure," said Mr. Lorette. "You mentioned on the telephone that you're interested in learning more about the Grand Central School of Art. We love talking about the subject, don't we, darling? The school was our child, in many ways."

"That it was," agreed Mrs. Lorette. "Irving took over the school soon after it opened and brought in teachers who were remarkable, forward thinking. The faculty, in turn, drew in some remarkable students."

Mr. Lorette beamed. "We have several well-known artists who found their footing while studying with us."

"I've read a little about the history of the school." Virginia placed her tea on a coaster on the coffee table and scooted forward on her chair. Her heartbeat had returned to its normal cadence, and the warm tea settled her down. "I understand one of the painting teachers was Levon Zakarian."

"Levon." Mr. Lorette sighed. "Mercurial, difficult, brilliant. What a sad tale. From beginning to end, I don't think he had very many moments of happiness."

"Yet he created great art," interjected Mrs. Lorette. "One hopes he found satisfaction in that. Even if he died young."

Her husband chuckled. "Whenever I did something that annoyed Levon, which was quite often, it seemed, he'd tell me that I had goats on my roof."

"What did that mean?" asked Virginia.

"I didn't find out until a year or so after he'd died, from one of his students, who used the same expression. Levon told him that the Armenian villages where he grew up had flat roofs, where the women set fruit out to dry. A perimeter of prickly branches kept the goats off. If you had goats on your roof, you hadn't bothered to fortify your fencing. The expression meant you were oblivious, foolish."

"He sounds like a very colorful man."

Mr. Lorette began to laugh. "I had goats on my roof then, and probably still do today!"

"Now, now, Irving." Mrs. Lorette turned to Virginia and whispered, "Maybe a little."

The Lorettes were sweet together and knew all the players. Janice at the Art Students League had steered Virginia in the right direction. "I was also wondering what you knew about Clara Darden, the illustration teacher at the school."

"She taught there early on," said Mr. Lorette. "Around the same time as Levon. Before the Depression. Clara Darden was not very ladylike. She could be shrewish at times. Unyielding. Something was always wrong, and I was often at the receiving end of her wrath."

Mrs. Lorette shook her finger at her husband. "You see what you're doing; you're making her out to be a harridan while Levon Zakarian gets away with the same behavior and is considered brilliant. Not acceptable."

She was right. The descriptions of both artists were two sides of the same coin. Levon was mercurial and difficult. While Clara was shrewish and unyielding.

"Please forgive me, darling. I live in the past."

Virginia addressed them both. "Do you know what happened to Clara Darden?"

"There were rumors she left town," answered Mr. Lorette. "Rumors that she was on the train with Levon, but her body was never recovered. In any event, she simply vanished."

"Isn't it strange no one knows what happened to her?"

"By that point, we'd had to close the school. Everyone was struggling, and I guess we lost touch."

Mrs. Lorette cut in. "When we shut the doors temporarily, to ride out the worst of the Depression, we struggled as well."

"But that's all over now." Mr. Lorette reached over and took her hand. "We're still in our home, still going strong."

"How did you manage, during the years it was closed?"

"We rented out our place in New York City, moved to Maine until it got too cold. Then wintered in Europe, staying with friends, hopping from city to city." Mrs. Lorette's eyes lit up. "We were well-dressed vagabonds, depending on the kindness of strangers."

The image brought Finn and Xavier to Virginia's mind.

"Even after the school reopened, it wasn't the same," said Mr. Lorette. "We lost our lease in 1944, right before the war. They told us to get out, gave us very little notice."

"Have you been back since?"

He shook his head. "We only go to Grand Central if we're taking a train somewhere. It's a dreadful place now."

"But you should have seen it back in the day." Mrs. Lorette clapped her hands together. "Students running about, so much energy and laughter coming from the hallways. Up to the school, down to the gallery. They held balls once a year, and they were grand affairs. There was nothing like seeing pairs of students dashing across the concourse, dressed in black tie and silk dresses."

How sad to think that chapter of the terminal was lost to history.

"It's a dinosaur, like us." Mr. Lorette rubbed his cane with his thumb.

"Would you say that Clara Darden and Levon Zakarian knew each other well?"

Mr. Lorette considered the question. "They were teaching around the same time. Yes, I remember quite clearly Levon advocating for Clara at some point. I was about to let her go, and he insisted she stay on. Glad I listened to him, in the end. It was right before she took off with all the fashion magazine covers. Before that, students were dropping out of her class right and left."

"Why would they do that?"

"They didn't like being taught by a woman, probably. But once she made a name for herself, everything settled down."

He regarded Virginia. "Why is it you're here, Mrs. Clay? Is there something specific you're looking for?"

She placed a hand on the portfolio but didn't open it. "I'm really interested in finding out more about Levon Zakarian and Clara Darden. In particular, I'm curious about their techniques. They were quite different, right, since they used different mediums?"

"Completely different," affirmed Mr. Lorette. "He was masculine, always chipping away at his paintings, scraping and then repainting, big, thick strokes. While she did watercolor, which requires great patience, forethought. You can't go back and fix a watercolor, you see. If you've made something too dark, there's no way to lighten it. You're stuck; you have to start over."

The watercolor by Clyde had strong, dark strokes. A combination of Zakarian's methods and Darden's medium. "Would they have shared supplies?"

"Now, that's an odd question." Mr. Lorette exchanged a glance with Mrs. Lorette. "What are you getting at?"

She couldn't hold back any longer. The Lorettes were probably the only people left from those days who might be able to help. She unzipped the portfolio and pulled out the watercolor, placing it on the coffee table. "I discovered this recently. I'd love to get your thoughts."

Even in the shadowy autumn light, the Clyde painting seemed to leap off the page.

Mr. Lorette leaned forward, his brows knitted together. "This looks like a Zakarian Clyde work. It's very similar to the one that's going to auction."

"But it's watercolor." Mrs. Lorette gently touched one corner, as if it were still wet with paint.

Virginia nodded. "I brought it to the curator at the Art Students League, and she recommended I show it to you." She turned it over. "Here's why. On the back, there's a sketch that's signed and dated by—"

Mr. Lorette cut in. "Clara Darden."

"Right. That's why I'm here. Why I asked about them sharing supplies. I'm curious if Levon Zakarian might have done this on the back of her work."

"Maybe. I really don't know."

"There's something else. A detail that the curator, Janice, and I found intriguing." Virginia was enjoying herself, building up the drama. She pulled out the auction catalog and opened it to the ear-marked page. "Look at the letter C on this signature and on the signature of the drawing."

The Lorettes did so. Mr. Lorette's eyebrows raised. "They're exactly the same."

"Right. They also match the way Clara Darden signed her *Vogue* covers." Virginia surveyed their reactions. "The drawing is dated two years before Clyde's New York exhibition in 1931. Maybe Clara Darden drew that first, then expanded on it for the watercolor. Maybe Clara Darden, not Levon Zakarian, is Clyde."

"Quite interesting," murmured Mr. Lorette. "We'd have to enlist an expert to compare it with the one that's at auction. Where again did you find this?"

They'd been so helpful and encouraging, she couldn't lie. "The truth is, I work at Grand Central, in the information booth. I was exploring the terminal and came upon the School of Art. This was behind one of the storage cabinets, in one of the studios."

"The school is still intact? No one's rented out the space in all this time?" Mr. Lorette's mouth dropped open.

She nodded. "Penn Central's planning on building a skyscraper on top of Grand Central, so there's probably no point in renting it out. The whole place is a disaster."

"How utterly sad." Mr. Lorette's eyes watered.

His wife patted his knee. "There, there. It was a place and time that's over and done with. We have our memories."

"My wife, always the pragmatist." He beamed at Virginia. "I'm thrilled that you discovered this watercolor. If it is a Zakarian, there's no family left to claim it."

"What about if it's by Clara Darden?"

"No idea about her. But lawyers can always take care of that kind of thing."

Expensive lawyers, most likely.

"Now, who do we know who might be able to help us?" Mr. Lorette said.

His wife answered without missing a beat. "Sammy!"

"Sammy, yes."

"Who's Sammy?" asked Virginia.

"An expert at the Museum of Modern Art. He'll know how to go about this. But I must call right now, this very minute, as he's off to Europe soon." Mr. Lorette disappeared into the adjoining room. Virginia tried to listen in, but his conversation was muffled.

Things were moving too fast. She turned to Mrs. Lorette. "What if I take it to Sotheby Parke Bernet and show them what I've found?"

Mrs. Lorette poured herself more tea. "They have a lot at stake, with the auction coming up. I'm not saying they'd do anything unethical, but it wouldn't be in their best interests to have the provenance of the Clyde painting questioned so soon before the sale."

"What if Penn Central decides it's theirs? After all, they own the space where it was found."

"Art belongs to the public, not a corporation. And certainly not a mercenary one like Penn Central. No need to involve them."

Virginia sighed. "I almost hate to let it go. My first thought was to hang it in my apartment; I figured it'd make me smile every time I passed by."

Mrs. Lorette picked up her teacup and saucer and wandered over to a painting above the fireplace, an oil of a woman in a fancy dress standing next to a greyhound. "I know what you mean. You become attached. Every time I look at this painting, I see something different, like a subtle aura around her head that I'd never noticed before, or the way the greyhound's eyes are flecked with yellow." She turned around. "But yours needs to be cared for. Poor thing's been sitting in a dusty room for ages. Sammy will know what to do, how to preserve it, restore it, if need be."

Mr. Lorette returned, looking triumphant. "Sammy's quite interested. We have an appointment on Monday at ten o'clock."

Virginia held up one hand. "I can't, I have to work then. Can we make it during my lunch hour?"

"He's off to Europe then, some kind of partnership with the Louvre in Paris."

"Maybe when he gets back?"

"He'll be back in the New Year."

More than a month away. "Do you think he'll be able to help?" She knew the answer but wanted reassurance.

"Of course. He knows that era well. Best man in town. Heck, in the world."

Virginia looked from one to the other. According to her temp contract, she wasn't allowed to take off work until she'd been there a month. A little less than two weeks had passed since she started, and she couldn't risk losing her job. She'd never find another. She supposed she could leave the watercolor with the Lorettes.

And after that mugging, it would be a relief to have it taken off her hands. But she should warn them. "Just so you know, I got a threatening letter, telling me to put the watercolor back. I think that mugger was after it as well. Someone wants it badly." She paused. "I worry that giving it to you may put you in harm's way."

Mr. Lorette didn't seem in the least bit concerned. "The ghost of Levon Zakarian, trying to fight for his legacy, perhaps?"

"Or Clara Darden's."

His smile faded. "Just goes to show that your instincts are on track. You've discovered what might be an important piece of art. We'll guard it closely and make sure it gets safely uptown to Sammy. Don't you worry about us. We've lasted longer in this city than almost anyone we know."

They had a point. The Depression, the war years. The Lorettes had seen it all.

Virginia placed it back in the portfolio. "All right. Take it to Sammy, and then let me know what he says."

"Are you sure you can't come?" asked Mrs. Lorette. "It could be a fun meeting; we'd learn a lot."

"Let's not get our hopes up too high, now," added Mr. Lorette. "Who knows? We might learn that it's all a hoax, that a student was copying one of his teacher's works in progress. Although I certainly hope not. It might be an important piece of the Grand Central School of Art's history."

Virginia agreed. "I'll call you on my lunch hour to find out what you learn."

"Very good. We shall speak to you Monday." Mr. Lorette held out his hand, and Virginia shook it. "Let's pray for good news."

CHAPTER FIFTEEN

July 1929

"And here are the bedrooms. You can fight among yourselves for whoever gets stuck in the one with the slanted ceiling." Mrs. Lorette stood in the center of the small second-floor hallway of the Maine cottage while Clara, Levon, and Oliver stared uncomfortably about.

The trio had left the city yesterday, headed for the Grand Central School of Art's summer program. The best students had been invited to take courses with the top instructors, all eager to replace the fiery oven of New York City in July with cool northern breezes.

A few days before she was supposed to leave, Clara and Oliver had attended a cocktail party at the Lorettes' town house, where Oliver had shared the news that one of his poems was to be published in a reputable literary magazine. Clara was thrilled—finally he was getting the attention he deserved. She was even happier when Mr. Lorette extended an invitation on the spot for Oliver to join them in Maine. "Our first 'poet in residence,'" he'd proclaimed.

Mr. Bianchi had loaned Clara a Studebaker for the month away, and after checking with Oliver, Clara suggested that Levon join them for the drive. She'd seen little of Levon since their brief interaction in the train station with Oliver a month earlier and was looking forward to catching up.

The ride had begun on a light note, Levon and Oliver teasing Clara for her massive leather suitcase, Levon holding forth in the back seat with stories and jokes, leaning forward every so often to clap Oliver on the shoulder and praise his driving abilities.

"This car is grand, isn't it?" Levon ran his finger along the brown velvet nap of the front seat.

Clara twisted around and playfully smacked at his hand.

"Stop it, woman," Levon said. "You should be thanking me for the chance to get out of the city like this."

"How's that?"

"If I hadn't saved your job for you, you'd be home drawing stockings right now."

Oliver laughed, and Clara sat back and watched as the landscape outside the car flew by, relieved the two men could finally enjoy each other's company, even if it was at her expense.

The tiny town of Eastport sat upon an island thick with pine forests and blueberry bushes, ringed by rocky coves, and linked to the mainland by a causeway. Clara had imagined a large boardinghouse where the faculty gathered for communal breakfasts, and she was surprised to learn that instead, they'd be scattered about in tiny cottages, some miles away from the town center. And that Levon, Clara, and Oliver were assigned to the same one.

Mrs. Lorette gestured again into the rooms, beaming as if she'd shown them around a palace. A few tendrils of hair had escaped her updo and curled around her neck. Clara peered into the gabled room, which was simply furnished with a bed on one wall and a small desk on another. About halfway across the room, the ceiling plummeted to the floor at a steep pitch. "I say we put Levon here, just to hear him smack his head every morning when he gets up."

"Very funny." Levon rubbed his head as if he'd already done so.

"We'll be fine, Mrs. Lorette," Clara said. "Please don't worry about us. I'm sure you must have to go wrangle the students."

"The students." Mrs. Lorette tossed up her hands. "I put them in one room and they always end up in another, if you know what I mean. But it's only five weeks, and I don't want to be a prison warden. It's an art school, after all." She started. "Oh, and I almost forgot, Mr. Lorette's goddaughter is going to take the fourth bedroom. Lovely girl, Violet. Working in summer stock for the local theater company."

"We look forward to meeting her," Clara said. "I'll take the gabled room. I'll just have to remember to get out on the left side of the bed each morning."

"I'll bring you coffee in bed so you can clear the cobwebs before you rise," offered Oliver.

Mrs. Lorette led them back down the stairs, where an enormous stone fireplace bisected the living and kitchen areas. Half a dozen drawings of the cottage from various angles decorated one wall of the parlor.

Clara studied them. "Were these done by the artists who stayed here?"

"Yes, my dear. Aren't they lovely? You're free to hang one of your own."

"We will certainly add to your fine collection," said Levon.

At a welcome dinner that evening at a rustic restaurant by the sea, Clara, Levon, and Oliver joined a few students at a picnic table. They feasted on barbecue as bald eagles nested in the neighboring trees and fishing boats rocked gently in their moorings. Mr. Lorette appeared, his arm around a striking young woman with blue eyes and black hair.

"I have the pleasure of introducing my goddaughter," Mr. Lorette announced. "Miss Violet Foster, a budding actress all the way from Los Angeles. I do hope you don't mind if she joins you, as the other tables are all full."

"Of course not." Clara waved her in. "We're sharing the same cottage, from what Mrs. Lorette mentioned."

Violet gave her godfather a quick peck on the cheek before sitting down. "We are. I just dropped off my things a moment ago. It's divine, isn't it?"

After introductions were made, one of the students asked what parts she'd played.

"Well, last year I had a teensy part in a movie called *Street Angel.*" Miss Foster, who insisted they all call her Violet, held up her index finger and thumb to show just how small the part was.

Both students gasped. "We loved *Street Angel!*" They peppered her with questions about the movie, about working with stars like Janet Gaynor and Charles Farrell.

Clara glanced over at Levon, who stared at the woman as if she were a living doll. The setting sun had turned her pale skin a warm rose, and several strands of her hair picked up the same hue. No doubt he was analyzing the light, trying to figure out how he might capture it. Or he was smitten by her glamorous beauty. Violet might as well have jumped right off one of Clara's magazine covers, with her tiny nose and ears, her big seal's eyes. Clara shifted closer to Oliver on the bench.

"How long are you acting up here in Maine, Violet?" asked Levon.

"It's a crazy schedule; we only have two weeks to rehearse, then

three weeks of performances. But I love it; it's much better than doing a movie where you show up, do a scene, and then move on to the
next one. Here I get to hone my acting skills."

"Not to mention your speaking skills." Levon pulled out his flask
and offered it to her. "Silent movies must be quite frustrating for
someone with your melodic voice."

She took a quick sip and handed it over to Oliver. "You're sweet.
But it's a different set of skills, in a way. I have to be much more expressive with my face in film, to get the idea across."

"Let's see that," said Levon. "Quick, before the light's completely
gone. Show me an expression that says you're deeply in love."

Clara cringed at his audacity, but Violet laughed. She took a
breath and then looked at Levon while fluttering her eyelashes.

Truly awful. Clara burst out laughing. Oliver nudged her in the
ribs, and she attempted to cover her rudeness by clapping her hands.
"Brilliant."

Violet smiled at the praise.

"And now, show me anger." Clara couldn't tell if Levon was goad-
ing Violet or if he was taken in by her dainty charm. "Come on, the
angriest you can do."

Another breath. Then Violet lowered her chin, gritted her teeth,
and glared up at him. He glared back, and everyone laughed.

After dinner, they walked back to the cottage in pairs—Levon
and Violet, Clara and Oliver—and said their good-nights. Oliver
tried to persuade Clara to let him into her bed, but she lightheart-
edly pushed him off, embarrassed by the thin walls and close prox-
imity to the other bedrooms.

The next morning, a bright sun woke Clara, and she lay in bed for
a while, listening to the morning chorus of birdsong. There was no
sign of Oliver with the promised coffee, so she dressed and headed

downstairs, making her own before stepping out into the front garden. A dirt road cut between the gentle slope to the sea and the
cottage, but the house was far enough out on a short peninsula that
traffic stayed at a minimum. The sea glistened in the morning sun,
and Clara quietly retrieved her easel and paints from the house, curious to see if she could pull off a sunrise in oils.

The water sparkled, dotted with whitecaps. Clara remained transfixed, unable to blend anything or put brush to canvas. The blues
reminded her of the watercolor she'd done during class the month before, the day she'd been angry at Levon. She wanted to try that again.

"To draw, you must close your eyes and sing."

Levon stepped out of the house, wearing a large straw hat and
carrying a rustic walking stick.

"What did you say?"

"Not me. Picasso. I'm off for a walk around the spit. Send out the
troops if I'm not back in an hour and tell them I've been eaten by a
bear."

"I will. Enjoy your walk."

She worked for a half hour, the only sound the maple tree rustling
overhead. The milkman drove down the street, waving, then back
up ten minutes later. Inspired by the water, she intensified the blue
of the girl's dress and didn't bother trying to delineate the form
from the background.

Oliver, bleary-eyed, staggered down the front steps and stood behind her. "All this fresh air is like hooch. I haven't slept that well in
ages." He put his arms around her waist. "What's that you're working on?"

"I'm not going to tell you. You have to guess."

He glanced at the painting, pointed out into the distance. "Stormy
seas?"

"No. Try again."

The next-door neighbor's dog, a pudgy yellow Lab, waddled over to check on them, panting heavily. Oliver picked up a stick and tossed it. The dog stared at him for a moment—Clara could have sworn she saw a flash of disdain—before lumbering off in the opposite direction.

She turned back to the painting. "Here's a clue: It's not a landscape. You have one more guess."

"Some abstract version of a bluebird."

"Wrong again. It's a reclining woman."

He sighed. "What's the point of painting something if no one can recognize it?"

"I'm experimenting. Isn't that why we came up here?"

"Of course. In that case, I'll write an abstract poem and you can guess what it's all about."

"I'd be delighted."

"Hello, young lovers!" Levon careened up the driveway, hat in hand, his face sweaty from exertion.

"Good morning," said Oliver.

Levon shook his hand before surveying Clara's work. Her cheeks flushed as she waited for his verdict.

He pointed to the right quadrant. "She's a siren. You must believe that with every brushstroke. Don't be afraid."

"You can tell that's a woman?" asked Oliver, his mouth agape.

"Of course."

Levon whirled about and walked away, taking the front steps three at a time, the screen door closing with a bang.

Oliver plunked down on a tree stump beside her and finished off the rest of her coffee. "Be careful not to let Levon influence you too much."

"What on earth does that mean?"

"He's stuck in the past, doing that painting with his mother over and over."

She regretted telling him about it; his flippant tone annoyed her. "You haven't even seen the painting. It's a masterpiece. Even Felix thought so."

Oliver lowered his voice, only slightly. "Levon's a superstitious peasant who wants to move on from the old world but can't. You oughtn't waste your energy taking care of him."

His sudden change in attitude didn't bode well for the rest of the month, all three of them holed up in the same cottage. "Levon seems to be doing fine without me. All I did was do for him what you did for me. You set up the appointment with the *Vogue* editor, and I did the same using my connections for Levon."

"Using your connections?" Oliver's blue eyes blazed. "You said you dropped my mother's name when you met Felix."

She had. "You're right. You're absolutely right. What's going on? Why all this resentment?"

Oliver stared down at his feet. "I'm finally going to be a published poet, and instead of supporting me and fanning the flame of my career, you're taking care of Levon." He paused. "I sound like a whiny child, don't I?"

His honesty moved her, and she knelt down in front of him. "No. I've taken you for granted, everything you've done for me." She touched her hand to his cheek. "I'm sorry for that, Ollie."

Inside the house, Levon's rumble of a laugh intermingled with Violet's high-pitched giggle.

"I promise I'll do more for you, for us, all right? Once the summer session is over, let's plan a trip to Europe. Just the two of us, no work, all play."

"What about Mr. Bianchi and your art classes?"

"They'll manage without me."

He kissed her. "I'll start planning our tour. Paris, London, possibly Madrid?"

She kept her grin plastered on her face, calculating how long she'd be away. "All three, my love. Whatever you desire."

—※◎

The days in Maine fell into a steady rhythm. Oliver had become the school's pet, encouraging the students and getting chummy with the other teachers. His social skills, cultivated at the best schools, offered him a seamless entry into practically any situation, whether by charming the cleaning lady when she delivered fresh towels and a mason jar of wildflowers, or taking Mrs. Lorette and Violet out for ice cream while classes were in session. Clara spent the early mornings in front of the cottage working on *The Siren*, teaching classes during the day, followed by dinners alfresco and bonfires that lasted well into the night.

She'd been partnered with Levon to teach a painting class held in an old schoolhouse, but every afternoon they'd escape the stifling classroom and take over a beach or a field, to allow the students to apply what they'd learned *en plein air*. Levon pranced about, making aphorisms that most often made no sense, throwing back his head and arms and shouting at the sky, while she quietly assisted with questions regarding technique. When not advising, she sat on a boulder behind everyone and stared out across the fields, basking in the natural light and brilliant colors, the elderberry and lavender, breathing in the scent of the sea.

She and Levon made a good team, and as the term came to an

end, Mr. Lorette often remarked favorably on the quality of their students' work. Out in the wilds of Maine, the director had lost some of his officious airs. It helped that Oliver had gone out of his way to chat up the Lorettes, overriding Clara's naturally abrasive manner.

Life with Oliver had settled into an easy calm after their discussion about Levon. His recently published poem had been praised by a distinguished critic, and the boost couldn't have come at a better time. Clara had made sure to read the review out loud at the bonfire that evening, and since then, Oliver had noticeably relaxed, retreated from offering career advice, and enjoyed his own acclaim. She was truly happy for him.

A few weeks into the term, Levon wrangled several students and teachers into attending Violet's play. Clara hadn't seen much of her, as Violet tended to come in very late and sleep in most mornings, but she'd heard Levon and Violet whispering as they climbed the creaky stairs together in the middle of the night. The play, a zany musical, wasn't Clara's cup of tea, but Violet's singing voice was melodic and carried well. After, they feasted on crabmeat and corn, as Levon literally sang the praises of Violet, having caught the musical theater bug himself, apparently.

Oliver whispered into Clara's ear. "Let's go back to the cottage now, shall we?"

They slipped out and wandered down the moonlit road, Oliver listing more European cities he'd like to visit on their trip, which had already lengthened from three weeks to four. He held open the screen door for Clara. "Come on, let's hit the sheets before the choir returns."

She whacked him on the arm and ran up the stairs, grateful they finally had the whole house to themselves. Later, they lay in her bed, the only sound the crickets chirping outside. Her eyes began to droop.

"Marry me, Clara."

She stayed still for a moment, unsure if she'd heard him correctly. He was looking up at the ceiling, his profile barely visible in the dark room. She touched his nose.

"What was that?"

He turned his head, his eyes gleaming. "Let's get married."

"We practically already are."

"I want it to be official. We can make the trip to Europe our honeymoon. I don't want to lose you."

She propped herself up on one elbow and studied him. "You're not going to. Unless your success as a poet goes to your head and you run off with a silly girl like Violet."

He didn't laugh. "I have something to confess."

She braced herself. A confession on the heels of a proposal. Who knew what was coming?

"I paid to have my poem published. Well, to be more specific, I offered to invest in the journal, and they understood what that meant."

Dear Oliver. He had tried so hard, and Clara's successes had most likely made him feel like a failure, simply by comparison. He'd done so much for her; he'd made her life as seamless as possible so she could churn out illustration after illustration, design after design. She was always the focus. Whenever they had a lull in conversation he'd ask her about whatever detail she was struggling with, whether the coy expression of a cover girl or the line of a car door handle.

And for that, his own career had suffered. She owed it to him to support him in a way that was less selfish. He had dreams of his own. There was no shame in that, or in the way he went about getting his work out in the world.

She told him so. "Look at the reception you've gotten. It was the right thing to do. I'm proud of you."

"Then you'll marry me?"

Their life together, so far, had been an easy ride, one of shared interests and many joys. Once Oliver reached his full potential as an artist, the small irritations would smooth over naturally. He was good for her, no question, and she would try harder to be a good partner to him.

She took his face in her hands and smiled. "Yes, Oliver, I will marry you."

On the last weekend before the end of the summer term, the mood among the students took on an almost feral urgency. Like children in a summer camp, knowing that restrictions would soon be imposed, they became boisterous and edgy. Levon, of course, encouraged the wildness, insisting that the class play leapfrog in the field when they should have been painting, or teaching the students a bawdy song that became the school's anthem, much to Mr. Lorette's chagrin.

Clara and Oliver hadn't made any kind of announcement about their engagement. Oliver insisted they wait until he tell his parents and buy her a ring before sharing the news. He'd asked if he should send a letter to Clara's father, formally requesting her hand, and she'd dismissed it as a bad idea. When he'd pushed back, she'd stood her ground.

Saturday morning, Clara woke early to finish her painting. Other than the milkman's truck, not a soul passed through. Clara stepped back, surveying her work, and couldn't have been more pleased. At first glance, the painting seemed like a jumble of shapes and colors, but eventually a woman emerged on the page. The figure wasn't much different from her first attempt, but the oils made the colors and texture even richer.

After dabbing her sable brush in black paint, she considered where to place her signature. She had painted the first letter of her name when the door to the cottage slammed, making her jump.

Oliver shambled over, two cups of coffee in his hand. He offered her one, but she motioned for him to set it on the tree stump, as both hands were occupied.

"Interesting."

"I'm just about to sign it. You've come at the final moment."

He grimaced. "I wouldn't do that. If this gets out, your career will be ruined."

She couldn't tell if he was joking. "That's unnecessarily cruel. Why would you say such a thing?"

He smiled and kissed her, but his voice remained serious. "I'm sorry. But we have to be honest with each other. You'll tell me when a poem is a horror, right? Promise me that."

He had a point. This was her first foray into expressionism, quite possibly her last. She was too close to it to be able to judge its worth. "Fine. But I've already written the first initial."

The yellow Lab from next door ambled over, a stick in his mouth. Oliver gently extricated the stick from his jaws before giving it a good throw down the driveway. The dog trotted off into the back-yard instead. "You can name it after our contradictory friend here. Clyde."

"You want me to sign it 'Clyde'?"

The sunlight caught the canvas at an angle, turning the surface into a series of peaks and valleys. Maybe Oliver was right. The painting was ghastly, an attempt to be artistic and modern. She should stick with what she was good at. She finished up the signature, and Oliver offered to carry her easel and supplies back up to her room.

That evening, they all gathered around a bonfire on the beach. Levon and Violet wandered out of the darkness and sat on a log across the campfire from Oliver and Clara. A frisson of jealously slid up Clara's spine at the way Levon touched Violet's hand, leaning into her and whispering some private joke. Violet threw back her pretty head and laughed as Levon studied her throat like a vampire.

"I'll be right back." Clara stood and brushed the sand off her dress, hoping that Oliver wouldn't follow. He was deep in conversation with one of the other teachers and hardly noticed her leave.

She wandered along the shore, avoiding driftwood and seaweed, the cold sand on her bare feet a paltry salve to the irritation burning inside her. But no, she told herself, it wasn't Levon and Violet. Her frustrations were to be expected. She was sad to be leaving this magical place, to be going back to the grind of the city and the machinations of planning a wedding. But perhaps it was time to stop fussing about and focus on what was right with the world. She was to be married, and Clara would be lucky to have Oliver as a husband, someone who tempered her rough edges and told her the truth.

"Wait."

Levon.

She turned and waited for him to catch up to her. "Where's your actress?"

"Where's your poet?"

She didn't reply. Together, they walked in silence for a while. She would miss teaching class with him once they got back to New York. His energy inspired her.

"You finish *The Siren* yet?"

"Today."

"I'd like to see it."

"I don't know, it's not very good." She took a breath. "But I have news: Oliver and I are engaged."

"Congratulations." He looked out into the dark sea.

"You don't sound like you mean it."

"Of course I mean it." Levon picked up a rock and threw it out into the water, the sound swallowed up by the breaking waves. "No, I don't mean it at all. Why bother with marriage? You don't need a husband."

"I love him."

"He'll drag you down."

"I disagree. If anything, he's made me the success I am today."

"You've made yourself a success. If he hadn't come along, you would have found another way. Who knows what will come along in a year, in five years?"

"What on earth are you talking about?"

"Stop playing it safe. You're coddled, tied down by convention, when you should be leaping into the abyss with me."

He stopped in his tracks and grabbed her. His grip was strong, certain. When he leaned down and kissed her, it wasn't like Oliver's kisses. This was a claim. She grabbed his head with her hands, threading her fingers through his unruly hair, and pulled him close. He tasted like moonshine and the salty sea.

They finally parted, panting with ragged breath, as if they'd completed several rounds of boxing.

"I'm sorry." Levon leaned over and put his hands on his knees, looking down at the sand.

Not the reaction she'd expected. She'd disappointed him. Just as she'd disappointed Oliver with the painting. Clara backtracked, trying to save face. "It's fine. We had to do that sometime. Now it's done. We know we're not a good fit."

"I suppose so." He rubbed his chin with his hand, staring at her strangely.

As she headed back to the campfire, her heart began to calm. She wanted to have some kind of hold on him, that's all. Who wouldn't? Such a charismatic, talented man. But complex, unyielding. Uncompromising. She and Oliver had a bond that was calm and civilized. That should be enough.

She looked up. Oliver stood thirty feet away, up on the seawall. He must have come looking for her.

Clouds that had been covering the moon parted, revealing his shocked face. He'd seen everything.

He took off running, back to the campfire. Clara called out and ran after him, but he was fast. By the time she got back to the rest of the group, Oliver was nowhere to be seen.

And neither was Violet.

CHAPTER SIXTEEN

July 1929

The morning after the campfire, Clara remained up in her bedroom until she heard Levon leave. She sat up in bed, lost in thought. The siren of her painting glared back at her from the top of the desk, where it had been left angled against the wall. Oliver hadn't come home last night.

Clyde came to the door and barked a couple of times before giving up. Finally, she dragged herself out of bed and tossed on a navy cotton dress before heading to class, where Levon offered a cursory hello. Her shame was complete: She'd made a fool of herself with Levon and caused terrible pain to Oliver within the span of fifteen seconds. Her head ached from the lack of sleep, but she struggled through, focusing on the students and avoiding Levon entirely.

Back at the cottage, she found Oliver sitting at the kitchen table, his hair tousled, his eyes blue as the sea. He glowed, still seductive in his anger, a man who had chosen her and taken good care of her right when she needed it most.

From where Clara stood, Violet's cloying perfume tickled her nose.

"I'm sorry, Oliver. It meant nothing. What you saw on the beach."

"I've been warning you about him for months now, but you couldn't help yourself, could you? You talk about him all the time; now you're trying to paint like him. I knew it." Oliver's tone cut into her. "You can have him. Good luck to the both of you. You'll tear each other apart."

"I don't want Levon; I want you."

"We're done. It's over."

"We can talk about this, can't we? You immediately took off with Violet, after all. Maybe now we're even." He lifted his chin to speak, but she cut him off. "I can smell her on you, for God's sake."

"We'll never be even. You'll always listen to what Levon says over me, because he has some kind of magnetic hold over you. He's an immigrant, a peasant, from God knows where, but he sucks you right into his delusions of grandeur. Both of you think that you're special, above the rest of us. That you can act on impulse and get away with it. Well, now you know I can, too."

There was no talking to him, now that his resentment had boiled over into vicious insults.

She went up to her room, needing a refuge so she didn't strike back in anger. But something was wrong. Missing. Her painting.

She searched for it in Oliver's room, then her own again, before storming back downstairs.

"My painting—where is it?"

"You destroyed me, and so I destroyed something you love. It's only fair." The coldness in his voice was unrecognizable. As if he'd turned into an entirely different person, one she'd never met before.

"You destroyed it?" She hadn't realized how much it meant to her until then. The painting was part of the sea and the Maine winds and the people who had surrounded her this past month. It was the key to a new way of seeing the world, interpreting it. She had been gathering up the courage to show Levon the finished painting, and now he'd never see it. "You're heartless, you know that? I would never have burned your poems to punish you, no matter what you did."

"That only goes to show that I loved you more."

"What twisted logic. You make no sense. I care for you too much to ever enact revenge in such a petty way." She paused, gathering her thoughts, trying to calm her breathing. "It was a stupid mistake, what I did last night. A moment that came and went and was done for. We aren't interested in each other, not like that."

"You could've fooled me."

"Please, Oliver. I'm sorry. Let's sit and talk and hash this out. I can't imagine life without you."

For a split second, pain carved through his face, but as her hollow words lingered in the air, he quickly recovered his composure. "You're saying that to get the painting back, aren't you? You're not saying that for me."

He knew her so well. She had no reply.

⎯⋘⊙

Back in New York, Clara spent the month of August catching up on commissions from the magazines and from Studebaker, a welcome distraction from the Maine debacle. She hadn't seen Oliver since he'd driven off with Violet, leaving Clara behind to finish up the last week of classes and endure the sympathetic looks and fevered whispers of the students. Once home, it had been a relief to hole up in her studio and work fifteen hours a day. That awful morning in Maine, when he'd looked at her with contempt and fury, haunted her in the dead of night when she couldn't sleep.

She missed him, and the loss of *The Siren* still stung. But she had to let both of them go, for the sake of her sanity. Now her work could take precedence, and the frenzy for her illustrations had only increased over the summer. But each new success was tinged with the sadness of not being able to share it with Oliver. With anyone, really. On the same day that a newspaper interview hailing Clara as the "highest-paid woman artist in the country" was published, Mr. Oliver Smith and Miss Violet Foster appeared in the wedding announcements. They were to honeymoon in Paris before settling down in Los Angeles. She imagined the newlyweds walking along the Seine, exclaiming over their good fortune.

Miss Lillie Bliss, the society maven who'd asked for Clara's advice just five months earlier, opened her modern art exhibit in the Heckscher Building to great fanfare in November, just after the stock market took a dive. Like most of her acquaintances, Clara dismissed the drop as a temporary adjustment. After all, the headlines trumpeted a return to normal quite soon, followed by an orderly, if not promising, end to 1929. The success of the art exhibit created an uproar of its own, convincing critics and buyers that modern art was exciting, something to take a chance on instead of dismiss out of hand. Clara heard that Levon had been invited to participate in the next Museum of Modern Art show, scheduled for the following spring, and that Felix was selling his works off at a great clip. But his success meant that he taught fewer classes that fall, and they rarely crossed paths. Probably better that way. Although she missed his kinetic energy, their encounter on the beach had left her depleted.

One dreary March day, when the heavens couldn't decide whether to rain or snow and instead dropped down a mucky combination of both, Mr. Lorette called Clara into his office.

"How are you doing, Miss Darden?" He spoke like a doctor with a dying patient, all concern and gravitas. He had never broached the subject of Oliver and Violet's marriage, and she prayed he wouldn't now.

"I'm doing quite well, thank you." Her illustration class, which began the term with a full herd of thirty, had dwindled down to five, like her first term in reverse. But this time the troubles were financial—fewer students could afford the tuition—and had nothing to do with her gender. "The students who've remained are quite enthusiastic and talented, I'm happy to report."

By the summer, she hoped, the city would be recovered and hum again like it had in the fall. In the meantime, her contract with *Vogue* hadn't been renewed. Which was to be expected, even without the stock market crash. Most illustrators went in and out of fashion, the editors rotating the cover artists so that their readers didn't get bored with one particular look. While all agreed her designs were smashing, one didn't need to see the signature at the bottom of the page to know that it was a Clara Darden. Her distinctive style meant that her tenure was shorter than most.

On to bigger and better things.

Mr. Lorette fiddled with the papers on his desk before holding up some forms. "Three more students dropped out of the illustration course today. I'm sorry, but we'll lose money if we keep you on. It's only for this semester, until the economy rights itself. I hope you understand."

"Of course." Only one semester. She'd have more time to branch out, pursue alternate avenues of income. But she'd miss mingling with the other teachers and students. Only then did she grasp how much she counted on the place to alleviate her loneliness. "Will you be all right? The school, I mean."

He chewed on his bottom lip. "I can't say. Let's hope we pull out of this quickly. There's a chance we'd have to shut down for the coming term, then reinstate the program next fall. That would be the worst-case scenario."

"You'd shut down the entire school?" She hadn't expected anything that drastic. Her heart drummed with anxiety.

Mr. Lorette leaned back in his chair. "Art means nothing when someone is out of work. We're a luxury."

"Maybe it's times like these when art is most crucial."

He smiled. "That's exactly what Levon said. Let's hope you're both right, in any event."

"What will you and Mrs. Lorette do?"

"We'll head to Europe, escape from the dreariness of all this. Don't you worry about us." Another teacher appeared at the door, looking pale. The next victim.

That evening, she met Mr. Bianchi over dinner to discuss the new line for Studebaker. She'd drawn a dozen sketches on a pad and brought it with her, determined to excite him with the possibilities and prove her value.

Inside Barbetta, on Forty-Sixth Street, the ceiling dripped with crystal chandeliers. The cool salmon-colored walls offered a protective cocoon for the diners who could still afford it. Somewhere to forget the dreary outside world and indulge.

"The best-paid woman artist." Mr. Bianchi gave a tight-lipped smile as they sat down.

"Well, now, I doubt it's actually true. I'm not exactly sure how they did their research. It's not like there's a list of women artists and their earnings published anywhere. You know newspapers, all that hyperbole."

"Of course. You're right about that."

During the first course, she waited for him to bring up the new line, but he danced around the subject, speaking of their competitors, the need to address the current mood of the country in their advertising. She offered up several ideas, but none seemed to take.

By the time they were drinking coffee—he'd waved away the dessert menu—a hard stone had lodged in her stomach.

He sighed. "I'm afraid I have bad news."

Not twice in one day. She braced herself.

"We can't afford to keep you on, Miss Darden. You can imagine, the kind of pressure we're under."

If she lost this job, she'd have nothing. No covers, no classes, no cars. Her voice shook. "I understand that things have changed. But you've seen, I can adapt."

"I'm sure you can. But it's all about public perception. We featured you in the ads: *Interiors designed by Clara Darden.* Who's now the highest-paid woman artist. It's not good for business. We can't afford to seem wasteful, not when four million people are out of work. We'll alienate whatever customers are left."

"You don't have to pay me as much. I can do more for you. I have additional time now, you see."

"We've decided to keep everything in-house."

"May I ask who'll be taking over?"

"Benjamin Mortimer—you remember him?"

She nodded. He was an engineer by trade, with no creative abilities whatsoever.

Mr. Bianchi called for the check. "In any event, he has a family to feed. It's either let you go or fire him, and I can't do that to a man with responsibilities." He put a meaty hand over hers. "You don't want me to put a man out of work, now, do you?"

She pulled her hand away and resisted the impulse to wipe it on her napkin. "I don't mean to be rude or contradict what you're saying, but the company's obviously still doing well, right?" She gestured around the room. "If you can afford a fancy dinner at Barbetta, things can't be so bad, can they?"

"You may know about art and design, but you don't know about running a company. It's all about appearances. We need to appear both successful and frugal. Not an easy task." He pulled out some bills and left them on the table. He rose. "But it's just for the time being. By the fall, all the worry will be over and we won't be able to keep up with the demand. I assure you. Trust me, will you, Miss Darden?"

As if she had a choice.

⁓✿◎

By October 1930, Clara had stopped going by the magazine editors' offices with mock illustrations in hand, keeping her tone as light as possible to prevent her desperation from seeping through. There was no point. They weren't going to hire her, and the walk to and from the offices only made her hungry.

She was one of the lucky ones, able to scrape by on her savings, as long as she was thrifty. When she remembered the silly trinkets she and Oliver had bought on a whim, spending hundreds of dollars at a time, she felt sick. They'd enjoyed an expensive lifestyle, and very little of that remained.

Her apartment, now empty besides a few boxes and her two

suitcases, was no longer possible on her tight budget. In the living room, her maid, Angela, folded up the curtains.

"Miss Darden, what would you like done with these?"

"Please take them. You can make clothes out of them, if you like."

The curtains had a metallic sheen that at the time epitomized all things art deco. Now they seemed outlandish, useless. What was she thinking?

"Never mind, I have no idea what I'm saying." Clara couldn't help but laugh, and Angela joined in.

"I'm sure I'll find a use for them, Miss Darden. Unless you'd like to take them with you? To decorate your new place?"

Clara shoved at one of the boxes with her foot. "No, it'll be fine." She wandered through the rooms for the last time. Without Oliver to insist Clara go out of her studio, she'd succumbed to a hermit-like existence. Which was fine when she had hours of work on her plate, but not so much now that her days were empty.

The letter she'd sent to her parents in Arizona had been returned, marked NO FORWARDING ADDRESS. Clara hadn't kept up contact, and she added that to her many regrets. Not that she'd go running to them for comfort; that wasn't her aim. But she'd wanted to know that they were all right, to confirm they all retained a connection, however tenuous.

Levon had also fallen out of touch. His April show had been a success, but since then, the city had folded in on itself, retreated from art, from music. No doubt he was suffering financially as much as Clara was, if not more so. The Grand Central School of Art had indeed been forced to shut its doors until the situation improved. The once-dazzling art scene of New York was like a golden sarcophagus locked away in a dark tomb.

What if, as rumors suggested, the current economic disaster was permanent? The daily breadline just down the street at St. Vincent's Hospital had doubled in length from last summer; newspaper accounts put it at five hundred people and growing as the weather worsened.

Angela broke into her morbid thoughts. "May I ask where you're going, Miss Darden?"

"Don't worry about me; I'll be fine." Clara took Angela's hands in hers. "Off you go, and thank you."

"Best of luck, Miss Darden."

"You, too."

She took a last look into each room, remembering the silly times they'd had, when what to wear for Oliver's dinner parties had been the most important decision of the day. She hoped he was well and his family's fortune safe.

Her two suitcases sat in the foyer. One was filled with her art supplies, her livelihood. The other contained her clothes, what remained after she'd taken dresses to the consignment shop in the summer. To keep her hopes up for a return to better times, she'd held on to the dress Oliver had bought her for the May Ball. Maybe one day she'd wear it again, appreciate it anew.

The October air sliced into her lungs as she covered the eight blocks to her new home on East Seventeenth Street, the unimaginatively named Hotel 17. A man leaning on crutches scooted out of the way as she walked up the front steps. Inside, she handed over a month's rent to a grizzled woman behind the front desk and took the elevator up to room 35.

She busied herself setting up her meager possessions, which took only five minutes. At least the hotel had good bones. The dark moldings were handsome, and with some polish she'd be able to make them gleam again. The room had once been larger, but now a shoddily constructed partition divided it in half. She tried not to think too much about the occupant on the other side.

There was nothing to be done about the sink, as no amount of soap would scrub away the rusty stains encircling the drain. Sure, the place was a dump, but it was cheaper than a boardinghouse. She'd manage. She always had.

A burst of sunlight came through the lone window beside the bed. For a moment, she considered asking for another room, one with northern exposure. But the feeble warmth changed her mind.

For now, she lifted her face, closed her eyes, and basked in the light.

CHAPTER SEVENTEEN

December 1974

Virginia ran into one of the phone booths at the end of her lunch hour the Monday after Thanksgiving, and rang the Lorettes to find out what the art expert had said. Mr. Lorette told her that their friend Sammy was quite intrigued by her find, but that it would take a few weeks.

Intriguing. That sounded promising. Newly energized, Virginia grabbed a bottle of Windex and spent the next few hours wiping down the glass windows that encircled the information booth. After all her hard work, the place was looking spiffy, if she did say so herself, and one of the supervisors had even remarked on the difference. Terrence kindly gave Virginia all the credit, and the supervisor had shaken her hand.

She had a final section to wipe down, including Totto's window, and she worked as quickly as possible. "You'll like this, I promise," she said to him. "You'll be able to see your customers much better."

"Why would I want to see them better?" He flipped over the WINDOW CLOSED sign and pulled out the newspaper.

"Virginia?"

Virginia froze. She knew that voice anywhere. Betsy.

She turned, clutching the Windex and rag close to her body, as if that would stop Betsy from noticing.

"I thought that was you. What on earth are you wearing? And what are you doing here?" Betsy's hair fell in perfect sausage curls along her cheeks; her eyelids shimmered a glittery blue. Virginia, meanwhile, was lost in her too-big blazer, her face bare.

"Hi, Betsy." She accepted an air kiss on one cheek, stammering for a suitable reply to her question. None came. Better to redirect. "What are you doing here?"

Betsy pointed to her umbrella. "It's pouring out there, and I figured I'd take my chances and cut through Grand Central, try to get a cab on the other side." She gasped. "Oh my God. Now it all makes sense. I was at the Carlyle over the weekend with some of the girls from the PONY committee and swore I saw Ruby working as a barmaid. I thought, 'That can't possibly be.' And now here you are, a cleaning lady at Grand Central? You must be in terrible straits. Divorced and now this? What can I do?"

"I'm fine. Really." What else was there to say? Her humiliation was complete. By the end of the day, everyone would know that she'd fallen on hard times. A cleaning lady whose daughter worked in a bar.

"I'm so sorry for you, Virginia. If you needed a cleaning job, I could have used you in the penthouse. Lucinda just quit. With no advance notice, I might add." She looked about, her mouth curling with disgust. "This place is revolting. I hope you're careful, with all the rats and roaches and dirty people wandering around."

"Hey. Watch it, lady. You have no idea what you're talking about."

Virginia turned around. Totto was leaning forward on his counter, his arms crossed.

"What?" Betsy looked from Totto to Virginia. "Who's that?"

"Get off your high horse, lady," Totto snapped. "Don't you come in here with your ugly blue eyeshadow and bad-mouth this place. We've gotta work here, day in and day out, and your attitude doesn't help one bit."

"Totto, enough," said Virginia.

"Miss Clay." Winston had come out of the booth and took the Windex and rag from her. "I'm so sorry to have forgotten these. I hope you won't tell the stationmaster."

Virginia stared, speechless.

"Miss Clay is running the whole place these days, you know, as the chief information officer." Winston addressed Betsy with his laconic southern accent. "She's a tough taskmaster, but we don't know what we'd do without her."

Betsy gaped at Virginia. "Chief information officer?"

"Well, yes." Virginia tried to sound confident. "Thought I'd see what I could do to help out, something to do with my free time." She looked over at Winston, who nodded in encouragement. "I decided there should be more to my life than shopping and going out to lunch."

"Well, isn't that something? I had no idea." Betsy nodded at Virginia. "I'll let you get back to work, then. I'm very impressed. Just wait until I tell the ladies of PONY."

After Betsy had trotted up the staircase and disappeared from view, Virginia followed Winston back into the booth. "Thank you, both, for that. For standing up for me."

"I was standing up for the terminal, not you," said Totto, switching his sign back around. "People like that make me want to scream."

"And scream you did." Winston handed back the Windex and rag and climbed onto his stool. "What a horrible woman. Is she one of your friends?"

"Ex-friends. Again, you guys were great." She kissed Winston on the cheek and patted Totto's arm. "Now back to work, both of you!"

"Don't push it."

Virginia could have sworn Totto smiled.

Grand Central exuded a completely different atmosphere on weekends. The people who wandered through did so at a more leisurely pace, which offered Virginia the opportunity to show off her workplace to Ruby without being trampled by passengers.

"You're practically giddy, Mom," said Ruby. "This is hilarious."

Virginia didn't care that she was coming off as a train geek. "You have to imagine what it was like back when it opened in 1913. Imagine this railing all painted and clean." She waited while Ruby snapped a couple of photos of the brass filigree. "And over here, check out the timetable in this waiting room. It's still a blackboard."

Ruby stepped back to fit it in the frame. "Those sconces on either side are glorious." More clicks.

Together, they meandered through the terminal, Ruby shooting not only the beautiful but also the ruined, like a Botticino marble water fountain filled with garbage. To Virginia's surprise, her daughter stopped a few of the workers, including a train conductor and a janitor, and convinced them to let her take their portraits.

"These doors, you've got to see these doors." Virginia brought her to the entrance to the small police station Dennis had taken her to. She'd read in the trainee handbook that it used to be a grand office called the Campbell Apartment.

In the hands of metal artisans, the heavy wrought-iron double doors looked like Irish lace, with an interlocking pattern of four-leaf clovers. They were massive and solid but somehow came off as weightless and transparent.

A woman's voice rose from behind them. "It'll work better close up. You'll get less reflection."

"Doris?" Virginia smiled and gave her coworker an awkward half hug. "Doris! What are you doing here on a Saturday?" She introduced her to Ruby.

"Nice to meet you." Doris looked tired, with dark rings under her eyes. Her wig was slightly askew. "I'm taking extra shifts. My husband got laid off."

Virginia understood the pressures she was under all too well. "I'm so sorry."

"Well, what are you gonna do? What's with the photos?" She gestured toward Ruby's camera.

"We're doing a little project. Trying to show the prettier side of the terminal. Ruby's studying photography."

"Hey, that's great. Good for you."

"Do you know a lot about photography?" asked Ruby. "You're right, the doors are even better close up."

"Nah. Just made sense, is all."

"Can I take your photo?"

Doris put one hand to her hair. "You want a photo of me?"

Virginia cringed inside, hoping Doris wouldn't lash out or be offended by the request.

"Yes." Ruby pointed to the wall. "If you stand here, the light is really nice."

Doris did as she was told, pasting a wide smile on her face, turning into a movie queen for the time it took Ruby to snap a few photos, offering a completely different side of herself from the scowling clerk Virginia knew.

They said good-bye, and Doris tromped off.

"She seems nice," said Ruby.

"Doris is one of the pricklier clerks, to be honest. A tough nut. I can't believe she agreed to have her photo taken. You must have the magic touch."

"You really like these folks, don't you?"

Virginia nodded. They were decent and smart, each and every one of them. "How about you, do you like the people at Bemelmans?" Since Ruby had started working, she seemed to have a newfound sense of purpose. She took her role as barmaid as seriously as she did her photography, chatting with Xavier and Finn about complicated cocktail recipes over dinner.

"Yes. Everyone's great. Ryan's known as the best bartender in all of Manhattan, the master of the martini. The tips are nothing to sneeze at, either."

There's an idea. "If the clerks in the information booth got tipped every time they answered a question, we'd be rolling in it."

Ruby rewound the film, another roll filled. "Hey, you could put out a tip jar."

"Someone would steal it within five minutes. Unfortunately, Grand Central is no Bemelmans."

A week later, Finn and Xavier were regaling Virginia with the plot of the opera they'd just seen, something involving a castle and a torture chamber, when Ruby burst into the apartment. "I stayed late at the darkroom at the Photography Institute, and the Grand Central photos are ready. Do you want to see them?"

"That was fast." Virginia was delighted with her daughter's enthusiasm.

"I was dying to see how they turned out." She laid them out on the dining room table, one after another.

In black and white, the original splendor of the terminal re-emerged. The ornamental motifs over the doors curved with shadow and light; the bare bulbs on the mammoth bronze chandeliers glowed like fireflies.

"What a shame," said Virginia.

Ruby turned to her. "You don't like them?"

She quickly reassured her. "I love every one. It's just too bad we can't get them out in the world, as they might change people's minds about putting a skyscraper over the terminal."

"Who says no one will see them?" Xavier put his hands on his hips. "Let's do an exhibit."

"An exhibit?" asked Ruby. "Where?"

Finn jolted upright. "Right here. We'll do it in one of the Carlyle's private rooms on the second floor. Invite everyone we know, and have a party after in Bemelmans. I'll talk to the manager first thing tomorrow."

"You'd really do that? You think they're that good?" Ruby bit her lip. "It's not like I'm anyone important."

"Not yet," said Xavier. "Leave it to us. We'll aim for a couple weeks after the holidays, when all the Christmas festivities are over with and everyone is bored and dying for an excuse to go out."

Ruby clapped her hands together. "I'll mount them on something stiff. That's easy enough."

"Exactly. Let's keep it simple. Let the photos speak for themselves."

Virginia hugged her brother and Xavier. "The best Christmas present ever. Thanks, guys."

Holiday madness hit the city, clogging the streets with tourists and shoppers. New Year's fell on a Wednesday, basically shutting down the entire week to post-revelry recovery while further delaying any update on the watercolor from the Lorettes. Virginia had tried them again after the holidays, only to be told by the maid who answered the phone that they were out of town, returning mid-January.

The morning of Ruby's exhibit, Virginia called their number. Mrs. Lorette answered, her voice more gravelly than Virginia remembered.

"The Lorette residence."

"Mrs. Lorette, it's Virginia Clay. I'm sorry to bother you on a weekend, but I was eager to find out if you've heard anything about the painting. I understand you've been out of town."

"Right. Yes." A pause. She seemed distracted. "I had meant to get back to you sooner."

"That's fine, of course. The holidays and all."

"That's true. I'm afraid I haven't been as attentive as I should have been to your inquiries. Mr. Lorette's been ill. The excitement from your discovery has taken a toll on his health. We had to visit some specialists, see if they could help."

"Oh no. Is there anything I can do?" A blister of guilt bubbled up inside her.

"My dear Virginia, you're too kind. But we're taking it day by day."

"I understand completely."

The Sotheby's auction was in two and a half months. Surely, they had plenty of time. She was saying so to Mrs. Lorette as Ruby walked in the front door, tossed her keys on the table, and rummaged around in her fringed suede purse. Virginia gave her a quick wave before turning away and lowering her voice. "Let me know how it goes, Mrs. Lorette."

"Of course. I'll get back to you as soon as I can on the watercolor. You're a sweet girl, so patient."

She didn't have much of a choice, really. Or maybe she did. "Why don't you give me the number to Sammy, the expert who's been looking at it? I can deal with him directly and that way you won't have to be bothered."

"Lovely idea. Give me a moment." Papers were shuffled, Virginia heard a drawer open and shut. "Mr. Lorette must have it on his desk. I'll find it and call you back in a couple of days. Do you mind, dear?"

"No, of course not. Speak with you soon."

As Virginia hung up the phone, Ruby placed a pile of letters on the table. "I swung by the apartment and picked up the mail for you."

"Great. Thanks. How's it looking?" The repairs to the apartment were only slightly behind schedule, and while Virginia would miss Finn, she was ready to be back in her home.

Except for one reason.

"It's looking good." Ruby glanced her way before grabbing a soda from the refrigerator. "What's wrong?"

Virginia sorted through the mail, her heart pounding. She'd received one threatening note a week since the first one. There it was. Her name and address scribbled on the envelope. No point opening it. "Nothing. Nothing at all."

"Where are Xavier and Finn?"

"They headed off to brunch in Chelsea."

"But what's up with you?"

"I'm cool."

Ruby laughed. "Look at you, trying to be hip. It's cute."

"Groovy? Should I have said groovy?"

"Please don't." Ruby had a silly grin on her face. "You'll ruin it for the rest of us." She twisted the top off her Dr Pepper and took a swig. "Who were you talking to?"

Until now, Virginia had been reluctant to discuss the watercolor with anyone else, figuring she'd wait until she had good news, or at least a great story. But unburdening her anxiety about the watercolor was tempting. Besides, Ruby should know what was going on.

Virginia explained how she'd found the painting at the art school, that it had slipped behind a cabinet and that she'd recognized the image from an auction house catalog. "Hold on, let me show you."

She grabbed the catalog and opened it to the correct page.

"This blue one?" asked Ruby. "It's breathtaking."

"Right. I think what I found might be an early study for that painting, and if so, it could be really valuable." She described her meeting with the curator at the Art Students League, followed by the one with the Lorettes, before elaborating on the complicated provenance. "What it all boils down to is that it might actually be by a woman named Clara Darden."

Ruby let out a low whistle. "You've been doing a lot of detective work."

"I didn't want to say anything until I knew more."

"These Lorette folks, they said they'd get it appraised?" Ruby cocked her head.

"They did. But then the holiday happened, and they're old and he's sick. Hey, maybe we can stop by and bring some chicken soup or something?"

"Let's do it. I'm a mess of nerves with the exhibit tonight. It'd be nice to get out of here and do a good deed."

After stopping at a deli for a quart of soup, they headed off to the

Lorettes'. Virginia didn't mention the mugging, but she kept an eagle eye out for her assailant. The day was brisk but sunny and the sidewalks busy, which helped calm her nerves.

"Have you seen Libby lately?" Virginia asked. If there were scandalous rumors flying around about Virginia's new job, Libby—Betsy's daughter—would have been sure to share them with Ruby.

"Nah, I haven't seen Libby in ages. She's hanging with a different crowd. They're always talking about stuff that I don't care about."

"I feel the same way about Betsy these days."

Ruby's eyes widened, clearly shocked by her mother's honesty. "Do you miss her? It's not like you have a lot of friends, Mom."

"True. My life is smaller than it was before. But it's richer, in a lot of ways."

"Not literally richer, though," Ruby teased.

"Don't I know it. Wait. There they are."

The front door of the town house opened, and Mrs. Lorette stepped out, followed by Mr. Lorette, who turned to lock the door behind him. The two stepped gingerly onto the sidewalk.

"Hello, Mr. and Mrs. Lorette!" Virginia's voice came out unnaturally bright, like a bad actor in a soap opera. "What a surprise."

"Virginia." Mrs. Lorette took a tissue out of her sleeve and sniffed into it.

"This is my daughter, Ruby, who I've been telling all about you." She turned to Mr. Lorette. "I understand you've been unwell."

"Right. I have."

She could have sworn he hunched over slightly, as if exaggerating his frailty. Mrs. Lorette put her arm through his, and they exchanged nervous glances.

"Well, we brought you some soup." She held it out, and Mrs. Lorette took the bag but made no move to return to the house.

"Thank you."

"I know you've been going through a lot lately, and I figured I'd get that name and number from you and take over the investigation again. So you don't have to be bothered."

"Name and number?" Mr. Lorette looked at his wife, confused. Or was he faking it?

"The art expert, dear. For that watercolor from the art school." She smiled at Virginia, but it didn't reach her eyes.

"We should have some news by now, I would think." Virginia took out a pad of paper and a pencil from her handbag. "What was that name again?"

Mrs. Lorette threw Virginia a sharp look. "I'm getting the distinct impression you don't trust us. First off, let me tell you a little about how the art world works: very slowly. You want something done correctly, you give it to an expert and you wait."

For a moment, Mrs. Lorette's withering reply left her chastised. She glanced over at Ruby, who gave an imperceptible shake of her head. Virginia wasn't imagining things. The woman's defensiveness was uncalled for. Suspicious. "We'd like the phone number as well, please."

Mr. Lorette regarded them both. "How dare you speak to us like that? We try to help you, and you turn on us? Not very kind, I must say."

Neither Virginia nor Ruby spoke. The silence dragged on.

"Fine. Samson Coutan. Works at the MoMA. I don't know the number offhand, but I'm sure the switchboard will connect you. If you ask politely."

Virginia's mind whipsawed with uncertainty. What if Mr. Lorette was right, that these things just took time, and she'd alienated the two people who had offered to help her? But she hadn't done anything but offer to assist *them* with the painting she'd discovered in the first place, and her heart raced at the thought of the painting being lost to her forever, after she'd only just rescued it from its hiding place.

Virginia and Ruby hightailed it out of there. In the subway, on the way home, Virginia leaned into her daughter. "They seemed so nice when I first met them. But after how they acted when I was trying to help, I think I'm being played."

"I got the same vibe. How much did the curator say the watercolor might be worth?"

"A hundred and fifty thousand dollars."

Ruby whistled. "That's a ton of money."

"This probably sounds strange, but the painting means more to me than that. What if I never get it back? This Mr. Coutan has no idea who I am; we've never spoken on the phone or met. I guess I'll dash over there during my lunch hour and hope for the best."

"Don't give up hope just yet," offered Ruby. "Monday's my day off. If you like, I'll go to the MoMA first thing and track down the mysterious Mr. Coutan."

No doubt her daughter would have a better chance of getting through to him. He'd smell the desperation on Virginia right off, especially if she was in a rush. "Would you?"

"I'd be happy to be your partner in crime."

Later that evening, Virginia stood in the corner of one of the Carlyle's private meeting rooms, where tasteful striped curtains and matching valences added a dash of color in a sea of creams and light browns. Ruby held court in the center of the room, where she belonged, flanked by two classmates from the Institute of Photography, the three of them giggling with delight. Finn and Xavier had outdone themselves, even convincing the manager of the hotel to throw in some champagne and a cheese platter for the exhibition of Ruby's Grand Central photos, which stood on simple wood easels arranged in a horseshoe pattern around the room. The two men were obviously in their element, surrounded by fabulous New Yorkers wearing leopard print and leisure suits, and Virginia was more than happy to take a back seat and watch the circus from afar.

Finn glided over, offering to refill Virginia's champagne glass. "The party's a big hit."

"How did you attract so many people? You don't even live here."

"Bemelmans Bar, baby. I mentioned the exhibit the past week during my show, and of course people jump to do my bidding."

"Why am I not surprised?"

"Where are all your coworkers? I imagine they would have loved this."

Virginia had considered inviting the other information booth clerks, especially with the lovely photo of Doris that was part of the show, but in the end she had decided against it. "I was worried about inviting them. This place is so fancy, then they'd think I was fancy, and that I was somehow treating my job and the people who worked at Grand Central as objects." She shook her head. "I'm not making much sense. But I didn't want them to think I was using them."

He clutched her arm. "Oh my God. Look. Over there."

A thin woman with dark chestnut hair stood with a couple of other ladies, studying the photo of the water fountain. She wore a biscuit-colored Chanel suit that fit in perfectly with the surroundings.

Jacqueline Kennedy Onassis.

Virginia had been besotted with Jackie O since she'd stepped into the political spotlight. Jackie was five years older, practically her contemporary, but maneuvered through the world with a grace and charm that had always eluded Virginia. And now here she was, in the same room as Virginia.

"I can't believe it. What is she doing here?" Virginia couldn't help staring, even though everyone in the room was doing likewise, with varying degrees of subtlety.

"I have no idea. Come on, let's go say hello."

"I couldn't."

"Why not?"

"I wouldn't know what to say." She held Finn back. "Look, she's approaching Ruby."

They shook hands, and Virginia swore Ruby did a small curtsy. *That's my girl.*

Virginia gathered up the courage to approach, and together she and Finn walked over, arm in arm, like a bride and groom on their wedding day. They were only a few feet away when another woman swooped in and whispered something in Jackie's ear. In an instant, Jackie and her two cohorts dashed out of the room and were gone.

"What? Where did they go?" asked Virginia.

The other woman, an elegant lady in pearls, overheard and turned to her. "Sorry about this. Apparently, there's a scrum of photographers staked out in the lobby. We had to get her out the back door fast." She held out her hand. "My name is Adelaide Parsons, and I work at the Municipal Art Society."

Virginia recognized the organization, an urban planning and preservation group, from her committee days. She shook hands and introduced Finn and Ruby. "My daughter is the photographer."

"Indeed? Your photos are glorious."

"It was all my mom's idea." Ruby slung an arm around Virginia. "She works in the terminal."

"You make a good team. It's a wonderful exhibition."

Virginia beamed with motherly pride. "We're hoping it might help raise awareness."

"I wish it were so. We've been fighting Penn Central on this since the late 1960s. Unfortunately, I don't believe there's much chance we'll win the court case at this point, but thank you for trying."

"You don't think they'll uphold the landmark status?" asked Virginia.

"Not the way things are going. The judge isn't very sympathetic to our cause. If he rules against us, Penn Central will be allowed to build on top of the terminal, or demolish it entirely."

She gestured toward the easels, before letting her hand fall limply to her side. "At the very least, we'll have a lovely record of the past."

CHAPTER EIGHTEEN

January 1975

The clerks buzzed with news at the information booth Monday morning.

"Did you hear?" Winston asked Virginia. "Penn Central won their court case. I heard them talking about it in the Station Master's Office. The judge declared that Grand Central isn't a landmark, so they can tear it down or do whatever they want."

Coming so soon after the success of Ruby's exhibition, the news was especially crushing. Virginia wondered about Dennis's reaction. He must be pleased. His colleagues were probably popping the champagne right about now.

But Virginia's fellow employees looked worried. Totto dug his hands into his pockets, ignoring the man gesturing outside his window, and Doris looked like she was about to cry.

"What will happen to all of us?" asked Winston.

Terrence shook his head. "It'll be the perfect opportunity to lay us off and replace us with younger folk. We'll have to find new jobs."

The unemployment rate was nearly 11 percent. Inflation was close to twelve. None of the information booth clerks were good for anything other than answering transportation-related questions, and they should be looking forward to retirement, not the unemployment line.

"I'll go find out what's going on in the Station Master's Office," said Terrence. "Virginia, cover my window."

Two months ago, the request would have struck fear into her heart. But by now, she knew the answers to the most-asked questions, and the few she didn't, she nudged Totto next to her and asked him. He threw her a glassy stare every time, but she didn't care.

Ruby appeared at the window. "Mom. Can you get away?"

"Give me five minutes."

As soon as Terrence returned, shaking his head and looking even more depressed than when he'd left, Virginia took a break and met Ruby on the West Balcony. "How did it go?"

"Samson Coutan doesn't exist. There's no one there by that name. The Lorettes have been lying the whole time."

Stunned, Virginia leaned over the railing, staring down at the swirls of people below. "I was so stupid."

Ruby touched her shoulder. "You had no idea they were crooks. You couldn't have known. You're not stupid. I just saw you answer eighty questions about this place in five minutes; you were amazing."

"You were watching me?" Embarrassed, she straightened up and brushed off her sleeves.

"Yes. You were great. Especially with the people who were rude."

"I guess you get used to it." But her daughter's compliments didn't make her feel any better. "I got a degree in art history, and now I answer questions about departure times."

"And your daughter's a barmaid. As Dad keeps on reminding me."

While the recent blast of honesty with her daughter had been refreshing, Virginia was liable to bring her daughter right down with her if she wasn't careful. That was the last thing she wanted. "Listen. Don't let Dad pick on you. You're working, and there are very few jobs to be had in the city right now. Ignore him. But at the same time, remember that he has a good heart, he loves you, even if he's sometimes caught up in that fancy world of his. We're not like that, and that's fine."

Ruby nodded. "What do we do now? We can't give up. Let's go back down there and confront the Lorettes again. Or go to the police and tell them that they lied to us and stole it."

Virginia hated to let Ruby down. Or lose this new connection with her daughter. She considered calling Janice at the Art Students League and ratting out the Lorettes, but if Janice telephoned them, they'd tell her that Virginia had taken it from the art school, had lied about finding it at her aunt's house. Which made her look as shifty as the Lorettes.

"I highly doubt the Lorettes would answer the door or talk to us on the phone, now that they know we know they lied. As for going to the police, we have no proof that we owned it in the first place."

"I have an idea." Ruby brightened. "Why don't you talk to Dad? He's a lawyer."

"You want me to ask your dad for legal advice?"

"Why not? That painting is yours, right? The Lorettes took it from you."

"I have no proof of that."

"Still. Meet up with him. Ask him for help."

Virginia studied Ruby, whose eyes were full of hope.

"I can't do that. I'm sorry. That's all over with."

Confiding in Chester would only make things worse. He'd laugh at her, dismiss it as a wild-goose chase. She hoped Ruby understood the meaning behind her words, that their intact, happy family was over with as well.

"You can't even ask him for advice?"

"No."

Ruby slumped over. "That's too bad."

"I'm glad you were here to help."

"Not that I did any good."

She pushed a lock of hair behind her daughter's ear. "You did. Thank you."

Virginia stopped by the apartment to collect the mail before going back to the Carlyle. Another threatening note, no surprise at that. She carried her mace in the side pocket of her purse now, just in case. Also in her mailbox was an official-looking letter from some law firm.

She read it and gasped out loud, drawing a scowl from the doorman. Her upstairs neighbor had retained a lawyer who was threatening to sue Virginia for damages to their apartment. She had never met the upstairs neighbors, just heard them clomp back and forth across her ceiling every so often. But these people, the clompers, claimed that all their clothes, draperies, rugs, and furnishings had been damaged by smoke and had to be professionally cleaned. The bill was in the thousands.

She'd never be able to come up with that much money. Heck, she didn't even have enough to hire an attorney to question their claims.

The only answer was the one that her daughter most wished for.

There was only one person left to ask for help.

⟿⟆⟆◎

"You're tan."

Chester took off his coat, laid it carefully on the back of his chair, and sat down opposite Virginia in the Oyster Bar. "I was in Mexico."

How strange to be strangers. Virginia stared at him while he went through the motions of folding his napkin on the table, crooking up one finger to the waiter to ask for coffee, all the while avoiding eye contact. He'd lost weight, looked healthier than he had in ages.

Before, she'd known what he was going to say before he even said it. She often finished his sentences, eager to show how close they were. How in tune she was. *On the same wavelength*, they called it these days. But now he was impenetrable.

They both ordered the oyster stew. She reminded herself why she was there and spent the next ten minutes inquiring about his work, their mutual acquaintances, ever so gently softening him up. For those ten minutes, it was as if nothing had happened between them. They made fun of Betsy and her husband, worried together over a recently widowed colleague of Chester's. When he brought up Ruby's stint as a barmaid, she made light of it and changed the subject fast.

He never once asked Virginia about her life. Just like old times.

The oyster stews came. Nerves made her unable to eat more than a few bites, but she stirred the lumps around while chewing on the oyster crackers, which had made up most of her early pregnancy diet. Then, Chester had been a true partner. She'd wisecrack about her morning sickness, using the language of a trucker because he loved it when she played up her working-class background. In private, of course, never around his family or their friends.

Her pregnancy and his attention had made her feel important, strong. Able to bear anything.

With her operation, it'd been the opposite effect. She'd joke, hoping to get a smile out of him, and he'd cringe. A baby was one thing. A breast, quite another.

When the conversation lulled, Virginia scrambled for something else to talk about. She wasn't ready to ask for his help, not yet.

"Did you hear about the Grand Central ruling?" The words sounded odd coming out of her mouth, like she was trying too hard to impress.

"I did."

"The people I work with are worried that they'll lose their jobs when they build the new skyscraper." In fact, Doris spent the lulls in the day reading the help wanted ads out loud, until Winston told her to quit it.

"They may lose their jobs, but in the end, it's all about progress. This city's a pit, and we need to remake it into something better. You can't live in the past."

His opposition didn't surprise her. "I read that the city will probably appeal the ruling."

"Don't believe everything you read."

"Why wouldn't they?"

He leaned back in his chair. "It costs money to appeal, and the city is barely squeaking by as it is. If the city appeals and loses, then Penn Central could countersue for damages. Mayor Beame would be an idiot if he exposed the city to that kind of financial risk."

She glanced around. "The judge called it a 'long-neglected faded beauty.'"

"'Faded beauty' is putting it mildly. It's a dump."

Virginia didn't answer. She was a faded beauty herself. The thought stung.

Back when she was sick, her doctors had told her that if they found cancer and didn't remove her entire breast, her prognosis would be poor, her disease terminal. Just like the building above her, from the Guastavino tiles of the Oyster Bar to the triumphal arch windows of the main concourse.

She'd survived, but the terminal would not.

"What did you want to meet about?" Chester had finished his stew and was eyeing hers. She pushed the bowl over to him.

She pulled out the letter from her neighbor's attorney and handed it over to him. "I'm being sued by my neighbor. They say they have two thousand dollars' worth of damage from the fire."

"If they had to get everything professionally cleaned, it adds up. Furniture, clothes, repainting the walls."

Not the answer she was hoping for. "I can barely afford to fix my place, with the high deductible on my insurance policy. I was hoping I could get a loan from you."

Chester shook his head. "I wish I could help. But I can't. I'm sorry. We're all strapped these days."

"Not too strapped to go to Mexico."

"It was a business trip, not a personal one. On top of that, the law firm is in financial trouble. We're hoping we can ride out the slump." A momentary flicker of humiliation crossed Chester's face. He wasn't lying.

She was embarrassed to ask him for money, and he was embarrassed to have to admit he didn't have it. "I understand. Thank you for considering it." There was only one other option. "There's this painting that I found, and I think it's worth a lot. I wanted to get your advice on that as well."

"Shoot."

"It's an early version of a painting that's up for auction in April, by this artist named Levon Zakarian, who died tragically. They don't really know if he's the true artist, because he signed it as 'Clyde' and died before revealing himself, but everyone assumes it's his." She explained about the Chicago show and the train crash. "This early version I found has a sketch on the back side that's by a woman illustrator. I think Clyde is this woman, not Levon Zakarian. If that's so, it would blow the minds of the art world people."

Chester perked up. "Have you had it examined?"

"That's the thing; I seem to have hit a speed bump. You see, I gave it to an older couple who ran an art school back then, and they were going to get it examined or analyzed or some such thing, but they took off with it and won't return it."

"What do you mean they won't return it?"

"Just that. They won't give it back. Even worse, the expert they said they sent it to doesn't exist. They've been lying the whole time."

"Do you have some kind of bill of sale for your sketch or whatever it is?"

"No. I found it, you see. Up in the old art school on the top floor of Grand Central."

He wiped his mouth with his napkin and motioned to the waitress for the check. "If you don't have proof that it's yours, I don't see what you can do."

"I was hoping you could help me somehow." She didn't have much time. Chester's mind was elsewhere, mulling over his next appointment, figuring out how long it would take to get there, probably relieved to have lunch over with. "I read in the paper a few months ago about the lawyer in your firm who recovered art taken in World War II by the Nazis. Maybe he could help prove that Clara Darden was the artist."

"It's much more complicated than that, Virginia. You have no idea what you're talking about."

"At least you could send a mean letter; you know how good you are at those, and then they'd realize I was serious and return it."

He pulled a ten-dollar bill out of his wallet.

She continued. "It could be worth a lot of money. One curator told me that it might be worth over a hundred and fifty thousand dollars."

He looked up at that. "Huh."

"Ruby and I have been working together on this, and we both thought maybe a mean letter from you would help." Her last chance, bringing up their daughter.

"First of all, stop calling it a 'mean letter.'" In the past, he'd laughed whenever she mangled legal language on purpose. Not anymore, apparently. "And it doesn't change my answer because you brought up Ruby."

"The painting means something to me. It's important."

"Lesson number one in negotiating: Don't get emotional."

"How can I not get emotional? I'm going to be in serious legal trouble with these neighbors."

Chester rubbed his eye with the meat of his palm, his habit whenever he grew annoyed. "You should've read the fine print in your insurance policy; then none of this would be such a surprise." He spoke to her as if she were a recalcitrant client, not the mother of his child.

Tears pricked her eyes. She blinked, trying to stop them. "I agree, it's been a sharp learning curve for me, after the divorce. I didn't handle the finances when we were married, and so I made some mistakes early on."

"We're no longer together, Virginia. You have to accept that and move on. I can't take care of you anymore."

He was right, of course. For the first time all lunch, Chester looked at her. Really looked at her. His eyes moved down her neck. Normally she'd cover herself, but this time she didn't.

He nodded to her chest, his face unreadable. "You've got a problem there."

She glanced down. Her mastectomy bra had ridden up, making her look lopsided, disfigured.

She jumped up, grabbed her purse, and headed to the women's bathroom. Once there, she locked herself in a stall and let the tears come, bawling without making a sound.

When she could cry no more, she unbuttoned her shirt and adjusted the bra, cursing her bad luck, her ex-husband, and the world.

—⁂—

When Virginia finally emerged from the bathroom, the energy in the restaurant had shifted, the same way the air thickens imperceptibly before a thunderstorm. Gone were the last of the commuters and tourists; all the tables sat empty, yet fifty or so men in suits and a few women milled about in groups, murmuring in low voices.

At least Chester was gone. Her humiliation complete, she wound her way through the crowd, keeping her arm pressed tightly against her chest, like a coat of armor.

An excited buzz went through the crowd. Curious, Virginia lingered behind them, wondering what was going to happen next. Five or six tables had been pushed close together in a long row. On the middle table, a bouquet of microphones had been set up, the wires dangling down and along the floor like steel serpents.

Virginia was in no hurry to return to the information booth. What did it matter if she did a good job or not, when it was all going to be over soon anyway? And the longer she took, the more time her red, swollen eyes would have to return to normal.

"Mr. Mayor, Mr. Mayor!"

The crowd called out as a group of seven walked through the front entrance and took up seats behind the long table. She recognized Mayor Beame right away, his thick dark eyebrows a sharp contrast to his snow-white hair. The reporters waited as the rest of the mayor's entourage settled in their seats.

She couldn't get a good view, but his words cut clearly through the crowd as he introduced the Committee to Save Grand Central: architect Philip Johnson, author Louis Auchincloss, and other names she didn't recognize. Until he got to the last one. "Mrs. Jacqueline Kennedy Onassis."

Virginia pushed her way forward, taking advantage of her small size to work her way up to the front row. The mayor introduced the group and praised the Municipal Art Society, which he said had spearheaded the effort to save Grand Central. Virginia spotted Adelaide, the woman from Ruby's exhibit, standing off to one side. The mayor continued. "We're fighting to save not only the terminal but the very existence of our landmark law. If we don't stand up now, nothing can be saved."

The reporters scribbled down his words.

They reshuffled places so that Jackie sat in front of the microphone. She wore a tan, fitted dress that draped her lithe body beautifully. A long gold chain hung from her neck, and matching earrings glittered against the black sheen of her hair.

The crowd leaned in as she began to speak, her voice breathy. "We've all heard that it's too late, that it has to happen, that it's inevitable. But I don't think that's true. Because I think if there is great effort, even if it's at the eleventh hour, you can succeed, and I know that's what we'll do."

Virginia couldn't wait to tell Ruby. She had no doubt her daughter's photographs had played a part in convincing the Municipal Art Society to put up a fight.

"Isn't it inevitable for the terminal to come down if it can't support itself economically?" shouted a reporter.

Congressman Koch, a tall, balding man with a sardonic smile, cut in. "Central Park doesn't support itself. God forbid we should ever think of it in that way."

"Europe has its cathedrals, and we have Grand Central Station," added Philip Johnson.

Terminal, Virginia corrected him in her head. Terrence would be very upset. Still, the sentiment was lovely.

Just outside the doorway, she spotted Dennis standing close to another man. They both wore dark suits and carried briefcases—a fellow lawyer, probably—out spying on the opposition.

As the press conference wrapped up, the mayor hightailed it out and the reporters surged after him, sweeping Virginia along. She found an eddy of calm in the passageway just outside the Oyster Bar and waited there, fishing in her pocketbook for a tissue, biding time until the crowds thinned.

"Ignore it, Jack, they're posturing. The story will die down in a week."

Dennis was right behind her. She twirled around, a fake smile plastered on her face, but he was nowhere to be seen.

Through the crush of the press corps, she spied Dennis and his buddy huddled forty feet away in the opposite corner, speaking quietly.

Of course. They were in the Whispering Gallery, where sound was telegraphed up and over the surface of the vault.

She turned her head to locate the sweet spot, where she could hear the voices clearly while still keeping an eye on the two men.

"We sure don't need this aggravation, though," continued Dennis. "You sure we're all set?"

"The judge will listen to numbers, not rabble rousers. The numbers are in our favor." The man took a yellow file from the side pocket of his briefcase. "Here's the original balance sheet for Penn Central. The revised one, which will include the railway operating costs, should be ready in a few days."

"Let's hope that does the trick."

"We prove economic hardship, the judge will understand what a millstone this place is around Penn Central's neck. Trust me, by adding in those expenses, Grand Central looks like a sinking ship." He put one hand up to shield his mouth from any observers, which only served to increase the clarity. "Creative accounting at its best. By my revised calculations, Penn Central lost two million just this year."

Dennis tucked the yellow folder into his briefcase. "Good work. Landmark, my ass."

They disappeared up the ramp, clapping each other on the back. Virginia waited a few minutes before following.

In the middle of the concourse, her information booth shone like an opal in a coal mine. Imagine if they fixed up the entire place, rubbed clean every marble surface like she had done? It would be magnificent. Like when it was first built, before hordes of people had spat on the stairways and scratched up the waiting room benches. Back when it was still a gleaming work of art.

She imagined a giant wrecking ball flying through the half-moon windows on the south facade. The shattered glass falling to the ground. The next blow would take out the thick stone slabs that had been painstakingly stacked on top of one another just after the turn of the century. The clock at the very top, where a statue of Mercury presided over Park Avenue South—would that be saved? Probably not. Nor the melon-shaped chandeliers. All smashed to pieces. The next building would stand upon the powdered remnants, as Dennis had cavalierly declared, the way the ancients built a new city on the landfill of the old. In a few hundred years, archeologists might come upon the golden acorn on the top of the information booth. They'd place it in a museum and mourn the past.

She'd lost the opportunity to give Clara Darden the recognition she deserved. But the terminal was still standing.

And maybe, unlike with the Clyde painting, Virginia could do something to save it.

CHAPTER NINETEEN

October 1930

Take a load off; with this rain, no one's coming in anytime soon."
Clara nodded to her boss—a former anarchist with the heart of a dove named Romany Marie—untied her apron, and settled into a booth at the back of the empty restaurant. A week after she'd moved into the fleabag hotel, Romany Marie had seen the desperation in Clara's eyes as she sat at a table and offered her a waitress position.

The restaurant had once been the artistic heart of the Village, but these days few folks came by. Those who did knew that Romany Marie would let them gorge themselves on free rolls and all the coffee they could drink. She clanked around the small restaurant with her jangly necklaces and full skirts and confided to Clara that she came from Red Hook, not Romania. But she lent the place an air of mystique that other diners lacked.

After an unseasonably warm couple of days that made winter seem far away, the temperature was supposed to plummet that evening. These days, cold weather was a threat, not a nuisance. The radiator in Clara's hotel room clanged constantly but emitted no heat, and a cold spell meant it would be impossible to paint, even if she wore fingerless gloves. Her waitressing shifts left her too exhausted to paint, anyway. Really, there was no point.

Closed galleries, slashed museum budgets. No one in their right mind would waste money buying a painting these days. Artists were at the bottom of the food chain. They had nothing of value to offer; they didn't bake bread or knit scarves. They put liquid on paper and watched it dry. That was it.

But guardian angels were out there, if you looked hard enough. Like Romany Marie, who frequently ushered pale, trembling artists into her back office—men who had been heralded twelve months earlier—and bought a work or two off them.

The reverberations from her father's fall from grace had stayed with Clara throughout the heady days of success, prompting her to sock away everything she could, but nothing could have prepared her for the futility of the times. The highest-paid woman artist in America. What a joke.

She looked up to see a blurry figure at the door. A man swept in as if on a tidal wave.

Levon.

She ran to the kitchen, told Romany Marie she wasn't feeling well, and hid behind a column where Levon couldn't see her, peeking out to watch their exchange.

He wore the finely cut jacket that had replaced his ratty wool one soon after he began to sell, and raindrops tipped off a sleek black fedora. In his stylish ensemble, she could have sketched him into one of her editorial illustrations back in the day, accompanied by a woman holding the leash of a slick greyhound.

She didn't want him to see her like this. Sallow. Skinnier than ever.

Miserable.

Romany Marie breezed by and shot her a quizzical look. "You go take care of him now. He asked for you."

Clara inched over like a child about to be punished. He looked up and bellowed, "Clara," before wrapping his arms around her and lifting her off her feet.

"Nothing's changed, I see." She pulled away and wiped the rain off her sleeves. "You're a beast still."

"I am a beast. But a hungry one."

Up close, she could see his cheeks were gaunt, his old ruddiness now a pallor. No doubt a stick figure lurked beneath his beautifully cut suit. His fine clothes had distracted her from the truth.

And here she was hiding from him. "What can I get you? Did you give your order already?"

"Just some hot water is fine."

She knew what he meant. The other artists did the same: Order hot water, then add to it whatever was on the table—ketchup, salt, pepper—to make a thin soup.

"No. You need something more substantial."

"Really, hot water will do. I don't have anything." The last sentence came out in a whisper.

She retreated into the kitchen and pulled a big chunk of cheddar out of the icebox and a roll from the basket. "For a dear friend," she said to Romany Marie. "You can take it out of my pay."

Romany Marie shrugged her off.

Clara sat down with two cups of coffee and pushed one over to him. "It'll warm you up." He took a few sips before picking up the cheese. The whole time, his left hand stayed in his lap.

"What's wrong?" She indicated his arm.

"Lead poisoning. Damn pencils."

A memory of Levon gripping a thick chunk of pencil lead in his fist popped into her head, the pad of his hand as gray as an angry ocean. He'd light a cigarette and take a smoke break without washing it off, practically ingesting the poison. For a fastidious man, such carelessness.

"I'm sorry. How are you doing? What do you do now?"

"No shows, of course. I teach some private lessons, mainly society ladies who feel sorry for me. I can't paint again until the numbness goes away."

"When does your doctor think that'll happen?"

"Soon, I hope." He lowered his voice. "I am sorry about what I did. In Maine. That Oliver left you because of my silliness."

His silliness, and her own stupidity. She'd been greedy, wanting both Levon and Oliver to herself. Her arrogance had rivaled Levon's, and in the end he'd found her disappointing. Which served her right. Even in the darkness, she'd caught the look of distaste on his face after they'd pulled away from each other.

How long ago it seemed. "Don't be sorry. Oliver didn't even give me a chance to explain. I hear he's out in California, now, with that actress girl."

"I ruined it for you, and you miss him, I can tell." Levon wiped his mustache.

"Not that, exactly. But it's hard." Hard to be alone. Hard without anyone else to share the burden of not knowing what was to come.

"What do you do?" Levon asked. "Besides this." He gestured around the empty restaurant. "Do you paint?"

She shivered involuntarily. "No. It's too cold in my room."

"Even Fifth Avenue landlords are being stingy?"

"I'm not living there anymore. I had to move out."

"Where, then?"

"The Hotel 17."

He took her hand. "You're freezing, even here. Come with me. We must warm you up."

After checking in with Romany Marie, she left with Levon. His studio was exactly as she remembered it, immaculate and ordered, except for a bowl of fruit rotting on a table. A blackened banana had caved in on itself, and three apples were patchy with mold. Fruit flies fluttered about, and a sickly scent permeated the entire room.

"How can you stand it?" She held her nose while he picked up the bowl of fruit and dumped it out a window. "Are you in a memento mori phase these days? I can't blame you."

But when she saw the canvas on his easel, she regretted her flippant response. Levon had attempted to draw the fruit when fresh, but the lines were shaky, feeble. He'd abandoned the drawing halfway through and, knowing him, refused to throw out the fruit as a fetid punishment for his ineptitude.

Levon put some wood on the fire and sat Clara in the armchair in front of it, draping several blankets over her.

"Coffee?" He held up a familiar blue-and-gold can.

"You have Martinson's?"

"Of course. I don't skimp when it comes to my coffee. Only the best. I have to keep up appearances."

"You do a good job of it. I was sure you were a wealthy man when you walked into the restaurant. How do you manage?"

"My private classes. My society ladies treat me like a pet. They bring me cans of coffee and their husbands' old hats, bestow gifts on me for my services."

"Your services?"

"An introduction to the world of beauty. They are my patrons, and I grovel accordingly."

She studied him as he made the coffee, tried to keep her tone light. "Why do I suspect the lessons involve a serious examination of anatomy?"

He shrugged but didn't answer her question.

"How thrilled the ladies must be to have a distinguished painter visit them in their parlors and provide attention that their distracted husbands cannot." She checked herself, her sarcasm unwarranted. "You've kept the studio, though. Must be worth it for that alone."

"True. My services are much appreciated."

She could have sworn that was a smirk on his face.

Clara pushed off the suffocating blankets. "Lucky you, remaining solvent by being able to charm old ladies." She hit the word *charm* hard.

He leaned against the table, waiting for his fancy coffee to brew. "You're angry with me for that?"

"Only because I don't have the chance. If the situation were reversed, and I was asked by the idle, rich men of New York to tutor them in the 'painterly arts,' I could never boast of it. I would be considered a disgrace, a prostitute, whoring myself out. Yet you get to indulge in the same behavior and strut about like a rooster with no repercussions."

A look of shock crossed his face at her crassness. "These women, they are sad. They are devastated and unsure. Just like you."

"Does that mean you're going to mess about with me, too?" She glared at him. "Don't even think about it."

Levon poured the coffee into two chipped, mismatched cups, set them on the small table beside her, and knelt down.

"Don't be angry, Clara."

Her anger came from all sides, from Mr. Bianchi's words, which still smarted, from Oliver leaving her to flounder, from the fact that she had had so much and squandered it all.

He took her hands in his. "You must live here, with me, from now on. I'll keep you warm."

She'd done everything she could to push him away. Her eyes burned with tears. "I have nothing to offer you."

"I have nothing either. But I've already lived through this kind of hunger, day in and day out. We sucked on stones, we ate grass, anything to fill that void, even if nothing would come of it. But there are other ways to fill the void. With painting, with art. I'll show you."

"How to suck on stones?"

"No, no. You don't understand."

"I do, Levon." Her tone softened. "I do understand." She studied the artworks against the side wall, where he stored his best. "Where's the painting of your mother?"

"It's in the bedroom, turned to the wall. I can't bear to look at it if I can't work on it."

He looked like he was about to cry, his eyes big and round, like the boy's in the portrait with his mother.

Clara's petty resentments subsided. "I shouldn't judge you on your students, your arrangements." She kicked off one shoe and rubbed the arch of her foot, wondering what to say next. She'd never been at a loss for words with him before, and their friendship would never be the same if she didn't address what happened in Maine. Best to get straight to the point. "The night on the beach, I'm sorry about that."

"About what?"

"Disappointing you."

"Yes, I was disappointed." His forcefulness made her heart sink. "With myself, for having stepped over the lines of friendship. I couldn't help myself, though, and I don't regret it. Well, yes. I regret not chasing after you, telling you to stay with me, not Oliver."

They sat in silence for several moments. She could hear her heart beating.

"I'd like to paint you, Levon."

He stared hard at her, a challenge, but she knew he'd give in.

He rose and gestured to the art supplies on the worktable. "Help yourself. Might as well get some use out of them. Where do you want me?"

"Sit on the model's stand. With your arms on your knees." He did so. The white of his shirt accentuated his darkness: olive skin, black hair falling over his forehead, the thick mustache above his lips. He gazed across the room at the rain falling outside, lost in a reverie as she worked. Satisfied with the sketch, she squeezed lines of paint onto the palate, mixed and remixed them, before dipping her brush and applying paint to canvas. She worked fast, knowing that he wouldn't sit for her again. This was her one chance.

Later, as the paint dried, they made love on the pile of blankets in front of the fire, a chaotic feast of long limbs, bony elbows, and hunger.

The next couple of months flew by. The painting Clara had made of Levon that first evening was stored in the tiny bedroom, as neither of them wanted any of their friends to see it. It was too personal, a window into their shared pain and pleasure. They satisfied their desires as often as they could as the weather grew cold, as if the friction of their bodies might stave off the harsh winter ahead.

Whenever Romany Marie had leftover food, she'd give it to Clara to take home, and she and Levon invited all the artists they knew over for dinner. Clara provided the household with food and cash, while Levon offered shelter and paint supplies. She harangued him when he insisted on the best: Lefebvre paints and Winsor & Newton brushes. At least once a week he came home with an art book tucked under his arm, an extravagance they could not afford, including a rare edition on Brueghel, which she threatened to toss out the window but surreptitiously curled up with in front of the fire whenever she knew he'd be out for the afternoon.

The only other fights were over his meticulous management of his art supplies. She was used to the chaotic splatter of watercolors, of the mess of paint on her work clothes. He put up with that, flinching whenever a drop of paint fell on the floor, but insisted she place each brush back in the correct pottery vase along the windowsill when finished, arranged by size, the bristles clean and dry.

When he was called for a lesson uptown, they didn't speak of it. He wandered off, and she didn't question him when he returned looking rumpled and abashed.

Sometimes, he had to give a lesson in the studio, and she'd return to find her painting of him turned to the wall, the covers of their bed pulled up tight, even though they never bothered to make it otherwise. Or she'd come home to him with his shirt off, violently scrubbing the studio floor, the easels and chairs and tables pushed to one side, as if he was trying to erase all signs that another woman even walked upon the parquet. A small price to pay, she told herself.

She continued painting, Levon strolling behind her every so often with encouragement or a suggestion, miming with his hand the correct brushstroke to use. Some days it was as if she were channeling him, channeling their energy together. She painted whenever she could, making up for his own lost time in a way, never knowing how long their luck would last. How long they'd be able to hold out here without the landlord raising the rent and sending them packing. Her work was more dreamlike than anything she'd done before, save *The Siren*. She was determined to push herself as far from illustration, from realism, as she could go.

On Christmas Eve, they invited several friends over. The celebration would be lackluster compared to years past, the china mismatched and the linens frayed, but at least it was something. A sense of humility permeated the discussions these days, as the economic devastation had leveled the field. Salacious topics—artist affairs, gallery scandals—were replaced with more elevated discussions on politics and art. Levon no longer spoke over everyone else with his commandments and pronouncements. Nor did anyone else, for that matter.

Romany Marie had offered two roasted ducks for their Christmas Eve celebration. Levon balanced them in his arms while Clara fiddled with the lock to the studio.

"Hurry up, woman."

"I am. It's not working. No, it's unlocked." She pushed open the door. "You've got to remember to lock it; what if someone came up here and stole everything?"

"Like what?"

"Your fancy art books. To burn in a fire to keep warm. You'd be upset."

"Now, now, children."

Felix stood on the far side of the room. He shrugged. "It was unlocked."

"You're an hour early." Clara walked over to give him a kiss.

"You both seem well."

"As well as we can be." Levon set down the ducks before pouring them all a drink from the bottle of wine he'd received from one of his Park Avenue students. "Any good news on the horizon?"

Felix wandered about the room, his eyes darting from canvas to canvas. Clara had planned on hiding the paintings away before anyone arrived. "The government is considering financing a program where artists get paid to work. To paint murals for new buildings, build sculpture for public spaces, that kind of thing."

"How much would they pay?" she asked, trying to divert his attention.

"Who knows? It's a long way off. Artists are low on the list of people to be propped up these days."

She put the drink in Felix's hand. "Here, come sit by the fire."

He dropped heavily into the chair and raised his glass. "I have good news for you, Levon."

"What's that?"

"I'm glad I came early, before you cleared the room. They're glorious. I can find a buyer for these. Even in this market, this is phenomenal. The Museum of Modern Art will want to see them. You've made great strides."

Clara froze.

Levon took a sip of his wine and responded coolly. "Do you think so?"

"Absolutely."

"What do you like about them? Why do you like them?"

"How do I sum it up? They're glorious, free, and yet they show so much pain. It hurts to look at them, but I couldn't stop. I can't stop." He leaned forward. "Your arm must be much improved. Thank God for that."

"They're not mine. They're Clara's."

"No." Felix blinked. He looked at Clara, then back to Levon. "Yes?"

"They're all hers. I can't paint yet. Soon, but not yet." He held up his bad arm, letting it tremble.

Felix sat back in his chair, contemplating the news. "That's a shame."

"What's a shame?" Clara wiped off her hands on a dishrag and joined them, leaning against the mantel above the fire. "You say they're good. They can be sold."

"Not until the Depression's over. Your timing is off. Heck, even if you were a man, the fact that you're known for drawing clothes and cars makes it an unlikely leap."

Levon stood. "It's the art that matters, not the person who made it." Clara held out her hand to calm him down, but he shook her off. "We've been talking for months now about the purity of art. How this Depression has rid us of our commercial obsessions. Her work is as pure as it gets."

"I agree, it's not fair. But in this climate, no gallery would take a chance on a woman illustrator these days." Felix turned a skeptical eye on Clara. "Even if she were as good as Picasso."

CHAPTER TWENTY

December 1930

The party dragged on well into the next morning. No one had anywhere else to go or anything else to do. Christmas was sure to be dismal compared to holidays past, so what was the point of rushing home? Levon drank more than usual and jumped up several times to perform Armenian dances. To the cheers of their guests, he lumbered about the room caterwauling at the top of his lungs, crashing into the table and sending glassware flying.

Clara didn't bother to hide her petulance from her place in the corner, where she sat on a pillow on the floor. Every so often, Levon looked at her with his big brown eyes, lips in a pout, trying to rouse her spirits. But she refused to engage. Not that anyone else noticed. Their guests were drinking heavily, the more successful artists in chairs, with various girlfriends and former students sprawled about on the floor around them. Again, the men in thrones simply because they were men. They had access to the best galleries and patrons, and because of that, they became better known, and because of that, they were rewarded with success.

It wasn't fair.

And not exactly true. Other women had done well. Georgia O'Keeffe, of course, and Mary Cassatt. Even Clara had experienced a blazing, if temporary, success.

One of the artists had brought his small dog along, a stocky terrier who curled up on Clara's lap. She ran a hand down his spine. The dog looked up at her with soft eyes, then he was out again, snoring softly.

He wore a thin leather collar, flaked with age. No tag. She wondered what he was called. When the crowd began to dissipate, she lifted him off her lap and placed him in the warm chair where Levon had been.

That odd dog in Maine, Clyde, came to mind.

Clyde.

The name she'd used for *The Siren*, after Oliver's peevish criticism.

Buzzing with excitement, Clara herded out the last of the stragglers, holding Felix back with another pour of wine. His face was flushed—even better, to break through his defenses. Convince him.

"We can show the work. My work." She stood, her feet slightly apart, in the middle of the studio. Levon cleared up a broken glass beside the sink, and Felix slumped at the table, hat in one hand and wine in the other.

"How is that, my dear?" Felix exchanged a tired glance with Levon.

"You say that it's by an unknown painter, one you've just discovered. Named Clyde. I sign all the paintings with that. You explain that the painter wishes to stay unknown."

"Unknown? Why on earth?" Levon laughed at her. Of course, he couldn't imagine staying anonymous. His big presence was part of his art. But hers was not.

"Why not? You said they're good. Everyone will assume they're by a man. They can be judged on what they are, not who I am. Or am not."

Felix shook his head. "It's not a parlor trick, exhibiting paintings."

"Maybe it should be."

Levon dropped the shards of glass into the trash. They tinkled like wind chimes. "Why not? What do you have to lose, Felix?"

Felix set down his glass. "Do you have any idea how much money it takes to put on a show? You artists, you all think it's a matter of hanging paintings on a wall and waiting for the crowds to come." He counted off on his fingers. "I must find a suitable space, arrange to have all the paintings framed, solicit potential buyers in a discreet yet unyielding manner. There's a kind of magic required. An expensive magic. I can't take that chance if I can't guarantee sales."

She stood her ground. "We know you can do it. You're the best, Felix, and you love the work. Shouldn't it come down to that? The work will sell. You'll be hailed as the man of the hour."

"Stop flattering me."

"If it's about the economics, I can help." Levon stepped closer. Together, the two of them were circling in on Felix. "I'll pay for the framing."

"How? How will you do that?" Clara asked, dreading the answer.

"I'll take up more private lessons."

"No. You don't have to do that."

Felix took off his glasses and cleaned them with the edge of a napkin. "If you can pay for the framing, we might be able to pull it off."

"We'll do it, don't worry," Levon insisted.

"I'm not promising anything." Felix stood and pulled his coat off the coatrack by the door. "And I'm drunk. So don't count on it, either of you. Stop ganging up on me."

Clara gave him a kiss before he headed out into the early morning. "Thank you, Felix."

"Clyde? Insane. Both of you. All three of you."

And he was gone.

—⁂—

"Where are you going now? And what's in the satchel?"

Clara didn't mean to sound like a harpy, but she'd been painting for two months straight, ever since they'd hatched the Clyde show idea, and had serious cabin fever. Felix had arranged for an exhibit to take place next month, early April, when he hoped the change of weather from winter to spring would encourage art lovers to open their wallets.

She'd let Levon and Felix handle all the details. Clara didn't care where, or when, the show would happen, because the pressure to create enough paintings to fill the room was enough to deal with. Some days she didn't venture outside at all.

Levon gave her a quick kiss. "I'm heading uptown. Do you need anything? More supplies?" The man was adept at changing the subject when it came to his mysterious errands.

But she knew what he was up to. Raising money from his Park Avenue ladies to help get the exhibit mounted, to get enough cash to pay for frames. Earlier that morning, she'd spied a note on the dresser signed *Nadine*, which had turned her stomach. Sharing him with anonymous old biddies was one thing, but a mutual acquaintance, especially that wretched girl, was quite another. Not that Clara had said anything, knowing she should shut up and be grateful for his efforts on her behalf. He'd even begun filching from his own bookcase when he thought Clara wasn't looking. The strap of the satchel strained against his shoulder.

"Please stop selling your art books," she implored, not for the first time. The books were like his children, each one precious. "You don't have to do that. We'll find another way."

He patted the side of the bag. "Never you mind. Besides, once the show's a great success, I'll buy them all back, first thing."

Any talk of the show made her squirm with irritation. "When you return, I want you to paint as well," she said.

Levon's doctor had declared his symptoms much improved on his last visit. Yet he'd resisted Clara's entreaties to pick up a brush. The more he resisted, the more she pushed him. Partly to offset her own nerves, and also because she feared the longer he put it off, the harder it would be to find his footing.

"Stop with that, woman." Levon waved her away. "Concentrate on your own work."

"But what about you?"

"I'm fine."

"Then paint with me."

He let the satchel fall hard to the floor. "You want to see me paint?" He was beside her in a flash and snatched the brush from her hand with his left hand. "I tried it the other morning, when you were still asleep."

He held the brush clumsily in his dominant hand. It fell to the floor after only a few seconds.

Such histrionics. "You didn't even try. You have two hands. Paint with your other one."

They'd been going at each other for the past couple of weeks, as the pressure ratcheted up. She shouldn't pick fights, should let him go about his business, but she was desperate for something else to focus on. Something that would take her out of the terrible images she was painting day in and day out. Of the world turned upside down, where no one cared about the child crying alone on the street or the man with one leg shivering in the cold. The works were expressionistic, imprecise, as far away from her earlier work as an illustrator as possible. She imagined the art crowd stunned into repulsion by the sight of them, ridiculing one after another.

"I will not paint with my left hand unless you paint with your toes. Leave me alone." Levon stormed off.

She let him go. Levon would paint again. Once the show was over, she'd have time to cajole instead of shame him into trying once more. Right now, her work crowded out everything else. It was loud and forceful and took up all the air in the room.

⁓✲☙

The day of the show, Levon and Felix spent the afternoon at the gallery, putting on the finishing touches, making sure everything was set. Clara had done a quick walk-through the day before, but Felix asked that she stay as far from the place as possible, to avoid giving anything away. He'd insisted they not hang the painting of Levon she'd done, to avoid adding fuel to the speculative fire. Which was fine with her. During her short visit, Felix pulled Levon and Clara into a back room to reveal good news: A third of the paintings had already sold.

The pride on Felix's face, and the joy on Levon's, made the past several months of agony well worth it.

Felix's approach had worked beautifully. He'd shown the paintings to a select group of still-wealthy collectors and the city's art critics that morning, and the mystery around the identity of "Clyde" had upped the ante.

The evening of the opening, Clara put on her peacock dress, her one fine frock, and headed uptown. A crowd surrounded the entrance to the gallery, and she slipped in unnoticed. She thought back to her first show, at the Grand Central Art Galleries, where her illustrations had been relegated to a back office. Not this time. She'd clawed her way to the top back then. Against all odds, she would be famous once more by the end of tonight.

She relished the idea as she wandered through the rooms, unremarked upon, invisible.

A young, new illustrator was now the hotsy-totsy *Vogue* cover artist. A man had supplanted her at Studebaker. Everyone could be replaced, but Clara refused to be forced down and out. Not by her father, by Mr. Lorette, nor by Oliver.

Oliver. If he hadn't destroyed *The Siren*, it would have been the highlight of the show. She'd tried to replicate it but couldn't and finally had given up. That painting had sprung from a particular place and time, of cool Maine sunrises and her rising awareness of her love for Levon.

Levon stood in the middle of the main room, surrounded as usual by admirers, men and women. A man nudged her on the elbow, and she turned to see Mr. Bianchi.

"Miss Darden, are you here to find out who this mystery artist is, like the rest of us?" He took out a handkerchief and wiped his shiny forehead. "They better do it soon or the place will explode from anticipation."

"I'm sure it'll be soon." She spied Felix in one corner, adjusting his tie and murmuring to the critic from *Art in America* magazine. "What do you think of the paintings?"

"They're exquisite. I'm kicking myself for having spent money on a painting just last week. If I hadn't bought that, I would pluck one of these right off. But times are tough."

Right. So tough he could only afford one painting, instead of two. She tamped down her anger. Not now. He'd learn the truth soon enough. "What painting did you buy?"

"A Zakarian. Felix turned me on to it. A private sale, and Felix said it's one of his best."

Levon hadn't mentioned any sale.

No. He couldn't have.

"Which Zakarian was it?" She knew the answer before Mr. Bianchi opened his mouth.

"One of a boy standing next to his mother. It's strange and kind of eerie, but Felix assured me it would go up in value in another ten years. That I just have to hold on to it."

She opened her mouth, but nothing came out. Levon had sold his best work so that her exhibit could go on. She looked around to find him, but he'd disappeared.

Mr. Bianchi continued. "I've stashed it in the carriage house on the estate for now. I don't want it in my apartment or my weekend house; it's not a happy painting, you know? I'll wait until the market recovers and it rises in value, before selling it to the highest bidder."

The thought of that painting sitting in a damp carriage house, abandoned and probably eventually forgotten, made her ill. How could Levon have done this?

She made her excuses and turned to go outside, to get some air, but it was too late. Felix was calling for everyone's attention. Levon stood a little apart from him, off to the side.

The time had come. She hoped she wouldn't be sick.

"I know everyone is here to learn the identity of my new discovery." Felix's eyes twinkled with mischief. "I have quite a secret and am very eager to share it with you."

The crowd was silent, almost worshipful. Clara hated them all.

Hated them for how easily led they were, not by artistic merit but by whatever was the latest craze. Clara was the next big thing, the fur coat on the cover of *Vogue*, the art deco door handle on a car. They would eat her up and spit her out again.

Felix held up both hands. "However, I can't tell you just yet." He waited until the crowd's groans and protestations died down. "We've been asked to do an exhibit in Chicago in two weeks. The works of Clyde are traveling across the country so that even more people will be able to see firsthand these astonishing and provocative paintings. Then, and only then, will we reveal the identity."

Somehow, Felix found his way to Clara through what was almost an angry mob. Levon caught up and pulled them into the back hall-way, closing the door behind him.

"What are you doing, Felix?" Levon demanded.

Felix patted them both on the shoulder. "This will widen our reach." He looked at Clara. "You'll not only be a New York sensa-tion but a national one. Trust me. Two weeks, and you'll be at the pinnacle of success. By stretching this out, we'll increase the value of the unsold works even more. We'll add in that one of Levon you did, sell out completely. You'll be rolling in it, have enough money to ride out this Depression in fine form."

"Why didn't you tell us about this?" Clara asked.

"I didn't want to raise your hopes before I knew for sure. They committed to us just now. We've done it, though." He was practi-cally levitating with excitement. "We've done it."

⚬

In the week and a half since the exhibit, Felix's predictions had come true. All of New York was talking about Clyde, and newspapers across the country had picked up on the story of the mystery artist, with experts weighing in on who the painter might be.

"Did you remember to pack your good suit?" Clara yelled out from inside the taxi, as Levon and the driver jammed their suitcases into the trunk of the cab.

Levon slid in beside her and pulled the door shut. "Of course I packed it." He paused, scratching his chin. "Or did I leave it hanging up on the bedroom door?"

"You left it. Since you'd already headed downstairs to catch a cab, I put it in my suitcase."

"You're a doll." He kissed her on the nose. "Grand Central, please."

The cab pulled out, the driver careening around the other cars as if they were in a race. She checked her watch. They had a good forty minutes before the train to Chicago—the 20th Century Limited—would pull out. Plenty of time. She couldn't help but tease. "I was tempted to toss it out the window to you. How could you forget your one good suit?"

"I have other things on my mind."

She couldn't tell if he was kidding her or not. Levon's name had been one of many bandied about in the press as a possibility. Better to address the situation now, rather than when they were trapped in a Pullman car with Felix. She shifted in the seat so she faced him. "A lot of people think you're Clyde, Levon. Do you wish you were the artist? Have I put you in a strange position?"

He chuckled. "I don't mind one whit. All the better to surprise them with the truth when the artist is revealed. To be honest, it's a relief not being the artist du jour for a change. I find I'm bursting with ideas these days. Once you're established, I'll be on my way."

"Once we have the money, we're paying for you to see the best doctor in town." She still regretted forcing him to pick up a paintbrush.

"I have a surprise for you. Look." He held out his left hand, palm down.

Even with the bumps of the taxi, she could see he had control of the limb, finally.

She yelped and hugged him to her. "No tremors! That's wonderful."

"Progress, my dear. When we return, we'll move to a bigger studio."

She shook her head. "You're probably sick of me by now. We could get two studios if you like." The city zoomed past; she looked out the window and watched it go by rather than check his reaction.

"One. I don't want to change anything." He threw his arm around her, and she curled into him, breathing in the scent of smoke and spice.

"We'll buy all your books back, and more." She paused. "And we'll get your painting back from Bianchi."

Levon went rigid with anger. She hadn't broached the subject yet, unwilling to break the charm of happiness between them, the glimmer of hope. "How do you know about that? Felix, running at the mouth again?"

"No. I saw Mr. Bianchi at the opening." She put one hand over his heart, unable to look up at him. "I know you did that to help me, and I also know how difficult it must have been. But I'll talk to Mr. Bianchi; he'll be happy to sell it back. We'll pay whatever we have to."

She took his silence for agreement and didn't press him further.

The cab lurched to a stop on Forty-Second Street, where a redcap took their bags and led them down the ramp to the main concourse. "Track 34, leaves six o'clock sharp." He pointed to the right. "Enter that way."

Levon gave Clara a sly smile. "Thanks, we know the station well." He tucked a tip into the porter's hand.

"I'm going to buy an *Evening Post* before we board," said Clara. "Do you want anything from the newsstand?"

"Not a thing. I'll march ahead and make sure Felix hasn't had any trouble with the crates."

"See you in a few."

The newsstand had an unusually long line for a Saturday. She paid for the magazine and turned to go.

"Clara."

Oliver hovered just outside the newsstand, his hands in his pockets. A rough stubble covered his cheeks.

"Oliver. What are you doing here?"

"I saw in the paper that Felix was on this train. I figured you'd be, too. Since you're Clyde."

She tried not to react.

"Clara, I'm here to apologize." Oliver's brightness and confidence had dropped away since they'd last seen each other, replaced with a weary heaviness that Clara knew all too well. "When I realized what you'd accomplished, how amazing this has been, I had to see you and say I was sorry. Can we talk?"

She looked at her watch. Ten minutes to six. "Only for a moment."

He guided her to the side of the doorway, out of the way of the foot traffic. "I knew the artist was you when I saw the paintings were by Clyde. The stubborn dog, up in Maine, right?" He scuffed one heel on the marble floor. "There I was telling you to quit, when it's what's made you famous."

"I'm not famous, not yet. How's your lovely bride?"

"Violet's still in Los Angeles. It didn't work out." His mouth started to twitch. "I miss you."

A memory of their last car ride together swept over her: the two of them skidding along a Maine dirt road, carefree on a windy summer day, Clara whooping for him to go faster. They'd shared an easy way of traversing through the world back then that had since been decimated.

Clara laughed harshly. "Really? Now, all of a sudden, you miss me?"

"I became too protective, like you were my creation, not a person in your own right. I shouldn't have done that. But I did help you, right? Early on?"

"You were very helpful, Oliver." He had been. As his ambitions had faltered, he'd tried to pull her closer to him, to tie her down. In return, she'd cut him open with that kiss on the beach. "I'm sorry for what happened in Maine."

"I acted like a fool."

"As did I. You were right to be jealous. I didn't understand myself what was going on between me and Levon. I was confused."

"I heard you're with Levon now."

"True." She didn't elaborate, not wanting to hurt him further.

He frowned. "You're too much alike. Do you think he's going to be able to take your fame? We both know he's full of himself. Always has been. Maybe for now it's working, but there's no way it'll continue without resentment."

She recoiled. "We're fine. You don't know the half of it. Don't forget that you're the one who destroyed my painting. Levon would never have done that. Ever."

"I walked down the beach to find you, to tell you I wanted to announce to everyone around the fire that we were engaged. I couldn't keep it a secret any longer. Only to come upon you kissing him."

"It wasn't like that. Not then." There was no point in explaining.

She began to walk away, but he grabbed her arm. "No, wait. I lied about the painting. The one you were working on in Maine. I never destroyed it."

The painting she'd mourned for the past year, watching it swirl by in her dreams, night after night. She shot him a hard look. "Where is it?"

"I hid it in the attic. I'll get it back; I want to make this up to you."

She had no idea if he was lying or telling the truth. Her watch read six minutes to the hour.

A strange look glinted in Oliver's eyes, one she'd never seen before. If she walked away, would he deliberately destroy it just to spite her?

Clara desperately wanted to have *The Siren* back. The artwork was the touchstone to everything she'd done since. She had two options: She could catch the train and never see her painting again. Or stay in New York, find out if Oliver was telling the truth, and possibly recover *The Siren*. If she took option number two, she could send a telegram to the Chicago train station, to be delivered to Levon and Felix upon their arrival, explaining everything and saying that she'd be arriving a day later. Of course, Levon would be fuming by then. Or crazy with worry.

She thought of Levon's lost painting, buried somewhere in Bianchi's carriage house. Levon had given that up, voluntarily, so she could have her chance.

And now she had to do the same. She'd give up *The Siren*.

"You can keep it. Do whatever you want with it. I don't care."

His face fell. "We were good together. I helped you; I helped you get to where you are now."

"Where I am now is late." She checked her watch. Five minutes. A man yelled out in the middle of the concourse, and Clara looked over in time to see a woman run into his arms in front of the information booth. As they kissed, her eyes traveled up to the large clock on top.

No. It couldn't be.

The clock read six o'clock on the nose. Which was when the 20th Century Limited to Chicago was due to depart.

Her watch read 5:55. Five minutes slow.

She took off, as fast as her Mary Janes allowed, sprinting across the marble floor and through the entryway to track 34. The train was still there; it hadn't left yet. But she tripped on the edge of the crimson carpet that lined the platform and lost time recovering her balance.

Imperceptibly at first, so that she wasn't sure if she could trust her eyes, the train began to move. She screamed for it to wait, but the roar of the engine muffled her cries.

She stared after it, tears in her eyes, watching as everything she loved disappeared into the black tunnel.

CHAPTER TWENTY-ONE

February 1975

G ot a big date?"

Doris swiveled around in her chair in the information booth and eyed Virginia up and down. Virginia tugged on her skirt, which was short and tight and had been riding up all day, and slid her clerk's blazer back on.

"I must've gained some weight," Virginia said with a laugh. She'd last worn this outfit to an anniversary dinner with Chester, hoping to light his fire, leaning over to apply makeup in the mirror by their front door so he could get a glimpse of the stockings she'd worn underneath. Real stockings, with a garter belt and all. It'd worked that night, at least temporarily, and she hoped it would do the same later today.

But the booth had gotten intolerably warm, stuffy with the heat in the tight space, and she'd draped her blazer over the back of the chair where she sat sorting timetables. Of course, Doris couldn't let it pass.

If they only knew she'd dressed this way in a valiant attempt to save their jobs, they might show a little more respect. She remembered Jackie, impeccably dressed, moving with such grace through the throng of admirers. This wasn't quite that—Virginia looked positively trashy—but she was performing her civic duty.

Virginia checked her watch. Time to go.

"I'm out of here. See you all tomorrow."

She hung her blazer on the back of her chair, grabbed her coat and handbag, and trotted across the concourse, taking care that her high heels didn't slip out from under her on the slick marble. A homeless man sitting on the floor beside the entrance to track 23 called out to her, holding up his palm, and she gave him a couple of quarters. She'd started carrying spare change to hand out to the men and women who made the building their home. It seemed the least she could do. Ever since her apartment fire, Virginia had seen the homeless in a new light, as folks like her who unexpectedly got tossed out on the streets. Thank goodness for Finn and Xavier's kindness.

The elevator opened on the seventh floor, and she headed straight for the law offices of Penn Central. The receptionist was on her way out, but she called Dennis's extension and gave him Virginia's name. After a few minutes, Virginia heard his heavy footsteps coming down the hall. Deep breath.

"Virginia?"

He peered at her over a pair of reading glasses. The fragility of the metal frames and glass were all wrong for his large features but gave him an air of vulnerability. That and the fact that he looked like he was about to be attacked. She could almost see his mind whirling, wondering if this was a trap, if that was indeed Virginia who'd called on Thanksgiving and spoken to his wife, and if so, why was she here?

The receptionist left, shutting the door behind her.

"Hi, Dennis. You look well."

He swallowed. "You, too, Virginia."

"I figured it'd been way too long and I should stop by and say hello." She shifted her weight onto one hip in what she hoped looked like an invitation.

"Is that right?"

"I missed you."

His shoulders dropped an inch or two. "Right. I'm sorry. I've been swamped with the court case."

"I heard the city's fighting back and figured you might need a little distraction." She walked closer and offered up a winsome smile. "What do you think?"

"You want to go to the art school? Now?"

She pretended to think it over. "No, it's too dusty there. But it's been a long day and I really need to relax. Let's go to your office and maybe we can figure something out."

"My office?"

"Sure. Why not? You have a door, right?" She lowered her voice. "I'll be very quiet."

And that was that. He took her gently by the arm, and they walked back down to his office. She wandered over to the desk while he shut and locked the door. Placing both hands on the desktop, she leaned over and scanned the files and papers on top while giving him a nice view of her backside.

"Wow. You look amazing. I wasn't sure . . ." He trailed off, distracted.

"Do you have something to drink here?"

He walked over and opened a drawer in his desk, took out a bottle of whiskey and two glasses, and poured a couple of fingers. She took hers and sashayed over to the couch, where a stack of redweld folders were piled up. Dennis stumbled over and began to set them on the floor.

She helped, flashing an inch of skin above her stocking, while eyeing the folders inside the redwelds. PENN CENTRAL TRANSPORTATION COMPANY V. CITY OF NEW YORK: APPEALS, LANDMARK STATUS, MEMORANDA, CORRESPONDENCE. All manila files, not the yellow one he'd patted that day in the Whispering Gallery, which showed the terminal's actual expenses. Not what she was looking for.

She kissed him, drawing him in, leaning back and letting his weight settle on her. He tried to touch her breasts, but she pushed his hand away, told him to unbuckle his pants, ordering him about until they were going at it. Virginia had rarely been the initiator when it came to sex. It just wasn't what girls of her era were supposed to do. But being the one in power exhilarated her. The arm of the sofa crimped her neck, but she didn't care; the pain and the pleasure were all wrapped up together.

When they finished, she shifted closer to the edge of the couch so he could lie down next to her.

They both were panting, and he laughed. "This was amazing. You're amazing."

"Shh. That's enough talking. Close your eyes and relax." She ran a finger up and down his forearm until he had drifted off and the snores were regular and loud.

She slid off the couch to the floor, in a way that brought to mind the Salvador Dalí painting of the clock. Once there, she scanned the folders, one after another, keeping her back to Dennis in case he woke up. She probably had ten minutes, if his past slumber was any indication.

No yellow folder. She tried his briefcase, but it wasn't in the outside pocket or any of the interior ones.

She crawled over to the desk, staying low. The drawer where he'd stored the liquor held more files, including a lone yellow one marked PRIVATE AND CONFIDENTIAL: ORIGINAL TERMINAL BALANCE SHEET.

Bingo. Mata Hari had nothing on her.

"What are you doing?" Dennis sat up on the couch, rubbing his face.

Virginia dropped the file to the floor and lifted out the whiskey bottle. "Looking to see if you had any other booze. Whiskey isn't really my drink."

As he got to his feet, she did the same, sliding the file out of his field of vision with her foot.

"What would you like instead?" he asked.

"How about some water? You really wore me out there."

It worked. Dennis strutted out of his office like a rooster, off to the water cooler, and while he was gone, she tucked the file into her purse.

- - -

A few days later, Virginia found herself seated across from Adelaide in the sunny Midtown offices of the Municipal Art Society.

"We're thrilled to have more volunteers." Adelaide picked up a pen. "What kind of work would you like to do for us? We have several options, including helping stuff envelopes for our mailings, inputting data, or assisting with outreach."

"Whatever I can do to help save Grand Central. All three, if necessary."

"You're enthusiastic. I'm not surprised, after seeing your daughter's remarkable photos."

"She really captured it. Since I work there, I see firsthand the beauty of the place."

"I wish there were more people like you in this city, ready to step up."

"I was at the press conference. It sure feels like there's a groundswell of support."

"We can only hope the appellate judge in the case takes that into account." Adelaide checked her calendar. "Can you start on Saturday? We're planning to hold a couple of demonstrations outside the terminal over the new few months, and it'll be a brainstorming meeting."

"You bet."

Out in the reception area, they shook hands. "Oh no, I forgot my umbrella." Virginia held up one hand. "I'll grab it and be right back."

She popped back into Adelaide's office, pulled out a large, unmarked envelope from her purse, and laid it on Adelaide's chair, where she couldn't miss it. Sealed inside was the yellow manila folder, proof of Penn Central's creative accounting. She could only hope that Adelaide understood the significance of the figures.

Virginia plucked her umbrella from the floor and left, closing the door softly behind her.

The first of March came in like a lamb, the sky a bright winter blue. Slightly buzzed after sharing a farewell mimosa with Xavier and Finn at Bemelmans, Virginia considered what to do next, the whole Saturday wide open in front of her. Ruby had served them, proud of her skill behind the bar, and they'd all hugged and kissed good-bye. Xavier and Finn were off to Europe and their next adventure, and Virginia was sorry to see them go. Even though Finn was due back in the summer for another long gig at the Carlyle, she'd miss her daily dose of her brother's silly wit and quiet strength.

After that dismal meeting in the Oyster Bar, Chester had surprised Virginia by writing to her upstairs neighbors on his firm letterhead requesting any and all receipts relating to the fire damage. In response, they'd dropped their demands considerably, and Virginia and Ruby had moved back into their apartment a couple of weeks ago. Virginia relished every nook and cranny, happy to have a home again, except the blank space on the living room wall, where she'd hoped to hang the watercolor.

"Hey, Virginia."

Virginia turned to see Ryan standing beside her on the sidewalk. He squinted in the bright morning light. "That scarf looks grand on you."

She pulled it closer around her neck, surprised by the compliment. "Thanks."

"What way are you going?"

She pointed south. "I thought I'd stop by the Museum of Modern Art."

"If you don't mind, I'll walk with you for a bit."

They fell into step through the early-morning crowds, mainly older folks wandering down Madison. A bike zinged past her on the sidewalk, and Ryan took her by the elbow and pulled her a little closer to him. "Careful, there."

"Thanks."

"I'm glad we have some time like this. I'd been hoping to talk with you." He shoved his hands into his coat pockets.

She frowned, thinking of Ruby, who was relying on the bar income to pay for her photography classes. "Is something wrong?"

"No, not at all."

But something was off. She couldn't tell what. Ryan buzzed with a nervous energy and had a spring to his step that she hadn't seen before.

"How's Ruby doing?" she asked.

"Great. Really good."

"I wish her father would give her a break. Chester seems to think that she's slumming it by working in a bar." She turned to Ryan. "I don't think that, of course. I'm thrilled she's working and happy."

"I understand his concern. I come from a proud line of publicans, so to me it's about carrying on a tradition. America needs more gathering places, like pubs. It offers a sense of community that otherwise we don't have, wandering about in our own little worlds, disappearing into our flats at night."

"I like that. A very refreshing take. My father would've certainly agreed."

"Of course, there's always a group of drunks getting plastered in one corner."

"As long as they pay."

Ryan laughed. "That's right. As long as they pay."

They wandered along, chatting about the neighborhood and what the city had been like when Virginia was young.

She pointed up at the skyscrapers of Rockefeller Center as they turned west. Her volunteer work at the Municipal Art Society had given her a new appreciation of the city's skyline. "Those were built during the worst years of the Depression and put forty thousand people to work. They hired out-of-work artists to decorate the lobbies. Imagine all those families who had enough to eat because of this?"

"A first-class piece of architecture," agreed Ryan.

"What do you think about this fight for Grand Central?"

He shrugged. "I haven't thought much about it, to be honest."

Time for the soapbox. "Grand Central has to be saved. It's an important part of old New York. I'm involved with the Municipal Art Society to do whatever I can to help."

"What are you doing for them?"

Probably best not to mention that she'd slept with the enemy in order to steal financial documents. Adelaide had never asked about the envelope Virginia left behind after her interview. Maybe she knew it was smart to be circumspect, or perhaps Virginia had overestimated the documents' importance. In any event, the subject had never come up. "I'm handing out flyers, mailing out press releases. Jackie O's involved as well, you know."

"Jackie, right. You two good friends?"

She batted at his arm. "You're teasing me."

"I like the way you light up when you talk about this. It's good to have a passion."

"True."

When they reached the Museum of Modern Art, Virginia stopped. "Here's my destination. Where did you say you were going?"

"I didn't, exactly." He shoved his hands into his pockets. "What are you seeing?"

"The Georgia O'Keeffe exhibit." She paused. He seemed a little lost, like he needed company. "Do you want to come in?"

"I don't want to intrude."

"Not at all."

Ryan followed after her, insisting on paying for her ticket. The woman behind the counter flirted with him, but he didn't flirt back. He was a very good-looking man, Virginia noticed. His hair was white but thick and wavy, and his face was still unlined.

Inside the exhibit hall, Ryan stood frozen in front of one of the paintings, an enormous jack-in-the-pulpit flower. "Oh my." He swallowed. "It's very . . ."

"No. It's not." Virginia tried not to blush, and laughed when she couldn't stop.

"How can you say it's not?"

She parroted the review she'd read in the newspaper earlier that week. "O'Keeffe dismissed the sexual interpretations of her paintings. She saw all these enormous buildings going up in New York and decided to paint her flowers as big as well. It got people's attention, startled them."

"So you're saying that Rockefeller Center inspired this?"

"I bet it did."

Virginia continued her lecture, unable to stop herself even though she sounded like one of the speakers from her preservation committee days. "O'Keeffe rejected the notion that she was a 'woman' artist. After all, no one calls Rembrandt a 'man' artist."

"That is a very good point."

They made their way through the exhibit chronologically, pointing out the works they loved. Virginia adored a set of mannequins wearing clothes that O'Keeffe had sewn herself: loosely draped wrap dresses, paper-thin white linen shirts, and austere wool suits. Comfortable and elegant.

They reached the end of the exhibit, where a few old books were splayed open in a glass case.

"Virginia, I did want to ask you something today."

Was he going to ask her on a date? Was that what this was? She still hadn't been able to determine how old he was. The white hair made it difficult to ascertain. But did it matter, in the end? He seemed like a nice enough boy.

Ugh. Boy. No doubt about it, Ryan had a boyish air to him that made her want to reach over and fix his collar, which was sticking up on one side, rather than toss him over a couch like she had with Dennis.

She shifted her weight from one foot to the other, defensive. "What's that?"

"I'd like to date Ruby."

Not what she was expecting. She rested one hand on the display case to steady herself. "What?"

"I know this is strange and possibly uncomfortable for you, with my being older than she is."

If he knew the least of it. She'd been worried that he was going to ask *her* on a date, acting like a schoolgirl, when in fact he wanted to date her daughter. Humiliation was a possible reaction. She tried it on, breathed it in, but for some reason it didn't stick.

Ruby and Ryan. "How old are you?"

"I'm twenty-six. I know this hair makes me look like I'm about to retire, but I'm not. It's a family trait. Happened to my dad as well."

"Let me see your driver's license."

He pulled it out of his wallet and held it up for her to inspect. Indeed. Born in '49.

She almost laughed out loud at the absurdity of her vain mistake, relieved by the fact that it really didn't bother her. Ryan was a good man. Her daughter was smart. They'd figure it out.

She stared down at one of the books in the display case. "Huh."

"Are you all right?" Ryan moved closer. "I'm sorry for the way I'm handling this. But I wanted to be forthright, not hide about."

She waved a hand in his direction but didn't look up. "No, no. I appreciate it."

The label in the display case said it was an old yearbook from Georgia O'Keeffe's high school. She read the caption out loud. "'A girl who would be different in habit, style, and dress.'"

"A modern lass, that Georgia," Ryan said.

Virginia barely heard him. She stared at the name under the photo, leaning in close to make sure she was seeing it correctly.

Georgia Totto O'Keeffe.

How odd. She'd assumed Totto was a nickname but had never questioned what for. What if the connection to an artist wasn't a coincidence? She thought back. Totto had been the one who'd mentioned the art school was haunted. What if Totto was the one going through crates? But why would he do that?

Then she remembered the black-and-white photo of Clara Darden she'd seen in Janice Russo's office. The long neck and translucent eyes. The two could be brother and sister, easily, and Totto was the right age to have been Clara's sibling or some kind of relation.

Confusion and elation ran up Virginia's spine.

What if Totto was the ghost of the Grand Central School of Art?

CHAPTER TWENTY-TWO

March 1975

Virginia showed up early to work on Monday, greeted the evening shift, and offered to take over for the supervisor. The early-morning commuters knew where they were headed, for the most part, so she busied herself by climbing up through one of the missing glass panels in the ceiling and up onto the very top of the information booth, not caring who saw her. From there, she had easy access to the four-sided clock. Taking great care not to disturb the face of the clock, she rubbed the brass sides with cleaner until they shone, before climbing back down and stowing away her cleaning supplies.

But even this didn't help alleviate her nervous exhaustion.

Last night she'd hardly been able to sleep, not only because of what she was about to do but also because Ruby had wanted to talk about Ryan into the wee hours, after the bar had closed for the night. Virginia supported her daughter's decision to date him but entreated her to stay independent for a while longer. Not to rush into anything. Sure, Ryan seemed like a lovely man, but she had her whole life ahead of her. That morning, Virginia left before Ruby woke up, eager to get to work.

Terrence arrived first, arching one eyebrow at her promptness—usually no one was in before Terrence. Soon after, Doris and Winston sidled through the door, arguing whether *The Stepford Wives* was boring or brilliant.

Finally, Totto showed up, balancing two coffees, handing one to Terrence.

Virginia tried to stay cool, as Ruby would say, and not stare, but she couldn't help it. His hair was messy, as if he'd just rolled out of bed. She'd assumed early on that he and Terrence were brothers, as they shared the same slim builds, gray hair, and height. They bickered all the time. She'd been corrected by Terrence but hadn't considered the matter further.

Totto's back was to Virginia as he settled in, adjusting his timetables, lining up his pencils just so. Imperceptibly, his shoulders stiffened. He straightened up and looked about, one hand covering the O'Keeffe exhibit brochure that Virginia had left there.

They locked eyes.

"What's this?" Totto's voice trembled, but he covered it with a cough.

"I went to a fascinating exhibit this weekend." Virginia spoke louder than necessary, so her voice traveled across the booth. "I learned a lot."

"Is that so?"

"Yes. For example, I learned what Georgia O'Keeffe's middle name is."

Doris tore off a bite of her egg sandwich. "Georgia O'Keeffe? Love her."

Winston's eyes gleamed with mischief. "She's the one that draws enormous lady parts, right?"

"That's enough, everyone," said Terrence.

Virginia made her way past Doris until she was right behind Totto. "Totto is her middle name," she whispered. Totto tried to ignore her, but she pressed in closer. "Right?"

"What about it?"

"We should talk."

Totto stood. "Terrence, I'm going to help Virginia with some boxes."

Totto led the way to the elevator at track 23. Virginia's heart pounded as loudly as her footsteps, as they walked toward the art school without speaking. Her hunch had been right. Totto pulled out a key ring, fiddled with it, and then opened the door.

She'd found her ghost.

Inside, Totto headed to the back storage room, the one with all the crates. He stood in the middle of it, his hands on his hips, surveying the mess of crates, some opened, some shoved to one side, the assortment of artwork pinned haphazardly on the walls. He plonked down on one of the crates and let out a harsh laugh, before putting his head in his hands, overcome.

Virginia perched on an old wooden chair. "I'm sorry. I didn't mean to upset you. Maybe we can help each other."

"I don't need your help."

"I think you do. Who are you really, Totto?"

"You don't know?"

"You're related to Clara Darden."

Totto threw back his head and laughed.

Something about the movement caused all the pieces to finally shift into place. The smooth white neck. No Adam's apple.

Totto wasn't Clara Darden's brother.

Virginia studied Totto with new eyes. A woman, not a man. The suit did a lot to conceal her shape, but the hands and neck should have given it away weeks ago. Her wrinkled, mottled skin masked the delicate bone structure of her face.

"You're Clara Darden."

"I am." She raised her head, glaring. "Where's my watercolor?"

Virginia sidestepped the question. "How did you know I had it?"

"I heard you in the booth, on the telephone, setting up an appointment. You mentioned me and Levon Zakarian. I realized that you'd found it, somehow. After months of me digging through these crates, you'd breezed right in and plucked it out from under me."

"How did you get a key?"

"From when I taught here, back when dinosaurs roamed the earth. Surprisingly, it still worked."

"You sent me threatening letters."

"Which you ignored."

"I had to find out more about the painting."

"You thought it would make you rich." Venom dripped from Clara's voice.

This wasn't going the way Virginia had imagined. She'd lost the upper hand. "How do I know it's really yours? Levon Zakarian is the painter, according to the rest of the world. Do you have proof?"

Clara turned to Virginia, hate in her eyes. "One of my illustrations is on the back of the watercolor, signed and dated at the bottom. The illustration is the basis for the watercolor, which was a study for the oil painting. Follow the clues, Sherlock."

"Why didn't you just sign the oil painting with your own name?"

She leaned back on the crate, her arms braced behind her, head cocked. "We decided to keep it anonymous at first. Me, Felix—my art dealer—and Levon. The Depression was in full force, no one was buying, especially from a woman illustrator, and we figured a big revelation would attract attention."

"Everyone assumed Levon was the artist, because he was on the train to the Chicago exhibit with Felix when . . ." Virginia drifted off, unable to finish the sentence.

"When it crashed." Clara spat out the words. "A flash flood took out a bridge, and the train fell into the river below."

Virginia didn't know what to say. "I'm sorry."

Clara nodded and pulled a tissue out from her sleeve, gently dabbing at the skin under her eyes. A habit Virginia had seen every day but only now recognized as something a woman would do, so as not to smear her makeup.

"I have to ask, why weren't you on the train as well, if you were Clyde?"

"I should have been on the train with them, but I missed it, because someone delayed me. Some would say it was a lucky break. I consider it a terrible tragedy."

"Don't say that. You're alive." Virginia pressed on. "Why didn't you claim the paintings back then, when it all happened?"

"There was nothing left to claim. They were all destroyed."

"Except the untitled one."

"I didn't know about that. Not until I saw it in the auction catalog." She eyed Virginia, sizing her up. "I'd been told it was still around, but I didn't believe the person who told me. Oliver originally said he had destroyed it."

"Who's Oliver?"

"An old lover. A jealous one. Once I'd recovered from the shock of the crash, I reached out to him to find out the truth. By then he'd killed himself." She stood, her arms crossed. "There, I'm obviously the painter. Do you need more proof? Where is it? I want it back. Now."

"What happened, after the accident? Where did you go?"

"Why do you deserve to know? Do you have the watercolor or not? It's mine."

"I thought I was rescuing it."

"You stole it."

"I swear I didn't mean to. When I discovered it, the watercolor had been collecting dust for decades."

"I must have it in order to claim *The Siren* as my own before it goes to auction."

"*The Siren?*" Of course. The title fit perfectly. Virginia pictured the painting's vague figure, which swam in and out of the viewer's gaze, the wash of blues. "Where did you go after the crash? Where did you disappear to?"

"I have to tell you a story and then you'll tell me where it is? Is that the game you're playing?"

After a moment, during which Virginia remained silent—not without great difficulty—Clara dropped her hands to her sides.

Her words came out slowly at first. "After Oliver made me miss the train, I exchanged my ticket and had a telegram sent to Chicago saying I'd be there a day late. I went back to the studio Levon and I shared, livid with myself. And with Oliver.

"A friend came by the next morning and knocked on the door. He said there had been an accident, and he'd come around praying we hadn't taken the Twentieth Century Limited. Showed me a copy of the newspaper saying it had crashed, fallen into a river, many killed. No mention of Felix or Levon. A few days later I got word that the paintings were all gone, that Levon and Felix were dead." She paused. "Everything I loved was lost."

"What did you do?"

"I wandered about, out of my mind with grief, blaming myself. They had done so much for me, taken risks, and paid with their lives. I had to get out of town, get away from everything that reminded me of Levon. I put on a pair of trousers and one of Levon's old jackets. He used to talk about how he'd dressed his sister like a boy when they were driven out of their village, back in eastern Turkey. Dressed as a man, I felt safe traveling alone. The jacket still smelled like Levon."

"That's when you became Totto?"

"Yes. Since I'd already tried on a new identity with Clyde, what was one more? This way, no one could find me and start asking questions about Levon. I could simply disappear, leave my fury behind me." A wisp of a smile showed, briefly. "I ended up teaching art back in Arizona, where I grew up, eventually settling in an old mining town called Jerome."

"Did you paint?"

"No. Never again. But I stayed tuned in to the art world. I'd get the auction catalogs from New York in the mail, subscribed to all the magazines. Watched as the brilliant few of our contemporaries hit it big. I read that the Grand Central School of Art had been closed, abandoned. Last summer, I saw the listing for *The Siren.*"

"Wait, just last summer? When did you come to New York?"

"In September."

Virginia remembered Doris calling Totto the "newbie." She'd assumed it meant he'd been working there for, say, sixteen years, versus Doris's seventeen. Not six months. The combination of Totto's advanced age and Grand Central expertise had thrown her. "Seeing your work up for auction must've been a shock."

"I went to a canyon and screamed until my voice was hoarse. It was mine, but how to prove it? No one would believe me. Then I remembered the watercolor, how I'd tucked it on top of the storage cabinet and forgotten about it. I had to come back, see if it was still there. It wasn't. When I saw the crates, I figured maybe it had been put away and began working my way through them on my lunch hour. I wasn't going to give up until I'd scoured every one."

"Why did you leave it up on top of the cabinet in the first place?"

"That was where I stored most of my work, after the students had cleared out for the day. I didn't want the director to know I was painting for myself during class. At the time, I didn't think any-thing of it. The oil was painted later, away from the school. Where did you find the watercolor?"

"Behind the storage cabinet. One corner was sticking out; we must have knocked it from its hiding place when we . . ."

"We what?"

Virginia was certain she was turning the color of rhubarb. "I was up here with a man."

"I see." Clara muttered under her breath. "The type of woman who's only good when she's on her back."

"It was from behind, actually." She couldn't believe she just said that.

One corner of Clara's mouth lifted, a dint of humor.

"Anyway, that blue color caught my eye. Why didn't you just look behind the cabinet in the first place?"

"I tried. Damn thing is anchored to the wall, there's no light, no way to tell." She threw up her hands. "For God's sake, have I proven

to you that I'm the artist? That I'm Clyde or Clara Darden or whoever else you want me to be?"

She had no doubt of Clara's story.

But even though Virginia had discovered the painting, she'd also
surrendered it.

Clara took Virginia's silence for doubt. "Follow me." They walked
deeper into the art school, down the long hallway. At each room,
Clara narrated a story. About her first illustration class, the students, the art exhibits. New York during the 1920s came to life
through her words, Clara's eyes sometimes blazing with anger, other
times wet with tears. The school truly was full of ghosts. Virginia
imagined them streaming through the hallway, whispering between
easels.

Clara pointed to one of the bigger studios. "This is where Levon
used to teach. I took his class once, on a dare."

"What was Levon like?"

"Passionate, sometimes bullheaded. Always engaged with whoever was in front of him. He'd suffered terribly as a child."

"And Oliver?"

"Privileged. Beautiful and knew it. He supported me early on.
Without him I might not have made it as far as I did, but he made
sure I remembered that. He thought he could live out a life of an
artist through me, I think, and resented my success."

"How did you get the job at the information booth?" They circled
back toward the entrance.

"I knew someone who knew Terrence." Clara stopped in the small
foyer. "How much do you want for it?"

"For what?"

"The watercolor."

"No, that's not it. I don't want your money. You should have it; it's yours, rightfully so."

"What have you been doing with it, shopping around for the highest bidder?"

"No. I wanted to find out more about it, about you. Over the past couple of years I've lost so much, and the watercolor gave me hope that eventually I'd be okay. I know that sounds strange. But I loved it."

"Loved?" She leaned forward. "Why past tense?"

"Well, that's the tricky part. I don't have it. It's with the Lorettes."

"Irving Lorette?"

"Irving and Hazel. I was told to talk to them. They said they were going to get an expert at the MoMA to examine it."

"And?"

"They lied, and now they won't give it back."

Clara's entire body went rigid. "Bastards. What were you thinking, giving it up like that?"

"I have no idea how the art world works. I assumed they were doing the right thing."

"You fool."

Virginia's defenses rose. "It certainly didn't help matters, you sending me threatening notes. I was terrified. You tried to come after me in the school that one time, right? When I ran out the door?"

"I came in to try to figure out where on earth you'd found it, then realized someone else was already in here. What you heard was me trying to hide inside one of the closets."

How ridiculous. "We were frightened of each other!"

"This isn't some zany comedy. It's not funny."

"No kidding. You had some guy mug me at knifepoint and try to steal the watercolor." Virginia grew indignant at the memory. "I could've been killed. You should know that right after that terrifying incident, I handed it over to the Lorettes, happy to be rid of it, at least temporarily. So it's partially your fault they have it now. Why on earth did you do that?"

"I watched as you waited in line at the Lost and Found, then didn't follow through. I offered the guy twenty bucks to follow you and grab the portfolio case. I didn't know he had a knife. I didn't want you to get hurt."

For a moment, the two stood off against each other. Until Clara hung her head. "It's all lost. Again. Without that watercolor, Clara Darden is just a footnote to history. If that. Levon gets to be celebrated and revered. I loved him, but nothing has changed, almost fifty years later." She leaned back on the wall, all fight drained away, fighting back tears. "You ruined it all, you meddling, ignorant fool."

CHAPTER TWENTY-THREE

March 1975

Clara should have never come back. She felt like a paper-thin shell of a person. An apparition, sitting in this abandoned art school. Better yet, a relic, just like the dried-up paint cans and brittle brushes.

All her savings had been spent on her big trip to New York. Just like last time, it had ended in failure. Clara's new life back in Arizona had been fine, rich in beauty. She'd found a town of artists on the edge of a mountain, most of whom made Indian jewelry, metal sculptures, or misshapen macramé webbings to sell to tourists. Her house had a sagging front porch and a tiny bedroom that was boiling in summer and freezing in winter. She made some friends but never got close to anyone. Teaching art at the local school paid the bills. No one questioned her clothes or voice, asked if she was a man or a woman. She was free to be Totto, the name she came up with on the train out west.

New York City, when she first returned, had thrown her off-balance. The crowds made her dizzy; the filth overwhelmed. But she'd settled into a routine with the job she got from Terrence, a distant relation of one of the teachers in Arizona. Her old knowledge of the terminal returned right away, although every so often, early on, she'd answer a question incorrectly, sending the inquirer to the newsstand near gate 37, when it had relocated decades ago. Her sole purpose had been to see if she could get that watercolor. She dreamed of it at night, rued the day she didn't take it home with her instead of leaving it on top of the cabinet.

She looked around. The sorry state of the old art school matched her own.

Virginia spoke cautiously. "Where are you staying?"

"I found a short-term rental. Downtown." Clara narrowed her eyes at her. "Don't tell anyone in the booth about me."

"I swear I won't."

The dimwit had handed the watercolor over to the Lorettes, just like that. Mr. Lorette, who'd had it in for her since the very beginning.

"I'm sorry for all the suffering you've been through," Virginia said. "The train crash, losing everything."

The girl wouldn't give up. It was as if she was looking for absolution, and Clara wasn't about to give her that. "It was the Depression. The whole country was suffering. Not like today, where they're moaning about gas prices or inflation. People were starving to death in the streets."

"Does anyone else know that you painted *The Siren*? Is there anyone else alive who could recognize you and stand up for you?"

She was stubborn, this one. Not about to back down. No matter how cruel Clara was. Clara grudgingly respected her for it, to be honest. Same for the way she'd showed up day after day in the information booth, cleaning it up and making herself useful, when she wasn't being annoying and prissy.

"Not a soul."

Virginia exhaled loudly. "Where was the last place you saw it, then?"

"In the cottage in Maine. Oliver told me later that he'd stashed it in the attic."

Virginia scrunched up her face. "Who else had access to the cottage?"

"An actress named Violet, who Oliver eventually married."

"Is she still alive?"

"No. She died in Palm Springs a decade ago."

"Anyone else?"

"Mrs. Lorette. She handled all the sleeping arrangements and kept the cottages stocked."

"Then the Lorettes must have the painting." Virginia spoke Clara's thoughts out loud, gathering steam. "That's why they took the sketch. They don't want it to come out, because it'll screw up the auction, rewrite history in the art world."

The logic made sense, but Clara wasn't about to thank her. "You delivered it right into the wolf's hands, just like a fairy tale." She stood. "I'm going back to work. I've come this far; I'll figure out another way to get it back."

"Let me help you. I owe you that, at least."

"Don't bother. You've done quite enough."

But the woman wouldn't let up. The day after their confrontation, Virginia approached Clara in the booth and whispered into her ear, "Meet me at the art school at one o'clock."

Clara ignored her, shoving a timetable through the window at an impatient young man with too-long hair who was carrying a backpack.

She turned to face Virginia, crackling with bitterness. Yesterday, Clara had stomped over to the Lorettes' town house. By the time she got there, she'd been ready to storm the ramparts. But her fury dissipated when a maid answered the door and said the couple was out of town. Her bored demeanor indicated she was telling the truth, that the Lorettes weren't hovering on the other side of the door. Clara had tried, lamely, to get inside, but she was rebuffed.

This morning, she'd awoken to the sound of the garbage trucks grinding away outside her window and decided she was done. New York had lost all the mystique that she'd constructed around it during her decades away. From Arizona, even the hard times of the Depression had acquired a dreamy haze, of the gang sitting around Levon's fireplace, talking about art in order to divert attention from their growling stomachs. The city had since recovered, gone to war a few times, risen and fallen. It was unrecognizable and had moved on without her.

Virginia's eyes were wide, like a doll's. Clara hissed at her, "Please stop acting like we're in a spy movie."

"Promise you'll meet me. One o'clock."

Doris glanced over, sensing the tension. Clara relented, just to get Virginia off her back. "Yes. Go away now."

At one, Virginia was waiting at the doorway of the school. "I thought you weren't going to come." She fiddled with the lock, swearing under her breath, before opening the door.

She ushered Clara inside. "Follow me."

An easel sat next to a worktable in one of the smaller studios, where a dozen tubes of paint were arrayed in the shape of a rainbow.

"What's this?" Clara stopped and stared.

"I went to the art supply store on Fifty-Seventh Street, picked up some things. Look." Virginia pointed at each item. "A palette, some brushes; they said we needed turpentine and a cloth, so I bought those as well."

"You planning on becoming an artist?"

"No. Not me. They're for you. I feel bad about getting in the way of everything."

Clara eyed the brushes. Not the best quality, but not the worst, either. The prestretched canvas was pedestrian but usable. The whiteness gleamed in the dingy room like fresh snow.

Virginia was positively giddy. "Do you like it?"

"What's there to like? I don't paint anymore."

"Aren't you an art teacher?"

"Doesn't mean I make it."

"Don't you miss it?"

Clara looked back at the canvas. She remembered the way Levon struggled to hold the brush the last few months of his life. "Levon couldn't paint, near the end. Lead poisoning. Made his arm go weak."

Funny how regret never let up, even years later. Certain memories still carved out her insides: The look on Oliver's face when she'd betrayed him on the beach in Maine. How she'd tortured Levon for not trying harder to paint. Learning that her parents had both gotten sick and died a few months before her return to Arizona.

Virginia was looking at her strangely. "Did you and Levon ever consider getting married? Having kids, that kind of thing?"

Clara picked up one of the brushes and ran her finger over the tip. "No. Back then, we were more like the hippies of today. There was no rush to make things official. And the last thing we needed was another mouth to feed." She pursed her lips. She didn't want to let Virginia in, the busybody.

"My daughter, Ruby, had a brief hippie phase when she was

fourteen. She was into tie-dye and swiped all her father's white T-shirts, turning them into these wild, swirly designs. Her plan was to sell them and buy a camera with the money." She shrugged. "My ex-husband yelled at her but then ended up buying her a camera anyway."

If the girl was going to jabber on, Clara might as well investigate the paints. She opened one, a sunflower yellow, and squeezed it out onto the palette in a brightly colored worm.

Virginia showed no signs of letting up. "Ruby was a lovely girl, but so shy. After I got divorced, she really lost her way, which maybe would have happened anyway at that age. Kids want to find their own space, and I was crowding her, telling her what to do with her life. Which made her resent me, which made me crowd her more, you know?"

Clara didn't reply. The chemical scent from the paint brought memories flooding back. Sure, she'd been around paints for the past many years, but not in this room, where it all began. She dipped a thick brush into the paint and drew a slash on the canvas, wanting to mark it up, to defile its brightness. "How much did all this cost?"

"No bother. Well, actually, Ruby lent me the money. Just until we get paid on Friday. She's making lots of cash in tips, working in a hotel bar. Now she's focused, gets to work early and stays late. Takes photography classes in her free time. She's energized. Kind of like I was when I found the watercolor."

Clara mixed in some white to soften the color, tried a different brush. The quality of the canvas was terrible, fighting against the oil instead of supporting it.

"Ryan, one of the other bartenders, was at the O'Keeffe exhibit with me when I figured out who you were. Funny thing was, I thought he was there with me on a date, sort of, when in fact he wanted to ask my permission to date Ruby. You can imagine my shock. I laughed at myself. I do that a lot lately."

Clara shot her a look. "Did you tell anyone else about me? Who I am?"

"No. Of course not."

"That's my secret. Not yours."

"I understand."

"I doubt you do. You're not the type to have secrets. You prattle away in the information booth all day, getting into everyone's business."

"That's not true. I have secrets."

"Name one."

Virginia placed her right hand on her left shoulder, diagonally across her torso, like the sash of a beauty queen. Clara had noticed she did it whenever she was nervous, like when the stationmaster stopped into the booth or when Doris mocked her.

Virginia's voice quivered. "You want me to name one secret?"

"Sure. You know all about me. My losses, my humiliations. What's yours?" Clara stabbed the air with the point of the brush on the last two words.

"You're being awfully dramatic."

Clara turned back to the easel and sniffed.

"I had an operation, about five years ago." Virginia's voice dropped to a husky whisper, as if her throat was closing up to prevent the words from reaching the air. "Before I got divorced. They had to take off one breast, and I didn't know it was going to happen, beforehand. They put me under, and when I woke up, I'd been mutilated. They carved me up."

Clara turned and studied her. "You look fine to me."

"I wear a special type of bra. Not very comfortable, and it rides up all the time." She grimaced, as if remembering something painful, but continued talking. About her recovery, the fear that the cancer would come back. At some point, Clara realized that the woman was talking to her like she would to a sleepy child. Because as she droned on—and no, that wasn't a kind thing to think now that the poor woman was pouring her sad little heart out—Clara was painting. Mainly to distract herself, and to not have to look Virginia in the eyes. But still.

She was painting.

CHAPTER TWENTY-FOUR

March 1975

Friday, Clara decided to give her notice to Terrence. She waited until Virginia took her afternoon break and then turned her WINDOW CLOSED sign around.

"Terrence, I want to tell you some news."

Terrence held up one finger. "Hold on, I just have to figure out the answer to this question on the crossword. 'Old Russian ruler known as Moneybag.' Do you know the answer to that?"

She shook her head.

"Anyone else in this godforsaken booth know the answer?" He repeated the question.

"What? Money what?" yelled Doris.

This would not do. "Terrence, it's important."

"So is this."

"Ivan I." Winston, of course.

"It fits!" Terrence yelped, scribbling in the answer.

Virginia emerged from the tube that hid the spiral stairway and barged over to Clara. "Come with me. Quick."

"I already took my break."

Virginia was panting as if she'd taken the stairs three at a time. "No. You have to come. Quick. They're here."

"Who?"

"The Lorettes. I spotted them heading up here from the lower concourse. Look."

She pointed to an older couple in coats with their backs turned. Clara couldn't be sure. She hadn't seen them in decades.

"Let's go." Virginia turned to Terrence. "I need Totto's help; we'll be right back."

They left Terrence beaming at his completed crossword and hightailed it across the concourse, skidding to a stop right as the couple was about to take the stairs to the West Balcony.

"Mr. and Mrs. Lorette." Virginia's voice boomed out, surprising even Clara. She didn't know the girl had it in her. "Stop."

The Lorettes turned around. Forty-five years had gone by since Clara set eyes on them. They each carried a handsome old leather suitcase and were similarly weathered, wrinkled and spotted with age, like shriveled crab apples. Not that Clara hadn't also lost the bloom of youth years ago. The dry heat out west had that effect.

Mr. Lorette's voice, when he spoke, had the same affected accent, a mix of Maine and continental Europe. The shakiness of age heightened the aristocratic effect.

"Who are you?"

Virginia stepped in. "Hello, Mr. and Mrs. Lorette. We'd like to talk to you. Come this way, please."

"Why should we? We've really had enough of your nonsense." Mrs. Lorette waved them away.

Clara edged closer. "You don't remember me, do you?"

Mr. Lorette peered at her. "Who are you?"

"You know who I am. Clara Darden."

"Clara Darden?" Mrs. Lorette peered at her through smudged glasses. "But Clara Darden is a woman."

Clara was about to answer when Virginia jumped in. "We can't talk here. Follow me." She led them around the corner to a small waiting area that Clara recalled was once known as the Kissing Gallery, where reunited sweethearts were allowed to kiss as long as the smooch lasted less than five seconds. Today, the ornate lamps flanking the departure board were dark, the room drafty. A couple of homeless men slept along one wall on thin strips of cardboard that offered minimal protection from the cold marble floor.

"How do we know you're really her?" Mr. Lorette drew closer. "No one's heard from her in years."

"Who else would know that you banished my illustrations at the faculty exhibit?" snapped Clara. "Who else would know that the sketch was done during one of my illustration classes, based on the model we were lent by *Vogue*?"

Mr. Lorette's face changed in an instant, from dark to light. "You are Clara Darden. I can see it. Your face, you're her." He came forward and held out his hand. "What a pleasure to know you're still alive. There's not many of us left. After all these years."

Clara exchanged glances with Virginia. This man was not to be trusted.

But maybe all was not lost. After all, they'd shared a history, of a time and place that could never be repeated. A love for art. They spoke the same language. Maybe now that the Lorettes knew they were dealing directly with Clara, they'd relinquish her watercolor. Indeed, the theory that they were the sellers of *The Siren* could be way off base. For all she knew, Virginia had alienated them and forced them to abscond with her work. They probably thought she was as nuts as Clara did.

"Why the disguise?" asked Mr. Lorette.

"It's an art project."

"Like Bowie." Virginia looked around, pleased.

The Lorettes answered in unison. "Who?"

"Never mind." Clara had to find out more. "What happened that summer? Did Oliver take the painting? Or did you find it?"

"Honestly, Clara, we don't know." Mr. Lorette leaned hard on his cane. "We have no idea how it ended up at auction."

"What about the watercolor?" Virginia again. "You took it from me." The woman had no idea when to tread lightly.

"You originally took it from the art school," said Mrs. Lorette. "We don't know who you are. If anything, we're protecting it."

Mr. Lorette grew stern. "This is about more than possession. It's about protecting art, protecting a legacy."

"Whose legacy?" asked Clara.

"Levon Zakarian's."

"The watercolor is mine. You can tell from the sketch on the back. Which means the oil painting is also mine."

"Did anyone else see you painting it?"

"Oliver, of course. Levon."

"Both are long gone. Did anyone who's still alive see you painting it?"

No. No one. There was no point in saying the words out loud.

Mr. Lorette shook his head. "Then there's really no proof at all that it's yours. I'm sorry, but how do we know you're not trying to claim Zakarian's legacy for your own? You were an illustrator. That's all. No one ever saw you paint, really paint. You did magazine covers and car advertisements and that sort of thing. Then you appear out of the blue, claiming a watercolor that you say proves you're Clyde? Fishy, all around."

Clara couldn't believe his audacity. "Why would Levon not use his own name for those works? You know as well as I do what an enormous ego that man had. Besides, he couldn't paint at that time. Lead poisoning. His arm was numb. I did the paintings. All of them. Including *The Siren*."

Mrs. Lorette shook her head. "Is that what you're calling it? But no one saw you paint any of them."

"What about the existence of the watercolor?" asked Virginia.

"The watercolor is nothing." Mr. Lorette dismissed her with a wave of his hand. "We had it evaluated. It's meaningless. Artists copy each other all the time. Levon was copying Picasso for ages, until he hit his stride. For all we know, you were copying Levon."

A policeman peered in on them. "Everything all right in here?"

Mr. Lorette continued, emboldened. "You were a second-rate illustrator, selling your name and your work for the masses. Not like Levon, who was a genius. Then you show up decades later, trying to ruin him?" He drew Mrs. Lorette closer to him and started edging in the direction of the policeman. "We are the protectors of his legacy, and we'll do everything we can to keep you from meddling. Including calling lawyers."

"I know lawyers." Virginia, barging in again. "I have friends who will take up our case. We'll track down the watercolor and get it back and prove to everyone that Clara is Clyde. Don't think we won't." But her voice trailed off as the policeman offered to escort Mrs. Lorette up to the street.

The Lorettes were right. The last thing the art world wanted was someone coming in and upending what would be a deliciously rich sale of a work by a master. How Levon would have loved this, being called a genius, selling a painting for gobs of money.

That afternoon, Clara gave her notice to Terrence. He pleaded with her to stay on past the Easter rush, and she relented. On top of not wanting to let down a friend, she also wanted to prove to herself that she wasn't running blindly away, like she had the last time.

Four weeks and then she could leave all this behind her.

It was time to seek solace out west, just as she'd done before.

CHAPTER TWENTY-FIVE

March 1975

As the weekend crawled by, Virginia replayed the confrontation with the Lorettes in her head, kicking herself for how stupid she'd sounded. When she'd spotted the couple on the lower concourse, she'd been sure it was a sign, that this was their chance to shock them with Clara's existence and force their hand. Now she was even more convinced that they were the sellers of *The Siren*. Their excuses for hanging on to the watercolor were thin. It had to be because they didn't want the auction interfered with.

On Sunday morning, as Virginia was drying dishes at the sink in her apartment, Ruby touched her arm and made her jump.

"Mom. Hello? I said your name three times." Ruby looked more confused than exasperated.

Virginia picked up the spoon she'd dropped into the sink. "Sorry, darling. What's up?"

"Nothing." Ruby perched up on the counter. "Ryan and I are going out for a bite before we open up for the day. Wanna come? You've been holed up in the apartment all weekend."

"No, I'm fine here. You go, enjoy yourself."

"You seem weird. Is something going on?"

Even though Virginia had promised not to reveal Clara's identity, Ruby had been by Virginia's side through some difficult months and deserved to hear the story. She could be trusted to keep the secret. Virginia threw the tea towel over her shoulder. "I found the artist. The one who did the Clyde sketch."

"Clara Darden?"

"Exactly."

Ruby squealed. "That's wild. What's she like? Where was she?"

"She was dressed as a he and was working in the information booth with me. Right under my nose the entire time. She was also trying to track down the watercolor, but I got to it before she did."

"Fantastic! Then she can claim it back."

Virginia sighed. "We tried that. The Lorettes won't budge. So now I've ruined her life."

"Come on, Mom. You're being dramatic."

She gave a rueful smile. "You're right. Here I thought you were the dramatic one. But still. I feel really bad."

"Can we go to the police?"

"Unfortunately, it's not really an option. No New York cop is going to stop fighting crime long enough to mediate an art dispute between a bunch of old folks." And neither she nor Clara had the money to hire lawyers. Her empty threat to the Lorettes was just that. Empty. Dead ends all around.

But it helped, having talked it through, and by Monday morning, Virginia was eager to try to apologize again, let Clara know that she was truly sorry for having mucked it all up. But Clara ignored her, turning away when she approached.

"Serious cold shoulder going on there," observed Doris. "Did you have a spat? Put the timetable in the wrong slot or something?"

"Very funny." Virginia backed off but kept a close eye on Clara when she left for lunch. Virginia waited ten minutes and then followed her path.

She found Clara in the art school, in the smaller studio, palette in hand, staring hard at a piece of paper on an easel. Clara looked up, and her forehead creased. "You."

"Sorry. I don't mean to bother you."

"Yes, you do."

"I do. I want to talk. Can we talk?"

"About what? About how you ruined everything?"

"Yes. I own that responsibility and want to apologize to you."

Judging by the furious look in Clara's eyes, she'd been stewing all weekend as well. "That's all you do, apologize. I came back to stake my claim and instead have been maligned, yet again, by the Lorettes. A 'second-rate illustrator.' How dare they! I'm worse off than when I started. I have no money left, no reputation. With no chance of reclaiming either."

Virginia stood her ground. She'd heard enough moaning from having a teenaged daughter over the past few years, and this was no different. "You're the one who ran away in the first place, may I remind you? Yes, there was a terrible tragedy, but you could have bounced back. Declared that you were Clyde, staked a claim. You had talent, but you took off for the hills and threw away your life."

"Far from it." Clara threw back her shoulders. "I taught generations of children how to draw. When I watched a child blossom during class, saw her recognize her own talent and feel special, it was well worth it. I might have lost my chance to make it big, but I did everything in my power to ensure other young girls could reach their full potential. The students at the Grand Central School of Art could be petty, competitive. Once I removed myself from the fickle art world, I began to appreciate art for its own sake, like I had long ago. In many ways, I was finally free. After I became Totto, I wasn't beholden to anyone. I had mad affairs, some thrilling, some not."

"You had affairs?" An unexpected admission. Clara as Totto was so tightly wound, Virginia couldn't imagine it.

A glint of pride shone in Clara's eyes. "Does that shock you?"

"Nothing shocks me anymore." Virginia envied Clara's life, suddenly. No longer trying to please everyone else, only herself. "But then you came back."

"When I saw the painting in the catalog, it was like seeing my own reflection. It made me realize I deserved more. This was my last shot."

She had a point. She did deserve more. "I'm sorry the Lorettes have stolen that opportunity from you and that I had a hand in it. But I'm still glad I found the watercolor. The watercolor, the sketch—they were magical when my life was not. They helped me get by." She stared up at the skylights, where a weak sun filtered through a thin coating of dirt. "I wanted to be like that woman, *The Siren*. The woman in the painting, mysterious and powerful." She paused. "How can I make it up to you?"

"You can take off your dress."

"What?" Virginia wasn't sure she'd heard correctly.

"Take it off. I want to paint you."

"No. I couldn't."

"You asked a question. I'm answering it. Take everything off, place the stool on top of the model's stand, and sit on it."

"You want me to be naked?"

"Stop being a ninny. Do you know how many people took off their clothes and posed in this studio over the years? Hundreds. Now do it."

They locked eyes. Clara stood warrior tall, the palette like a shield in one hand, the brush a spear. After everything that had happened, it was the least Virginia could do. She untied her wrap dress and let it drop on the floor as Clara began organizing the supplies. After taking a deep breath, Virginia took off her bra, the air cold on her skin but not on the thick scar tissue, where she had no feeling, only numbness.

"Sit down."

"I'm really not sure about this." She covered her chest with both arms.

"You want me to paint? Well, I've found my subject. If you want to make it up to me, sit yourself in that chair and uncross your arms."

Virginia placed the stool on the model stand, checking to make sure its legs weren't near the edge.

"Stop stalling."

Clara had put down the palette and was sharpening one of the pencils, her nose scrunched up like a bunny. The thought made Virginia smile.

"Stay like that." Clara's commands grew less severe as she became engrossed in the work. When she looked up, she didn't look into Virginia's eyes, but everywhere else. Her thighs, her feet, her hairline. But not in the way that Chester or Dennis had. Nothing ravenous. More an intellectual examination of her muscles and skin, hair and bones.

To her surprise, Virginia fell into a quiet meditation. Free of all clothing, she was like a child again. Pure and open. The minutes ticked by, but she didn't care. The only sounds were the pencil scraping the canvas and the quiet whir of the terminal, as if it were breathing in tandem with her own lungs. She closed her eyes and let her thoughts roam.

"What the hell is going on in here?"

Three men in suits stood in the doorway. Virginia dashed to her clothes, clutching them to her, the stool sliding off the model stand with a loud bang. She ran behind one of the easels and tried desperately to get back into her bra and dress, her hands shaking with shame.

"We're making art," Clara thundered. "What are you doing here?"

"We're doing an inspection for Marcel Breuer. For the new building."

"Inspect away. We won't stop you."

The taller man stepped forward. "Who are you?"

"We work for Grand Central. We're on break."

"This area is off-limits. I won't tell the stationmaster that you were here, but you better get out."

By then, Virginia had pulled everything on but her underwear, which she stuffed into her handbag.

"All right. We're going." Clara waved to her, and Virginia scooted over, keeping her eyes on the floor in front of her.

"Wait a minute. How did you get in? If you have a key, hand it over, now." The man held out his palm.

Clara did so without saying a word and began shoving the supplies into the storage case. Virginia's hands trembled; her face burned at the thought that these men had seen her disfigurement. Clara put a protective arm around her shoulders, and together they walked out. The sound of the men chuckling to one another echoed down the school's hallway.

"Bastards." Clara slammed the door on their way out and headed to the left, away from the elevator.

"Where are you going?" Virginia yanked her dress closed at the bosom and stared after her, shell-shocked. Her worst nightmare had come true, and Clara couldn't care less.

"Follow me. It's quicker this way." Clara opened a door at the very end of the hallway and went down a stairway, the pad tucked under one arm and the painting kit in the other.

Virginia stopped, her shoulders heaving with sobs, her humiliation complete. "They saw me."

Clara turned to her with a sad half laugh. "Do you really care, though? What does it mean to you that they saw you?"

Virginia considered the question. "They know I'm not a whole woman."

"And?" She shrugged her shoulders. "Look at me. No one knows what I am. But I don't care, because I love the way I move in the world. I love my perspective on the world. I've earned it, and anyone else can go to hell. I wouldn't have wanted to paint you if I didn't think you were a fascinating subject: a woman of a certain age, with the wounds to prove it. That's what interests me. Desperate to cover those wounds but still carrying them capably. A woman who is just learning her own strength.

"Besides, it's a great big world out there. Living in the West, surrounded by ancient mountains and a huge sky, shows you how inconsequential you really are, in the grand scheme of things. I find that reassuring." She pointed to the right. "Look."

They were standing at the edge of a frosted-glass catwalk sandwiched between the double-paned east windows. Virginia stepped onto it. Below her, the entire concourse spread out. People darted in all directions, one man running, another strolling, a woman herding three small children. All were miniature figures of themselves;

the clock above the information booth glowed like a lighthouse beacon.

Virginia's tears had dried. "It's magnificent."

"If you wanted to see magnificent, you should have seen it in the 1920s. Like a European cathedral."

"That's what they said at the press conference."

A dull roar thundered through the passageway.

"What was that? The subway?" asked Virginia.

"No. It came from Forty-Second Street. Let's see." Clara walked away, leaving Virginia to hurry after her retreating back. They turned another corner, back up the stairs, and into a tiny room where a ladder rose up through the ceiling. "Leave all your things here. We're going up."

"Leave them?"

"Yes. This way. Levon and I used to sneak up here on breaks, to get away from the students."

After ducking under a low beam, Virginia followed Clara up a narrow metal ladder, then another, until she finally stepped out onto a tiny platform. Looming above them was the reverse side of the massive Tiffany clock that adorned the very top of the terminal's south face. Clara clicked a latch at the base of the clock, and the oval containing the roman numeral VI opened inward. Another roar. They poked their heads out.

Below, on the elevated roadway that encircled Grand Central like a belt, stood a rabid crowd. Normally, taxis would careen by in a yellow blur, but today the street had been blocked off.

"I'd completely forgotten. It's one of the protests to stop Penn Central." Virginia pointed to a man with a bullhorn. "That's the mayor. Look, right beside him is Jackie O."

"Impressive crowd. Too bad they can't do anything about it."

"Do you really think so? You think that the collective voice of all these people doesn't count?" Virginia stuck her head out farther. "There must be hundreds, thousands. If enough of us protest, then they have to do something about it. It's our city, after all."

"Then you ought to be out there protesting."

Virginia withdrew her head just as the clouds cleared and sunlight hit the clock full on, beaming jewel-colored rays into the chamber, turning it into a giant kaleidoscope. Both she and Clara stood still, looking about, transfixed by the glorious show.

The words Jackie had used in the press conference came back to Virginia: Even if it seemed too late, maybe it wasn't. That with great effort, you can succeed, even at the eleventh hour. Jackie O really believed it, and that made the rest of the city believe it, too.

But what if this wasn't just a fight to save the terminal? Maybe everything Jackie said in the press conference applied to artists like Clara, and possibly dozens of others, who'd been lost in time. Artists whose works had been cannibalized by the greed of others.

As the light swirled around Virginia, a plan clicked into place.

The art auction was still a month away, so maybe the fight wasn't over quite yet.

She could save Clara, save Clyde.

And she knew exactly how.

CHAPTER TWENTY-SIX

April 1975

O n Clara's last night in New York City, Virginia insisted she
join her for dinner.

The invitation had come out of the blue. In the weeks since they'd
been caught in the art school, Clara had made plans to pack up and
head back to Arizona. The clerks at the info booth had thrown a
small going-away celebration party for her that afternoon, with Doris passing around homemade cupcakes that tasted like glue, and
Clara had accepted their kind words and good wishes. Virginia
showed up late. Not a surprise, as she'd pulled away recently, disappearing during lunch hours, coming in late and leaving early. No
longer harassing Clara. Which at first was a relief—the woman was
a nutjob, after all—but then hurt more than she would care to admit.

Clara had told Virginia she couldn't possibly go out to dinner,
that she had far too much to do before leaving, but Virginia had refused to take no for an answer. In truth, all Clara had to do was put
the suits hanging in the small closet into her suitcase and pack up

her art gear. She'd been painting, up in her hotel room, but hadn't told Virginia about that.

Something about being forced to paint again opened the flood-gates. Her mind whirled with thoughts of the work at hand: how to shape the shoulders, what colors would capture the intense white-ness of the scar. She'd been painting, from her memory, Virginia. Remembering the sad, faraway look in her eyes as she stared up, trying not to cry, so exposed. If anything, Virginia's bravery in that moment had made Clara feel closer to her than ever. She'd been proud of the woman, of the shocking display of her vulnerability.

But then the men had come barging in, and after that, Virginia had completely withdrawn.

Virginia wasn't alone at the table when Clara entered the restau-rant, an Italian place with checkered tablecloths and candles stuck in wine bottles, wax dripping down the sides like white lava.

"I'm so glad you came." Virginia was breathless. She put her arm around the girl next to her. "This is my daughter, Ruby."

"The one who took your boyfriend?"

Virginia turned red. Clara should have held her tongue, but she was peevish about Virginia's cold shoulder over the past few weeks. Now she thought she could make it up to her by taking her out to dinner right before she left?

"Mom?" Ruby turned to her mother, confused.

A bit contrite, Clara shook her hand. "I'm just kidding. Your mother mentioned that you'd found a new beau. She said he was de-lightful."

Ruby gave a shy smile. "He is."

They sat and ordered wine, which helped melt some of Clara's bitterness. That and the way Virginia looked at her daughter as

Ruby spoke about her photography and the bar where she worked—like she couldn't believe this stunning child was her offspring. Sweet, really.

The wine was making Clara loopy. They ordered pasta, and that helped steady her.

"Your daughter is lovely," she said to Virginia.

"Isn't she? The two of us have been through a lot these past several months." Virginia looked over at Clara. "But then again, haven't we all?"

Virginia carried on, telling Ruby about the going-away party. How Clara had returned from her lunch break to find her seat decorated with ribbons and balloons—a ridiculous idea in that small space, in Clara's opinion—and how excited they'd been to surprise her. As if Virginia was there the entire time and hadn't blown in late, gasping her apologies.

When dinner was over, Virginia insisted that Clara join them in a taxi.

"I'm not going your way. I'm downtown; you're up."

Ruby and Virginia exchanged a strange look. Ruby spoke up. "We insist. Come on, it's your last cab in New York. We want to treat you."

The girl's sweet smile was hard to turn down.

Once in, with Clara squashed between Ruby and Virginia, the cab headed north. "Where are you taking me?"

"Just one stop and then we'll drop you off." Virginia stared straight ahead. In fact, all during dinner, Virginia had seemed out of sorts. Usually she reminded Clara of a sparrow, hopping aimlessly about. Tonight, her energy was more like that of a woodpecker. Noisy, yet focused.

Never mind. It wasn't as if Clara had something important to get back to.

The cab pulled up in front of a low gray building on Madison Avenue. The home of Sotheby Parke Bernet auction house. Clara's stomach flipped when she remembered what day it was.

April third.

The day the Clyde painting was going to auction.

"No. I'm not going in there." She braced one hand against the front seat of the cab, as if expecting them to yank her out.

"Please," Virginia pleaded. "We've come this far." She and her daughter held both doors open.

Clara got out only because she was worried Ruby would be run down by a passing bus, standing in the middle of the street like that.

She'd catch another cab home, and silently cursed Virginia for the additional expense.

"Now that we're all here, why don't we pop inside?" Ruby took Clara's arm.

Clara resisted. "Unless you have the money saved up to buy the painting, what's the point?"

Virginia stepped close, her face serious. "I know you don't trust me and that I've disappointed you at every turn. But I sat for you when you asked. You know how hard that was for me. I'm asking you to do something that's just as hard for you."

Clara looked over at Ruby, who was biting her lip. God only knew what was really going on. "Fine."

Inside, they took the elevator up to a cavernous room, at the front of which stood a dais and a large easel. Smartly dressed men and women filled most of the seats, but Virginia nabbed three near the back. Clara began to leaf through the auction catalog that had been placed on her seat as a prim-looking man with a mustache spoke out from the lectern.

"Ladies and gentlemen, thank you for joining us today for Sotheby Parke Bernet's American Art Spring Auction. Our first artwork is Edward Hopper's remarkable watercolor *House on the Shore*, signed by Hopper, dated 1924, and inscribed *Gloucester*. I'm going to start the bidding at sixty-five thousand dollars."

The auctioneer spoke with an English accent. As he motioned with his hands, he kept his fingers together, so they resembled fins. He indicated to each bidder as they raised their paddles, left fin, then right.

"He looks like a robot," said Clara under her breath.

But the man's mastery of the room impressed her. When the bidding paused, he didn't rush to fill in the space but left them all hanging until another potential buyer jumped in to relieve the tension.

A de Kooning pastel went for $40,000. Seeing it was like seeing an old friend again. She remembered drinking and laughing with him around Levon's fireplace. Next up was a Stuart Davis gouache. He'd been working on that for ages, complaining to Levon that he couldn't find the right perspective. The memories brought tears to her eyes, and she wiped them away. This was torture.

She started to rise.

"No. Not yet."

Virginia's words were a command, not a request. Clara sat back down.

Only then did she notice that Virginia was quietly communicating with the other people seated nearby. She exchanged a whisper with a woman with long braids sitting in the row in front of them, while Ruby nodded to the man on her right. In between auction items, the people in the rows behind murmured to one another, leaning forward to check in with Virginia.

"How do you know all these people?" Clara asked Virginia.

"What people?"

Two art handlers wearing white gloves lifted the next work onto the easel.

The Siren.

Clara sucked in her breath. She hadn't laid eyes on it in forty-six years, and analyzed it with a fresh perspective. Even from this distance, the strength of the composition was evident. As was the power of the colors, the blues and the blacks. It had been her best work. Now a packed room of strangers ogled her painting as if it were just another item on the auction block, not an open wound. She suddenly understood, viscerally, Virginia's reaction to those men barging in on their session together. She wanted to snatch it off the easel and run off into the night.

The auctioneer piped up. "Next we have an untitled painting attributed to Levon Zakarian, signed as 'Clyde,' the only such work to survive. Bidding will begin at seventy thousand dollars."

Clara tried to swallow, but her mouth had gone dry.

Virginia stood and held something up above her head.

The auctioneer blinked a couple of times and opened his mouth to speak, but Virginia cut in. "My name is Virginia Clay, and I am here to protest the sale of this painting. First off, it has a name. It's called *The Siren.* I believe *The Siren* was stolen from the painter by the anonymous seller."

What on earth was she thinking? This was mad. No one interrupted an auction. Already, the auctioneer was waving to the security guards in the back.

Virginia continued, her voice loud. "I believe the sellers, Irving and Hazel Lorette, stole this painting from the artist."

Clara stared up at Virginia. She was taking a huge chance here. No one had confirmed that the Lorettes were the sellers. Stupid girl.

"How dare you?"

A man in the very front row stood. Mr. Lorette. The auctioneer asked for everyone to please take their seats, as Mr. Lorette and Virginia glared at each other across the crowd. Clara made out Mrs. Lorette next to him, straining her neck to look back.

"Mr. Lorette," said Virginia, "I'm here with dozens of family members of alumni of the Grand Central School of Art, all of whom accuse you of theft."

People in the three rows around them also stood, many clutching large posters in their hands, which they raised high above their heads, just as Virginia had done. Clara glanced about. They portrayed images of artworks with the artist's name in block letters at the top. Several press photographers snapped photos as the crowd rumbled with unease.

Virginia's voice rang out. Louder now, clearer. "These twelve paintings were stolen from students at the Grand Central School of Art during the 1920s, thirties, and forties. After the artists' deaths, they were all put up for auction by an anonymous seller. Irving and Hazel Lorette."

Clara looked back at the auctioneer, who glanced down at the Lorettes with a raised eyebrow, his face ashen. Virginia had called it correctly.

"The Lorettes pilfered the work of the top students over the twenty years the school was in session and have been living off the proceeds ever since." Virginia yanked Clara to her feet. The flashes from the cameras blinded her. "This is 'Clyde.' The artist of *The Siren* was not Levon Zakarian but Clara Darden, the famed illustrator and industrial designer. She's alive and well, which is the only reason this fraudulent scheme was discovered."

Clara looked around, stunned. The Grand Central School of Art had a long list of distinguished students. How had Virginia tracked these people down?

The woman with braids stepped into the aisle. "My name is Janice Russo, the curator of the Art Students League. The past several weeks, we've been accumulating the proof to show that these allegations are true and should be taken seriously. We are asking for the opportunity to present our documentation to the auction house before this work is sold."

Reporters hurried forward, notebooks and pens in hand. The auctioneer banged his gavel a few times to try to restore order, as if they were in a courtroom, but gave up as the noise level rose. "We'll stop the bidding and reconvene at a later time." He rushed off quickly, trailed by several assistants carrying *The Siren* out of harm's way, and disappeared out a side door. The Lorettes weren't far behind, with reporters giving chase.

"What just happened?" Clara turned to Virginia, who was hugging her daughter close. The people in the crowd behind them were shaking hands and hugging, too.

"Jackie O said that it's never too late, that even at the eleventh hour, you could change the course of events." Virginia glowed with triumph. "That day we looked out the clock and over the rally, I realized she knew the secret: There's power in numbers. I figured if the Lorettes had done this to you, they'd probably done it to others. I went back up to the school and searched through the crates to find anything that was administrative, including names of former students, listed by year. Janice helped out, going through the class lists and highlighting any alumni who had made it big but were no longer alive."

Ruby piped up. "Then we went through old Sotheby Parke Bernet auction catalogs and cross-checked our list of names against any lots by anonymous sellers."

Clara remembered the random thefts while she'd been a teacher at the school, usually blamed on the cleaning staff or jealous students. The Lorettes had total access, of course, and the most promising students were easy enough to spot. An insurance policy for their later years.

"So then," said Virginia, "along with Janice, we contacted the living relatives of the artists. None of them had even seen the paintings before, because the Lorettes always waited until the artist died to bring it to auction."

Clara nodded. "They'd assumed that I probably died by now, or disappeared into the ether. How did you get all this done so fast, in time for the auction?"

"It wasn't easy. All hands on deck. Janice even enlisted some of the students from the Art Students League to help out."

"In the end, you didn't even need the watercolor." Clara's single-mindedness had prevented her from seeing the bigger picture. She had to hand it to them. "You've pulled off quite a stunt."

Virginia smiled broadly. "We figured out an end run around it. The Lorettes were never going to let the watercolor go once they had their hands on it, because by questioning the painter's identity, it would have attracted a lot of attention."

"And press."

"Right. That was the key. I figured I'd use the press the same way Jackie did. To make a splash."

Three reporters appeared in the aisle. "Miss Darden? We'd like to speak with you. Do you have a moment?"

Clara looked at Virginia.

"Thank you."

"My pleasure." Virginia gave her a hug. "Now, go and take your place in the spotlight."

CHAPTER TWENTY-SEVEN

December 1975

Virginia's legs shook as she maneuvered her way through the revolving door of the Museum of Modern Art. She gave her name to the woman at the desk, who directed her to a third-floor gallery where a sign outside read CLOSED TO THE PUBLIC. She pushed through and stood still, unsure of where to begin.

Clara stood at the far end of the room, towering above the art handlers and gallerists in her dark suit and shock of gray hair. Even from far away, Virginia could see Clara's face was animated, her words coming out in a rapid clip.

In the eight months since they'd stormed the auction house, Clara had garnered lots of press, about her history, her legacy, and her artwork. The museum had offered up a show of not only her work but also Levon's and some other artists from the period's. But Clara was the only woman, and had the starring role, as she deserved. She'd invited Virginia to stop by in the afternoon before the official opening, a chance to see the show before the public swarmed in.

Virginia worked her way around the room, unnoticed and unob-served. The exhibit began with some of Clara's early illustrations and, of course, *The Siren*. Nearby, in a display case that allowed both sides to be exhibited, hung the watercolor for *The Siren*, the link between Clara's early work and her turn to oils. The piece had been recovered from the Lorettes' possession after a police investigation into the sale of stolen paintings that electrified the art world.

Soon after being arrested, Mrs. Lorette admitted she'd discovered *The Siren* in the attic of the Maine cottage while putting away bed linens at the end of the summer term. The cleaning lady had told her it was by the "tall, skinny lady painter," and she and Mr. Lorette had held on to it in case the value rose, just as they'd done with the other works of art that had "disappeared" at the school over the years.

Due to their advanced ages, they were each sentenced to only twenty-six months in prison.

Virginia, emboldened, had applied to the part-time master's de-gree program in art history at New York University and, to her shock, was awarded a full scholarship. She still worked a few days a week at the information booth and was even more involved with the Municipal Art Society.

In fact, just before coming to the MoMA, she'd presented some of the raw materials for her thesis to Adelaide and the board of the Municipal Art Society, a slide show she called "Grand Central Ter-minal: Past, Present, and Future." It began with photos of the inte-rior and exteriors when it was first built, followed by Ruby's powerful shots to show what it was like now. For the big finish, Clara had created renderings of what it might become with a little TLC. Or a lot, to be honest: a new roof that wouldn't leak, windows scraped of paint and dirt, the marble walls cleaned, and, most spec-tacularly, the celestial ceiling restored to its original turquoise. The board had gasped out loud at the renderings, exactly the effect Virginia had hoped to achieve.

Now, though, her elation was ebbing fast. Virginia stiffened her spine before moving deeper into the exhibit, knowing what lay ahead.

Clara's exhibit included three nudes Clara had painted of Virginia, including the one begun in the Grand Central School of Art. Together, they formed a fleshy, bold triptych. The figure in the paintings was definitely her, with her pixie haircut and wide eyes, but the look on her face was otherworldly, as though she were a seraph. The scar was just that. A scar. To think that her big secret, the one she'd been ashamed of these past five years, was out in the world for everyone to see. Fine. It was a part of her body, and she wasn't going to pretend anymore. She'd been sliced open and put back together in a different way, and it had made her wise. A woman who'd fought her own wars and survived.

"Virginia!" Adelaide came careening toward her, holding the afternoon paper in her hand, her face flushed.

"Adelaide, what are you doing here? Is something wrong?"

"I remember you said you were coming here. I had to find you. Have you heard the news?"

"No. What news? Is it about the presentation?"

"No. Well, yes, in a way. It's been saved!"

Adelaide had attracted the attention of several people nearby. "What has?" asked one of the gallerists.

"Grand Central!"

Adelaide read aloud. *"The landmark status of Grand Central Terminal was reinstated earlier today when the Appellate Division voted three to two to reverse the trial court's decision. In his ruling, the judge challenged Penn Central's accounting methods, saying the company wrongly assigned railroad expenses to the terminal operating costs, instead of the railway business, in an attempt to demonstrate economic hardship. Specifically, Penn Central's claim that it was losing millions of dollars a year was found to be unsubstantiated. The decision is sure to advance to the New York Court of Appeals and perhaps the Supreme Court, but is a victory for the Municipal Art Society in its crusade to stop the construction of a 55-story tower atop the terminal."*

As a cheer broke out around the room, Adelaide mouthed *thank you* to Virginia, and they exchanged knowing smiles.

An arm wrapped around Virginia's shoulders. She looked up to see Clara beaming down at her. "Congratulations."

Virginia slid her arm around her friend's waist. "It's a huge win, for now. But who knows what kind of fight is looming down the pike. It might go right up to the Supreme Court."

"I know that your side will prevail, most certainly."

Virginia's life up until last year had been about mitigating risk, doing nothing out of the ordinary, all while holding the people and things she loved as close to her as possible. Too close, it turned out. She'd learned the hard way that growth and change were unavoidable. Only once she'd undertaken her own crusades had everything fallen into place.

Most important, Clara Darden was finally recognized as a seminal artist of the twentieth century. She'd gotten the respect she'd deserved, almost too late. Using Clara's life as her template, Virginia was now able to see a future unfold before her, one that didn't involve loneliness or fear. She'd work in a gallery or teach art history, have mad affairs of her own—she'd already embarked on a burgeoning romance with a witty NYU linguistics professor—as well as deep friendships to see her through the difficult times.

Clara motioned across the room. "What do you think? Are you okay with this? I'll take the triptych down if you're not."

"No. I love it."

Clara smiled. "I wonder what Levon would have thought of all this."

Together they surveyed the room. "I bet he'd have eaten it up," said Virginia.

"He'd tell me I have goats on my roof. And he'd probably be right." She barked out a laugh, and everyone in the room turned and smiled, acutely mindful of the celebrated artist in their midst.

But only Virginia could see the tears in her eyes.

AUTHOR'S NOTE

On June 26, 1978, the Supreme Court of the United States ruled 6–3 in favor of Grand Central Terminal's landmark status, guaranteeing that it would never be demolished nor dwarfed by Penn Central's proposed skyscraper. The splendid building we see today was restored and rededicated on October 1, 1998, after a renovation led by the New York architecture firm Beyer Blinder Belle. A plaque dedicated to Jacqueline Kennedy Onassis for her role in the preservation hangs in the main entrance of the terminal.

The Grand Central School of Art, founded by the painters Edmund Greacen, Walter Leighton Clark, and John Singer Sargent, opened in 1924 and enrolled as many as nine hundred students a year before closing in 1944. While this is a work of fiction, I was inspired by two former faculty members at the Grand Central School of Art—Arshile Gorky and Helen Dryden—and by the real-life fight to save Grand Central Terminal in the 1970s. Penn Central did incorrectly allocate their expenses to try to show economic hardship, but the stolen balance sheet and scenes involving the Municipal Art Society are fiction. Several books were incredibly helpful during my research, including *Arshile Gorky: His Life and Work* by Hayden Herrera; *Rethinking Arshile Gorky* by Kim S. Theriault; *Lee Krasner: A Biography* by Gail Levin; *Women of Abstract Expressionism*, edited by Joan Marter; *An Evening in the Classroom* by Harvey Dunn; *Grand Central Terminal: 100 Years of a New York Landmark* by the New York Transit Museum and Anthony W. Robins; *Grand Central: How a Train Station Transformed America* by Sam Roberts; *Grand Central Terminal: City within the City* by the Municipal Art Society of New York, edited by Deborah Nevins; and *Grand Central* by David Marshall. I'd especially like to thank Sarah Marie Horne, who provided me with research from her groundbreaking dissertation on Helen Dryden.

ACKNOWLEDGMENTS

I'm incredibly grateful to everyone who helped bring this story to life, especially Stephanie Kelly and Stefanie Lieberman, who were by my side every step of the way.

Thank you to everyone at Dutton, including Ivan Held, Christine Ball, John Parsley, Amanda Walker, Carrie Swetonic, Alice Dalrymple, Liza Cassity, Becky Odell, Elina Vaysbeyn, and Christopher Lin. The team of all-stars also includes Kathleen Carter, Molly Steinblatt, Nikki Terry, and Julie Miesionczek. In terms of research, I am indebted to Francis Morrone, Wendy Felton, Karen Spencer, Erin Butler, Don Morris, Sarah Marie Horne, Jillian Russo, Stephanie Cassidy, Alfred G. Vanderbilt, Frank J. Prial Jr., the Art Students League of New York, the Avery Architectural and Fine Arts Library at Columbia University, and the Municipal Art Society of New York. Finally, I'd like to thank Brian and Dilys Davis, Tom O'Brien, Cynthia Besteman, and Linda Powell for your support and love.

ABOUT THE AUTHOR

Fiona Davis is the nationally bestselling author of *The Dollhouse* and *The Address*. She lives in New York City and is a graduate of the College of William and Mary in Virginia and the Columbia University Graduate School of Journalism.